D0961967

THE CROCODILE AND THE CRANE

Also by Arthur Rosenfeld...

Novels

The Cutting Season
Diamond Eye
A Cure for Gravity
Dark Money
Dark Tracks
Harpoons
Trigger Man

Nonfiction

The Truth About Chronic Pain
Exotic Pets

Forthcoming Novels

The Cutting Season – Series

THE CROCODILE AND THE CRANE

ARTHUR ROSENFELD

YMAA Publication Center
Boston, Mass. USA

ARTHUR ROSENFELD

YMAA Publication Center, Inc.
Main Office
4354 Washington Street
Boston, Massachusetts, 02131
1-800-669-8892 • www.ymaa.com • ymaa@aol.com

Editor: Leslie Takao
Cover Design: Axie Breen

ISBN-13: 978-1-59439-087-6
ISBN-10: 1-59439-087-8

10 9 8 7 6 5 4 3 2 1

Publisher's Cataloging in Publication

Rosenfeld, Arthur.

The crocodile and the crane / Arthur Rosenfeld. -- 1st ed. -- Boston, Mass. : YMAA Publication Center, c2007.

p. ; cm.

ISBN: 978-1-59439-087-6

1. Apocalyptic literature. 2. Technology and civilization in literature. 3. China--History--Fiction. 4. Medicine, Chinese--Fiction. I. Title.

PS3568.O8124 C76 2007 2007933253
813/.54--dc22 0709

Printed in USA.

For Camilla May, mother and philosopher

Acknowledgments

My students helped me a great deal with this book, in particular Kit Bredahl and Jennifer Beimel. Nine bows to each of you. Thanks also to Steven Beer for his contract work, and to Axie Breen for such a lovely cover. My brother, Dr. Stephen Rosenfeld, helped me navigate medical intricacies, and my great old pal Dr. Henri Lichenstein translated otherwise incomprehensible points of genetics and microbiology.

Britin Haller gave me good story inputs, and my editor, Leslie Takao, did a stellar job of wrapping her mind around the complex construction required to knit together several main characters, a global biological catastrophe, and 3000 years of Chinese history. Tim Comrie remained patient with me through literally hundreds of last-minute changes and polish points, too, and my publisher, David Ripianzi, kept stayed cool, calm, and collected for all us. What a team!

Again, Master Max Gaofei Yan kept me on track with historical details and aspects of Chinese culture and martial esoterica, and Janelle made it possible, as she always does, for me to disappear into an imaginary world for months at a time.

**"I command the earth to stop spinning so wildly.
I command all storms to look quietly to their center.
I command all things to become clear to me."**

Gao Sanfeng–2009

Dramatis Personae

Annabelle Miller–Dalton Day's business manager

Brush–executive at Crocodile and Crane Holdings in Hong Kong

Dalton Day–*Gongfu* teacher, writer, coach

Dr. Gary Broten–Centers for Disease Control scientist

Dr. Henri Eonnet–French scientist

Gao Sanfeng–Immortal, *qigong* and martial arts master

Gao the blacksmith–Father to Sanfeng and Zetian, *qigong* creator

Gao Zetian–Immortal, *qigong* and martial arts master, sister to Sanfeng

Huangfu–Zetian's chauffeur

Jimmy Ngo–Billabong books IT employee

Jou Yuen –Pharmaceutical company director, Crocodile & Crane Holdings Indonesian division, Zetian's lover

Leili Musi–Executive assistant to Jou Yuen, nurse, mother of Lombo

Lombo Musi–Six-year-old son of Leili, first plague victim

Monica Farmore–Marketing executive, Billabong Books

Rachel Kleinman–Billabong Books Senior Vice President, Monica's boss

Reggie Pritt–Australian born Hong Kong police captain

Tony Tunstall–Australian Tea Merchant and father of Lombo

1

Henan Province, China–Shang Dynasty, 1426 BCE

The moon is always swollen above this valley, and the cloying smell of the forest rides the back of night like a cavalryman. Steep walls sandwich the valley. The eastern throw of a vast isolating plain, a country of scrub brush and howling winds, lies beyond. A blacksmith named Gao and his two children wearily walk the edge of the ravine, navigating by the stars until they can walk no more. They make camp, and sleep deeply, undisturbed by the myriad creatures of the forest.

In the morning, they rise and Gao makes a fire. He takes leaves from a pouch and brews a weak tea, which he gives to his children to drink. The elder is an arresting girl of fourteen, with high cheekbones, piercing eyes, and a nose atypically aquiline for her tribe of origin in the far west provinces. Her brother, seven years younger, has handsome, regular features, but is more remarkable for his bird-like crown of thick-shafted hair. When they are properly alert, Gao takes his children to a spot in the clearing, where he leads them through a complex set of exercises, his late wife's ancestral *qigong.*

It was not unusual in those days for families to have martial traditions incorporating breathing and stretching: exercises designed to manipulate biological energy. Gao himself came from a long tradition of such training, as did his late wife, whose death in childbirth had been accurately predicted by a village oracle who read the future in the lines of a burnt tortoise shell. Before she died, she contributed to Gao's practice as well, and the blacksmith built on what he inherited and learned, devoting himself to the perfection of the *qigong* because he was above all a practical man who understood the benefits of self-reliance and medicinal self-help.

More than practical, it turned out that Gao was an energy

savant, a true genius in the ways of meridians and meditation. While only his children would ever herald him, he kept at the practice long enough to synthesize a system effective beyond any previous. Over time, he noticed he could work longer and harder than others, and that he barely seemed to age. He noticed his children seemed frozen in time as well, changing barely perceptibly over the years. He might have worried about prolonging their immaturity had they not proven utterly immune to drought and famine, and excesses of heat and cold.

Tenacious and seemingly invulnerable, the little family would occasionally stop wandering and settle in a village, staying only so long as the villagers did not notice their peculiarities, did not wonder why the children seemed not to age, and why the family rarely slept or suffered so much as a sniffle. When questions arose, the family would leave quietly in the night, and in this way as well as all other ways, their *qigong* came to define them.

They practice together now, near the rim of the valley, amidst the birch trees and the rising sun. Gao gleams with a morning corona, and his children do too, but less brightly. The *qigong* movements mimic those of animals, but with an additional dimension of mind an animal could never possess. The routine begins by settling the torso into the pelvic girdle like placing an egg into an egg cup. Next there is breathing timed with stepping, focusing heavily on cultivating strength in the diaphragm and keeping the chest from any involvement in the movement of air. After that comes a kind of twisting that evokes wringing water from a towel.

The spiraling wave seizes the heart and lungs and the intercostal muscles, vivifying and energizing these key components of youth and power. After the chest, the arms are engaged, waving and circling until the muscles literally turn around the bones to which they are attached, creating a degree of freedom that is of great value in martial grappling. The head comes last, and with the wave and the breath timed to match, the sense organs and the brain are themselves suffused by a revitalizing bath, one which the trio perform each and every morning.

When the set is completed, the children shine with sweat and satisfaction. Their father, who has worked at least as hard, does not perspire at all, for his life force, his *qi*, is settled and calm and cannot be disturbed.

"When will you show us something about fighting?" the girl wants to know.

"Not today," says Gao. He is torn by how much martial application to show his daughter. On the one hand, he believes such skill to be the province of men–he shows his son often, usually in the afternoon when the girl is mending clothes or fetching water–but on the other hand the girl is beautiful, and for a life far longer than Gao can imagine will fend off the attention of admirers.

"You said that yesterday," the girl pouts.

The boy and his father exchange a knowing glance. The girl notices and flies into a fury.

"Why do you show *him* then," she rages, pointing at her little brother.

Gao winces. His daughter has had this temper since infancy, and was wont to cow her mother with it.

"Settle down," he says.

The girl stalks off. Father and son watch her shimmy up a birch tree with scarcely believable ease. High up in the branches, hoping only for distance from her family, she settles into a crook in the tree. A flying squirrel comes close to her, for she has nuts in her pocket and it is autumn and the rodent is on a mission to gather food from every available source. She reaches out and grabs the rodent by the neck and pinches the life out of it. She hurls the still-warm corpse to the ground, hitting her brother on the back of the head hard enough to drop him.

"Come down right now," her father commands.

She does, but not before she spies the squirrel's nest, and in it, baby squirrels. She reaches in and takes two out and brings them down with her, pelting her brother with the first one, then picking it up and wringing its neck.

"Stop!" her brother cries. "They're helpless creatures."

"The world is full of helpless creatures, and I refuse to be one of them," she says, chasing the second baby squirrel, which takes refuge between her father's legs.

"Stop being so cruel."

"You're the one who's cruel for not teaching me what you teach him. You think I don't know you practice *gongfu* together? You think I haven't come home and seen you?"

Before her father can answer, she darts between his legs and kills the second baby squirrel with her foot. "That's what happens to the weak in this world," she says. "Do you want that to happen to me?"

"I fear giving you power, seeing what you do even without it," Gao says.

The girl stamps her feet, and screams in frustration.

"Listen to me," her father says. "You are too often angry at the world. Someday you must become a wife and mother. No man will have you until you get the better of your temper."

"I won't belong to anyone then," the girl says. "Not now, not ever."

Sighing, the blacksmith gathers their meager belongings. The boy buries the three squirrels. As the morning warms, they continue their circumnavigation of the valley. They hear the clamor of a community below, and are struck by the unique frenzy of the village, by the smells that issue from the valley, the smoke and the noise.

"Wait here," says Gao, positioning his children in a copse. "I will return before nightfall. If I do not, climb out of the valley and follow the stars as I have shown you."

"To the sea?" asks the boy.

"To the sea," confirms his father.

"You'll come back," says the girl. "I know you will."

Gao creeps down into the valley. He spends the day reconnoitering, and observes a great deal. He has never seen such a density of population, the people literally tripping over each other; their huts built only inches apart.

He discovers that the tribe living there call themselves the Banpo, and the sensitivity to energy the *qigong* has developed within him tells him they have been inbreeding for generations, and are of a weak constitution. He sees they are too numerous for the valley, which can support them no more. There is no tree the Banpo have not stripped of bark, no parcel of land they have not tilled and seeded, no rivulet they have not fished dry. There is no weed they have not tasted, no grass they have not used in soup or in hut making, and no vein of ore they have not mined. Yet even as they exhaust every resource and suffer increasingly crowded conditions, Gao learns the Banpo will not strike out for new territory, as their talk is of the monsters beyond the confines of the valley; a tradition of fear has them cowed and pinned down.

At dusk, he returns to his children.

"In the morning we will visit the village for supplies," he says.

"Can't we stay?" pleads the boy, who is tired of wandering.

"Not long," says his father. "A few days, no more."

2

It was a summer morning even children recognized as evil, a punishing demon that blanketed New York City, crippled the overweight, killed the elderly, forced parched teens to open fireplugs, and tortured the city's row after row of withered flowers. Inside Bloomingdale's Department Store, powerful air conditioners created an oasis for a television news crew filming seventy-three white-coated aestheticians, all perfectly coiffed, moving through a series of gyrations and bends.

They were following the lead of their spiritual concertmaster, Dalton Day. Pale, willowy and tall, he wore a *gongfu* suit of black cotton–the jacket closed by frog buttons–the pants cut loose so he could leap and bend unfettered. His hair was the color of mead, and pulled back into a ponytail, exaggerating his gray eyes, and making him look boyish despite his thirty years. His lips were full and soft, but the rest of his features were angular and flinty, suggesting they could cut if you went at them the wrong way.

"Okay people," he said, his voice amplified by the store's public address system. "Let's stop and breathe: slowly and deeply: in through the nose; out through the mouth. Hold your arms out in front of you as if you are hugging a tree. Now touch your tongue to the roof of your mouth behind your front teeth. With a little practice, you can exhale past your tongue. This circuit of breath keeps tension down, and makes an energy circuit up your spine and down your midline, following meridians the Chinese call *Ren and Du.*"

He moved smoothly through the crowd, fixing stances here and there, chastely massaging a stiff neck or two, helping raised shoulders drop, and tight hips relax.

"Get comfortable," he said. "Fine. Now I want you to focus your attention on the soles of your feet, on the spot the Chinese call 'The Bubbling Well.' You can find it just behind the middle of the ball of your foot. This is your energetic connection with the ground, and I want you to imagine roots emerging from it, anchoring you firmly so you can relax without worry."

His audience sank perceptibly, and he nodded to himself, satisfied.

"Right. By now these roots of yours are thicker than the largest phone pole you've ever seen, but tipped with little digging fingers. Each time you inhale, the roots bring you energy from the Earth. Each time you exhale, you send the roots deeper and deeper into the ground, through the tile floor below you, through the wooden sub-floor and the concrete foundation, and right into the bedrock of Manhattan Island. Exhaling, you drive the roots toward the liquid, bubbling, molten center of the Earth. Inhaling, you bring up enough energy to heat your feet. I know that sounds god-awful on a steamy day like this, but it's good, believe me, because what you're doing is charging yourself up like a big sexy battery."

Dalton saw his audience smile; saw the TV crew grinning. Encouraged, he went on.

"Now the roots are the size of giant Sequoia trees, and as they twist and dive deeper you can feel the energy coming up your legs. You are powerful, ladies. Not even a bulldozer can move you from where you stand. You're one with the Earth, in contact with a whole new kind of Mother Nature, and it feels peaceful and exciting at the same time. You're more relaxed by the minute."

Sure enough, it was clear to him the meditation was working like magic. The normally frenzied sales staff was happy, relaxed, breathing deeply and easily, unaffected by the fact they were live on national television.

"That's all for today," Dalton told the group. "But the energy you have brought up from the ground will stay with you. Now it's time to slowly let your hands down, and open your eyes."

Surprised and refreshed, the cosmetic clerks mobbed Dalton. Panning and zooming, the TV cameras caught him shyly smiling, flushed with success beyond his expectation. A newspaper reporter cornered him, and thrust a voice recorder at his chin.

"A moment of your time?"

"I really have to catch a flight. I'm afraid a moment is all I have."

"Do you consider yourself religious?" the reporter asked.

"I consider myself spiritual."

"Do you believe in God?"

Dalton hesitated. "If you mean a personal god who watches over me while stroking his beard up in the clouds, the answer is no."

"You're an atheist, then? You go it alone?"

"I don't like labels much. Seems to me they do more to drive people apart than bring them together."

"What would you say is the distinction between religion and spirituality?"

Relaxed, Dalton sank a bit more deeply into his stance. "The way I see it, religion is organized and taught; spirituality is experienced directly."

"I'll have to think about that one. Can you at least tell me what got you started in all this? I can't find much background on you."

"A girl named Grace set me on the path," Dalton answered. "I thought of her just now when I got a whiff of patchouli; she used to wear it."

"Was she Asian?"

Dalton laughed. "She was a Haight-Ashbury hippie, but she read Daoist texts and taught me all about yin/yang theory."

"Give me that in English."

"Daoists were the wooly mountain men of China. They meditated in caves for years at a time, and tried to live life as naturally as possible. They had the idea that the universe is all about opposing forces playing against each other. When things are going well, the interplay is harmonious. When everything seems rough and difficult, it's because opposites are out of balance."

"I'll have to think about that too."

"You asked about my beliefs. I believe you're here for a reason. At this interview, I mean. I don't think anything happens by accident."

"What else did that young lady teach you?"

"To be dissatisfied with my education, even though I went to a brand-name college, to question everything, to always dig deeper. Grace fell in love with another guy, and I fell in love with the Chinese classics."

"Which are what, exactly?"

"Works of philosophy, and political tracts masquerading as novels."

"You don't strike me as very political."

Dalton put his hand on the reporter's shoulder. "Politics are yet another thing that drives people apart. There's a lot of great material in those books. That ancient world was gritty and tough–average people didn't live very long–but it was also full of loyalty and honor, compassion and fighting."

"Gongfu?"

"First you dream it, then you want to do it. These days, of course, *gongfu* training is for the body what meditation is for the mind. It's all about strength, balance, health, and longevity."

"Not self-defense?"

Dalton shrugged. "Self-defense against your inner demons, self-defense against the degenerative diseases of aging. Guns are so widespread; I don't sell the combat side too much. Once you become competent, violence loses its attraction."

"Easy for a master to say," the reporter countered. "But lots of folks out there are scared these days, particularly in the cities."

"Violence is never the solution. It only makes problems worse. We have the power to choose non-violence, to steer clear of our animal instincts and become an internal boxer, which is to say, someone who uses fighting competence to build self-confidence and avoid fighting because he, or she, has nothing to prove. I'm advocating self-cultivation, not a path to pugilism. And by the way, please don't call me a master. I've trained with masters. I know I'm not one."

"Give me your message in a nutshell,"

"The nutshell is the book."

"Please?"

Dalton sighed. "Anything worth doing is worth doing slowly."

"That's the message?"

"Seed the body with physical practice, fertilize the mind with meditation."

"In other words you need both philosophy and movement to be healthy and happy."

"You got it," Dalton nodded, giving a cheery wave.

He made his way to the store's Third Avenue exit and into his waiting limo.

Anabelle Miller was in the back seat. She was lean with a square Welsh face–copper hair, freckles everywhere, and a firm chin. She had met Dalton at one of his seminars and become an instant fan. Initially, he had hired her to do the books for his small school, but she had taken over more and more of his career, finally becoming more of a manager than an accountant, directing him to lucrative corporate speaking gigs and expensive private lessons for well-heeled students looking as much for transcendence as martial competence.

"You looked great on camera," Anabelle enthused

"I thought I was stiff."

"You thought the same thing about *Good Morning America*, but it was a triumph."

"Chasing the limelight is your idea," said Dalton.

The limo came to a traffic light. Annabelle leaned forward until her elbows were on Dalton's knees. "You want to help people, right?"

"You know I do."

"The limelight lets you help more than you've ever dreamed. Media appearances give you credibility."

"Credibility comes from experience and skill, not from cameras," said Dalton.

Annabelle spread her hands. "Fine. Then go back to teaching in a dirty little corner of the Lower East Side."

"The school was never dirty."

"Quit your grousing. You were earning a few hundred bucks a week and doing your laundry at the Laundromat."

Dalton smiled a reluctant smile. "I'm grateful for everything you've helped me do. I just miss the quiet time to practice, and the opportunity to make meaningful connections with people."

"You can make those connections," Annabelle said. "Your book will help you."

"The book was also your idea."

"I'm glad it turned out to be a good one."

The limo took the FDR Drive north, and crossed the Triboro Bridge. Dalton stared out the window, lost in thought. Annabelle watched him. Sometimes she worried she had pushed him too hard too fast. Fresh out of business school with a head full of entrepreneurial ideas, she knew her job was a dream come true, an opportunity to put everything she had learned to work. She didn't want to blow it.

"You might consider following your own advice," she said softly.

"Meaning?"

"Stop wishing you were a monk. Go with the flow. You're the real deal. The fallout from Letterman is fantastic. Five grunting bodybuilders pushing against your arm and you just smiling sweetly at the camera like you're getting your toenails done. If you need more time to train, just say so. If you need more time to meditate, tell me that, too."

"I have to recharge sometimes, that's all. If I keep going and going without quiet time, I lose touch with the source of what I know. Life gets superficial. I don't like myself."

"I understand. When you get back, we'll put meditation and practice times right into the schedule on my PDA. Now, tell me, have you thought about my clothing line idea? I've already talked to one manufacturer in Thailand. You'd have to do the modeling, though. No way we can sell product without your image attached."

"I'm no model. If we do the line, we'll hire beautiful people."

"You're a hunk, boss. You know you are."

"A hunk who knows brown-nosing when he sees it. Now brief me on Hong Kong. Did you get me an aisle seat? I've got to be rested for the meeting and I do better if I can move around a bit."

"Aisle seat it is, but don't sweat the meeting. Foreign rights don't amount to much; you're just going there for PR. The publisher used to be Australian-owned and stodgy, but the Chinese entrepreneurs who took it over are hip and savvy. They understand marketing, and they know that a personal appearance can get the buzz going in Hong Kong. Do me a favor, though. Just remember the Chinese put their last name first, and first name last. I know you know that, but it's easy to forget, and remembering will save embarrassment."

"I'll remember. But selling *The Boxer Within* in Asia still feels like preaching to the choir."

"I bet the book does well. The way the publishers explained it to me, young people in Hong Kong favor Western culture, but are proud of their heritage. You offer them access to old knowledge in a new, American way."

"The publishers told you that?"

"I paraphrase."

"Of course you do. I've got only one thing to tell you."

"And what's that?"

"Practice the *qigong* I showed you while I'm gone."

Annabelle closed her eyes and waved her hands like a windmill in a faint breeze.

"You're holding your breath," said Dalton.

"That's right," Annabelle grinned. "And I'll keep holding it until you come back."

3

Gao and his children blaze a trail downward until someone from below catches sight of them. The Banpo cannot remember the last time someone came in from the terrifying land beyond the valley; they treat the travelers as great heroes. There are days of celebration, and the celebration entails drinking. The alcohol of the Banpo is made from fermented fruit, and it goes to the blacksmith's head. In order to clear himself and stay alert, he performs his *qigong* ritual by firelight, when he believes all the villagers to be intoxicated or asleep.

In the days that follow, the children move freely about the village. The girl attracts a crowd of suitors, but she frigidly rebuffs them all. The boy draws younger children to him, and amuses them with tricks. Meanwhile, Gao finds a forge and makes tools to earn money for supplies. In a few days, he has enough herbs to season into palatability even the toughest game, and he clothes himself and his children in rugged skins for the coming winter.

The family has been in the village for only a week, when a terrible sickness crops up in the village, spreading as savagely as a wildfire. Within the first two days it has crippled the village, destroying the weak and the strong, the young and the old, all horribly and without distinction. Beginning with sneezing, it rapidly leads to joint pain, seizures, and death characterized by a gruesome facial grimace. A sentry goes to the village chief and reports that the blacksmith is dancing in a strange way by firelight. The chief reports this news to the high priest of the village, who concludes that the horrible killing smile must be a curse brought by Gao.

"Bring the blacksmith to me," the priest orders.

Gao fights valiantly but is no match for the horde that drags him to the temple, where the priest binds him fast to a stone table. Certain a sacrifice to the gods will end their trial, the Banpo gather in their temple. As darkness falls torches flicker, animating the shadows of the devout and drawing stick-like insects to the light.

Gao writhes against the deerskin bonds. He knows he has nothing to do with the disease and fears that when his death brings no cure his children will be killed too. When the villagers are distracted setting up the ritual, his daughter sneaks to him and struggles against his bonds.

"Forget about me! Take your brother, and run!" Gao hisses.

The young girl sets her jaw. "No."

"Will you listen to me this one time?"

"If I can just loosen those deerskin bonds, I can set you free."

"You would disobey me?"

"Only to save you, Father."

Nearby, her brother sits near a great bronze gong and plays with a hardwood top. Certain she was pregnant with a boy, his mother carved the toy for him while he was still in her belly, but never had the joy of giving it to him. He has carried it every day of his life. His father beckons him over.

The villagers cluster at the other side of the temple, thirty paces away. Some of their faces are already grotesquely distorted by the affliction, but all are raised in prayer to stone gods. The village priest gyrates in a ritual dance before the worshippers.

"It's too late," the blacksmith whispers to his children. "Help me die in peace by knowing you are both safe. Get out of this valley, and follow the river east. Practice your *qigong* every day. Every day, do you hear me?"

"Yes, Father," says his daughter.

"And you?"

"Yes, Father," says the boy.

"Never, *ever* neglect our family practice–not the meditation, not the breathing, nor any of the rest of it. Repeat it every day, no matter what happens, no matter what else you do."

The girl attacks her father's bonds with renewed desperation, but her fingernails find no purchase. "I'm going to kill everybody in this village to avenge you," she says.

"Just flee," the blacksmith implores. "There is no need for vengeance. Nature will exact it for you. Get your brother to safety. He's too young to be left alone."

Headstrong and stubborn, his daughter continues to gnaw the deerskin the way a wolf chews bone. The blacksmith feels her hot breath on the back of his hand, and sees her white teeth grow dark from the tannin. The boy creeps up, but the blacksmith waves him away.

The boy retreats instantly. He has none of his sister's rebelliousness. Obedience is all he knows. He has been trained to it well, following his father across the face of central China. He has crouched by the fire of his father's smelting furnace, and worked to bring firewood. He has done the *qigong* with his father every day, living for his father's loving glances, knowing that his father values him above all else in the world.

"Make me a promise," the blacksmith whispers, looking at his daughter's face, her lips swollen from fruitless biting and pulling. "Our *qigong* is for the two of you only. Never share it with a soul, so long as you both shall live."

"I promise."

"Remember, too, to protect your head and your heart. Those are the two places our *qigong* cannot regenerate."

"Protect the head and the heart," the girl repeats.

The Banpo priest draws near the sacrificial table, forcing the girl to retreat. In his hand, the priest carries the blacksmith's own *guan dao*, a seven-foot halberd with a hooked sword blade at the end. It is a fearsome weapon, conceived for use on horseback. "Our gods demands your life," he says, as the crowd stomps their approval.

"I've told you before, I have nothing to do with the plague that's killing you," Gao replies.

"You came, the smile came. You practice evil dances when you think nobody is watching, and your body stays strong and unblemished while the rest of us perish. Nor do your children get sick, even though our own children die. Your arrangement with your gods has brought sorrow to our village. When you are dead, this plague will run from us like a frightened tiger."

The villagers hoot in agreement. Gao grinds his teeth in frustration. "Know this," he says, straining to lift his body a few inches off the table. "We have not brought your misfortune. You are dying because there are too many of you here, and because you go against nature by mating brother and sister. Put too many chickens in one coop, and they too sicken and die: too many fish in a pond, they float belly-up to the surface. You have outgrown your valley, but you lack the courage to leave it. The forest and the plain are filled with animals to hunt, rivers to fish, fields to farm. I have seen them, but you have not because you are too fearful to venture there. My children and I are not killing you: you are killing yourselves. Set yourselves free! Spread out!"

In response, the priest raises the *guan dao* and brings it down on Gao's neck. The blade cuts all the way through to the stone table, and the impact shatters the bones in the priest's wrists, setting him shrieking. Gao's severed head rolls to the end of the table and falls to the ground, landing on one ear. In the last instant of consciousness, the blacksmith's eyes catch sight of his daughter, crouched beneath the table. Impossibly, he winks.

The villagers cheer, certain their suffering is over. The Gao girl wants to throw herself on the people and bite and scratch and kick and hit. Her brother restrains her. She breathes vengeance, but he pulls her out the front door anyway. The children run past the clearing and into the dark woods, their wounded hearts pounding, sobbing for their father, because he is dead, and for themselves, because they are alone. They run until they can run no more, rest, get up and run again. Their fear and their stamina take them far, far away from the hamlet, farther than the Banpo have ever been.

"Are they following?" the girl pants, taking shelter in thick underbrush.

"I don't think so," her little brother replies, peeking out from behind a thick trunk.

"You should have let me stay and fight them."

"You don't know how to fight. They would have taken your head too."

"I would have avenged our father and taken some of them with me."

"Look," the boy points. "There's the river!"

The morning light is upon them. Warily, they creep down to the bank. When they have drunk their fill, the girl pulls her brother close. "Listen to me," she says. "There is nothing more important than our secret *qigong.* Our father died for it, and he made us promise we would practice every day."

"I will. Every day."

"And you must promise never to show it to anyone."

Terrified, bereft, hungry and feeling horribly alone, the little boy nods.

"Say it aloud!" his sister shakes him roughly.

"I promise!" the boy cries.

"We must honor our father forever."

"Forever," echoes the boy.

A high-pitched squabble erupts on the riverbank. A crane has speared a catfish and brought it out of the water, but the fish is too large for the bird to manage, and it twists and flops in a desperate bid for life. Suddenly a crocodile explodes up the bank, and takes the fish in its jaws. The crane will not back down. It pecks at the crocodile's eyes until the reptile retreats, leaving half the fish. The crane, now able to lift the spoils, flies away with the catch. Each predator has gotten half.

"What will become of us?" whispers the boy.

"We will go forward together and share the world," says his sister. "Just like the crocodile and the crane."

4

The long-haul Airbus 340 passed the limit of the Arctic Circle with Dalton Day doing quiet meditation in his business class seat. Flight attendants were in the aisles with champagne and cookies when the plane flew into a storm. Dalton kept his eyes closed as a gust hit the plane, but he registered the bump.

"Sorry about that, folks," the pilot announced. "Radar showed this system much farther out than it is. We've got a few of these embedded storms in front of us: unusual for this time of year, frankly, and not on our weather advisory. We're going to blaze the trail for other flights by picking our way through the cells. There's no real danger, but there will be one beautiful lightshow for you weather buffs back there."

A couple of people grumbled about wanting safe transportation, not entertainment, but Dalton brought his seat back up, and raised his window shade to scan the night sky.

"Some champagne, Mr. Day?" a flight attendant inquired softly.

"Half a glass, please."

The flight attendant smiled. "I thought you might say no, spiritual teacher and all that."

"I won't tell if you won't."

"I read the blurb about you in *Time* magazine," she said.

"You're nice," said Dalton.

"My gosh but you're a shy one. Not used to being recognized? I bet you're going to have to get used to it. Your inner boxer idea is cool. Is it true you've taught movie stars?"

"My secret."

"Which ones?" She leaned forward eagerly. "I promise I won't tell anyone."

"Of course you will," Dalton smiled. "You'll tell everyone."

The flight attendant giggled. "You're right. I'm a terrible gossip. I watched your Bloomingdale's broadcast in the crew lounge this morning. I tried doing the standing meditation along with you, but I got needles and pins in my feet."

"Were you wearing high heels?"

"I always wear high heels."

"Heels aren't the best meditation shoes."

"Could I do the standing meditation on long flights? There's usually time, you know, after all the passengers have gone to sleep."

Before he could answer, a blue flash filled the cabin, and the plane suddenly dropped. The flight attendant tumbled away, and the overhead bins popped open. Thunder clapped.

While lightning charges generally dissipate across an airplane's skin without doing any real harm, occasionally–if the strike is uncommonly strong and there are composites in the fuselage–electrical circuits are affected. The charge that hit the Airbus was of that magnitude, and it devastated the craft's autopilot. The plane pitched to starboard, sending it into a steep uncontrolled dive. Emergency floor lighting appeared and people screamed as oxygen masks dropped from ceiling panels. Champagne corks popped in the galley.

The smell of ozone filled the cabin, and the door to the cockpit burst open. The purser came out, his eyes wide, his mouth agape, his voice lost to the labored shriek of the jet engines. He ran past Dalton, leaving the door open and swinging. Smoke billowed out of the cockpit as Dalton rose and ran forward. He found the pilots fighting the yoke, and the overhead switches smoldering.

The tempest shook the plane like a puppy shakes a shoe. Balancing against the navigation console Dalton used his meditation skills to scan his body. The deep, true Dalton observed the agitated Dalton's shaky legs and sweating palms and issued a calming order. Breathe, Dalton told himself. This kind of storm may be perfectly routine in these far north crossings.

A slim Asian man with a high forehead and peculiar thick hair jostled Dalton from his morbid reverie, pushing him aside and sliding up to the controls. The pilots shouted angrily while the man played a silent symphony on the switches, his fingers moving inquisitively over the panels as if exploring the creases and buttons of a lover. A strange keening came from his throat, and something red and crackling–not fire, not static–leapt from his fingers to the avionics. As if in answer, the whole instrument panel suddenly came alive. Needles stabilized, lights came back on, the pitch of the engines steadied, and the airplane's nose gradually came up.

Bewildered, the pilots began to question and quarrel and sputter and yell, but the man quieted each of them with a gentle touch on the forehead.

Then he turned to Dalton.

5

Leili Musi and her six-year-old boy Lombo came aground at Sunda Kelapa, Jakarta's back door, and maritime gateway to the world's fourth most populous nation. The historic port, named for the original Hindu spice-trading post, was decorated with the flapping sails and hulls of multicolored *pinisi*, the wooden Buginese junks that plied the Indonesian archipelago, most often laden with sawn Kalimantan timber, but occasionally also carrying passengers on a shoestring.

Leili's junk docked with a gentle bump, running intentionally aground against the dirt piles that substituted for a pier. A long plank was laid down, and bare-chested sailors began unceremoniously offloading cargo. By the time the single mother and her son came out on deck with their shoddy bags, there was already a hubbub around the ship. A couple of seamen dove into the fetid water to cool off, and splashed around in the dawn, shouting happily. Leili wanted nothing so much as to escape the ferocious heat by diving right into the water beside them, but she was a striking woman with a sultry look, and had already suffered enough of their leering. She took her child by the hand, and left quickly.

Mother and son trudged along the waterfront with their suitcases, the little boy carrying his favorite stuffed elephant. They stopped by the old Dutch lookout tower just long enough to clean the mud from their shoes before catching one bus to Merdaka Square, the heart of the city, and then another to the rabbit warren that was Glodok, Jakarta's Chinatown, south of the city's colonial European center.

Communism had been crushed under the forceful heel of Islam and President Soekarno in the 1950s, and the Chinese–their written and spoken language strictly forbidden–were still pariahs. Leili lived in the unlikely location because of what was now clearly a poor career decision. Needing more money when Lombo was born, she left nursing for an executive assistant position with a Chinese pharmaceutical concern. When she was little, her mother had seen China's rise and insisted her daughter learn Chinese. The increase in salary made Leili glad she'd stayed in practice.

At first, her new boss, Jou Yuen, had been decent, but in time his appetites had become clear. His persistent brand of charm had led to one sexual liaison, and then another. When it became obvious Jou wanted a mistress not merely a secretary, Leili succumbed. To clinch the deal, Jou bought her an apartment.

When she learned it was in Glodok–for discretion's sake, he said–Leili threatened to leave. In response, Jou furnished it opulently, put in new windows for a panoramic view of the city, and even made renovations to the building so she had perfect plumbing and reliable electricity. It was now a beautiful place, perhaps the best in the area, and everything in it, from flatware to wall-hangings was absolutely first class. By the time Leili came to loathe her benefactor, she was too smothered in debt–the expensive sexy lingerie Jou demanded she buy, private school and special classes for Lombo, a new car–to get out.

"Please can we have air conditioning?" Lombo begged.

"Of course," said Leili, setting the switch on the thermostat, then rushing to bring the boy a wet towel for his brow. "I'm sorry, baby. I know it's hot, but we had a great vacation in the out islands, don't you think? And you got to swim with dolphins."

"In the same *ocean* with dolphins. I didn't get to actually touch one or anything."

Leili knew Lombo was disappointed. His keen interest in animals was at least partly responsible for their itinerary, and the dolphin swim had not worked out exactly as planned. Still, the trip to Taman Margasatwa Zoo in Medan was a great success, and the stuffed elephant she bought him there had stayed in his grasp since.

"I'll take you on other trips," she promised, silently cursing her employer for the tight vacation policy that would force her to wait at least another year to do so.

Lombo was an academic prodigy, and Leili spent freely on trips, piano lessons, books, and educational toys for the boy, who by the age of two, was able to calculate the projected path of every planet in the solar system, and by four, speak Mandarin and French, on top of his native Malay.

A fit of sneezing took Lombo. "I don't feel well," he said.

"You look pretty happy," Leili ventured.

"My body hurts," he said.

The nurse in Leili took over. She bathed him in rubbing alcohol, and poured two big glasses of water down his throat. Then, as he drifted off into what seemed like a contented sleep, she kissed him, closed the door, and began her exercises. They made her feel good, they really did, although she had a thousand questions about them–more every day.

She had learned the routine six months earlier when the gorgeous chairwoman of their parent company visited Jakarta. Everyone in the office was terrified of Madame Gao Zetian and spoke her name in reverential whisper. Leili should not have been surprised when she came home in the middle of the day and found Zetian with Jou in her apartment, but she was. She followed Zetian's trail to the bedroom door–high-heeled Italian shoes, designer dress, silk stockings, finally, skimpy panties–and peeked through the keyhole. There were rumors Zetian took men as sport, and watching her sexual gymnastics with morbid curiosity, Leili was sure it was true.

When Jou fell asleep, Leili saw Zetian move to the middle of the room and begin a bizarre sequence of movements. She had read that headstands inhibit pregnancy and wondered if perhaps Jou's prophylactic had ruptured. It soon became obvious the exercises were something different; they involved indistinct grunting, singing and chanting along with violent twisting, writhing movement punctuated by quiet meditation. Knowing Zetian's reputation, and sensing some kind of mystical power in the routine, Leili did her best to mimic the sequence silently on the floor outside.

Her boss's liaisons continued all week, and each day at lunchtime, Leili took the trek home, slipped silently into her own apartment, and took revenge by watching Gao Zetian's exercise routine and mimicking it. At first she told herself she was doing it to become as flexible as Zetian obviously was, or as powerful or smart or rich or lucky. She told herself if she could move like that she could have any man, even one who really loved her. After three days, however, something began stirring in her, and all she could think about was the exercises. Almost addicted to them, she practiced the breathing at odd times, and alone in the stall in the ladies' room at work, practiced the spiraling movements, and the way Zetian emptied herself of breath and then pulled up on her abdomen so as to massage her inner organs one against the other.

Long after Zetian went home, Leili practiced, and although she knew movements were missing and wished she could ask her unwitting mentor certain very specific questions, she soon found she could go almost as low in her postures as Zetian had, and could turn her body almost as far around.

If Jou Yuen perceived the results of the practice in Leili, he did not mention it. In the months that followed, however, Leili realized her periods were light and regular, her skin glowed, old bathing suits fit, and she never suffered from so much as a sniffle. More than that, she found she possessed a newfound resolve in all things, an ability to follow through on projects she started, and the strength to stay optimistic in the nightmare her life had become. She believed so deeply in the routine she performed it every day, sometimes twice, sometimes three times. The effects seemed miraculous, and the better she felt, the more she wondered about Zetian and her exercises.

Jou Yuen looked across his vast malachite desk at the panoramic view of Jakarta. It was already mid-morning, and the sights were already out of focus, thanks to the burnt orange layer of hazy smog created by internal combustion fumes. Horrible city, he thought–unsanitary, overcrowded, and desperate–but no worse than Beijing, where aridification caused dust storms that blanketed the city at least once a month. Working here was worth it, though, as he was getting rich in Jakarta without having to bribe the entire Chinese Communist Party. The complete lack of regulation and the systematized government graft were great for business, making it easy to manufacture herbal products cheaply and export them directly to the growing American market. His superiors at Crocodile & Crane Holdings were delighted with his numbers.

Beyond that, he was thankful for Leili. Nothing could compare with his one-time fling with Gao Zetian, but Leili was still a gifted and generous lover, and she looked better and moved more lithely all the time. Of course he had interviewed many women in search of just the right combination of looks, science background, and business savvy. He hadn't wanted a woman with a kid, but Leili was so perfect in every other way, he'd hired her anyway.

He checked his watch. It was time. His chauffeur was at lunch. In China, he would have trusted his personal driver to take him to a romantic meeting; here, he never did. The chauffeur took Jou's wife shopping sometimes, and was just the type to let something slip. Jou went down to the garage as he always did, got into his bronze Jaguar coupe, and drove to Glodok. He knew the twisting streets better than most, in part because it was his hobby to immerse himself in the local culture whenever he was posted to a new city.

"We just came back," Leili apologized. "Lombo isn't well."

Jou frowned disapprovingly. "Is he asleep?"

"Yes, but I'll have to listen for him," Leili answered, knowing Jou would ask her to be vocal in her sexual appreciation, and loathing the prospect.

Jou nodded, and began taking off his pants. Leili turned away, unable to watch him. No wonder the Indonesians hated the Chinese: their industry, their cleverness, the way they liked to control things.

"Momma!" Lombo suddenly moaned from the other room.

Leili gathered the bedclothes about her. Jou froze, scowling.

Sometimes he wished the little bastard would just die.

6

Monica Farmore first visited Hong Kong in 1998 as a college freshman on a student exchange, arriving on the very last international flight to land at infamous Kai Tak airport. She experienced the dizzying descent into the middle of town, and gasped as the landing gear seemed to scrape the rooftops of Kowloon, a part of town kept low, literally, by the approach and departure corridors. As the wheels touched the tarmac, the pilot waxed philosophical about how the old Hong Kong would soon be gone forever, and commented that the only constant in the universe was change.

Kai Tak was now the site of an Elysian housing development, and as Monica waited for Dalton Day in the new arrival hall at Chek Lap Kok, she decided the pilot had been right. Despite most outward appearances, Hong Kong was not the same since the handover. Communism was spreading over what had once been the glory of a Crown Colony. The town had an increasingly agrarian edge to it, and Hong Kong's capitalist princes, now facing a new master in Beijing, had turned downright mean. She could see it in the way they looked at her at the airport entrance, the security checkpoint, and at the bar, where she sat thumbing through Dalton Day's book. One after the other they approached and suggested she might enjoy something stronger than the orange juice she was drinking. Occasionally, they pointed at her copy of Dalton's book and asked if she did *gongfu.*

Monica handled them with ease. Mistress of the icy rebuff, she was a tight-bodied beauty from Enid, Oklahoma, a testimonial to hybrid vigor, with green Asian eyes and blonde hair worn braided in neat rows to show her scalp, Generation-Y style. Barely five feet tall, she felt bigger in Hong Kong than she had at home. Chinese were taller these days, but they were still tiny tykes compared to the men in overalls she had known as a girl: oil-derrick-sized farmers who strode across the endless Oklahoma panhandle looking positively Gulliverian against the New Mexican butte.

She expected pretty much the same predation from Dalton Day. Even though his authorial voice was humble and even-keel, by the time authors got the kind of coverage *The Boxer Within* had received, they were usually pretty taken with themselves. Monica wanted, *needed* the book to sell well, but she was not looking forward to meeting the author and having her illusions shattered.

She glanced at her watch. The plane was late, with no word of why. That was the Beijing way. Let the proles suffer. Monica was all set to call the office and tell them she was going home, when she recognized Dalton ambling distractedly through the arrival door, a black raincoat slung over his arm.

The other passengers passed him in a rush. Thinking he might be drunk, Monica stepped up to meet him and pushed out her hand, trying to cost him his balance. She worked hard at the gym, was proud of her strength, and this was a little power game she played, pushing outstretched fingers nearly into a man's chest at first meeting, so as to rock him back onto his heels and defuse a bone-crushing grip.

"Monica Farmore," she said. "I'm with Billabong Books."

"Dalton Day," he replied, gently pulling her forward.

Now that was a first. Usually it was the *guy* who looked like a lurching fool, not Monica. Maybe he did know a bit of *gongfu* after all. Being busted at her own game amused her. She hoped he missed her little grin.

"Our Senior Vice President, Rachel Kleinman, wanted to be here to greet you personally, but she's in the hospital with asthma," she said. "A lot of people have trouble breathing here. The pollution is terrible."

"I'm delighted it's you instead."

"You must be exhausted. It's a long flight even without the delay."

"Delay?" Dalton blinked.

"You're nearly two hours late. If they leave late, they usually make the time up en route, unless there's a wind. Did you have bad weather?"

"Not that I recall. Seems like I slept most of the way. So where did you learn English, Monica? You have no accent at all."

"My father was Chinese, but I grew up in the Midwest."

"I wish I had some Chinese blood," Dalton said as they began to walk. "I've been in love with the philosophy and martial arts of China for more than two decades, but I always feel like an outsider looking in through the window at a big happy family."

"I don't know that I'd call China a big happy family."

"I work hard to keep my rose-colored glasses firmly on my nose."

"Really? I found *The Boxer Within* very sober. Funny in places, but a serious work with a serious message."

"So you're an editor?"

"I'm the marketing director."

"Do you predict my book will sell?"

Before Monica could answer, a group of men in dark suits surrounded them.

"Professor Day!" Their leader bowed.

"Hello," Dalton blinked. "Actually, I'm not a professor."

Monica's first and nearly instant thought was that he might not be a professor, but there was the seriousness of an academic geek about him. She kept her counsel.

"I am Robert Fong," said the Chinese group leader. "Assistant Director of Home Affairs. These masters have come from all over China to join me in welcoming you to our country. We are grateful for what you have done to bring our most treasured traditions to the West."

Monica stood on tiptoes to whisper quickly in Dalton's ear. "Home Affairs means he's some sort of cultural attaché. The new government does this kind of thing sometimes. Five years ago, it would never have happened, but they're big on protocol now. Be nice to these guys. Do what they ask."

Fong introduced his delegation: practioners of Shaolin Long fist, Monkey style, White Eyebrow, and Praying Mantis *gongfu*, along with *Shuai Jiao*, *Xingyiquan* and *Taijiquan.* Dalton was thrilled. These men were the sort Dalton had seen in movies when he was a kid, although no film could have prepared him for the sour mash smell of the thick-bellied wrestler, the willowy *gongfu* master's wall eye, the missing fingers of the Shaolin master, or the star-shaped white cicatrice at the base of the sword master's throat, the mark, no doubt, of an opponent's blade.

Dalton gave a deep bow. "I don't deserve this. All I did was take some old Chinese ideas and express them in a modern, American way."

"You have devoted yourself to our traditional ways and our beliefs," Fong said. "And you've been on big television shows. That is not a small thing."

When this brief exchange was over, Dalton found the masters jockeying for position, each trying to walk closest to him as the entourage navigated the airport.

"We have arranged a banquet!" Fong cried happily. "We shall have roast pork together, and smoked duck. Also lobster! Also monkey brain!"

"Join us?" Dalton took Monica's hand.

She surprised herself by saying yes.

7

Dalton swung his legs over the side of the bed, and smiled to himself at the memory of the previous night. He had eaten far too much–monkey brains had been the least of it–and the endless toasts had required endless drinking. Monica Farmore turned out to be both smart and sweet, and the masters seemed less intimidating with a bit of wine in them, or perhaps with a bit of wine in *him.* He reached back and rubbed his kidneys 81 times with his palms, drew a few controlled Daoist breaths–tightening his belly in and up as he inhaled, letting it drop easily as he let the air out–and then worked through a routine of his own design, something he had come to by changing and furthering the movements taught to him by his teachers

The primary theme to his movements was the spiral, a notion that had come to him after he saw an ancient Chinese text illustrating variations of the classical yin/yang symbol. The oldest of these, the original from which the others sprang, showed the dark and light halves intertwined in a spiral, growing tighter around an empty circle at the center. The explanation said the empty center was a symbol of the primordial universe, the emptiness gravid with infinite possibility, from which sprang the world organized into its component parts. Dalton came to think of the empty center as what the Bible described as the ether from which God created the universe. In practical terms, he decided it represented meditation.

The spiral also interested him because years of combat experience had taught him that while it was best not to meet force with force, it was also essential to not simply retreat and yield. The third alternative was to go around incoming force by spiraling behind it in much the way a snake climbs a tree. Dalton practiced this technique with his teachers and his students, and eventually incorporated it into his *qigong* exercises, his daily health routine. He was confident his personal sequence had great power, and he rejoiced in the growing vitality he experienced since he had refined the moves to their current state.

When he finished his sequence, he noticed the message light on his phone was blinking. Annabelle had called. He called her back.

"Dinnertime there, yes?"

"That's right. Where are you? I called your hotel."

He didn't want to tell her he had put a do-not-disturb on the phone precisely because he knew she would call in the middle of his exercise.

"Taking a shower."

"Your hotel all right?"

"Perfect."

"And the flight?"

"They said something about weather, but I didn't notice it."

"Billabong contact you?"

"One of their people met me at the airport."

"Rachel Kleinman?"

"Someone she sent."

"You're being secretive. Must be a pretty young girl."

"Annabelle."

"I know, I know–you're a grown-up. What are you going to do today? Get some rest and stay close to the hotel, whatever you have in mind. You have to save your strength for the signings."

"Sure," said Dalton. "I'll do that."

"And think about that clothing line. It's a winner. I feel it in my bones."

Dalton promised he would, hung up, and showered and dressed. He ate a light breakfast, and stopped by the desk for a map. He wanted to see something of Hong Kong before the promotional work began, and his plan was to start at Possession Point, where the British had taken ownership of the city at the end of the Opium Wars.

"Unfortunately, that spot is unmarked," the hotel's fresh-faced concierge informed him. "But if you are interested in getting a view of the city, you could take the Star Ferry across to Kowloon. There's a fine view of Victoria Harbor from the boat, better than what you could get from any one point in Central."

Dalton had a nose for life, and it led him around shamelessly. Aromas burned a hot wire right into his brain stem, overarching everything, commanding his experiences. When he stepped out of the hotel–in the Wan Chai district, near the water–the pungent smell of fermented soy struck him. He recognized it from New York's Chinatown, but it was much stronger here, more alive. In fact, there was life everywhere he looked. Even the buildings were alive, growing mold on their facades from the humidity, and the sheer bustle of the place was amazing. Every face brimmed with a preoccupied determination, as if the task at hand–whether it was sweeping the street, driving to work, or pushing a cart full of plastic dolls–was the most important thing in the world. He also noticed that personal space was an alien idea here. People pushed and shoved and rubbed past each other, and drove their cars with no margin of safety whatsoever. Feeling like he really was on another planet, but an exciting, even welcoming one, Dalton walked all the way to the Star Ferry dock with a grin on his face.

He boarded the boat, a green and cream affair with a dark wooden interior and its own unique aroma of sea and salt and sweat. The lower compartment was full of backpackers on a budget; affluent tourists and well-heeled locals used the upper deck. The captain barked commands, and Dalton watched the blue-clad deckhands joking happily as they manipulated their hooked docking poles.

The waterfront skyline of Kowloon was intriguing–the colonial days, the surging markets of Asia, and the Chinese Communist's proletariat all converging on one port. Dalton stayed on the bow of the lower deck, arms out in his favorite meditative posture, knees slightly soft. Inhaling the harbor air, and listening to the gulls, he closed his eyes, and checked his joints, relaxing from top to bottom, shoulders first, rib cage next, then hips, making an inventory of tension, and letting it go.

His thoughts went to his first teacher, D. D. Mo, an instructor in the close-quarter *gongfu* style known as *Wing Chun.* The hundred-pound fighter led classes in a cramped loft space above a Bowery Soup Kitchen in Manhattan, and with the aid of precise stepping and punching drills, gave Dalton an understanding of movement, rhythm and power. Too, he introduced him to the benefits of meditation, teaching him about breathing, and guiding him through inner journeys. Dalton listened, practiced, and learned, and would probably have risen to the top of Mo's heap, had the little master not been set upon by a Triad gang in an alley one night, and murdered with a common shiv; the sharpened end of the busted-off handle of an iron skillet.

Having his teacher die in such a useless fashion brought Dalton up short. For a time, he stopped practicing and went through an examination of mortality unusual in a man so young. When he resumed his training, it was with a more sensitive approach, more of an awareness of both the wonders and limitations of physical techniques, and a keener interest in the health and spiritual dimensions of the martial path.

He wished the old man could see him now, promoting *The Boxer Within* in Hong Kong. He sighed wistfully, with a little smile of remembrance on his face, began concentrating on his breathing. Listening to the soft whistle of his inhales, and the slow whoosh of his exhales, he let his mind wander to his favorite boyhood spot, the calico couch in his grandfather's study. Mentally gone from the prow of the Star Ferry, he became more relaxed and alert, experiencing, as he always did, the interconnectedness of all things, and the delicious dance of energy and matter.

Unexpectedly, Dalton's stogie-chewing paternal grandfather appeared. Chronically depressed–every one of his laughs ended with a sigh–he was, nonetheless, the kindest man Dalton ever knew, perhaps because of his intimate acquaintance with life's worst kind of pain–the death of his own children. After Dalton's parents were killed in a car accident, Dalton lived with the old man for two years before going to college, and was sorry his grandfather hadn't lived long enough to see him graduate.

Never before had the old man strayed into Dalton's quiet space, yet here he was. Puff, suck, puff, suck; he labored to keep his Montecristo torpedo cigar alive, drawing flame from his battered, golden Dunhill lighter. Blue smoke wafted across an endless expanse of green leather desk blotter. The flame grew brighter. Larger. No longer in his meditative state, Dalton felt his feet prickle with sweat inside his walking shoes. He wanted to come up out of it, but he could not force his eyes open.

In fact, he could not move at all. He heard his breath quicken, saw the flame from the lighter billow until it filled the room, engulfing the couch, the desk, the bookshelf, the green carpet, everything. The flame grew reddish and electric, and it smelled not like tobacco at all, but like something completely different, something that crackled and smelled of ozone, but still stayed cool.

Dalton tried to slow his breathing. He tried to tell himself what was happening was a result of jetlag, or maybe food poisoning, but he could not bring his own rational voice to the fore, especially not when he saw what was happening to his grandfather.

He was growing hair. The old man had always been bald–Dalton had never known him any other way–and yet a thick black mop of odd-looking hair was suddenly growing out of his scalp. The imagined face began to change. Wrinkles disappeared. The chin firmed up. The rheumy, sad, pale blue eyes–perhaps this was the oddest thing of all–began to morph into cold black ovals with only a thin brow above, hooded by epicanthic folds.

At the same instant that Dalton's grandfather turned Chinese, the dim, smoke-filled borders of his grandfather's study disappeared, replaced by dials and gauges and glass. The airplane cockpit. The thunderstorm. Suddenly, Dalton was not safe, invulnerable, or at peace; he was terrified. He tried to move, to duck, to turn, to run, but there was no escaping the huge storm cloud right in front of the Airbus' nose, nor the flame, originally born of his grandfather's lighter, now emanating from the hands of a Chinese man in a business suit and an open collar. Dalton felt completely paralyzed, trapped in a trance by something entirely beyond his control. The memory was so skillfully hidden, it might well have remained buried forever in a mind less adept at meditation, but Dalton yanked it out by the roots, fracturing fragile axonal terminations, re-connecting synapses, and re-establishing damaged pathways.

As it all came back, Dalton leaned over the front rail just as a recorded voice announced the boat's arrival back at Central, and chundered his breakfast into Victoria Harbor.

8

Leili Musi's nature left her no choice but to be a nurse. She was so soft-hearted and kind that her grandfather–a *dukun*, or fortune-teller of the old Indonesian school–proclaimed the girl's future profession, in no uncertain terms, by the time she was four years old. The old man made his home in the village where Leili's father had been born, not far from Tanjung Pinang on the island of Pulau Bintan, the largest in the Riau chain. There were other mystics in the Musi family tree. The best known of these, Pangeran Musi, had been an 18th century Javanese leader famous for his heroic, but failed, rebellion against the Dutch.

Leili's grandfather prognosticated freely about all manner of things. It was his job to do so, his veritable mission. Villagers followed his instructions for everything from arranged marriages to herbal cures. Nobody within ten miles did anything without the *dukun's* blessing. His son, Leili's father, a sharp, eager and modern man, moved away from the *dukun's* tyranny to attend university in Jakarta, inspired to do so by glorious pictures of a world he did not know, rendered in a magazine left under a tree by a German tourist. In the capital, he drove a taxi, started a tourist business, and married an American girl.

His new wife could not abide the *dukun*. She took the old man's mutterings for gibberish, and was not sufficiently afraid of his black magic to keep from saying so. She forbade little Leili to visit, but the medical prophecy was indelibly imprinted upon the girl's mind anyway, and in the end it came to pass, though not as the *dukun* intended, for Leili studied nursing, not fortune-telling, herbs and spells.

After school, Leili went to work at Cipto Mangunkusomo General Hospital, which despite being the best in Jakarta, was understaffed and overwhelmed. She spent some time each day teaching–her friendly manner and unexpected blue eyes found a welcome audience in every nursing student–and some time in the wards, battling AIDS, typhoid fever, cholera and malaria. In the early hours of the morning, she saw young men with knife wounds, elderly people with heart attacks, and overdosed teenage drug addicts. In the evening, she saw asthma attacks–sometimes fatal, because of Jakarta's horrific smog–trauma victims, and diabetics in insulin shock. She fought hard for her patients, and usually won, but the work wore on her, especially the hours, because she was separated from Lombo. When Jou Yuen offered her the job at the pharmaceutical company, she jumped on it.

The doctors all remembered Leili because she had been a skilled and hard-working nurse, and was distractingly alluring. They admitted little Lombo without the customary paperwork and delays. While Leili waited with him in the treatment room, she showed him a couple of moves from Zetian's *qigong* set.

"Mommy's exercises," Lombo said in an exhausted voice.

"Do you think you could try to do them with me?"

If Lombo had been an American city kid, a child raised on a diet of cynical television and the sort of humor that feeds by taking bites out of others, he might have given her a sarcastic answer. But he was sweet and he loved his mother. "I don't think I can do that right now, Mommy," was all he said.

Leili had tried to get Lombo to do the exercises with her when she first learned them; purely to share an activity with him. More mental than physical, he found the routine challenging, and resisted. As she began to notice the benefits she had tried again but he showed no interest, and perhaps because she hadn't been entirely sure of the long-term safety of the practice she hadn't pushed the point. Now she was filled with regret. She was sure that whatever was ailing him would have hit him more softly if he had fortified himself with the movements the way she had.

At last, one of the medical residents examined him, touching the vague spots on Lombo's calves and moving his knees around. He frowned when the child winced, because bilateral joint pain in one so young was alarming, and hoped the problem was merely angry epiphyses–growing pains.

"Has Lombo gotten much taller lately?"

"One inch in the last seven months."

"That's not so very much at his age. Perhaps he took a fall? Playing with his father, or on the soccer field?"

"My daddy left because he didn't love me," Lombo said.

The resident winced this time. Leili tried to cover. "Lombo isn't much of a sportsman," she said. "He's going to be an astronomer."

"Do you climb trees, Lombo?" the resident inquired.

Lombo shook his head.

"And you haven't fallen down hard on both feet, or maybe jumped off a high place?"

"Mommy washed my stuffed elephant, and it was hanging on the clothes line. I climbed up to get it and I tripped. It didn't hurt, though."

The resident worked hard not to smile. The boy sounded so serious and mature. He palpated Lombo's ankles, and then the top of the hips, where the heads of the femur met the acetabulum. "I remember when your mother worked with us she told us you liked looking at the night sky," he said. "Do you still look at the stars?"

"The sky is dirty here in the city," Lombo said. "I can only see stars in the country."

The resident did not like what he found. There was no tonus to the muscles, and no integrity to the tendons. What should have been a hard, sinewy, meaty joining place was mushy instead, like noodles cooked too long.

"Ouch," Lombo grimaced, his face contorting in pain. The expression lingered a moment.

"When did you first notice the spots on his legs?"

Leili frowned. "I didn't. They must be new."

Lombo sneezed.

"And the pain?"

"This morning. I brought him in because it's grown steadily worse all day. And his hands are shaking."

The resident nodded. He did not want to find a collagen disease in the boy, nor MS. He decided to run a screen for measles, and a standard panel.

"I'm going to take some of your blood," he told Lombo. "But don't worry, you'll make more."

Lombo smiled. "I know. I've got corpuscles and leucocytes and platelets and lymph. The life cycle of the red blood cell is one hundred and eighty days."

The resident laughed, although he could swear the boy's leg blotches were darkening before his very eyes.

"Stick around until we run some of the blood work," he told Leili. "That should tell us more."

The first run of tests took two hours. By that time, there was another doctor on duty, an intern who could scarcely hide his shock at the speed of Lombo's decline. The little boy was trembling violently now, and his orbits were inflated as if from parasitic elephantiasis. He had a bug-eyed look, and his lips pulled back as if he were in a wind tunnel.

"He's burning up. Can't you do something?" Leili implored.

The intern looked through Lombo's chart, noted the negative measles test and the normal white count. "He doesn't have an infection. I'm afraid I have to look this up."

At the nursing station computer, with Leili watching, the intern ran an Internet search for anything that presented with a facial distortion. He came across Bell's palsy, but that was wrong because it caused facial muscles to relax, giving a loose, hangdog, vacant expression. Tetanus was a better possibility–it caused spasms–as were acoustic neuromas–tumors that involve the facial nerves–and Tourette's syndrome. The problem was, none of those ailments presented with high fever.

"When did the facial tension start?" he asked Leili.

Leili tried not to cry. "I noticed he was smiling inappropriately yesterday when we got back from our vacation, but I didn't think anything of it. It was nothing like this."

"Where did you go on your trip?"

"The out islands. Doctor, please tell me what's happening to my child."

"Were you swimming?"

"Of course. He's a boy. It was hot."

"Any bites? Snakes, bugs, jellyfish?"

"No. He would have told me."

"Are there allergies?"

"I don't know of any. Doctor, about his face...."

"I know. I'm going to arrange for an intravenous muscle relaxant. That should relieve the spasm."

A hundred feet away–behind rails that made his bed look like a cage–Lombo Musi drew a last shuddering breath, and died.

Two flights down, the Emergency Room began to fill.

9

Near the Capital City of Hao–Zou Dynasty, 780 BCE

Exhausted, hunted, and weak with hunger, the Daoist monk leans against the rough trunk of a spidery willow tree growing near the bank of the Yellow River and contemplates the way his life and the river's have been intertwined for as long as he remembers. He has lost many friends to the brutal cycle of floods and droughts that have prompted the people of Xi'an to refer to the river as "China's Sorrow"; now he himself is about to die on its banks.

A posse of Zhou warlords on horseback chases him, their resolve strengthened by testosterone, sharpened by the odor of horse sweat, made keener by warrior talk, and transformed into rage by the monk's clever evasions. He is ahead, but they have finally cornered him by the river's edge. Quite simply, there is no place left to go.

The monk closes his eyes, and remembers his youthful trek to the high peaks of Tibet, across the western plain of yellow sand that gave the river its name. He was so young then, so strong and energetic, able to walk for days on a crust of bread, drink sparingly, sleep little. Now he is a man of sixty, and has managed, by following the flow of the *Dao* or "The Way," to keep most of his teeth and a physique that is the envy of men twenty years his junior. Still, after so many days on the run his beard is tangled, his clothing is rank with sweat, his feet are tired, his hair is knotted, and his skin cries out for a long soak and some strong soap.

The monk hears a sound: not the thunder of hooves, but something closer, smaller, more delicate. He peers cautiously out from his hiding place in the trees, and catches sight of a crazy-haired boy standing at the river's edge, scanning the water carefully, a lute and a sword by his feet. The boy turns and waves casually. The monk is mystified. Have his stillness and hiding skills failed him? Have all those years standing in quiet meditation fled him so that a peasant boy can see him easy as that when he tries to hide? Curious, the monk walks down the bank. "Good morning," he says.

The boy puts his finger to his lips and points at a dark shape, perhaps twenty feet out, just past the reeds. When the reptile's head emerges from the water, the monk recognizes it as a softshell turtle, an alert, evasive, species whose vegetarian habits make for tender flesh.

"Don't let your shadow fall on the water," the boy whispers. "I'm going to catch him without a net."

"Such turtles are fast," the monk whispers back. "He'll dive before you get him."

In response, the boy jumps in, showing the tanned and leathery soles of his feet. The monk smiles. He tried the same thing when he was young. He is surprised when the boy suddenly breaks the murky surface, grinning in triumph, gripping the turtle in a way that prevents its jaws from finding a purchase. The monk applauds as the boy scampers up the bank and uses a fine broadsword with emeralds on the hilt to behead the turtle. When the monk nudges the severed head with his toe, the boy swats him away.

"Please leave the head alone!"

"Of course," says the monk.

"If you start a fire, we can share the meat," the boy offers kindly, his expression softening. "The smoke will bring your pursuers, though. Are you a criminal?"

"I am a Daoist," replies the monk. "I respect the natural way."

"I've heard of your clan. An harmonious interplay of opposing forces. *Taiji. Wuji. Yin and yang.* Who is after you?"

"Tax collectors."

"You have not paid?"

"I will not pay taxes on air, water, and food. They are my right."

"If you really believe that, you *had* better hide," laughs the boy.

As if on cue, two warriors ride into sight.

"We could make you a raft," the boy muses calmly. "There are plenty of reeds. The current is strong, and there's a thick forest around the next bend in the river. Probably you could float downstream, and lose them."

The monk considers this. His pursuers will torture him before they kill him, and drowning has a certain poetry. "I would be grateful if you would help me do so," he says.

Staying low, the two move quietly from the bank. The boy slices reeds effortlessly with his blade.

"Tell me more about your Daoism," urges the boy, as more riders gather.

"Perhaps this is not the best time for a spiritual discussion," the monk whispers, lashing reeds together with grass as fast as the boy can cut them.

"If your system fails you when life is difficult, what's it worth?"

The monk chuckles. "It is precisely my system that tells me that there is a time to talk and there is a time to act," he says. "But perhaps we can do both. Do you see how the river flows in one direction all the time, varying only in speed and temperament? Nature flows along like the river. People react differently to it. Some deny it exists; others ignore it and swim for shore, ending up at a point quite far from where they intended to be; still others acknowledge the flow, but swim upstream against it."

"That last one would be you, right?" interrupts the boy. "Not paying your taxes, I mean."

The monk laughs again. "No, it would be the soldiers. I go with the flow, following nature, living my own life and not forcing others to my will. I have chosen to live according to the *Dao.*"

"But the *Dao* has failed you," the boy says, tying the last of the reeds together. "I mean, here you are about to be caught."

The monk smiles tolerantly. "On the contrary. The Dao has provided both you and this beautiful raft."

Although later in his life the reverse will be true, the boy is more pragmatist than philosopher, and this makes sense to him. Over the centuries, he has noticed how, if he is calm and patient and keeps a low profile, things happen for him. His needs are effortlessly fulfilled, as if by magic. The monk's ideas are consistent with the boy's own experience.

Suddenly, the riders spot them. They shout. They gesture.

They thunder in. The boy pushes the raft into the river. Looking fearfully over his shoulder at the riders, the monk climbs onto it.

"Don't paddle too hard," advises the boy. "Just float, and you'll be fine."

The soldiers wear leather armor. They carry heavy spears, and bows and arrows, and ride giant black beasts slathered in sweat and foaming at the mouth. Their leader, protected by headgear, rides the biggest horse. A girl accompanies him, floating behind him on the saddle like a little white cloud.

"Come out of the water!" The warlord calls after the monk "It will go easier for you."

When the monk fails to obey, the warlord raises his bow.

"No!" The boy rushes forward, his blade in the air. The warlord kicks him in the chest, and lets his arrow fly. It hits its target, knocking the monk off the raft. The boy jumps up and charges again.

"Are you in the mood to die with him, boy?" the warlord demands, raising his spear.

Without warning, the girl strikes the weapon from his hand.

"Are you mad?" the warlord snarls.

"He's just a child, my lord. "Don't do something you'll regret later."

The warlord almost allows himself a smile. He loves the girl's fire, the way she makes him feel when she rides along with him. Still, interfering with battle is something he cannot allow. He slaps her out of the saddle. The boy rushes to help, but she brushes him away, and staggers to her feet. The warlord gallops off, signaling his men to follow. He will come back for her when she has learned her lesson, when she is tired and cold and hungry.

"He might have killed you," the boy says, once they are alone.

"Never," she sniffs, swinging the emerald broadsword. "He's completely mine. This is a pretty blade. Did you make it?"

"I did."

"You're getting better. Maybe some day you'll be as good as our father."

"I doubt it," the boy shakes his head, wading out into the river.

"Forget that old monk," his sister says.

"I like him. I want to see if he's still alive."

"He's just a thief," she scoffs.

"He's not a thief," the boy calls over his shoulder. "He's a Daoist. He didn't pay taxes because he doesn't believe in them."

The raft has already been swept far down the river, but the monk's body has come to rest along the bank. Snagged by his robes, he bobs like a duck amongst the reeds.

The boy turns him over. There are floating river plants in the mouth, mud on the cheeks, and scratches across the forehead. The boy pulls the body ashore and lays it out beside the dead turtle. He pounds on the chest until water dribbles from the lips.

"Did this monk tell you that he held secret meetings to organize the other monks?" the girl asks.

"He did, and it's all the more reason to save him."

"Fortunately, you're too late."

With that, she sets off after her man, ruminating about how he will pay for hitting her. Perhaps she will kill him outright, or perhaps she will just continue to usurp his power, little by little, until the other wives bow to her, the soldiers take her orders, and the warlord is just a pitiful, weak old man with joints that hurt, a limp phallus, and a heart she has broken in more ways than one.

When his sister is out of sight, the boy pulls the barbed arrow carefully out of the monk's lower back. He blows into the monk's lips, squeezes his chest, blows again and squeezes again. The old man twitches, and his eyes come open.

"I'm done," he whispers, blood bubbling from his lips.

"Not until I say you are."

The boy places one hand on the entrance wound and another on the exit. As he does, he feels a current like a tiny lightning bolt run between his hands, passing right through the monk's brittle body. He closes his eyes, and envisions the needed repairs. He has seen dead bodies cut open before; he knows the arrangement of bones and organs and muscles inside, knows what has been perforated by the arrow, what has been torn, smashed or shattered. Where the tissue is angry, raw and heated, he imagines a small blizzard cooling it down. Where things are broken, he lets the energy between his hands knit them together. It takes some time–he will get better and faster at it in later years–but gradually the inflammation subsides.

At last, the boy removes his hands and inspects his work. Nothing but two faint patches remain; the one in the front redder than the one in the back, to mark the entrance and exit points of the arrow.

"I'm afraid," the monk announces, stirring.

The boy picks up his lute.

"Then let me play for you," he says.

10

"The little bastard gave me the flu," Jou Yuen hissed, looking at himself in the mirror. It was only a few hours since Leili took Lombo to the hospital, and here he was with the same damn pain in his joints, the same skin lesions, the same tremors, and a fever too. Jou Yuen rarely got sick, and the way his face kept contorting in an involuntary grimace had him wondering if he hadn't caught some venereal disease from Leili, something she brought back from her travels to the backward islands.

"Cheating bitch," he muttered, picking up the phone to call his doctor, one of the top internists in Jakarta.

The room jumped as he dialed, and Jou Yuen realized his eyes were twitching. A voice message prompted him to leave a number. As he did, the light to the phone's back line lit up. He watched it for a few moments before answering, unable to entirely trust his senses and unsure if someone was really calling. His fingers fumbled as he pressed the button.

"Yes?"

"Jou?"

He knew right away that his wife had been crying.

"Hello, darling," he said weakly.

"They told me you were in Kuala Lumpur. I tried all the usual hotels, but I couldn't find you! I asked for Leili, thinking she would know where you were, but they told me she didn't come in to work today. Have you seen the news? There is some kind of killing flu in Jakarta. I'm terrified. I took the children out school. Please come home!"

"I'll be leaving shortly, dear."

"Are you all right?"

"Of course," he said, lying reflexively.

"I can't believe you didn't call me today."

Jou suddenly found it hard to draw a breath. "The report to Hong Kong's been keeping me busy," he managed. "I told you I'd be working on it."

"Come home now. Please. The news is frightening me."

He wanted to tell her to call for help, but could not get the words out. No words out; no air in. He felt the same compressing squeeze pearl divers feel when they are struggling for the surface, swimming for the light. He was suffocating. The world was so quiet without the noise of his lungs. He never realized how loud breathing was, nor how terrible life was without the comforting rhythm, the satisfying whoosh. His whole life lay just outside the glass–his future, his loves and regrets. There was so much to do and say–but not without oxygen.

Jou's wife heard him fall off his chair. Because the cord had wound around his arm, the receiver stayed close, transmitting his death rattle over the line.

Mercifully, she was spared his ghastly smile.

11

Among Asian gardeners, the Japanese are the most famous. Perhaps it is because they feel that as their territory is tiny, they must control it utterly, even banish from it nature's tendency toward maximum entropy. The Japanese prune and fuss, and arrange every rock, leaf and stem, thereby creating a refuge where the unpredictability of life can be mitigated, the ravages of time erased, and man's impotence in the face of inevitable death temporarily ignored.

The Chinese Daoist garden, by contrast, shows as little of the gardener's hand as possible. The Daoist's goal is benign neglect. He shuns interference with nature, and strives to be sensitive to the subtle doings of the Dao, thereby to represent the universe fractally. As a result, Daoist gardens always look unkempt; vines run amok, walkways sink, and hardy invasive plants thrive to the detriment of delicate flowers as if in evidence of horticultural lassitude. In the Daoist garden, man's efforts and nature's will exist in realistic balance.

Gao Zetian did not care about the Dao. She didn't care about Zen either, nor about Buddhism. Despite being quintessentially Chinese, she treated her yard like one enormous Japanese bonsai. In fact, her whole spread would have looked more at home in Tokyo, than gracing a stone estate on Hong Kong's elite Victoria Peak, a place which until the 1960s, had been barred to Chinese by the British. Zetian's garden, set in the estate's enormous courtyard, was her refuge. She tended it every morning before she dressed for work. Sometimes she fussed with the line of the hedge, or with the low hangings of the camphor tree, or the Chinese Banyan, or the stem fig. More often, she tended her orchid collection.

The courtyard was made visually complex, not only by the extent and intricacy of its plantings, but also by the view, through the house, of the out islands and the South China Sea. It was home to praying mantises, caterpillars, black butterflies, and lizards, which basked in the mosaic patches of sunlight just after sun up, and lasting until midday.

That particular morning, a green pit viper made its way to the warm sun too, and on its journey encountered Zetian's hand. *Trimeresurus stejnegeri* was a small green serpent with a red tail and golden eyes. Its venom was hemolytic, meaning when it sank its fangs into the fleshy base of Zetian's thumb her blood was instantly under attack by enzymes designed to digest her, soften her hard parts, liquefy her viscera, and melt her body from the inside out. Had she been a mouse, the venom would have made her easier to swallow.

Banana leaves swayed in the slight breeze. Zetian dropped her pruning sheers to the courtyard floor and stared. She knew something about snakes; after all she had shared the world with them for a long time. She beat back panic and calmed her breathing, and as she did, the viper swiveled its hypodermic-like teeth into combat position and bit her again, hitting a major vein in her wrist. Zetian felt the venom rise up her forearm like acid. Smiling, she grabbed the snake. It twisted madly as she crushed it, and its last meal, a small arboreal lizard, emerged half-digested from its mouth. Chalky urine and foul-smelling feces squirted from the vent near the tail. As it died, Zetian threw it away in a high arc.

While the venom inside her was not among the most potent in the world, it was enough to be fatal. Zetian retrieved her shears, finished a trio of carefully chosen snips on the hedge, and then moved deliberately to a clearing in the heart of the courtyard, where she began to heal herself. First, she stopped the sweating that attended the bite, and drew her vital essence, her *qi*, up from its primary reservoir–the *dan tian*, just beneath the navel–melding it with the venom, diluting it, diffusing it, rendering it harmless. Then, to replenish her energy supply, she twisted and stretched upward, opening her rib cage, stimulating the organ system known in Chinese medicine as the "triple burner." Next, she executed a series of deep, circling bends to activate *dai mai*, the belt channel, a circumferential energy pathway around the waist. Toe touches came after that, then spiral punches, and a rising and abrupt dropping motion that slammed her tough heels into the most expensive real estate in Hong Kong.

The venom was already neutralized, but Zetian did not stop there. She continued through another twenty minutes of moving, breathing, vocalizing and visualizing, until she had addressed every organ and every anatomical structure. She concluded with a bow full of reverence for her father, his memory, and the sanctity and power of the practice.

At last she went inside, remembering to take her shears with her so they would not rust in the humid summer air. In the privacy of her bath, she applied a light layer of makeup, and went downstairs, where her chauffeur and adjutant, Huangfu, was anxiously waiting. Not once in the seven years he had worked for Zetian, had she ever been late. He could, and did, set his wristwatch by her 7:45 appearance, convinced she was more accurate than an atomic clock. In his eyes, she was also more intelligent than any other captain of industry in Hong Kong, and more beautiful than any fashion model.

"Is everything all right, Madame Chairwoman?" Huangfu inquired.

"Everything is perfect," she replied.

"I'm afraid we are running a bit late for the board meeting."

She smiled. "The others will wait; don't you think?"

Huangfu guided the Bentley Arnage saloon car through the crowded streets of Hong Kong's Central District. The straight-line distance between Gao Zetian's estate and the tall black Crocodile & Crane building was minimal, but the switchbacks down The Peak, not to mention the downtown traffic, made the morning drive a chore. Inside the car, Zetian relaxed in air-conditioned comfort. From time to time, Huangfu glanced at her in the rearview mirror. Usually, she read three or four morning papers during the course of the ride, but that morning she kept her eyes closed, and snoozed against the Connolly leather headrest.

Huangfu forsook the usual leapfrogging from one opening in traffic to another, in favor of a pace less likely to disturb her.

At last, they reached the building. Huangfu entered the parking structure, and pulled the car into the spot nearest the elevator. The space was unmarked, but no employee would dare park there. Huangfu went around to open her door. "We have arrived, Madame Chairman."

Zetian came up from sleep slowly. She stretched, pushing her bust against her gray suit. Huangfu averted his eyes to avoid staring.

They rode the elevator to the 51st floor in silence. Huangfu treasured the morning ride with her, enjoyed being so close in such a small space, but now her usually sweet aroma held something rank, and he found himself edging to the far side of the car.

As always, three secretaries stood at attention when the doors opened. The first handed Zetian the agenda for the meeting, the second offered her tea–always the same finest white buds from a northern estate–the last asked if there were any special instructions. The girls appeared relaxed around Gao Zetian, but Huangfu knew they were not. At the moment, his mistress was docile and smiling, but underneath lurked a human crocodile.

Zetian led the way into the conference room. Normally, the waiting executives exuded competence and relaxed power, but today there was a nervous buzz in the air. Huangfu sensed right it right away. Something was wrong. Zetian noticed it too, and her eyes narrowed, and her shoulders rose almost imperceptibly.

Huangfu closed the door, which sealed with a hiss. Decisions made inside the conference room held sway over fates and fortunes, and the room was an airtight chamber, an information coffin supplied by a filtered ventilating system. The floor-to-ceiling window, which afforded a view of Central Hong Kong and the harbor beyond, was comprised of two pieces of plate glass sandwiching a Kevlar matrix. It simultaneously garbled sound to defeat listening devices, and provided protection from bullets and typhoon-force winds.

Zetian sat down, and addressed her brother, who was seated at the opposite end of the table. "Sanfeng. I hear you had some trouble on the flight in from New York"

"A piece of bad weather. Nothing too serious."

"I see. And you are well?"

"Quite well, thank you."

An old man stood up, wearing a body so thin that his shoulder blades protruded from his suit. He was a skilled calligrapher. The others called him Brush. He cleared his throat. "Madame Chairman."

"Sit down, Brush. Your turn will come."

"But…."

"I said sit. Chan, you may begin."

Kai Chan rose. He was round and young, and took tranquilizers before these weekly meetings. "Shipping profits are way up for the quarter," he began. "Our new route through the Suez Canal has proven even more lucrative than I promised it would be. Now that the retrofit of the older container ships is finished, and the two nuclear-powered supertankers launched, we should be able to move far more cargo from Pyongyang and Shanghai."

"With the usual insurance discounts?" Zetian inquired.

"Of course."

"Good. What else?"

"The Koreans are fighting us for the Kowloon mega-mall contract. A certain city administrator now has a tidy Swiss account, so we will prevail. Metals and oils and refinery businesses are without incident. Last week I identified a competitive American concern of interest. This company imports used tires from Central and South America, and melts them down for boat dock bumpers. Although they recently procured a contract we had bid on to equip all the ferry docks in the state of Washington, they don't have the credit to procure operating capital. My acquisition offer was welcome."

"You will merge them with our existing rubber and plastics business?"

"Yes, Madame Chairman. Because they recycle, they had beaten us on price, and as such will be a good addition to our portfolio. Already, I've secured the dock bumper contract for all of Hong Kong Harbor for a thirty year period, offsetting their purchase price nicely."

Brush swayed back and forth in his chair, chewing on his knuckles in obvious eagerness to speak. Zetian ignored him, and turned next to Hop Ting, a tiny, arrogant man tolerated only because he had a genius for marketing any of Crocodile & Crane's numerous holdings.

"Our European newspaper holdings are experiencing the usual challenges," Hop Ting reported. "But our domestic publishing division looks very promising."

Zetian turned to her brother. "We're in domestic publishing now?"

"Billabong Books: a small house, formerly Australian. We've owned them for years. I like their editorial sensibilities."

"Your sensibilities and profits rarely mesh."

"In this case they do," Sanfeng said. "The franchise includes book outlets, so they're in both wholesale and retail. They have their own imprint, so they cut out the middleman on certain titles. They've done a nice job of picking store locations, too."

"You shouldn't be involved in small projects," Zetian shook her head. "Never mind. It's time to hear from Won."

Ping Won owed his job to the seamless information management system he had developed for Crocodile & Crane. He was venturing gingerly into international contracts, but having trouble, as he was young and understood computers better than people.

"The American Food and Drug Administration won't accept any of our claims," Ping whined. "They call our studies primitive."

"In those words?" Zetian's brow furrowed.

"Not exactly, Madame Chairman, but that was the meaning."

"Americans worship profit," said Sanfeng.

"I wish the same were true of you," Zetian replied.

The executives shifted nervously.

"Madame Chairman," Brush stood up.

"I'm tiring of your interruptions, Brush," Zetian snapped. "Are you trying to make me angry?"

"But it's about our Indonesia pharmaceutical holdings."

"What's the problem?" Sanfeng asked.

"Jou Yuen is dead."

There was a stunned silence. Before moving to Indonesia, Jou had been a member of this very inner circle, one of the trusted elite who helped Zetian and Sanfeng run Crocodile & Crane. He had sat at that very conference table hundreds of times.

"What? When?" Zetian demanded.

"Less than 24 hours ago."

"I hope his passing was easy," Hop Ting said.

"On the contrary," said Brush. "There seems to be some kind of deadly outbreak in Jakarta."

"What kind of outbreak?" Zetian asked.

"Apparently it's awful to look at. There are blotches, and fever, trembling, and a facial grimace that looks like a smile."

Sanfeng suddenly looked up. "I beg your pardon?"

"Facial muscles are involved," Brush explained. "The last stage is some sort of uncontrollable grin."

Zetian seemed suddenly to focus in on what Brush was saying. She looked at her brother. "A grin?" she repeated slowly.

Brush nodded vigorously.

Sanfeng rose abruptly, a worried look on his face. "Thank you, gentlemen," he said. "Today's meeting is over."

12

The Pan Pacific Mall, a Crocodile & Crane property, was the most prestigious and centrally located in Hong Kong. Despite the construction of larger properties in the New Territories closer to the harbor, it continued to be the preeminent address for high-end retail businesses. Billabong Books' flagship retail location was in the mall. It was a sprawling, wood-paneled store, resembling a Victorian library and standing in stark contrast to the neon displays and fluorescent boutiques.

The store manager–a Chinese man with a long gray beard and an elegant dark suit–asked to put Dalton Day in the front window to draw a crowd, but Monica Farmore wanted her author at the back of the store. She knew that according to *feng shui*, this would position Dalton perfectly for book sales. Her company's clever ad campaign, moreover, had brought people to the store in the first place.

Hong Kong was hungry for Dalton because they identified him with *wushu*, performance martial arts. Because of the great success of Hong Kong cinema, children see such martial art acrobatics as a ticket to stardom, and start training early. The fascination with heroism, athleticism, grace, power, and beauty seeps through Chinese culture to such an extent that any new permutation of the game–a tall, literary American, for example–intrigues everyone from land-shark businessmen and cell-phone-toting teenage toughs, to hunk-hungry Hong Kong housewives

Monica wanted to whip up the crowd by giving Dalton a fancy introduction, but he wouldn't hear of it. He took the podium in front of about a hundred people, and leaned into the microphone.

"Good evening. My name is Dalton Day, and I am 96 years old," he joked.

The crowd laughed.

"And that's not all. I was only 4' 8" when I started Chinese *qigong* exercises, and look at me now."

The crowd laughed again.

"Seriously, Chinese philosophy, *gongfu* movements, and Chinese medicine are real life changers, and I talk about all three in my new book, *The Boxer Within.*"

He went on to talk about the meat of the book, and many of his own experiences gaining proficiency in the arts, and learning the philosophical principles underlying them. He talked for half an hour then opened the floor to questions. The first came from an ostentatiously dressed lady who obsessively fiddled with a diamond ring the size of a fishing lure.

"If this intuitive part of the mind is so important, why do you call it the boxer?"

"Because there's a match going on. The two minds duke it out in the ring of consciousness. The intuitive, or spiritual mind, is guided by values and judgments not learned, but deeply seated in our animal experience and programming. The rational mind gives us bullet trains and jets, and unfortunately also gives us nerve gas, nuclear bombs, environmental savagery, and mass murder. What we're looking for is balance between the two."

"This sounds like mystical talk."

"Thank you," Dalton smiled.

"Mystics make people nervous," the lady said.

"I've noticed that. Perhaps that's because a mystic is a rebel, someone who doubts what everyone else accepts, often without critical analysis. The mystic challenges beliefs, tries to cut through what he sees as the veil of illusion, and attempts to move people's out of their so-called comfort zones."

"So you're a mystic?"

"I'm eager to help my readers cultivate a sense of wonder and appreciation for the world and their place in it, right here and right now," Dalton answered. "It would be great if we could all go meditate in caves for a month every year, or lie by a field of flowers and marvel at the beauty of nature, but modern circumstances demand otherwise. We must participate in the world: get the kids off to school, get to work on time, balance the checkbook, get to the gym, and bring home a paycheck. I'd be in a cave somewhere myself–or at least hiding in my little New York school–if my manager didn't push me to get out in the world and do the work, so in that sense, I guess you could say I'm a mystic wannabe. But my manager is right. If I'm really walking my talk, I shouldn't need that cave. The inner boxer is the mind in balance between intuition and reason, between wonder and cleaning the toilet, between racing around to get things done and sitting quietly listening to your breathing."

A pudgy man with thick glasses stood up. "You seem to have a curiously pacifist position for a pugilist. Have you ever competed in a martial arts tournament?" he asked.

In response, Dalton danced around the dais for half a minute, punching the air, kicking high, and generally hamming it up. The audience loved it, and Monica found herself grinning at the unexpected imp in Dalton.

"To answer your question, sir, I did compete in a few tournaments on the US East Coast in the 80s," Dalton answered at last. "This isn't *really* a martial arts book, though. It's more self-help."

"How did you fare in the competitions?"

"I write better than I fight, thankfully, although I got lucky with a few trophies."

"I've skimmed your book. You write a lot about following a natural path. Aren't you just ripping off Lao Zi's *Dao De Jing*?"

"Some great thinker, maybe it was Shakespeare or Einstein, said there is no such thing as an original idea. I'd have to agree. Most philosophical and religious traditions sing the praises of a simple, balanced life."

"And what happens when you meet someone who just doesn't want to change," the man went on. "Someone who is a staunch materialist and doesn't believe in any airy-fairy philosophy, someone who believes in violence, power, money and self-gratification? Don't you think there are plenty of people like that out there?"

"I know there are," Dalton said calmly. "And it's not my job to change anybody."

"Then why did you write the book?"

"To help people who want to help themselves. The sort of

people who come to one of my book signings."

The crowd gave a gentle round of applause. The pudgy man sat down. A young woman with a notebook raised her hand.

"I'm with the Ming Po Daily News. What's your favorite thing about Chinese culture?" she asked.

"It's a tie between dim sum and *gongfu* movies."

The crowd chuckled, but the reporter pursued him.

"Are you ever serious?"

"I just was! Look, I know the new China is all about capitalism and science and industry, but for me the compelling thing is the mythology of Old China, the system of honor and discipline, the unique combination of selflessness and self-mastery. I'm happy if I just help my readers quiet down, and listen to their inner voice."

So saying, Dalton was surprised to see Denise Howard, a very visible and vocal American senator from Wisconsin, standing at the edge of the crowd. He smiled at her, and she smiled back.

"A United States Senator, ladies and gentlemen. The honorable Denise Howard."

The senator strode up to the dais, and took the microphone from Dalton's hand. "Good afternoon everyone," she said. "I'm here on vacation in your exciting country, and walking past this bookstore just now, I was happy and surprised to find one of my favorite philosophers, and one of my favorite people talking to you. Well, as Dalton says, there are no coincidences, so I'd like to take a moment to tell you how Dalton's teachings, and his book have made a profound difference in my extremely stressful life. I am still just as busy, but I have found that following Dalton's exercises and ideas have reduced my stress, helped me establish my priorities, and gotten me in closer touch with who I am. As a politician, I give my endorsements carefully, but I can't exhort you strongly enough to listen to Dalton and read his book. Now, I'm off to find some of that delicious dim sum. Thank you."

"Thank you, Senator," Dalton said as she moved off with a wave. "On that happy note, my inner boxer says it's time to sign books."

The session broke up to applause and laughter, and nearly everyone in the audience lined up to purchase two copies. The long-bearded manager went to keep an eye on the cash register, leaving Monica to assist Dalton with the spelling of difficult Chinese names.

Leaning over his shoulder, Monica suddenly realized that although she had expected to play the typically boring role of babysitter, she really liked this guy, and truth be told, was secretly hoping he would invite her to dinner after the signing. Her one real relationship in Hong Kong had ended in disaster, a dragged-out, guilt-ridden mish-mash of depressed phone calls, lonely dinners, waiting in taxis, and crying in the tropical rain. Thus far, the idea of simply spending some time with this American writer seemed a definite improvement.

The China Club was a step back to 1930s Shanghai. Rosewood furniture surrounded vintage posters of beer, bicycles, and biplanes on the walls. Monica led Dalton to a cluttered, clanking art-deco bar, lit in neon, and filled with tapping wingtips and pumps. They took a booth in the back, and ordered drinks.

"So, what turned you on to the martial arts?" she asked.

"Not what, who."

"Who, then?"

"A girl named Grace."

She raised her eyebrow. "You got your ass kicked by a girl?"

"My heart, actually."

"Ahh."

"The dumping was worth it though. Grace got me interested in Chinese philosophy. I'd still be poking around in the dark if she hadn't given me the boot."

"And philosophy led to *gongfu*?"

"They're far more intertwined than most people realize. Martial arts are philosophy in motion. *Taijiquan*, for example, is based on a harmonious interplay between opposing forces, teaching you how to balance those forces in real life. But, I'm sure you know all that. Anyway, tell me about you. I can't imagine *you've* been dumped."

"Are you kidding?" Monica ran a hand through her tightly braided hair. "I grew up half Chinese in the Oklahoma panhandle."

"But you're so lovely."

"You're sweet. But it's redneck central there, even now, and there is no Asian population. Hardly anyone would talk to me, especially since my dad knocked up my mom, and took off."

"Ouch."

"Yes. I have never seen or heard from him–don't even know his name."

"So rather than hiding your head, you held it high, and learned everything there was to learn about your father's culture."

Monica smiled. "My mother gave me a wok and a Chinese cookbook when I was twelve. That was how much *she* knew about the Middle Kingdom."

"And from there to here?"

"Harvard in between. I did well in high school, and I was the first minority girl ever from Enid. To tell the truth, I was one of the first *ever* from Enid. It was my own idea to apply. I traveled to the big city of Tulsa for my alumni interview."

"Which was, of course, a rave."

"Speaking of raves, I have a question about something you said at your book signing."

"Shoot."

"You talked about comfort zones. You said being a mystic means avoiding them, or helping other people stay away from them. What did you mean?"

"Let's take busy-ness as an example," Dalton replied. "Folks who are busy all the time are usually dodging being alone with themselves, alone with their partner or their family. They're dodging because they don't like the feelings that come up, fear of intimacy maybe, or some sort of self-loathing or sense of unworthiness. The mystic, the person who gives free reign to their inner boxer, *wants* to engage those feelings, wants not to lose the opportunity to grow and learn and face the coldest, darkest places, so as to banish weakness, or at least try to build strength."

"That's fascinating," Monica leaned forward.

"Not really. All this is pretty self-evident. People the world over are stunningly similar. That's why great books in one culture are great books for all cultures, and why so many of the greatest thinkers converge in their ideas. The best ideas are universal. It doesn't matter if you're a regal Chinese or an everyday Joe like me."

Their drinks came, a glass of Merlot for him, a martini for her. She cupped the cold glass in her hands and looked in Dalton's eyes. "I'm enjoying your company," she said.

"And I'm enjoying yours. So tell me, how was Harvard?"

"Total culture shock after Enid–mostly rich kids from the Northeast preparing for a career at Morgan Stanley, or thinking they'd start an Internet business and make fifty mil the first year out."

"Nobody wanting to cure cancer, or write the great American novel?"

"I'm only 24. You've got the wrong generation. Don't you know this one is obsessed by the almighty dollar?"

A hostess told them their table was ready, and they followed her into a dining room decorated with tapestries and red lamps.

"Boyfriends?" Dalton resumed, when they were settled.

"Not at Harvard. I worked too hard. I had too much to prove."

"And here?"

"An ex."

"Banker?"

"An Australian cop named Reggie Pritt. His great-grandfather was a convict at Port Arthur, on Tasmania, and his father was a lumberman. That island still has miles of timber. Reggie always wanted to come to Southern China because it's warm. Things get pretty cold and gray over there, which may be why he started drinking. That and the fact Australians take beer seriously. Reggie has a captain's rank now, although with the handover, the Beijing Chinese have really clipped his wings. He likes to fight bad guys. I don't think he gets to do that any more."

"Bad guy fighting is my favorite too," Dalton grinned.

"I'm not surprised, the way you nearly pushed me on my butt at the airport."

"Ah, your handshake trick. Sorry about that. All instinct, no intention."

"I don't believe that for a minute."

"Just a little rooting, a martial arts basic."

"Speaking of rooting, your bio doesn't mention a family."

"I'm single, Monica. But I'm also old enough to be your father."

"No you're not."

"Your older brother, then."

Monica smiled ruefully. "Yikes."

"Anyway, I'm flattered."

"Is Annabelle in the picture? She calls the office every hour, middle of the night for her, and she's always on the phone with Billabong to ask how you're doing. Somehow she got my cell phone number. She rang twice during your signing."

"She's my manager, not my girlfriend, if that's what you're asking. More of a mother hen."

"During your remarks, you made it sound like she's the architect of your career."

"That's because she is."

They ordered their food. Dalton wanted to try shark fin soup. Monica ordered steamed vegetables. Finally, Dalton mentioned the man on the airplane. "There's someone in Hong Kong I'd like to find. I don't know his name, but I'm sure he practices an internal martial art, which means energy work in addition to physical movement. Do you know where I might start looking for him–maybe a certain part of town where there are a lot of schools?"

"That's all you know about him? That he does martial arts? There have to be a million martial artists in this town. Everybody and their brother practices *gongfu*. It's in the culture."

"I don't have a name, just what he looks like."

"Dark hair, middle height, smooth moves," she said sarcastically.

Dalton laughed. "I know it sounds ridiculous, but this guy has special skills. Not the run-of-the-mill master. I don't have those skills myself, but I know them when I see them."

Monica thought for a moment. "Grossport's computer guy

might know. He majored in computer programming at MIT, and loves watching *gongfu* movies. You two have a lot in common. He's plugged into the city in ways you can't imagine; he really stalks the fringe. I'll talk to him for you. His name's Jimmy Ngo."

Their food came, and their conversation grew wings. Monica tried to help Dalton pronounce some Chinese words; the attempt didn't go well.

"I can't tell you how much my wooden ear embarrasses me," Dalton confessed. "I can't help thinking I'd understand everything Chinese so much better if I could get just a little handle on the language. It's infuriating."

Monica was about to tell him she'd be happy to translate everything for him on his trip when she noticed Reggie Pritt enter the dining room.

"Oh boy," she said.

Dalton looked over and saw a thick, wet-eyed, large-chinned, ruggedly handsome man in a dinner jacket.

"Tell me that's your ex."

"Yes."

"Is he stalking you?"

"No. He's a member of the club."

"So we came here because you hoped you might see him?"

Monica flinched. "That's awfully direct."

"I wouldn't like to think you're using me to make him feel jealous."

Monica took a sip of wine and tried to look cool. "It's over between us," she said. "There's none of that."

"You're sure?"

"He's blue all the time. I can't take it. When I met him, he was so confident and self-assured. But the Beijing Chinese have taken him down so far he can't breathe; another peg every day. It's humiliating in the extreme, but somehow he won't let go."

"Couldn't he get a cop job back in Australia?"

"That's just it. He could. Melbourne or Sydney would be glad to have him. But he's stubborn and he's got some kind of pride thing about his unit and his force: that and he just about loves China to death."

Reggie caught sight of Monica then, and wandered over. "You're sitting at my table, luv."

"Reggie, this is Dalton Day, a Billabong author on book tour from the States. Dalton, meet Captain Reggie Pritt. "

"Monica told me about you!" Dalton pumped Pritt's hand forcefully. "Must be hell dealing with Beijing after all those years of the crown."

Pritt blinked, extricated his hand, wiped the back of it across his mouth and looked at Dalton uncertainly.

"What's your book about, mate?"

"Just a guide to keep us neurotic Americans from taking ourselves too seriously."

"What are you doing here, then?"

"I stole some ideas from the Chinese. Came to thank them, that's all."

"What sort of ideas?" Pritt asked suspiciously.

"Have a seat, and I'll tell you."

Pritt ordered a Scotch. Dalton ordered more tea, and then began to talk, using a soothing tone. He rambled on in lulling detail about philosophy and meditation, quoting sources, and throwing out technical terms.

Monica watched incredulously, as Pritt's eyelids began to flicker, watched as he supported himself on his elbows, watched as his face sagged under the weight of Dalton Day's sheer volubility. At one point, he interrupted Dalton with a wave of his hand.

"All this is nice for your fancy customers, but the world is full of shit heels, ne'er-do-wells who don't care a whit for your philosophy."

"The more pain you're in, the more you want to get out of it. Philosophy is a way out of suffering, and the right movements make the philosophy real."

"The folks I'm talking about don't know they're in pain; they're too busy looking to cause it in others."

"Are you talking about Beijing bureaucrats, or about criminals?" Monica asked.

"Don't see much difference, luv."

"There's no forcing people," said Dalton. "It's a book, not an enema."

Pritt stared at him, then let out a guffaw. "A book, not an enema. I like that. He's all right, your American. Out of touch, with his head in the clouds, but all right nonetheless."

Dalton smiled, taking the comment for a victory, and Monica visibly relaxed. Reggie had another Scotch, and Dalton talked some more.

"Show me your moves," Pritt slurred, suddenly standing up from the table. He reached out to steady himself, and Monica moved a highball glass out of the way so he didn't spill it.

"This isn't the best place, Reggie," she said.

"I'm not going to hurt him, luv," Pritt said in a loud voice. "I just want a demonstration."

Dalton stood and put Reggie's hand on his chest. He began to relax his torso, sinking down until his sternum seemed to draw Pritt forward and down. Monica recognized the body mechanics as those that had stolen her balance during the airport hand-shake trick.

"What's this?" mumbled Pritt. "You're disappearing."

"Look at my knees. You'll see they're soft, but not bending much."

Pritt did so, and pitched forward. Dalton caught him, and propped him up. "It's just a matter of relaxation," he said. "Letting go of tension in the body means letting go of tension in the mind. Do that, and you abandon resistance to useful ideas."

Pritt looked confused as he sat down. "Some sort of brainwashing, that's what it is," he said.

More talk. Another Scotch. Dalton rolled on. Reggie's head began to nod. His chin kissed the tablecloth as Dalton added some academic references. A few more words, and Reggie's forehead went down. Monica wiped the drool off his chin.

"You still care for him," said Dalton.

"We've got history."

"Well, thank goodness he passed out," Dalton exhaled. "I was worried I'd go first."

13

Every Saturday, between ten in the morning and two in the afternoon, Gao Sanfeng took a stroll on Hong Kong's Hollywood Road, a place known to tourists for antiquities, mostly over-priced, occasionally genuine, and always purveyed with the air of musty superiority at which Chinese artifact vendors excel. Sanfeng's experience of shopping was unique, both because he was wealthy beyond the wildest dreams of even aristocratic European collectors, and because he had an intimate familiarity with the objects for sale, having used them, or ones like them, when they were new. His knowledge was unequalled except by Zetian, but his interest was greater than hers, and more sentimental. This sentimentality might have clouded the critical eye of a lesser man, but it gave Sanfeng an unerring and instinctive sense of the real.

The morning Indonesia began to die, Sanfeng had a cup of coffee on a side street, at a café owned by a French couple who worked it together, serving passable croissants for breakfast and better crepes for lunch. Coffee drinking was new to him, in part because it was new to China–at least from his long-range point of view–and in part because the *qigong* he had practiced for so long had always obviated the need for caffeine.

He was dressed comfortably in a red baseball cap, sweat pants, a T-shirt, and a pair of Nike running shoes with air in the bottom. The Nikes were an indulgence–they damaged his lymphatic system, because lymph drained to the soles of the feet and needed to be squeezed back up into play by firm pressure from the ground–but he loved the luxurious feeling they provided, and the way they saved his knees from the effect of walking on asphalt.

"I'm getting soft in my old age," he muttered to himself.

He thought about his sister. They got along better when they did not see each other so much, when he was not forced to contend with the person she had become. It was easier when she ran her businesses, and he just lived quietly. He saw his being as a tiny stitch in a tiny corner of a vast fabric, holding no critical seam together, interacting with no important border. If Zetian had been willing, he would simply have left China years ago when Mao Zedong and the Communist Party came to power. He had seen many rulers, but judged Mao the most nefarious threat to the country in thousands of years. Zetian refused to go, unwilling to abandon her father's country, and so he stayed, not wanting to leave her alone.

Sanfeng was aware his mood was darkening, and it surprised and frustrated him. Most of the time, he was able to hold such feelings at bay, to live in accordance with what Daoists called "The Way," and pass his days in a state of grace, but the news of the smile in Jakarta shook him, especially in combination with his dream. He had been a doctor in more than one of his many careers–had cared for the weak and the sick using both his hands, and the vast Chinese pharmacopoeia–and he understood the fragility of the human condition. He knew perfectly well that if his father had never given him the magical family *qigong*, he would have suffered like everyone else, and died like them too.

He paid his bill, and left. Today his shopping was to be a meditation on the chaotic ways in which goods disappeared and reappeared in his native land. He matched his pace to that of the tourists, doing a perfect job of blending in, bringing his breathing into play.

Hen.

Ha.

In.

Out.

There. It was simple, really. He was feeling better already.

After a time, Sanfeng came to his favorite shop. The owner, a man named Chou, knew he would see his best customer on Saturday, and knew that when Sanfeng bought something–usually an old musical instrument, porcelains, weapons, and other antiquities too–he always paid with cash. Chou was certain Sanfeng was some kind underworld kingpin, a master thief perhaps, arch-blackmailer, assassin, or spy. He incorrectly presumed Sanfeng resold what he bought, figuring nobody could know as much as Sanfeng did about every era and province in Chinese history without actually being in the antiquities business.

Chou led Sanfeng into his tiny back office, where he kept the really valuable goods.

"I'm going to make you happy today, sir," Chou beamed.

Sanfeng circled his hand impatiently.

"Am I right in believing you have always coveted a sword from the armory of Gou Jian, the King of Yue?"

"Of course you are," Sanfeng said.

"Well, I have one."

"Really? From whom did you acquire it?"

By law, ancient artifacts belong to the government in Beijing, and digging without official permission is a criminal act, even if it is common. As such, there is generally some pretense involved in the provenance of a Chinese antiquity, some muttering about an old collection, some evasive words about whereabouts unknown. Chou did not bother with that kind of thing with Sanfeng. If the immortal had been some kind of investigator, Chou would have gone down long, long ago.

"It was unearthed last month in a private dig in Wangshan, Hubei Province."

"Condition?" Sanfeng swallowed, trying to appear nonchalant.

"Beautiful." Chou smiled, drawing the moment out to enjoy a bit of theater in his trade.

Like Sanfeng, the King of Yue had been a connoisseur of swords. It would have astounded the merchant Chou to know that at one time, the king and Sanfeng had been rivals in the fancy. Sanfeng's heart pounded so loudly in his chest he was afraid Chou would hear it. After all these centuries, could he possibly have a chance to buy the blade he had so long coveted?

"Let's have a look," Sanfeng said.

Chou had a red lacquer chest behind the counter. He opened the doors and reached in. What Sanfeng could not see, was that the chest had a false back, behind which was a large wall safe. He pushed the buttons to open the safe, reached in, and pulled out a black porcelain cup. He handed it gingerly to Sanfeng.

"The sword?" Sanfeng prompted.

"Patience," soothed Chou. "Have a look at this first–a Dawenkou tureen dated 2300 BCE."

Sanfeng ran his finger gently around the rim. The cup was impossibly thin, and in astounding condition. It predated his birth by nearly a thousand years, and was the oldest and finest piece of antiquity Chou had ever produced for his consideration.

"It comes directly from a gravesite," said Chou. "I have complete confidence in its provenance."

"Does that mean you know the grave robber?"

Chou winced. "Such an indelicate question."

Sanfeng held the cup up to the light. He could see the striations in the porcelain, tiny traces of the fingers of the potter who had turned it all those centuries ago. The lines were slightly off horizontal, and there was a tiny bump down near the bottom, suggesting an insect might have been caught in the clay before firing. If his mind had not been so intent on the sword of the King of Yue, he might well have purchased it, for he was a great fan of the delicacy of porcelains. This day he handed it back. "Very nice," he said.

"Truly a rare find," Chou confirmed.

"Tell me, what do you know about the use of swords?" Sanfeng asked.

"I am a merchant, not a warrior."

"Right. Well, the straight sword is a thrusting weapon. You could think of it as a long-bladed spear with a short handle. To be effective with it, you have to be a target master, accurate in the extreme, aiming for the weak points in a man's armor and his body: the top of the leather coat where it comes to the throat, or the inside of the thigh where the big blood vessels run. The hands themselves are also excellent targets, for when you cut them, your opponent cannot hold his sword against you."

"Naturally not," said Chou.

"The broadsword, by contrast, relies on strength for slicing. It can remove a man's arm, leg, or head. It requires less skill to wield dangerously, which makes it the best choice for the common soldier. Tell me: the sword you have to show me, is it a king's straight sword, or an infantryman's saber?"

"The sword is straight," Chou answered, relishing keeping Sanfeng in suspense. "A king's *jian.*"

Just then, the door buzzer sounded. Sanfeng handed the cup back to Chou, who hurried to put it way in the safe before opening the door. When he did, it was Brush who entered. Sanfeng's eyes narrowed in suspicion.

"You are following me, Brush?"

"I would not dream of it, sir."

"You know my haunts, is that it?"

"Some of them, sir."

Sanfeng looked at Brush intently, but the reedy old man gave nothing else.

"Well, what is it then?"

"It's about Jou Yuen, sir. And Indonesia."

"Ah. You sensed something, did you?"

"I have had the honor of being in your service all these many years."

"Yes, yes. And I appreciate you, as I hope you know."

"You are too generous. It is just that…."

Chou moved in, sensing something about his mysterious client was about to be revealed.

"What is it, Brush? I have business, here."

"I've never seen such a look on your face, sir. When I described the disease, you seemed to know it."

"It was a terrible description."

Brush nodded. "I have family in Indonesia, sir. You may recall that my daughter's husband works for Jou Yuen."

"Managing the factory, yes?"

"I'm honored you remember. I was just thinking that if you knew something that might help them avoid getting sick…."

"Tell them to leave," said Sanfeng. "Tell them to pack light bags and come here as quickly as possible."

Chou watched in amazement as Brush kowtowed to his master

in the old way, touching his forehead to the floor.

"Thank you, sir. Thank you so much."

"About my haunts, Brush. Tell me honestly, what others do you know?"

Brush glanced at Chou. "I know where you most like to burrow, sir, but it was not because I followed you, but because I happened to be sailing with my brother on his pleasure junk when I witnessed you speed by. Complete coincidence, I assure you."

Sanfeng waved him to silence. "I'll trust you to keep my secrets. You will, won't you?"

"Of course, sir."

"Good. Now go make your call. Save your family if you can."

Brush kowtowed even lower this time, and then made for the door. When he was gone, Sanfeng turned impatiently to Chou. "Let's dispense with pottery and get to the blade. Can we do that?"

Chou knelt to the safe once more, felt around for the sword and brought it out, cradling the scabbard in one hand and the handle in the other.

"King Yue's treasure," he said, offering it to Sanfeng.

Sanfeng picked up the sword. Hardly able to breath, he sliced the air with the blade, noting the perfect balance. The steel had been folded over and over in the forge in the style of a Damascus craftsman. There were jewels in the hilt, but these paled beside the masterful Daoist etchings of dragons on the blade, not the elongated, effeminate creatures seen on later work, but short, squat devils with tails and horns. Sanfeng believed this more powerful interpretation to be an accurate representation of dragons, creatures he had always hoped to one day see in the flesh.

He tested the edge with the hair on his thumb. He was just beginning to allow himself believe it was possible, when he found a flaw. Anyone else might have missed the tiny repair, but he was Gao Sanfeng, rival of the King of Yue.

"Not genuine," he grunted, tossing it onto Chou's desk.

"What?" Chou cried.

"There's a solder mark at the base of the blade."

Chou picked up the blade. "I don't see anything."

"Look more closely. It is small."

"A later repair, I'm sure," Chou countered desperately.

"You said it came right out of the ground, just like the bowl. In any case, this is not a repair. The solder is not visible except to exceedingly close inspection. It has been poured into the gap around the ricasso, right where it fits into the guard, revealing new technique. Whoever crafted this blade was not such a master. It is a good sword, but not a great one, and it is a fake."

"Impossible!" Chou paled, trying desperately to think how he would find the Iranian dealer who had sold it to him for an astronomical price.

"When all else has been dismissed, sometimes the impossible is all that remains," Sanfeng said wearily.

14

Indonesian Moslems are required by law to believe in God. Leili Musi broke that law the first morning she woke up alone in a world without Lombo. During the six years of his short life, the brilliant little boy was Leili's fountainhead. Lombo enabled her to smile while wiping moaning cancer patients clean, or stitching the skin of car accident victims closed. He gave her the will to lay little babies inside burn tanks, and save patients from succumbing to diabetic comas. Now he was gone, she was alone in her Chinatown apartment, and people all over the city were dying with the wrong kind of smile on their faces.

Leili rose from a sleepless night, showered mechanically, wrapped a towel around her head, and walked naked into Lombo's room. Not caring that the construction crew working on the building next door had gathered on one end of the scaffolding to ogle her, she picked up a toy that used cranks and gears to move tiny planets in accurate orbits around a model sun. If there had been a leitmotif to Lombo's life, it had been astronomy. It was almost as if the boy understood at birth he would be a human meteor, showering those around him with light and love but burning out too quickly.

Leili lay down on Lombo's little bed and turned her face into his pillow, inhaling the last of his scent. After a time she rose and gently trailed her fingers over his clothes and shoes, schoolbooks, lunch box, and pens, before returning to her own bedroom to wrap herself, to the enormous disappointment of her audience, in a towel.

Overnight, the plague–that was what the news media were calling it now, because it was a far less specific term than fever or virus, bacteria, poisoning or flu–was cutting a swath through the city. How randomly and nonsensically it struck–oh Lombo! –like God's scalpel in the hands of a homicidal drunkard.

Everything was happening so fast Leili could not seem to find a steady breath. There would be a service for her son later, and her answering machine was full of urgent messages from friends, most of them from nurses at the hospital. She returned none of the calls, not wishing to talk to anyone, having no idea what to say. She needed to be at work, immersing herself in the suffering of others as a salve for her own pain.

Arriving at the hospital, Leili learned non-plague patients had been moved to specialty wards. The Internal Medicine wing was filled with plague victims. Some writhed in the grips of the disease, weak in the limbs, sneezing and feverish. Others were already smiling–the final stage. Leili saw bodies being carted down to the morgue, but pressed on to the nursing station, knowing that to return to her lonely apartment would be worse than staying to help.

"I'm sorry about your boy," said the medical intern under whose care Lombo had died. His eyes were rimmed in red from hours of entering data into a computer, and he wore blood and coffee stains on his white coat.

"Thank you," said Leili. "I'm here to help. I know I don't officially work at the hospital anymore, but I have to stay busy. Is there some analysis? What is this thing that has killed my son?"

"Bacterial cultures have come up with nothing," the intern said. "We're thinking it may be a virus, something like Hanta or Ebola. Casual human-to-human viral transmission is rare, so there has to a common source."

"What can I do?" asked Leili.

"I've told the other nurses to put everybody on anti-viral meds, and get the pharmacy to start stockpiling all the AIDS cocktails in the city. Would you call those pharmaceutical reps that are always hounding us? We need every drop, and capsule, of anti-viral medication within a hundred miles in our hands by noon, samples included."

15

Eastern Qi Province, Qin Dynasty, 228 BCE

The prow of the little fishing boat slices through the winter China Sea like a butcher's cleaver. The hull is constructed of a special wood from the southern provinces, where trees are engaged in a fantastic life-long battle with pestilence and fire, but never with drought. This is a wood that resists the area's torrential tropical rains, a wood that repels the biting mouths of giant insects, that fends off the acid in the dung of the birds that built nests amidst its branches, that is impervious to the claws and teeth of the rodents that spread its seeds by eating its fruit. It is, in short, a magnificent shipbuilding material and Ahn, the fisherman, had paid dearly for it.

"We sail into that, we don't make it home," declares Gao Sanfeng, pointing at an approaching line of black squalls.

Ahn pushes the tiller so the bow of the fishing boat points right into the storm. "I want a big fish," he counters.

With his foot, Sanfeng prods the slippery pile of silvery fish they have already caught. A tasty variety of snapper, they are small, but numerous. Ahn is simply greedy. He has the best boat in the village beneath him, and the ablest deck hand in Sanfeng, and he works six days a week, growing richer than he needs to be.

"This is a fair load, boss," Sanfeng says mildly. He doesn't care about fishing glory. He's more interested in making music with his stringed *ehru*, and listening to the wind and the water.

"It's a fair load when I say it is."

The waves pick up, and so does the wind. Sanfeng, glances at the thick, yellowed sail. He sees it tugging at the boom, sees the fibers on the leading edge twitch in the wind. An hour earlier they had pulled in the net for fear of losing it in the current, but the stern line is still out for big game. The line gives a jerk and Sanfeng is on it at once, feeling the tension with his fingers, judging the size, the power, the speed, and the will of the fish.

Mostly the will.

"He'll fight," Sanfeng announces.

"We'll fight harder," Ahn retorts.

The boat goes down into the valley of a swell, and for a moment the coastline is lost from view. They are miles out, and the water is cold. Plankton float on the surface, making it grainy, and seaweed does too, creating lumps. It is a visceral, shivering thing, this ocean. A bird with broad feet could stand on it, were it not heaving so.

The boat goes down in another trough. Sanfeng plays the line, winding it in slowly, watching it, touching it. The boat rises again. It is late in the day, and the clouds are low and thick, and rain is coming. Sanfeng searches for a landmark, but finds none.

"Tuna or shark?" Ahn inquires.

Sharks usually go straight down from the boat; tuna run away. If the sea were calm, the answer would be obvious, but the breakers and the bobbing and the inscrutable surface make it hard to read the line. To be certain, Sanfeng reaches way out, to touch the spot where the line meets the water. Holding fast to the gunwale he leans as far abeam as he can, and just as his fingers reach their target, Ahn gives the tiller a mighty shove. The boat pivots, and the boom knocks Sanfeng overboard. He bobs gasping in the freezing water, trying to clear his blurred vision, his porcupine hair looking like a jellyfish turned upward.

"Help!" he cries.

"Drown slowly, you bastard!"

"What?"

"You're sleeping with my wife!"

Sanfeng blinks the stinging salt out of his eyes and spits. He touches his temple, and his fingers come away brilliant red.

"You're crazy! Zetian is my sister!"

"Don't you think I know that? You're perverts, both of you! After you've been dead a few days, I'll kill her too."

The wind is driving the boat further away. Panic grows in Sanfeng slowly, like an opera curtain rising. The water is frigid, he is miles from shore, a storm is nearly upon him, and he is bleeding into shark-infested waters. He has seen the fins, has seen the action of shark teeth on the last catch.

The sea picks Sanfeng up, and drops him. He takes a deep breath, trying to get his lungs to relax against the cold. He swallows more water, gags, and comes up on the crest of a wave just in time to see Ahn bent beneath the sail like a hunchback racing the storm to shore. Sanfeng takes a stroke to follow him and then another, executing a lazy pattern that two thousand years later, off another continent thousands of miles away, will come to be called the Australian Crawl.

He is not worried for Zetian. She can handle Ahn. If he were not growing numb in a frigid November ocean, Sanfeng might find the charge of cuckolding and incest amusing. Of course he and Zetian are intimate–how could it be otherwise after more than a millennium together–but they are not lovers. The plain fact is the fisherman has no inkling of the real secret the brother and sister share. He is small-minded and jealous, a mean-spirited miser onto whom the pair has latched in order to weather a famine that might otherwise have taken them, for even *qigong* cannot stop one from starving.

Sanfeng juggles the variables involved in getting safely to shore. He tries to calculate the force and direction of the current he has seen at work on the net, the distance the boat has traveled under sail, and his ability to keep moving in the icy water. He crests another wave and looks for Ahn's sail as a pointer to shore, but the squall line hits just then, and the rain is so fierce he is not able to see his own hand in front of his face. He realizes going out in the storm is part of Ahn's set up, intended to kill him faster, to obviate any chance he will make it ashore.

The horizon is gone, the sky is black, and the rain stings his face painfully. The worst part of his predicament though, is the alchemical reaction between the ocean and the air. Right at the interface of the two the distinction between the fluid and the gaseous state vanishes, and Sanfeng is caught in air so wet it yields no oxygen. He scissor-kicks upward, thinking that if he comes higher out of the water like a porpoise he might be able to breathe. It works, but as he goes down again, a blast of wind pushes a gallon of water down his throat. He struggles mightily, but the raging darkness and the thunder and lightning descend on him, and he loses consciousness.

His father awakens him.

"Sanfeng, wake up," he says. "The giant carp are going to eat you."

Sanfeng smiles, as he floats face down.

"They are not carp, Father. They are sharks."

His father's noble visage wrinkles at the unfamiliar term. The long-dead blacksmith Gao–a lifelong denizen of China's vast interior steppe–never saw the ocean. He knows nothing of fish the size of smelting furnaces.

"Call them what you will, you must wake up, and swim. They are taking you for dead, and will soon rid the sea of you. Come, my son–I raised you better than this."

Consciousness returns to Sanfeng as hard as the boom that hit him, and he jerks his head up, gasping. The squall has passed over him, leaving large black fins circling ever closer.

There is nothing in the *qigong* to prepare him for this, but his father always said to defeat an opponent you must know him, so Sanfeng brings his hands over his head, and sinks down to greet his killers. He sees their black eyes and he reads that they have not yet made up their mind about him. He struggles to the surface, takes a gulp of air, and sinks down once again. Holding his intention, his *yi*, in his palm, he gathers his *qi* into his right hand, concentrating it there so that even in the freezing ocean, his fingers, waving gently like coral fans, are hot enough to generate waves of *schlieren*. When the first tiger shark rushes him, mouth agape, Sanfeng exhales violently, projecting everything he has into one thick bolt of energy aimed down the beast's throat.

Its swim bladder ruptures, and the big fish is disoriented. It rolls over and over, blood escaping from the gills in a stream that makes the trickle coming off of Sanfeng's temple seem a mere wisp in comparison.

Sanfeng breaks the surface again. He wipes his face. There is no sign of Ahn's boat, although it could be in a trough, and the shore is still dishearteningly far away. He can barely make out the village, and the stand of tall trees behind the beach. He draws a deep breath and goes down again. The remaining sharks are eating the one he has wounded, ripping pieces from its head, its tail, finally its guts, which leak out, snake-like, in an ever-expanding circle. When that shark is gone, they turn on each other in a frenzy. As the violence below him intensifies, Sanfeng swims as fast as he can to be clear of it.

He is unable to maintain the pace for long. The *qi* emission has cost him a great deal of energy, and the cold is stealing what little remains. His arms are hopelessly heavy, his legs frighteningly weak. He finds a bed of kelp, and attaches cantaloupe-sized floating bulbs to his four limbs by wrapping their stalks about him. Their buoyancy keeps him afloat while he kicks gently for shore. Numb, he rests for a time, and then kicks again. A leaf from the stalk around his right arm floats next to his head, and he bites into it. It tastes rank and salty, and is fibrous and hard on his tongue. He gags but tries again, understanding he has to fuel himself if he's going to make shore. He swims, he eats, he swims some more. The plant gives him an aching thirst.

Darkness falls. Sanfeng watches the stars come out, and he uses them to take a celestial bearing. He is as good with the stars as his father was and he is confident of his heading. Hours pass, and with no way to measure his progress his grip on reality slips. At times he feels dizzy and he always feels cold. He struggles to keep his mind sharp. He tries singing, but it disrupts his breath. His head throbs from the bite of the boom. He can no longer feel his arms or his legs. He tries to force his eyes open but they keep fluttering shut.

"We have much to discuss," his father says, spreading arms that were partly imagined flesh, and partly starry sky.

Sanfeng puts his arms out to return the embrace. As he does, his fingers touch the hard, sharp littoral. Shells bite his forearms, and gravel abrades his back. His father retreats, and the surf pushes him gently onto the brown beach, where he lies for some time, vomiting chunks of rust-colored seaweed into the cold hard sand.

Dawn pushes the night away tenderly, and the early rays of the sun fall across Sanfeng's face. The first thing he sees is a crab staring at his seeping head wound, clicking its claws together in anticipation of a meal. Twice he staggers to his feet, and twice he falls.

After some time, he reaches the fishing boat. Ahn has off-loaded the catch: business as usual. Sanfeng fingers the sail, and finds it still damp from the storm and the dew. Shedding his stiff and sopping clothes, he drags himself another fifty yards, to the shack where Ahn lives with Zetian.

He pushes aside the cowhide flap. Ahn is fast asleep inside, snoring. Zetian is beside him, her legs pulled up, wrapped in fur. Her face is tear-stained and swollen, her eyes closed.

"Sister," Sanfeng whispers.

Her sleep has been fitful and troubled, and Zetian jerks awake instantly. She takes in his form, naked, shivering, in the doorway. She leaps to her feet at once, and embraces him, kissing him all over, touching him up and down as if to be sure this is no dream. Gently, she pulls a piece of seaweed from the corner of his mouth and touches the wound on his temple questioningly.

"Ahn said you were lost!"

Sanfeng buries his face in her hair, thinking how wonderful she smells, how beautiful she is after all these centuries. Wherever their father is, Sanfeng hopes he sees how much his children love each other still.

"He tried to kill me," he explains.

Her eyes narrow. Her expression grows dark. She pulls away from him.

"What do you mean?"

"He knocked me overboard many miles out, in a storm."

"But without you, he is no fisherman at all!"

"Even so, he left me to the sharks. He thinks we are lovers. He's jealous."

At this, Zetian lets out a roar of rage, and yanks the skins back from her husband's sleeping form. Ahn comes slowly to consciousness, and sees the brother and sister standing over him. He gives a horrified start, then recovers.

"Are you back from the dead to mock me?" he roars at Sanfeng, scrambling out of bed.

Zetian knocks him back down, and leaps astride him. She wraps her thighs around his neck and silently squeezes. The seaman claws bloody lines in her thighs with his nails, but she ignores the pain and squeezes until his face blows up like a hard red puffer fish. He bucks and arches, trying to be rid of her. She digs her fingers into his sockets. He shrieks when she pries his eyeballs out so they dangle along his cheeks, their stalks moist and pulsing, then finally screams in sheer agony as she pops them so their vitreous humor streams out.

Zetian gives a sudden twist of her shoulders, breaking Ahn's neck. The fisherman sags, instantly limp.

"Let's go," Sanfeng urges. "We have to leave this place!"

"It's early," she says. "You need to rest."

"Your thighs are bleeding."

"I'm fine."

He turns her by the shoulders, and puts his hands on her wounds, using the last bit of energy left in his freezing and battered body to close them, then collapses onto the bed. Zetian covers his body with fur, and crawls underneath with him, pressing tightly along the length of him until his shivering stops and his breathing slows and he grows warm.

At length she rises, slings Ahn's corpse over her shoulder, and carries it outside. She strides naked across the beach, in the new morning, and dumps the body in the fishing boat. Taking a rock, she pounds a hole in the tough wooden hull, down low by the keel, and pushes the vessel out to sea. At first, she is afraid it will sink close to the beach, but the wind catches the sail at the last minute and takes it offshore.

When the top of the mast disappears from view, she makes a fire, and bending to it, cooks breakfast for her little brother.

16

At five o'clock in the morning, two days after the inhabitants of Indonesia began to self-destruct, Monica Farmore brought Jimmy Ngo–a thick-bodied young man with abnormally small ears and a few seething pimples–to the lobby of the Grand Hyatt Hotel to meet Dalton.

"So you're the bum responsible for waking me at this hour," Dalton grinned, extending his hand.

"I was just thinking the same about you."

"I'm sorry. It's probably worse for you than for me. I've still got a bit of jetlag going, so my inner clock is off. Anyway, thanks in advance for the help."

"No problem. Victoria Park is popular for morning martial practice. We have a fair chance of finding your man there."

"Jimmy read your book," Monica said as they piled into a taxi.

"I liked it," Jimmy said slowly.

"Sounds like you have reservations," Dalton observed.

"Only about passion," said Jimmy. "I'm a creature of emotion, I know I am, but not all my emotions are negative. The picture I get from your book is of a detached, dispassionate guy. I'm not sure I want life without my feelings."

Dalton frowned. "The inner boxer feels everything, plus and minus, good and bad, positive and negative. The issue is what you *do* with those feelings. The whole point is to watch yourself, observe the ebb and flow of thoughts and feelings, observe your habits and your trends, notice them, and that's all. Don't let them rule you."

"I wouldn't want to be with a man who isn't passionate," said Monica.

"Maybe a Buddha can avoid *ever* being ruled by his feelings," Dalton smiled. "For the rest of us perfect equilibrium is just a goal to work toward."

"That's a relief," said Monica.

"Hmm," was all Jimmy managed.

A few minutes later, the cab pulled up to Victoria Park. Hong Kong was so luxuriantly tropical that Dalton expected the place to be lush, but the park was a flat dusty grid awash with people chattering like birds on a wire. Jumping, twisting, and stretching, they did their exercises quickly, with none of the stiff and secretive reverence of a traditional training hall. Their *qigong* and *gongfu* were part of their daily routine. There was no ego in it, no hidden martial agenda, no holier-than-thou expressions, no anger.

The three sat and watched the proceedings for the better part of an hour.

"You don't see this much zest for life in the average American skateboarding teenager," Dalton said.

"I wonder why that is," said Monica.

"Blame a sedentary culture."

"We have that too," said Jimmy. "The kids are all glued to video games."

"And then of course there's diet," Dalton added. "Asia lacks the food infrastructure we have in America, where food grows one place and is preserved and shipped somewhere else. The food is fresher here, but lack of exercise will bring obesity here too. At home, people lavish more attention on their cars than they do on their bodies. It's one of my pet peeves."

"The elderly are fitter in China, that's for sure," said Monica.

"The Chinese venerate the elderly," said Jimmy. "At least they used to. Ancestor worship is built into Confucian culture. Even the communists couldn't change that. If you're respected, you have something to live for. That's why these folks get up and move every morning."

In the central field, not far from a line of short trees and just beyond the entrance to the obviously popular swimming pool, Dalton watched a shirtless bald man in his seventies dip and split on the dusty ground. His washboard abdominal muscles and his energy and flexibility would have been the envy of any athletic teenager in the world. Nearby, a youngish woman dressed in black danced for a small crowd, a sword in her hand. Her cutting and stabbing was lithe and magnetic.

"Ben Hur!" she cried, smiling at Dalton. "You're so handsome!"

"You don't see so well, but your *Taijiquan* is beautiful," he called back.

"Come push with me," she replied, inviting him to a round of sparring.

Dalton hesitated.

"Go on," Monica urged, eager to see him move.

He did. The woman set the pace and Dalton followed, bending deeply to stay with her low stances. He could tell she was a performance artist, not a real martial player. She was not able to let her ancillary muscles release, and thus couldn't sink her center of gravity the way Dalton could. Sweating and grinning, she tried to end the game quickly by giving Dalton a mighty shove. He allowed himself to be lifted and thrown a good ten feet back.

"You really are an actor," she smiled.

"Actually, I'm a writer. And I'm in Hong Kong looking for a particular master. I know what he looks like but not his name or where to find him. Can you help?"

The woman handed him a business card. "This is my teacher. Tell him Sherry sent you. He knows all the high level players."

Dalton accepted the card with a grateful bow.

"Are you going to go see this guy?" asked Monica, as they made their way out of the park.

"Sure," Dalton nodded. "It's a lead, isn't it?"

17

Hotel concierges happily send tourists to Macau. They extol the Portuguese colonial architecture, particularly the churches of Sao Domingos and Sao Paulo, allowing that it gives the colony the most European feel of any place in Asia. They praise the creative cuisine too, and of course the casinos. Privately, however, because they know the Triad organized crime groups own the city, they refer to Macau as a beautiful woman with the clap.

The Gao empire had grown organically across the centuries, and had achieved a permanent state of truce with the secret societies that had become the Triads. The wispy tentacles and fluid corpus of Crocodile & Crane were so omnipresent the Triad bosses regarded the Gaos and their companies as forces of nature. Fighting them was like shooting the wind or cleaving a river: there never seemed to be any measurable effect and men were known to drown or be swept away in the attempt. In any case, the Triads had their hands full contending with the police, Beijing bureaucracy, and the Russian *mafiya.* While some Triad official always knew when the pair was in Macau, the Gaos were left alone.

That Saturday afternoon, Zetian arrived first, at Macau's Bela Vista Hotel. She wore a black skirt and purple blouse separated by an elegant, corded belt with a moonstone clasp. Black pearls dangled from her ears, and the tooth of a particularly virile African slave she purchased from the British East India Company in 1814 hung around her neck, merely because she liked to be reminded of how much he had pleased her.

Zetian waited for Sanfeng on the veranda, at her favorite table, between the Doric columns, in the corner by the low railing. The Bela Vista had a history far shorter but almost as varied as her own. Built at the end of the 19th century, it had been a health resort for French Troops, a secondary school, a

Cantonese language academy, a Portuguese refugee shelter, a British military club, and finally an exclusive inn. She loved it for its decadence, its adaptability, and its evocations of things past.

She produced a cigar from her purse, lit it, and took a few puffs. When the bald Nebraska farmer at the next table stared at her, she moved the cigar in and out her mouth until the farmer put his elbow into his salad and his wife slapped his arm.

"Cigars," said Sanfeng, sidling up. "They're not just for smoking any more. What is that, anyway? A Cohiba?"

She smiled. "It's a Montecristo from the Dominican Republic–very smooth. Times have changed. Cuba's soil is depleted. That boy Castro's too greedy to take care of the land."

She took a smaller one from her purse and handed it to Sanfeng. Usually, he refused to smoke, but he still did things he did not want to do when he was around her. He wondered idly when exactly had the shift occurred, when their forbearance with each other had given way to opposition. He couldn't identify a point in time, he could only notice the trend. He hoped some day his sister could come to accept him rather than control him, but he doubted it would happen in much the way he doubted the moon would turn purple. In truth, their struggle had begun at conception; they had been born yang and yin.

Smoke rings rose above them as they gazed out over Praia Grande Bay at a supertanker bound for the mouth of the Pearl River. The ship bore the Crocodile & Crane insignia–a gaping reptile and an elegant bird with spread wings bound together inside a circle–on its stern.

"Korean cars heading for Guangzhou," Zetian mused.

"Trucks, I think."

"If your eyesight was better, you'd see they are cars. Perhaps you will pay attention to that at your next practice?"

"My eyes are fine, Sister. Tell me, any luck with the antennas?"

He was referring to a new cluster of satellite dishes near Zetian's villa on Victoria Peak, ruining her view west toward Lantau Island.

"Huangfu had a conversation with the broadcasting

authority. My understanding is that the foul things will be dismantled and moved to Pak Kok by Thursday."

"I'm surprised Huangfu was so persuasive."

"You shouldn't be. He's mine."

Sanfeng smiled wryly. A Hoklo junk out of Aberdeen Harbor–far afield, and looking vulnerable in the middle of the shipping lanes–appeared to be on an intercept course with the Crocodile & Crane supertanker.

"Too small for the radar," Sanfeng muttered.

"What's too small?"

"That junk. The tanker's going to hit it."

Zetian had been watching the Americans, waiting for another chance to torture the farmer. She turned lazily to look.

"Just the angle," she said dismissively.

"I don't think so."

She crossed her legs for the farmer, driving her skirt up her thigh.

"If it hits, it hits. We're insured."

"Why do you suppose you still smoke?" Sanfeng asked, crossing to the railing.

"That should be obvious," she said loudly. "I like having something long and stiff in my mouth."

The farmer's wife pushed back from the table and stood glaring indignantly. A moment later, she and her husband left the veranda.

"I've been thinking about our father lately," said Sanfeng. "About the feel of his skin, the way he smelled. Do you remember the way he smelled?"

"Who?"

"Our father."

"I think about the future, not the past."

"Probably because he didn't carry you the way he carried me."

"You can't remember that," she scoffed. "It was thousands of years ago, and you were too young to know what was going on."

"I was too young to know about the world, but I wasn't too young to love my father."

"Oh, stop going on."

"I think I was closer to him than you were. That's what it is that bothers you when I talk about him."

"You were not closer," she leaned forward, her eyes dangerous. "I was with him before you were even born. And don't try to provoke me with childish games just because you're feeling sentimental about this thing in Jakarta."

"I'm not sentimental, I'm worried. And you should be too. What if it's the Banpo Smile?"

"Relax, brother. Go listen to music. Think happy thoughts. The Banpo are long gone. They've been absorbed into your precious Dao, into the flow of time, into the huge mass of humanity. There is nothing left of them, least of all their smile."

"I'm not so sure. Everything I hear tells me it's the same: the shakes, the splotches, the joint pain and fever. I've got a bad feeling about Indonesia."

"Why wouldn't you? Indonesians are the creeping parasites of the Pacific Rim: multiplying on island after island, crammed into that filthy shithole of a city. They're spilling out into the Timor Sea because they don't have enough to eat. They support terrorism, make women dress in black, and force children to pray twenty times a day. Chinese carry the whole burden of their economy, and yet the Moslems treat them like dogs. Why do you care what happens in Jakarta? If it *is* the Banpo Smile, I say good riddance. The only thing I'll miss is the profit from our operations."

"And Jou Yuen?"

She reaffixed a loose piece of wrapper tobacco with her tongue.

"Since when do you care who I take for a playmate?"

"I don't. And neither do you. Never have. We both know that."

"If you're trying to provoke me, it isn't working."

"Fine. Forget Jou. What if this thing spreads? If it is what I fear, it is the thing that cost us our father."

"No, a bastard priest did that, and a bad piece of timing, coming into that place when we did. And as far as I'm concerned, that thing killed the Banpo because they needed killing. Do you remember that valley? How crowded it was? It was the planet fighting back, that's all. Cleaning a clogged toilet. Nature is frustrated, even you should be able to see that. It tries with terrorism and war, but the United Nations intervenes. It tries with AIDS, but new drugs slow that down. It tries with heart attacks and cancer, but now we have transplants and pharmaceuticals and gene therapy, so now it has pulled out the big gun, the Banpo plague. If that's what it takes, that's what it takes. It's all about balance, and you of all people should understand that. You should be rejoicing, Brother. You should be dancing in the street. This is nothing but the Dao at work."

"But the suffering," Sanfeng protested.

"We have our *qigong.* It's not going to bother us. Why do you worry about the rest of the world so much?"

"Why don't you worry more?"

"Because it's a waste of time."

"Something you have plenty of."

"A waste of energy, then."

"You have plenty of that, too."

"Never too much, Brother."

Offshore, the tanker had drawn perilously close to the Hoklo junk. Sanfeng leaned forward to watch. He could see three men on board, one desperately hauling in a fish net, the other two leaning down into the engine compartment. The gigantic shadow of the tanker's bow fell like night over the little boat.

Zetian came up behind him. She stroked his head indolently, as if he were a dog. "Your cigar has gone out."

"I'm finished with it."

"You've lost your fire."

"I haven't lost anything I didn't want to lose."

"This plague of smiles will run its course, like all rivers, like all little boats, like all supertankers, like all diseases. When it's finished, you and I will still be here."

"What if we're the only ones left?" Sanfeng asked, as the three fishermen ran to the bow of the little junk and dove into the warm blue water.

Zetian took a long draw on her Montecristo.

"I'd relish not having to move from town to town," she said. "And not having to wear ugly makeup, and not having to occasionally pretend to be sick. I'm a little tired of all that, if you must know."

The tanker devoured the small boat. Sanfeng thought he heard the splintering sound of the impact across the water but he could not be sure. He searched desperately for some sign of the swimmers, but could see only debris, bobbing and twisting, slowly soaking and sinking.

"So many of the people I loved are gone," he said sadly.

She touched his face gently. "Why should you care, Little Brother. You will always have me."

18

Annabelle left message after message, but Dalton was following Sanfeng's scent and not ready to talk about the clothing line proposal. When the phone rang that morning, he left the room without answering it and headed off for a Hardee's off Queen's Road in Central Hong Kong.

The restaurant smelled like the one in New York or Los Angeles or Omaha or any other American city, and after just two days traveling, Dalton found the familiar smell comforting.

He bit into a slightly soggy sausage sandwich and thought about what he had seen on the airplane. On one level, he distrusted his own senses, particularly when it came to seeing energy projected, a skill that was the stuff of legend. There were people who claimed to know people who had seen energy projected into others, and acupuncture physicians and hands-on healers routinely claimed to manipulate *qi* in patients, but there were always other possible explanations. Precisely because Dalton wanted so badly to believe, he had always been a skeptic.

But Dalton believed little in coincidence and greatly in destiny. Having spent the first part of his life aimless, he found great power and focus in his passion for Chinese philosophy and martial arts, and had felt the pull to China for as many years as he had been engaged in the study. He couldn't help feeling that if there *had* been a supernaturalist on the plane, and he *had* performed a miracle, then Dalton had been a witness for a reason. In any case, he wouldn't rest until he had done his utmost to find the electric man.

He took a last sip of bad coffee, and then went for a walk. He spent several hours taking in the sights, then went down to the waterfront, meditated for half an hour, practiced his *qigong,* and went to meet Professor Fong, the functionary who had greeted him at the airport. Fong was a bona fide academic with a degree in cultural anthropology, and he suggested lunch at One Harbour

Road, the Cantonese restaurant at the Grand Hyatt.

"I'm interested in *qi* emission," Dalton told the professor.

"Ah," said Fong, sipping shark fin soup.

"I'm not saying I believe it exists, I'm just saying I am interested."

"Your interest is martial?"

"Of course, but also for healing. Do you know anyone with that level of skill?"

Fong smiled. "You would like to see it, or you would like someone to teach you?"

"Of course I would love to learn the technique."

"Emission requires the cultivation of an enormous energy reserve. I myself do not have this power."

"But you know someone who does."

"The government in Beijing made a big effort to extinguish martial practice under the late Chairman Mao," Fong said carefully.

"I've heard that. I've also heard that while many high-profile teachers were either killed or forced into other lines of work, some people left the country and others continued teaching, but only underground."

"In our modern life it is hard to find teaching that will lead in the direction of this kind of skill. More than that, social and financial realities make the ten hours per day of practice such expertise demands quite difficult."

Softshell crabs arrived, and other exotic seafood. "Good for the *jing*," Fong explained.

Dalton knew *jing* was sexual essence, the precursor of *qi* in the body. He understood Fong couldn't ordinarily afford such a meal and was using it to build his own health. He gave the professor the lion's share, and watched him eat it with gusto.

"A monk might become such an expert, yes?" he asked when Fong took a break from the huge lunch.

"Monks in China are not what they used to be. The Shaolin Temple has become an outlet for the sale of plastic souvenirs, and the acolytes who train there more often have a film career in mind above a spiritual one, and venerate Jet Li and Jackie Chan more than they do the Buddha. There are few rural areas that are so inaccessible that absolutely nobody wanders there anymore. Even the tallest mountains are used for military posts, and the most remote forests are penetrated by foreigners seeking rare species of animals or birds–cranes, for example, or panda bears."

"You're saying there are no teachers who know these arts anymore, and no place to go to practice them in peace?"

Fong spread his hands. "I'm saying I don't know any such people. "I'm saying if they exist, you will not find them in Hong Kong."

The only other lead Dalton had was the Kowloon address of the teacher Sherry had given him in Victoria Park. After lunch, he took the mass transit railway to get there. Underground, he found a refined, civilized universe of finely laid tile, comprehensible maps, and user-friendly vending machines. The combination of British propriety and Chinese ingenuity had produced a fast, cheap transportation system, highlighted by a train which stopped exactly where it was supposed to, doors lining up with yellow arrows painted on the floor. The car was full of people ignoring each other and talking animatedly on cellular telephones despite the roar of the train. One in every four people on the planet is Chinese, Dalton thought, scanning the faces. China's power is all about biomass and numbers. As capitalism continues to take hold, the nation will simply buy up all the latest technology, and never look back. He closed his eyes and listened for the energy, heard the pulsing moan of the city itself; the underlying rhythm of the organism called Hong Kong, and he stayed that way until the train had whisked him under Victoria Harbor to Kowloon.

He emerged from the station to find the waterfront behind him. The long throw of Nathan Road stretched out as far as he could see, and he glanced at the address on the business card Sherry had given him. The map said he had no more than a mile to go. On the way, he took in the aviary at Kowloon Park, then continued north, passing jewelry stores, tailor and camera shops and boutiques. The address he was looking for was in an alley hung with laundry. "Lu's Taijiquan Emporium" was on the second floor, above a discount electronics store.

He climbed the stairs, and entered a cavernous, sweat-filled hall. The mirrors were moldy, and the gray carpet was bare enough in some places to show the rubber mat underneath. At the far end, a group of women wearing traditional black *gongfu* uniforms went through the same sword sequence Dalton had seen in Victoria Park. They moved in unison, like synchronized swimmers, all their blades slicing and parrying at precisely the same angle. New students sweated in deep stances, their legs trembling. Opposite them, grim men strained against each other in a macho version of the same dance Dalton had performed with Sherry.

Suddenly, a youngster in a tank top gave his partner a shove that sent him hurtling through the air. The victim crash-landed against a mirror, cracking it. He lay stunned and bleeding on the carpet, but nobody seemed to care. Seeing that the man's shoulder was dislocated, Dalton went to him and cradled the joint, intending to restore it to normal alignment. A squat, rough-faced Chinese, wearing black trousers and a white jacket with a long green tea stain, interrupted him.

"What do you want here?" the man asked, clearly irritated. His English was crude but understandable.

"My name is Dalton Day. Are you Master Lu?"

The man inclined his head, but barely.

"I met a student of yours named Sherry at Victoria Park. She seemed to think I should meet you."

"Beginner class at night. Come back later."

"I'm looking for a friend. He is a master."

"A friend? What his name?"

"I don't know his name."

"What kind of friend not know friend's name?"

"A forgetful one, I guess. We met on an airplane."

Pushing Dalton aside, Lu relocated his student's shoulder with a quick, brusque movement. The student did not make a sound.

"The man I'm after makes flames with his hands," Dalton went on.

Lu shrugged and started off, but Dalton held him back, violating martial etiquette and putting himself in a dangerous position.

"Please, it's very important. He has hair like a porcupine."

"Go home. Don't come back," Lu commanded.

There was a boom box sitting on the floor, and the sight of it gave Dalton an idea. As the students watched warily, he went over and switched it on. The fine slow strains of Strauss's Acceleration Waltz reverberated through the hall. Smiling, Dalton began a low, fluid dance with an imaginary partner. As the tempo picked up, he began punctuating his graceful, easy, low and natural movements with explosive traps and sweeps and kicks and throws. As the waltz built toward its climax, his martial techniques grew more and more subtle, more and more seamlessly integrated into what looked, for all the world, to be a man waltzing by himself. The display was as fresh as a baby chasing a butterfly. Lu's demeanor softened as he perceived the character of a man entranced by *gongfu*, genuinely in love with the energy and the history and the purity of the practice, and a man able to risk judgment at the hands of those who knew what he knew and could also see what he lacked.

"Please help me," Dalton said when his dance was over. "Does anyone know my friend with the crazy hair?"

The maneuver won him some laughs, a smattering of applause, and even a reluctant smile from Lu, but no one claimed to know Dalton's electric man.

19

The lights in the hospital were bright, but the mood was black. Cots from intern offices and staff quarters had been wheeled into the nursing station, where a gurgling coffee machine and steaming teapot were the only symbols of comfort and normalcy in a hospital rapidly becoming a portrait of perdition.

Leili Musi was galvanized by how much work there was to do at the hospital. Nobody questioned her presence. The staff was fighting a losing battle, and they knew they needed the help. Patients were dying right and left, and morale and moxie were at an all-time low. Leili set up to making herself some lunch at the back of the nursing station, cooking the rice, boiling coconut milk, and brewing coffee.

"Go help the lady in E-33," someone told her.

When she entered the room, Leili recognized the kind old beautician who did her hair when she was a little girl.

"You were so young then," the beautician murmured when Leili identified herself.

"And you were like a magician," said Leili. "You made people beautiful with your scissors."

"Look who's beautiful now. Of course, you have *dukun* blood, so I shouldn't be surprised. Can you save me? Would you cast a spell for me and make this smile go away?"

"I'm afraid that's beyond my skill," Leili bit back tears as she increased the woman's morphine drip, "but I *can* make you feel better."

"Your grandfather made a prophecy," the beautician whispered.

"He did that a lot."

"He said I would die smiling in my seventy-fourth year. Two months ago, I turned seventy-four. Now it is my turn to predict something. I have spoken with Tuyul, the ghost of infant boys."

"Yes?" Leili said, thinking of Lombo.

"A terrible force is at work in the world. Tuyul has told me it is the work of the Bunyan. Do you know the Bunyan?"

"The soft people," Leili answered, referring to forest gnomes of legend, the leprechauns of Indonesian folklore.

"Tuyul says that the Bunyan want the islands back, and they will kill us one after the other until the islands are free for them to roam once more."

Leili forced a smile. "Let's hope Tuyul is wrong."

The old lady drifted comfortably off, and Leili went back to the nursing station, where she found Lombo's young intern typing on the computer.

"Can the Ministry of Health help us?" Leili asked him.

The intern shook his head. "Right now, the ministry is deciding what to do with the bodies. The city doesn't have morgues for everyone, the hospitals are filling up, and blood analysis in our best labs is confusing at best. When it comes to viral outbreaks in the Third World, even the World Health Organization is slow to help. For one thing, there is bureaucratic red tape. What's worse, seventy-five percent of their labs wouldn't even recognize something as well documented as Ebola if it bit them in the ass. That's why I'm on the Internet. I'm inputting data. We are the epicenter, unfortunately, so what is happening here is important."

"Epicenter?"

"Hub of the outbreak. Usually, diseases spread out from a central point like the shockwaves of an earthquake, but this plague of ours is not following any known pattern, at least not one we can fathom. It seems to show up at random, first here, then somewhere far from here. Maybe it will help when someone figures out the mechanism of transmission. Is it by water? Air? Physical contact? Food? Without answers to the most basic questions, we're whistling in the wind."

"Is there anything you want me to do?" Leili asked.

The intern looked at her thoughtfully. "Can you type?"

"Eighty words a minute with no mistakes," she answered, thinking of the long hours at the desk outside Jou Yuen's office.

He stood. "Then you do this. I'll tell everyone to bring the data to you. Just keep entering it. Lab tests, casualty numbers, everything. Keep the channels of communication flowing. Let the world know what is going on here. What do you say?"

"All right."

"One more thing. Forgive me, but what was your little boy's name again?"

"Lombo."

The intern patted her shoulder. "That's right. I remember now. I want you to know I sent Lombo's blood to the Centers for Disease Control in Atlanta, Georgia. That's in America. They have some of the world's best facilities. If they can isolate and beat this thing, it will be because of Lombo. He will save us all."

Unable to stop herself, Leili cried.

20

The facility at Harbor Plastics resembled a melding of the Taj Mahal and a quonset hut. Outside, a barbed wire fence protected the compound from the poverty and need of surrounding Sheung Shui–a city very close to Hong Kong, but about as rural as industrial southern Chinese towns get. Sanfeng stood on the catwalk high inside the factory dome, and wrinkled his nose at the fumes of carcinogenic oleoresins drifting upward. It was an outrageous work environment, and Sanfeng wondered how many other Crocodile & Crane operations treated their workers so shamefully. He would have to look into it. Still, he had seen pep talks win wars, and getting his new publishing company to send its important author to give a presentation might help worker morale while giving the immortal a much needed opportunity to see the American strut his stuff.

He watched Dalton's arrival through optically precise opera glasses. The American was tall, which meant he would command attention, and he wore his hair in a tight ponytail the way Sanfeng had until the last hundred years or so. Sanfeng saw Monica come in. The sight of her familiar face never failed to unnerve him. In recent nights he had dreamed her grinning the Banpo grin. He felt his footsteps grow unsteady at the mere idea of it.

Neville Ngo, the plant manager, came up alongside him.

"This is the American's own *qigong*," Ngo said softly, pointing at the movements Dalton had begun to perform. "It is detailed in his book, *The Boxer Within.* It's a bestseller."

"I'll be interested to see if an American's *qigong* makes our workers more productive. "

"The *qigong* is just part of the program," Ngo replied nervously. "Day's ideas are inspirational."

"He certainly seems to be enjoying himself," Sanfeng observed, watching Dalton's relaxed form.

"So does the staff," Ngo added hopefully.

Everyone did seem relaxed. Sanfeng had seen the phenomenon before. The greater the number of individuals doing *qigong* movements, the easier they were for everyone. This was not simply a herd syndrome, but something more metaphysical–the sharing of *qi*.

"What do you think of him, sir?" Neville asked.

Sanfeng watched Dalton subtly circling his hands in a fashion impossibly close to the Crocodile and Crane *qigong* routine.

"Are you all right, sir?"

"Of course," Sanfeng said.

Rubbing his face with his hands, the immortal took refuge in a moment of quiet breathing. He made it his business to live every day expecting coincidence precisely because he knew there was no such thing. Still, this simply could not be. He continued to watch. Aha. There was an incorrect movement–and another one. That turn was not right, nor was the position of the hands. The attitude of the torso was not quite correct either. There was too much intentional squeezing of the *zhong men* acupuncture points below the ribcage. Sanfeng was unsurprised at the errors, but remained confident of his secret plan.

"Mr. Gao?" Neville Ngo touched his elbow timorously.

"What? Oh. Yes. He's very good. Wonderful."

"I am going to make sure the employees follow this routine every day. I am confident it will decrease sick days, and strengthen the crew."

Dalton finished his warm-up, and took the microphone. "Today, I'd like to talk about *The Boxer Within.* This is just my fancy term for your intuition, the voice of your subconscious mind. The subconscious is a powerful force; it is just as powerful, just as insightful, just as intelligent, and every bit as important as the logical, conscious mind so celebrated in the West.

"Overemphasizing the conscious mind leaves us distracted, depressed, preoccupied with material things, reliant upon instant gratification, confused, and unable to reach our potential. Only when we cultivate our intuitive mind, what I call the inner boxer, can we achieve a healthy equilibrium. Through movement and meditation, I can show you how to do that, and thereby become more peaceful, more productive, and more prosperous. Is anybody interested?"

To Sanfeng's surprise, the workers cheered loudly. Smiling, the immortal trained his glasses on the American's face. Suddenly, he realized where he had seen the tall man before.

Close up.

In the cockpit of a plane.

21

Reggie Pritt nursed a Balvenie Scotch, and waited for Monica. How appropriate the Beijing bastards had turned the Wan Chai Gap Police Station into a museum, he thought. Nothing could have been a more fitting and bitter symbol of what the Communist Chinese had in mind for what was once the finest team of investigators and enforcers anywhere. Now even formerly ardent Filipina hookers spurned him, recognizing that there was nothing so pathetic and miserable as a fallen god, albeit a minor one.

"The new assistant commissioners are cruel," he said to Monica when she finally arrived. "And they're in bed with the Triads. It's true in Macau, it's true in Kowloon, and pretty soon it will be true on the island. Speaking of bed, what say you and I go off to my place?"

"You promised you wouldn't talk like that," she sighed, settling down onto the stool next to him, and pulling down on her hem to hide the tops of her thighs. Meeting her ex for a drink before taking in the Teawares Museum with Dalton Day had put her in a pretty pickle about what to wear. She wanted to avoid titillating Reggie, but in the end, her desire to impress Dalton won and she chose a tight yellow sundress and heels.

"Promises, promises," he said. "You've made your share too."

Monica looked around. Like its patrons, the pub was old and dark, and English and sad. The walls were of dark wood, the floor matched them, the lampshades yellow, the bulbs inside them low wattage. The bartender was a former racing driver. Young, thin, and jaunty in his leather helmet and thick goggles he waved from old XK Jaguars in black-and-white pictures on the wall. A dirty British racing green banner for Morris Garages hung behind the bar, a backdrop for dusty bottles on a narrow shelf. In one corner was a giant poster for Watney's Red Barrel, in another a tattered Union Jack.

"I shouldn't even be here, Reggie," Monica said.

A couple of Reggie's cop friends were in the back at a booth with a pitcher of beer. They smiled at her. She waved her fingers. She liked most of them, and felt for the fact that with no one to bully and no crimes to solve, they had become paper-pushing geldings with guns.

"Aw, give a man another chance, luv. I'm only depressed with the booze in me."

"And that's why you choose to meet me at a bar?"

He looked up at her. His eyes were red rimmed, his chin darkened by his two-day beard. "I have nowhere else to go."

"Reggie, stop feeling sorry for yourself."

"I know what this is about. You're after the American, right? What's he got? Some fancy *gongfu* moves in bed?"

"Stop it Reggie. You're drunk."

"You're the one sweet, good thing in my life, luv."

She picked up her purse from the bar. "I have to go."

Reggie took her hand. "Please don't."

"I have a date."

"A date?"

"An appointment."

"Well, could it wait a few minutes? I got something to ask you."

Monica felt her chest grow tight as Reggie sank to one knee on the bar floor before her. The bartender had seen men go up in flames on a racetrack, but not kneeling in sawdust in a pub. Shaking his head, he moved away.

"You shouldn't be doing this," she said. "This isn't right."

"Monica, please be my missus."

Monica looked down at him. His temples showed traces of gray, and there was a small bald spot growing at the top of his scalp. She felt like she was going to cry, and she fought it because she knew it would just make everything harder and worse.

"Get up," she said, taking his elbow. "Please?"

"That your answer, then? 'Get up'?"

"It's the middle of the morning," she said softly. "You shouldn't be drinking so early."

"I drank to screw up the courage."

"Marrying me won't fix your life. I'd be a problem for you, not a solution. And in all fairness to me, you're not ready to be with anyone. You need to fight this battle for yourself."

"I can't win it without you," he said.

"Yes you can."

"You'd make everything better," he sighed. "I know you would."

"I want you to be happy, Reggie. I really do."

Even the bartender winced at that one. Pritt staggered halfway across the room, and addressed his comrades in a loud voice.

"She wants me to be happy, lads. That's what she says."

Collecting herself, Monica made for the door. It seemed just plain wonderful that the sun was shining outside, and impossible too. She was almost in that radiance, when Pritt touched her on the shoulder. She turned to him.

"If I can do what you ask, what then?" he said.

"Then you could ask me again," she said. "But you mustn't do what you need to do for my sake, you have to do it for you."

She couldn't bear the pain on his face, so she turned and hailed a taxi and went to meet Dalton Day at the tea museum.

22

Dalton loved tea because he knew that the medical and energetic properties of the leaf supported his training. He also loved the taste. Over the years, he had come to favor first flush Darjeelings for their balance between flavor and jolt, but he also enjoyed watching anemone green or fine gunpowder unfurl. Occasionally, he would splurge on a lychee black or an Earl Gray with mallow flowers. When Monica sidled up to him at the tea museum, he was in the gift shop, carrying a paper cup of some oolong, sipping it, and looking at the display of teapots for sale.

"These are from Yiqing," she told him. "It's a region with a special clay that fires well, and makes the best earthenware for steeping. It's neutral, contributing nothing to the flavor, and taking nothing away."

"I've heard of it," said Dalton.

"Well then you're ahead of me. Before I moved to Hong Kong, all I knew was Lipton."

"Bagged leaf is generally awful," said Dalton. "It's the dust on the floor after the good stuff is heated."

Monica picked up a small blue ornamental pot with upswept handles. "I've had great tea since I've been in Hong Kong," she said.

Dalton noticed a streak of mascara from below her eye. "Are you all right?"

"I turned down a proposal of marriage from Reggie Pritt."

"I didn't realize things were that serious. You told me he was an ex."

"It made me sad, Dalton."

"Sorry to hear it."

She stared at him. "You'd rather keep to business, wouldn't you?"

"I didn't say that."

"I can see it."

"I've never been good with boundaries. You're good company, and I'm grateful for all you're doing for my book."

Monica looked away, checked her compact, wiped her face, and turned back to him. "It's a relief, really. The way things have been going I'm better off untangled."

Dalton started to demur, but she waved her hand and walked out of the museum. He followed. The heat of the day was building, and the park–a series of sculpted terraces and ponds–was empty but for a few people eating bag lunches under the shade of palm trees.

"Any luck finding your master?" she asked.

"I wish I could say yes. Listen. I'm sorry. If you need someone to talk to I'm happy to listen."

"Forget it. By the way, since you're going to stay on a few more days, my boss wants you to do another corporate seminar. The higher ups apparently liked what you did at Harbor Plastics."

"Ah. The mysterious Rachel Kleinman. I'm beginning to think she doesn't exist."

"She exists, trust me. She's out of the hospital, too, but all puffed up on steroids from her asthma attack. She'd shoot me for telling you, but the only reason she's not meeting with you herself is that she's peeing every five minutes."

"What's the corporation?"

"They make industrial lighting. Bulbs for stadiums, I think.

"Sounds like fun. Did we get any sales from the plastics company?

"Two hundred books."

"Not too shabby."

"Are you kidding? A lot of those folks probably can't read English."

"Let's do another presentation then. I'm not leaving town until I find this guy."

Monica sat down on a bench. "I'm glad you'll be staying around. That way I can spend more time not telling you things."

"Don't be that way. Tell me what happened with Reggie."

She turned on him with a ferocity he hadn't expected. "You want to hear about him? Fine. He got down on his knees and I turned him down. I love him but I'm afraid of him, afraid of this great big dark cloud that always hangs with him, that follows him in impossible ways, wherever he turns and wherever he walks, just like it was tied to his neck by some fine, fine thread."

Dalton sat down beside her.

"You don't talk like a girl a few years out of college."

"What do I talk like, then?"

"A girl who's pretty clear on wanting to be happy."

"You preach dispassion," she said. "I've listened to you. I wouldn't expect you to understand."

"I don't preach dispassion. I try not to preach at all. Most of the time, I'm just trying to get back to a quieter life, to spend more time at my practice."

"I don't believe you," she said. "I don't believe any of that. A guy like you doesn't let a woman push him. I've talked to Annabelle on the phone. She's smart but I don't see her controlling you, making you do things you don't want to do."

"I like the way my life is going, but a little push doesn't hurt. Maybe Reggie needs a push too."

"I'm not Annabelle."

"Annabelle's motivated, strong, independent. You're not so different. You left home, excelled in school, got a job on the other side of the world…"

For a long time, a minute or two that seemed to both of them like an eon, Monica didn't move and she didn't speak.

"It's a big responsibility," she said at last.

"Only if you don't want to do it. If you love him, it's just the necessary work."

"I'm the one that's scared, not Reggie."

"Perhaps you both are."

"By the way, it didn't happen the way you said."

"What didn't?"

"School, this job, my life. I know this sounds strange and I can't prove it, but I've always felt like there's a fairy godmother looking out for me. Someone's moving me around. My mother denies it, won't ever say anything about it, but I've had the feeling for years now. I can't put my finger on it, but things just happen for me. I'm doing nothing right and I'm doing everything wrong and then somehow the dominoes line up and poof, I get into Harvard. A few years later, poof, I land a Hong Kong gig."

"You're saying you didn't have the grades for Harvard?"

"I had them. But so did other people."

"Not so hard to figure out–minority, or half-minority, small town. Those places have quotas and demographics."

"I know, I know. That makes sense. It all makes sense. Everything that happens makes sense. I love publishing, I wanted to be here, wanted to get to know China because it was in my blood. What you're saying is right; I've thought it through a thousand times. It's just that there's something else."

Dalton took her hand. It was a friendly gesture, not an intimate one, but because of the conversation, it was a touch with power, like a punctuation mark on a sentence.

"My success feels the same way to me. Maybe it's what Lao Zi called the Way, the *Dao*, precisely that thing I talk and write about and think about all the time. When you're going with the river, the scenery seems to flow by incredibly smoothly, and you have the sense that you've hardly kicked and hardly paddled, the sense that you're doing nothing but somehow everything is getting done. Maybe what you feel is the power of the universe, the river, the *Dao*, call it what you want. Whatever it is, it supports you and moves you forward."

"That might be it," Monica sighed. "I've read Lao Zi, but I can't say I understand him."

They sat a few more minutes. "The way you're chasing this *gongfu* master, it doesn't feel like you're flowing with the river," Monica said. "It feels to me like you're pushing too hard. Why is this guy so important to you?"

"He knows things I'd like to learn."

"You seem to know everything already."

"Very funny."

"What could he know that's going to help us sell more books; that's what I'd like to know."

Dalton took a breath. "All right, I'll tell you. But you're going to think I'm crazy."

"Shoot from the hip, cowboy."

He got up and started to walk through the lush gardens abutting the museum.

Monica followed him. "Well?" she prompted, when he bent down for a closer look at a flower.

"There was a bad storm on the flight over."

"When I met you at the terminal you said you didn't remember any bad weather."

"I didn't; and that's part of the story. Lightning hit the airplane, and burned some circuits out of the controls. We were in a terrible dive–I mean it really felt like the end was near–and I went up to the cockpit to see if I could help. A man pushed past me and went to the controls. He stood in a martial posture and red bolts came out of his hands."

"Dalton."

"He pulled us out of the dive, and the controls came back. Then he touched me, and I didn't remember anything until later, when I was meditating."

Monica frowned. "You're saying he affected your memory, somehow?"

"That's what I'm saying, yes."

"Healing an airplane, and then stealing your memory. That's pretty far out. Maybe he was electrocuted in front of you. You know, electricity was going into him instead of coming out?"

"I thought of that, but it simply isn't what happened. The classics of traditional Chinese medicine and internal martial arts are full of references to *qi* transmission, externally conducting the energy of life. I never met anyone who could do it, though. I asked Fong, the guy who took us to dinner, and he doesn't think there are such men in Hong Kong."

"Maybe whoever he was continued on to another location. Plenty of people pass through this town."

"I thought of that, but I have to proceed on the presumption he's local. If not, I'm lost."

"You *were* kind of spaced out when I met you at the terminal. I figured you'd been drinking."

"I had half a glass of champagne. I never booze on planes; it makes me feel terrible."

"What an awesome thing to experience, Dalton. I'd be looking for the guy too."

Dalton smiled in relief. "Thank you."

23

Jakarta was a madhouse. Although the international community was still paying no more real attention to the outbreak than they had to the Dili massacres, Indonesians themselves were scared witless. There were soldiers in the streets, and every television was barking. If people had to go out, they did so carrying PDAs, or glued to transistor radios. Parents and children regarded each other with suspicion. There was an overnight swell in black market surgical masks. Through all this, and through the death of nearly the entire hospital staff, Leili Musi sat resolute and immovable at the nursing station computer terminal. The kind young intern who put her to the task passed away of the disease while watching her type, but not before she promised to keep going until her own last breath.

Leili was the information queen. Family, if any of them were still alive, were out of touch, and had, in any case, vanished into a deliberate barrier she put up between herself and feelings she determined she could ill afford. In truth, part of her thoroughly *passed* the breaking point. All layers of normal consciousness and conscience had receded, leaving the physical Leili a biological machine of naught but eyes and fingers; she had not eaten a proper meal in thirty hours, but seemed not to notice. The spiritual Leili was something else–compassion, grief, and humanity poured into her documents.

The hospital staff turned over virtually continuously as many fled and the rest died. The fleeing was unpredictable, as people would just suddenly put down what they were doing and walk out, struck in the moment by all they had to do or had not yet done. The progress of the disease was inexorable, and at the same time, since the vector had not been found, there was no way to know how the smile was communicated, nor how to protect against it. In the resulting chaos, Leili, sitting in front of her calm, cool computer screen, was the eye of the storm.

Perhaps that was why staff members kept the information coming: records of the dead and dying, observations about symptoms, numbers, too, including blood levels of tell-tale enzymes and liquids and salts. In the beginning, a steady stream came to her, but that stream eventually dropped to a trickle, and then finally stopped. Even so, the reams of lab results and body counts outpaced one woman's efforts to transmit them.

Despite the abundance of raw data, Leili's e-mail messages sparked more questions than answers, and so the faculties of medicine both in Jakarta, and at Airlangga University in nearby Surabaya, largely ignored them. As a large and coherent body of data, however, the messages received plenty of attention at the CDC in Atlanta, the London Institute of Hygiene and Tropical Medicine, the Geneva office of the World Health Organization, the French relief organization Doctors Without Borders, and the Pasteur Institute outside Paris. It was this latter outfit that made the first move. Representatives of the august institute arrived at the hospital during the third day of the plague's outbreak, and they went straight to Leili Musi in hopes of gaining more personal insight from what was obviously a trained medical observer.

The team was led by Henri Eonnet, an epidemiologist chosen not only for his canny field ability, but because he had been to Indonesia before, and had worked in Liquica, Ulmera, at the hospital in Baucau, and at the displaced persons facility in East Timor's Dili stadium. Eonnet secretly hated the Indonesian government, and was almost gratified to see things in total collapse. At the outset, before he realized the magnitude of the Banpo Smile, he thought the outbreak might ultimately make things better in that country by bringing down a ruthless and totalitarian regime. He told his team to fan out and take stock of what was going on in the hospital, while he himself went to find Leili.

Walking through the wards, Eonnet felt like an aquanaut in the bowels of a sunken submarine. His faceplate was fogged over, and he could hear his breath. The survivors took one look at his yellow biohazard suit–the team had borrowed the suits from the military–and knew they were doomed. The soon-to-be-dead had a different response, regarding him hungrily, as if he were an enormous banana, a source of health and power, of minerals and sugar and life-giving calories, of something foreign and magical. Striding down the corridors, Eonnet was afraid they might fall upon him like cannibals. When he finally located Leili, he found her nearly catatonic. Her shoulder felt bony through his double-walled gloves, and she barely reacted when he touched her.

"I'm here to help."

"Help," she repeated.

He noticed there were spots on her legs, but they were so faint as to be almost invisible. He noticed too that her nose was chafed. "I need you to come with me," he said.

Leili shook her head. "I can't leave. I have to keep the lines of communication open and continue inputting the data."

Eonnet sat down on the edge of the counter. "You can stop all that now," he said. "We're here."

She pointed her chin at lab results and charts. "There's still more data to put in."

There was mania in her. He saw that now. How could it be otherwise? It was amazing she could still string a sentence together after what she had been through.

"We have all we need now," he told her gently.

"The blood sample at the CDC. That's my son."

"I know."

He knew a lot more than that. He and every other doctor at the crisis facilities abroad knew Leili's entire story, because in her long hours in front of the computer she had created a stunning human document.

"Please," he said, gently touching her arm.

She looked down at his glove. This was what the world has come to, she thought, a place of hard black plastic where no warmth shines through: a place where the most regular and commonplace of human interactions–the tender touch–is denied.

"What's your name?" she asked.

He heard that her voice was flat, and saw crusty lines of dehydration around her lips, as if she had been drinking from a salty margarita glass. She noticed that through the suit, his voice sounded like a robot's.

"Doctor Henri Eonnet of the Pasteur Institute," he said formally.

"Dr. Henri Eonnet has arrived," she wrote on the screen. "He is a yellow plastic man with black gloves and blue eyes."

"Leili," he said. "You can tell your story right to me. You don't need to type it any more. I am your audience. I am here."

She glanced at him, then began to type: "Dr. Eonnet thinks well of himself. He thinks he is the whole world."

"May I write something?" he asked, gesturing at the keyboard. His voice sounded hollow through the pane of the suit, but even so it was kind. She regarded him a long moment then pushed her chair out of the way. There, under the desk, he saw the bedpan she had been using so as not to leave her post.

"I am here with Leili Musi," he said. "There is a plague afoot in Indonesia, and we don't know what it is, but we will isolate the agent, and develop a cure. Leili is going to stop typing now, because she has something more important to do. She is one of the few people in Jakarta who has been exposed to so many patients, and has not succumbed. She is going to help by lending us her body. She may have special antibodies we need to understand the nature of this plague. She is also going to help me sift through the reams of test results she has put into the computer, so that I may find some answers there."

Leili read the message. She scooted her chair back in front of the keys.

"Leili doesn't believe Dr. Eonnet," she wrote. "There are plenty of others alive in Jakarta."

"Not so many, I'm afraid," he said. "In fact, very, very few. And at this point, you are the only one who has been exposed to so very many and not gotten sick. Show me someone else in this hospital who knows everything you've written, and who remains free of symptoms, free of blotches, pain, fever, or the smile. I will ask that person to help me, and leave you to your typing."

"I won't be tricked," she said.

"Show me!" he demanded.

Slowly, Leili turned back to the computer.

"Goodbye," she typed with a sigh.

24

The Imperial Palace, Chang'an, Han Dynasty, 111 BCE

Liu Che, otherwise know as Emperor Wu Han, climbs out the window of the imperial bedchamber and drops silently to the ground. He is confident that he has thought of everything. If he can beat back the marauding Xiongnu nomads by mounting repeated campaigns of better than 100,000 men, he can deceive the palace guards by sending them away on a training mission to a Daoist retreat. If he can consolidate power through the imposition of Confucian reforms, he can remember to have the grounds swept free of snow so he will leave no footprints. A harsh wet wind from the west brings flurries, but the snow is not sticking. He knew it would not. He consulted both the oracle of the *I Ching* and his most trusted and erudite advisors in picking this night for the murder.

Liu Che is wrapped against the weather in a mustard cloak chosen in honor of the Yellow Emperor, the ancestor of all Chinese kings. Beneath the cloak, he wears a red silk suit, a color against which blood will not show. He carries a curved broadsword sharpened so it will cleave a falling leaf with ease. The emperor chose the weapon because it was a crude weapon forged for a common foot soldier, and he clandestinely stole it while reviewing the palace armory the previous month. It was perfect. Nobody would ever guess that the Son of Heaven would employ such a low-class blade.

Following the line of lighted torches, Liu Che steps lightly along the hard Xi'an ground. He is careful to stay in the shadows as he makes his way to the compound of concubines. His mouth is dry and his heart is racing, because unlike the heathen Xiongnu nomads, and unlike his forebears, this emperor is a strategist not a warrior. His brilliance in military campaigns comes from his mind, not his might. He is no combat-hardened veteran, but he *is* a man with a weakness for women.

He pauses by his intended victim's window, thinking of all the times he stood on the other side of those shutters, sated and proud, surveying his land. A thin silk curtain blocks his way, and he parts it gently with his fingers. He has decreed that all his women keep their quarters dimly lit so that he can come to them in the night without fear of what might lurk in the shadows, and without suffering the indignity of stumbling around. By the torch burning in the corner, he sees Zetian in her bed, lying flat on her back, her legs slightly spread, her arms out at her sides, her palms up.

How marvelous that even on the night she is to die, she sleeps so fearlessly! Do not his own men, seasoned fighters all, sleep curled up so as to present their hard backs to the world as a turtle might his shell? Why even he himself, architect of the Silk Road and commander of oceans, passes the night on his left side so that his heart and meridians will not have to work overly hard in circulating blood and *qi*.

He climbs carefully in through the window and draws a thin deep breath, filling his nostrils with Zetian's scent. Memories of her come rushing in; the first taste of flesh, sweet and firm as peach meat–although perhaps even then she had been older than time–her sultry low voice, so different from the chiming giggles of the other girls, her cunning tongue, her ideas about government, her suggestions he erase rivals. How many men had died because of the words she whispered into his ear? How many other ears had she breathed into before she breathed into his?

Has she been with other emperors? Now that he understands her secret, Liu Che is certain that she has. No wonder the eunuchs fear her, and other women turn away when she appears. If she had only borne him a son, he would have made her empress long ago. They would never have been at odds, there would have been no polarization in the court, and she would have drawn to her no powerful ministers and generals. If only she had not been barren, she would have had chambers next to his, with her own guard to command, and a regiment of servants and maids to supplant the strange thin man with the porcupine hair who always attended her. But barren, she could not be his queen, barren, she could only be his enemy, staying young as he grew old, staying strong as he grew weak.

There is a large, locked lacquer chest in the corner, decorated in filigreed gold, a crocodile and a crane rendered on its heavy lid. In the beginning, he assumed she kept inside those tools of a concubine's trade which allowed her to smell fresh at all times, to keep smooth and clean, to keep her breath sweet. Later, as he began to suspect what she really was, he nearly commanded her to open it, but something always stopped him. It was almost as if he were afraid to know, afraid of what she might do if forcibly revealed. She was, after all, stronger than any man he had ever met, and able to play herself like an orchestra when he was inside her.

He forces the clasp.

Snap.

He freezes. If she wakes now, it will be more difficult. He will have to speak to her. He will have to look her in the eyes while he takes off her head.

He waits.

She inhales deeply, rolls once, and then returns to her open, trusting pose. Under the dim light of the torch, he unpacks the chest. Inside, he finds strange vials of dirty-clay darkening potions, and other items he does not understand. He puts his imperial forefinger in one of the vials, and rubs the unguent it contains between his fingers. He goes to the torch to examine the result, and although the color he sees is not accurate–only sunlight could show the truth, or sometimes moonlight, especially during the solstice–he notices that the lines on his fingers, the tiny whorls which made his hands different from all others, are deepening, aging before his eyes.

Liu Che considers his discovery for a moment, and then rubs the salve on his forearm. It stings, and it smells like rotting beans, but more importantly it seems to loosen the flesh, creating wrinkles where there have been none, confirming what he has come to know, that Zetian uses her potions differently than all other women; they have secrets for looking young, Zetian has them for looking old.

He moves to her bed, and pulls his ugly blade. It glints ominously, despite the pork fat he has put into the scabbard to quiet the draw. Holding it in his right hand, resolving to gaze upon her one last time, he yanks the bedclothes back. Liu Che is tough with eunuchs, fortunetellers, and sons, but in the face of such a woman, he is feeble. He slides his hand under her gown, rationalizing his procrastination by telling himself that every emperor should take his fill of an immortal. He knows he will never again partake of her aeonian milk.

She stirs, but he does not withdraw his hand. Her flesh is so smooth. It has always been thus, and although at first he had thought her ill, she has never sickened, never weakened, and, indeed, never truly aged. He has seen younger girls come and go, and has watched them thicken and sag. He has even kept a few around and made marquises of their offspring, while all the while Zetian pretended to stoop and wither, but in bed remained as perfect as the day she came to court.

He puts the sharp steel against her throat, and she opens her eyes. He cuts ever so lightly into her flesh, warning her not to cry out. Bending, he puts his lips to her navel, licking and kissing and chewing her little button.

"I will make a legend of you," he whispers, his voice muffled by her skin. "I will call you Queen Mother of the West. You shall forever be remembered as you appear now, young, perfect, beautiful, and immortal."

The emperor sees the thin line of blood dribble down her neck, and then watches incredulously as the flesh knits together before his very eyes. So it is true! Hers is not earthly flesh! He begins to tremble with cotton-tongued awe, and is about to cut her again, more deeply this time, when Sanfeng creeps up behind him, and with one finger collapses his imperial carotid artery, depriving him of consciousness.

"He almost had my head," Zetian mutters.

"Your sleep was heavy," says her brother.

"I should have known something was going to happen. He has been coming to me many times in one week, like he used to years ago, ignoring the other girls, and putting his seed in me night after night. Why did you come here?"

"I can't say," Sanfeng answers, sheathing his sword, and tucking it into his robe. "My own sleep was troubled. I thought I heard a noise. Get dressed. We have to leave."

"I shall miss this place," Zetian sighs.

"You've had enough palace luxury for a while. He's your sixth emperor, after all."

Zetian dumps the lacquer chest containing her potions and creams onto the bed, wraps them up in the silk sheet, and slings them over her shoulder.

"He's a man of vision, you know," she says, pausing to look at the unconscious emperor. "I think I'll let him live."

"Believe me, he'll remain a man of vision without you murmuring sweet nothings in his ear," Sanfeng dryly replies.

"He's going to make a story of me."

"So I heard."

"Queen Mother of the West. I like that."

"The real reason you spare him, of course. I, no doubt, shall be King Father of the East. Immortals seem an intellectual curiosity to him, interesting so long as they don't interfere with his rule."

They trundle out into the snow. A palace guard approaches, recognizes them, bows and backs away.

"Where are we going?"

"Wudang Mountain."

"Oh no! Not the Buddhists! You know I hate Buddhists. I can't stand all that talk about coming back as a cockroach."

"No Buddhists." Sanfeng smiles slightly.

"No Daoists either. They're almost as bad. It would be nice if they took a bath now and then, or combed their hair."

"Don't be silly. They're just wild men unburdened by cares. They have their suspicions about me, knowing I sparred with their grandfathers–but they like my martial style, and I have some new moves I want to work on with them. I'll train up there in the snow, and you can live in a cave and find a good-looking teenage boy to keep you warm."

"Caves are for bats. I like the fast life of the city, or at least the finery of court."

"Just be patient. Right now we have to lie low."
To the west, the mountains beckon.
They ride.

25

Despite admonishing Zetian for her bigoted nationalism, Gao Sanfeng was a visionary patriot. He knew that in order to take its rightful leadership position in the modern world, China needed to be integrated into the global financial community, to open a realistic dialog with capitalist nations, to inform and educate a people who had been kept in the dark for years. But Sanfeng's plans involved more than just Chinese history; a far more personal and less theoretical plan had been taking shape in the immortal's mind for some centuries, and in particular during the past twenty-five years. Billabong Books and Dalton Day were part of this plan, and Sanfeng wanted to see the American give one more presentation, this one to executives rather than floor workers.

Unlike Harbor Plastics, End Zone Illumination EZI was a prized Crocodile & Crane holding, a cutting-edge facility with top-drawer products, excellent distribution and an energetic marketing team. High employee turnover was hurting the company, however, because the business was complex, and there was a steep learning curve. New people had trouble getting shipments out on time, and customers were dropping off. Once again the immortal suspected Dalton's presentation might actually be a good thing for the company.

Ten minutes before the program began, Sanfeng was in the observation booth usually used for monitoring sales training. He watched the ten people in the room mill about in anticipation. Rachel Kleinman ate three yogurts and a piece of Jarlsberg cheese. *Small wonder she has trouble with her lungs*, Sanfeng thought. *Dairy products are the worst things for an asthmatic.* Sanfeng had no idea that yogurt and Jarlsberg were the least of it, as Kleinman personally imported two crocks of strong Stilton from London every month, and kept them in her office pantry to eat with port wine.

Finally, Dalton walked in. Sanfeng switched off the music, and leaned forward to listen. The executives came quickly to order. Dalton began talking in English, but this time no translator was needed as the high-level crew had come to the fore under British rule.

"Corporations are fractals," he said without preamble. "That means they express, on a macro level, the characteristics, strengths, weaknesses, failures and triumphs, of all the people who comprise them. My purpose here today is to help End Zone Illumination by helping you get in touch with the intuitions that have subconsciously served you for years in business. If you do this, then the corporation will reflect your new insights, your new confidence, your new perspective."

Rachel Kleinman took Monica's praise of Dalton as a sign of stardust in the eyes, but it looked like the girl was right. Dalton was solid and convincing, and his message was clear and down-to-earth. What's more, he might not have been as tall as some of the Masai warriors Rachel had seen on the Mara when she ran safari insurance in Kenya for Lloyds, but he was not far behind.

Dalton went on. "To hear the voice of the inner boxer, you have to tame your hot-rod heart. That's my term for the impulse to run off and do this or that. I'm going to show you a meditative technique that helps. Ready? Stand up, and put your arms in front of you as if you're hugging a tree."

Rachel snuck a piece of cheese, chewed it silently, and took in the way Monica watched Dalton's every move, hung on his every word. She was sure they were sleeping together, and she found that unprofessional. Girls these days. Shapely, pretty girls. She would have to say something to her.

"Before I share my *qigong* energy exercises, I want to talk to you a bit about being a leaf in the river," Dalton said when the meditation was over. "The river is the flow of information in the world, the flow of culture from west to east. America is exporting materialism to China just as fast as you folks can gobble it up. We are exporting fast food, a hunger for gas-guzzling cars, a keen desire for a townhouse and a maid. The irony is Americans have had fifty years to learn that none of this leads to happiness. Lusting after luxuries and sex and money–not to mention worshipping celebrities–leads only to frustration and self-loathing. The vanguards in America are coming to the conclusion that the wisdom and techniques of the very traditional Chinese philosophy Mao Zedong tried to expunge in his Cultural Revolution hold the answers for us in America in the 21st century. I hope the irony of me coming to teach you things I learned from your own country isn't lost on you. Take the cue from someone who has gone down the road you are going. Health and happiness are to be found inside, not outside. Joy and satisfaction grown from the work you are doing rather than the imagined result. Focus on the process, not the goal. The ideas in my book are seeds. Let's use this *qigong* to prepare the earth of you so those seeds will grow."

Dalton began his exercises then, and Sanfeng leaned forward to watch. He was eager to see Dalton move again, to watch his hands, see his belly and chest empty and fill as he breathed, hear his sounds. It was not Crocodile and Crane *Qigong*, but it *was* damn close. Amazing. The American was a *qigong* genius. No wonder he was famous. More, Sanfeng knew Dalton was quite right in his cultural observations; he had noticed the very same irony. No wonder the lanky man's audience was growing. As he hoped he would be, Sanfeng was increasingly sure Dalton was the right man for the job he had in mind.

26

The Kowloon Canton Railway was ever so slightly seedier than the Hong Kong subway. It was neither the worn faces of commuters, nor the equipment itself that gave this impression, but the brown dust from the New Territories that crept past the rubber seals of the cars as soon as Dalton and Monica departed the antiseptically clean, air-conditioned tunnels under the city.

"Rachel told Annabelle we're having an affair," Monica announced.

"What? Why would Rachel have that impression?"

"The extra time I'm spending with you. The fact that you've extended your visit."

"But there's a certain police captain I somehow sense remains very much in your heart."

"Ha," said Monica.

"Tell me he doesn't."

"Depressing, but true," she said glumly.

"Love shouldn't depress you. I'm sure there's a way to work it out."

"Couldn't we get together as an experiment?"

Dalton took her hands. "You're desperate for me to say no. You wouldn't know what to do if I said yes. You'd go home and spend a sleepless night thinking it over and then you'd call me on the phone and say you were sorry you asked and I was right and, at least until things with Reggie were really over you couldn't do anything with me. What's more, you know I'm going back to New York and you don't really want to leave Hong Kong. I'm not well-connected enough to get you the kind of job you have right here right now. On top of that, you'd say, we don't really know each other."

"I hate you," said Monica, pulling her hands away.

"Of course you do, which is all the more reason you should try to work things out with Reggie."

"I expect you think you're being clever."

"Logical, anyway."

"All of this is really just your way of saying you're a serious guy who takes women seriously."

"That too."

"You could have just said so and saved us both a lot of trouble."

"Markets are the cultural core of cities. I didn't want to miss our little shopping expedition. Tell me. Does Rachel drive an Aston Martin?"

"What? No way. Nothing but Mercedes. She's always ranting about how nobody builds 'em big and heavy like the Nazis."

"There was a blue Aston in the parking lot at the presentation today. I recognized it from Harbor Plastics. I figured she might have been checking me out over there without telling."

"Hong Kong's the richest place on Earth. There's probably a bunch of those cars around."

"Is Rachel a good manager?"

"She knows books that sell, I'll say that for her. Hey, this is our stop."

They got off the train at Tai Po Market, and headed for what Dalton expected to be an open-air bazaar. What he found instead was a fetid maze of indoor stalls. The ceiling was low, the lighting poor, the doors permanently open, and the floor filthy. The stalls at Tai Po featured slabs of pork, live chickens, and anything that crawls or swims in the water. There were frogs, crayfish, shrimp, and eels. A man walked by with a sweet-smelling pig heart in his hand.

"You shop here?" Dalton asked.

"I heard it was great," Monica answered faintly.

Dalton pointed at a pair of white-headed langur monkeys crammed into a filthy carrying cage reeking of scat. They clung to the thin bars, their fingers raw and bleeding, their eyes glazed, their fur bare in patches, their tails twitching back and forth. "Look at those poor guys," he said. "Senseless abuse and suffering like that makes me crazy."

"When I first arrived, Reggie took me out into the countryside on one of the major rail lines," said Monica. "China's rural areas look like a nuclear bomb hit them–they're an environmental wasteland. If it moves, the Chinese eat it. If it grows, they chop it down and replace it with a vegetable patch. There's plenty of green out there, but it's all the green of vegetables. There are hardly any more native plants. There's no protection for endangered animal species, either. Deer antler, bear gallbladder, turtle shell, they're all fair game for folk remedies."

"A lot of those folk remedies work," said Dalton. "But they have no future if the sources dry up, not to mention the moral issues."

"Kill all the bears, and no more gallbladder," Monica nodded. "China is going to pay dearly for its rate of growth, because the government won't invest in infrastructure or renewing resources. A shift in consciousness has to take place, not only for managing resources, but for recognizing suffering. Animals feel loss and pain, I know they do, but the Chinese just deny inconvenient truths."

Dalton nodded. "Denial is a coping mechanism, an adaptive skill. If we didn't have it, we couldn't put up with the incredible injustice of the world, or its monumental indifference."

Gingerly, Monica touched one of the monkeys. The vendor appeared out of nowhere; a fat young man wearing a gold Rolex, open shirt, and two gold chains. Rivulets of sweat ran down his chest. One of his eyes was covered by a pale film, and when he smiled, Monica noticed he was missing teeth.

"Very special price," the vendor said. "Just today."

"Tasty, I'm sure," Dalton said.

The vendor pointed a pudgy finger at Monica.

"Eat monkey before love," he grinned. "Make smart baby."

"Good to know," said Dalton.

"Very beautiful girl," the vendor went on.

Dalton nodded. "You're right about that."

After they walked a couple of feet, Dalton leaned over to Monica. "Want to save those monkeys?"

"What? Of course!"

"Ask him how much they are. He'll give you a better price than he'll give me."

He moved off, and Monica stepped close to the vendor, so he could smell her perfume. Women who looked and dressed like Monica shopped at the European boutiques, high-end jewelers, silk merchants and department stores in Pacific Place in Central, or at exclusive locales in Kowloon. They didn't come to Tai Po Market.

"We would like to buy the monkeys," she said.

"How many?"

"All of them.

"Monkey meat very good for love," the vendor said, smiling.

"You said that already. How much are they?"

"American dollar?"

"Yes."

The vendor smiled, then gave a price. Monica shook her head. The vendor pouted.

"Let's go," Dalton called.

The vendor dropped his price. Monica shook her head again. He dropped his price again. Monica beckoned Dalton over.

"Not just beautiful, tough businesswoman," the vendor said.

Dalton paid, picked up two cages, and hailed a cab. The driver was reluctant to take the monkeys, but Dalton convinced him with a few more bills.

They drove out of town with all the windows open, and in less than 30 minutes were at the entrance to Tai Po Kau Nature Reserve. There were *Litsea* and sweet gum trees there, and giant beans. Joss stick trees gave the area a wonderful fragrance, and raucous bulbuls called from distant bushes. Monica jogged to keep pace with Dalton's stride, the monkey cage swinging wildly in his grip.

Finally, they found a peaceful glade away from the main path, and pushed aside the pale green leaves of a small acacia to lean the cage up against a paperbark tree. They were on the slope of a mountain. The Lower Lam Tsuen River ran quietly in the distance.

"How's this?" Dalton asked.

"Perfect," Monica said.

"I'm going to take a little time in meditation before we let them go–just to mark the moment, bring us to the present, and help us realize what we're doing and appreciate it more deeply. Follow along, if you like. Just keep your tongue on the roof of your mouth behind your front teeth."

"Why?"

"Energy flows up your back and down your front in many independent channels, but two major ones. Those two are connected when you put your tongue in place. Also, try not to use your ribs when you breathe."

"My ribs?"

"Your chest. Breathing is best done with the belly. There's a lot more to it than that–many, many different ways to breathe–but let's start with keeping your chest out of the picture, and try to relax."

"Most men close their eyes and want my chest *in* the picture."

"And I'm one of them. But discipline rules, and besides, the monkeys are watching."

Monica found she could actually do what Dalton suggested, or at least she thought she could. After a few minutes, she felt very calm.

"It's so quiet," she whispered.

"Listen to the bugs and the birds," he said. "Listen to the sound of the blood rushing in your ears. Listen to your heart. Hear the sound of your breath."

She did all that, and felt the tension go out of her upper body. Her internal world grew warmer and softer, but beyond that she did not have words to describe to herself what she was feeling. She sensed Dalton next to her, but didn't know how she did, being too far to feel his body heat or even hear his breathing.

At length, Dalton roused her.

"How long was I out?" she wanted to know.

"You weren't out. You were in. Or I should say, you were here. People make the mistake of thinking they've gone somewhere when they meditate. The truth is precisely the opposite. You are never more here than when you are standing quietly like you just did, never more aware. It's the rest of the time we are somewhere else, our mind filled with worry, anticipation, imagination, even passion. Observing yourself and your place in the universe is about as 'in' as you can be."

"I'll have to ponder that," said Monica.

Dalton opened the monkey cage. The animals had been confined so long, they did not know an escape hatch when they saw it, but finally poked their heads out.

"I thought they'd make a mad dash," Monica said, as the langurs moved slowly and carefully for the trees.

"Our meditation calmed them."

"You really believe that?"

"We were creating a certain flavor of energy," he shrugged. "You felt it. Why would you imagine they couldn't feel it?"

"So we did a good thing," she said, following the newly free with her eyes.

"It's not enough just to have compassion," Dalton said quietly. "You have to act on it. Principles without action are not enough. Without translation into movement in the world, nothing manifests."

Monica wanted to hug him, but she kept her arms to herself.

27

"We're too late to save our people in Jakarta," Huangfu said, glancing in the Bentley's rear view mirror.

"Really?" Zetian queried, putting on her lipstick.

"The city is closed and under quarantine. Some of the factory workers have called relatives here, but communications are sporadic, even by e-mail. I planned an airlift, but I'm not sure there will be any survivors. The whole world is watching Jakarta. There was talk of sending United Nations forces, but now there are reports of disease in Ireland. The thing is leapfrogging around the world. The downside of air travel, I suppose, people moving such great distances in such a short time, taking germs with them."

"I don't think this is about air travel," Zetian said.

"Water, then, or prevailing winds."

Zetian did not care to hear any more. She leaned forward until she was almost touching Huangfu. She had been thinking about him since news of Jou Yuen's passing, and was almost ready to make her move. "Sooner or later people die," she said.

"Jou Yuen was a good man."

"He was. But his importance to the company, and to me personally, has been exaggerated. Do you hear what I'm saying?"

"Yes, Madame."

They came to a traffic light. "I want you to go in with me," she announced.

He tilted the rearview mirror so he could see her.

"Madame?"

"Let the valet take the car. I want you to escort me tonight."

Huangfu had never attended a social function with her before, and he was not certain what the invitation meant.

"As your chauffeur?"

"No."

"As your *charge d'affaires*?"

"No."

"As a senior Crocodile & Crane executive?"

"As my date."

Her date? Huangfu at once began to think about his *toilette.* Thankfully, he always did his nails, and had not been on duty all day, so he was in his evening suit, a clean, well-pressed navy single-breasted with a somber tie, and cufflinks Zetian herself had given him in recognition of five years of faithful service. They were gold. She had said they were antiques, had mumbled something about the opening of the Silk Road.

"As you wish, Madame Chairman."

"And no more 'Madame Chairman.' You must call me Zetian."

"I beg your pardon?"

"You heard me. Say it now."

He watched the windshield wipers go back and forth and tried to force his mouth to work.

Click. Swish.

"Huangfu!"

"Zetian," he managed.

She smiled, conscious that her smiles were precious, and reserved for ministers, kings, lovers and prey. Before the light could change, she climbed out of the car, moving quickly through the rainy night, and joined him in the front seat.

She reached up and removed his chauffeur's hat.

My date. The words were still ringing in Huangfu's ears when he pulled into the roundabout at the Peninsula Hotel, and let the valet take the car. Zetian hooked her arm through his, squeezing his biceps. He began to perspire, unable to believe what was happening.

They took the elevator up one floor to the mezzanine. The Chinese restaurant was directly in front of them, decorated with dark fixtures and shaded lamps and mahogany tables. Waiters and waitresses scurried efficiently in every direction. The hostess drifted forth from the front podium to greet them. She barely looked at Huangfu–unusual in Hong Kong, where young girls played to the appetites of some of the world's richest and most powerful men–but he did not blame her. She could spend the rest of her life in Tahitian luxury with the proceeds from Zetian's emerald earrings and necklace.

She bowed. "Madame Gao. Please come this way. Everyone is waiting."

They moved past the "Private Party" sign, and into the dining area. A small dais at the back of the room was festooned with orchids, and the hostess led them past it to the central table. Huangfu recognized fifty of Hong Kong's power elite scattered about.

They sat down next to each other, Zetian at the head of the table. People came up and whispered in Zetian's ear. She nodded solemnly to some, shook her head to others. She appeared to enjoy the attention, but Huangfu knew her well enough to sense that it was all a sham.

Then he felt her foot on his shin.

She moved it up slowly–without so much as missing a beat of conversation, or shifting in her seat–until her toes were between his legs. He struggled to keep his composure as she stroked him, never so much as glancing his way but using her silk stocking the way some women might a mink glove, or a vibrator. He knew she was trying to prime his pump, to tease him and make him crazy. He understood it was a challenge.

Gently, but firmly, Huangfu pushed her foot away. He registered the surprise in her eyes, and saw the slightest flicker of a satisfied smile cross her lips.

He had passed the test.

The pre-arranged meal began with a twice-cooked pork in a fabulous, rare, mushroom sauce. Everyone cooed, but Zetian was as unimpressed with that dish as she was with the thousand-year-old eggs. Halfway through the soup, the director of the Chinese

Children's Project rose to make a toast. She was the wife of an industrialist whose information technology holdings were in direct competition with those of Crocodile & Crane. Huangfu noticed that her jewelry was not as impressive as Zetian's.

"I know we are all enjoying this wonderful meal," she began. "But I want to take a moment to raise my glass to our guest of honor. As you all know, Madame Gao has done more for the cause of Chinese orphans and orphanages than any world bank or international agency ever has. People say she is stingy, but due to her ongoing and generous support of our organization, starving and abandoned girls all over China find love in the our orphanages. As an expression of our appreciation, and on behalf of the board, I hereby present this Boda crystal sculpture of an angel, CCP's lifetime achievement award. Thank you, Zetian, for being China's angel of mercy."

After a moment of uncertainty at the backhanded compliment, the guests erupted in applause.

"Now," the director went on, "I am delighted to introduce living proof of what our program has accomplished."

More applause. A young matron led in two thin, pale children in pinafores. They bowed to Zetian, and she inclined her head in response. The matron pushed them forward. Zetian kissed them, and then took up the microphone as the girls were led away.

"In some quarters, I am criticized for not giving enough to charity," Zetian said in a strong voice. "In truth, I don't give as widely as I might because I see that many of the so-called causes for which people solicit funds are no more than the search for solutions to problems we ourselves have created. The answer to most crises in this world is discipline and forbearance, not merely generosity. When it comes to children who have no parents, however, all intellectual and academic considerations disappear. Children cannot know how to behave without our guidance. It is up to us to teach them. I don't give to orphans and orphanages because I have some ulterior motive; I give because I feel the pain of children all alone in the world. It's that simple, really."

Zetian and the director embraced theatrically, and everyone got back to the business of eating. Huangfu's mind raced as he tried to figure out what was in Zetian's heart. Was she really interested in him all of a sudden? Was she really concerned with orphans? She did not care about her own employees in Indonesia, did not seem to care that Jou Yuen, her former lover, was dead, and yet here she was making an impassioned speech about abandoned children. He was still trying to decide whether this was just a public relations ploy when the servers brought out a main course of curried shrimp.

Huangfu blanched. Anyone who had ever dined with Zetian–and that included the project director–knew she hated shellfish.

Zetian pushed her plate away. The project director looked her squarely in the eye. "Oh, that's right. I forgot you don't eat shrimp."

Zetian raised her hand for a waiter, and when one came, she requested the wine list. The food and drink had been arranged in advance, and the waiter started to protest, but Zetian shut him down with a look.

He brought the list. Loudly, she named a magnum of 1961 Chateau Petrus, with a price tag far greater than the food for the entire event.

The director gasped.

"Bring it quickly," Zetian commanded the waiter. "We want it to have time to breathe."

28

Gao Sanfeng loved the Bank of China Tower. He loved the angles and the glass and the twin rooftop antennae, which from afar looked like beetle pincers. His thirty-ninth-floor suite was special to him, and lately he had been spending more and more time in it. While Zetian was sipping exorbitant wine, Sanfeng sat in silk boxer shorts before an array of optical instruments–Leitz Tinovids, digitally steadied Starlight glasses, and Meade and Celestron telescopes–to monitor the city as a doctor might a patient. With music playing, classical for the most part, but occasionally blues, jazz or traditional Chinese tunes, he scanned the harbor, registered the faces in the windows of high-speed ferries. He noted the pectoral muscles of shirtless fisherman in small rowboats, saw cigarette-smoking captains sitting tall in the bridge chairs of liners, even noticed the flotsam of the day bobbing in the swell–bottles mostly, but hard plastic items and Styrofoam fast-food containers too. Remembering the days when the waters of the South China Sea were so pristine you could see a jellyfish draw a fish into its mouth from ten feet away, he sighed and swiveled the lenses past the teenagers holding hands on the streets below, past the red taxicabs running the overpasses out to Wan Chai, and brought them to rest on the window of Monica Farmore's apartment.

He had known Monica's address since her first day in Hong Kong, but had never spied on her before. He didn't spy on any of them, even though he felt cold as an ocean fish for his sacrifice. He was glad none of them would know how much he suffered, and hoped–although he knew his wish would forever remain unrequited–that they would not think him disinterested.

Now, however, he had a reason to bring Monica into focus, to listen to her voice, maybe even her breathing, with a hypersensitive parabolic infrared listening device that could sense the tiniest vibrations in glass. Sanfeng turned off the stereo, and donned headphones just as Monica's doorbell rang, and he saw her rush to answer it. He listened to her footfalls. She was dressed in heels, a diaphanous skirt, and a green tank top that matched her eyes. He felt a twinge of something when he saw Dalton Day at the door.

He watched Monica's body language, saw how she felt about Dalton, and realized it had been decades since he had felt the pure blush of romantic pleasure; his affairs after his first couple of centuries had always been tainted by an unpleasant habit of projecting into a future where he would have to leave before his love discovered his secret.

He felt those losses keenly, and remembered the pain as much as anything. He remembered the few times he stayed around to the end, and the inevitable resentment that superseded the wonder, the deathbed bitterness that poisoned love. He also remembered the special trysts, the later ones, after he put his life plan into action. Those liaisons were especially difficult to contemplate, all the more because it seemed to him he had spent an endless succession of days mostly alone. It was true that empty days zipped by, while days full of love were the source of cherished memories, but even so his loneliness would have been unfathomable to a mortal. He ached to someday, just once, express it and be comforted.

"So you're thinking that if this airplane master can really project *qi*, he's beyond anyone you've ever trained with?" Monica said, putting a bowl of steaming handmade crab dumpling soup down in front of Dalton.

"Not only anybody I've ever trained with, but anybody I've ever heard about or known."

Emitting *qi* in the airplane? Stunned, Sanfeng leaned forward. The American should not be able to remember that. Sanfeng had used an acupuncture technique he and Zetian developed together–a specific version of the much-vaunted *dim mak* death touch–to clear the mind of short-term memories. The technique had come in handy many times over the years.

"And you're sure you saw it."

Dalton took a sip of the soup, gave an appreciative roll of his eyes at the taste, and nodded. "Fong made a good point about this when he came to see me at the hotel. Martial artists don't develop power like that anymore, because life has become too fast and complicated. There isn't time to do the required meditation and physical training. There is no limit to what I could learn from a man with that kind of discipline and focus."

So the American was looking for him, Sanfeng considered. That was interesting.

"The good news is that the world has noticed you now," Monica said. "So if you *do* find him and learn what he knows, you'll be able to transmit it to a huge audience."

"Maybe, but there's a certain etiquette about sharing. I'd have to get his permission first."

"But if you had it."

Dalton grinned. "That *would* be pretty incredible."

Monica brought out two bottles of wine. "Red, or white?" she asked.

"No thank you."

"No wine?"

"No thanks."

Monica sighed. "I suppose I should be grateful for that. Do you mind if I have some?"

"Of course not."

He opened the red for her, and poured a glass. She drank it quickly. He smiled, and poured another for her.

"Tell me about the training you do have," Monica said. "I'm not a *gongfu* expert or anything, but I'm sure you have great stories."

"I started with *Wing Chun*, did a couple of other styles, and then settled on a form of *Taijiquan* that traces back to a chance meeting between two masters on Song Mountain in the early seventeenth century."

"What's *Wing Chun*?"

"A close-in fighting art that protects the center of the body. It means 'beautiful springtime.' It's named after a nun, and is the basis of Bruce Lee's system. You remember him, right? The movie star?"

Sanfeng clucked. He knew all about *Wing Chun*, as he and the nun had been lovers, and he had put the moves together for her as gift, so she could protect herself from unwanted advances.

Monica finished her second glass of wine, took away the soup bowls, and brought out a steaming plate of chicken in black bean sauce. "I bet Anabelle Miller never cooked you a dinner like this."

"She's an excellent cook, actually."

"And you know that because…."

"She cooked for me."

"You said she was a manager, not a girlfriend."

"I also said she was a mother hen."

"If she cooked for you and nothing came of it, she isn't much of a cook."

Sanfeng smiled at this. He had to say she was right.

"You're a piece of work," Dalton said.

"Anabelle called me today."

"She called me too," Dalton said. "She's very eager for me to get back to New York."

"To start the clothing line?"

"She told you about that?"

Monica picked up the wine bottle, looked at how much was gone, considered a moment, and poured a third glass. "The fact is, she calls me constantly. After a while, we run out of things to talk about. That's when she starts in with her great plans for you. Reaching out is her way of keeping tabs, of getting to know me too. Keeping her enemy close and all that."

"You're not her enemy."

"She thinks I am," Monica sniffed. "Tell me she hasn't asked about me."

"Lately she seems preoccupied with the plague in Indonesia. She's worried it's going to spread to New York."

"From what I've read, it's not a spreading thing," said Dalton. "It's cropped up in Europe now, in Ireland, and there is no discernable link to Indonesia."

"So poor Annabelle wants you to rush home and protect her?"

Dalton smiled. "She likes me in baseball jerseys. I think she has a sports fetish."

Across town, Sanfeng unconsciously touched his Nikes, and wondered if he had a sports fetish too.

Monica finished her third glass of wine. When she got up to clear the plates, she stumbled. Dalton caught her and let her down gently into the chair. She put her arms around his neck. He gently disentangled himself.

"Any dessert?"

"I have lychee nuts in honey glaze," she slurred.

"Let's bring them out together," Dalton suggested. "And no more wine, okay?"

He carried the dishes into the kitchen. As he did, she poured herself one more.

"I thought we said no more."

"You said no more. I tried meditating today. I couldn't do it without you there, couldn't stand still for more than a few minutes."

"You have to cultivate the habit. It's worth it though, and much better for you than drinking."

"I never drink this much. If you had some, there wouldn't be so much for me."

"Try harder with the meditation. It'll calm you down, make life sweeter, and once in a while give you insight into how things really are, like a peek behind the curtain, a sense of being part of something larger."

She went over and sat in his lap. Sanfeng watched intently. Dalton stood up, holding her arms in front of her.

"How about those lychee nuts?" Dalton asked.

"You can teach me to meditate, but first I'd like to learn some self-defense."

"Looks like I'm the one who needs self-defense," Dalton smiled.

Monica put her hands on his chest. "You don't like me?"

"We've been through this."

"But I'm drunk. I'm not responsible for my actions."

He removed her hands from his chest. "Exactly."

While she sulked, Dalton cleared the rest of the plates, took what was left of the wine to the kitchen, and then came back and sat down.

"Do you ever use your *gongfu* on the street?" Monica asked.

"Not much. We live in a world of guns and bombs. Hand-to-hand combat isn't as important as it was ages ago, and violence is, in any case, the lowest common denominator of the human experience. But the discipline is helpful, and the systems are beautiful."

"I know that from *gongfu* movies."

"You watch *gongfu* movies?"

"I love them," she clapped, her hands nearly missing one another. "The campier the better. People leaping into trees, flying with cloaks, battling for half an hour without sweating. How do they do that? Not sweat, I mean?"

"The code of honor is the thing," said Dalton. "The emphasis on loyalty, the clear distinction between right and wrong, the worship of wisdom and justice and power."

"Do you know how to use a sword?"

"Sure."

"Tell me a sword story."

He came back and sat by her. "I hate to disappoint you, but I've never raised sharp steel against another human being."

"You're such a straight arrow. Make something up."

"One day, I was practicing in the park. A bird landed on a low branch right next to me, like it wanted to watch. Probably it saw a worm. Anyway, I took a swing at it, and before I knew what happened, I had chopped the little guy clean in half. No kidding. It was like surgery, like a textbook picture of organs and bones. Of course I never thought I'd actually hit it. It upset the hell out of me. Honestly, Monica, I cried like a baby. I had nightmares."

Sanfeng leaned forward. He found himself interested in a martial artist who cried over accidentally killing a bird.

"Cried like a baby," Monica repeated.

And then she was out.

Dalton carried her to the couch, laid her out gently with her head on the pillow and spent a few minutes washing the dishes.

Sanfeng kept his telescope trained on Monica's sleeping face until Dalton turned out the lights, and left the apartment. Long after that, the immortal sat silently gazing out at the city.

29

Tony Tunstall knew tea in the same way seasoned, grizzled, charter boat captains know marlin. The ultimate cup perpetually eluded him, but the day-to-day purveyance of the commodity was his livelihood nevertheless. He was a white Australian with a proud convict heritage, and he hailed from Darwin, where his father operated a safari camp for tourists out on the edge of Kakadu, the park made famous by the *Crocodile Dundee* movies. Unlike his friends, most of whom became ranchers, and some of whom moved to Brisbane or Melbourne or Sydney or Perth hoping for corporate work, Tony remained in the Northern Territories. What kept him there was neither sloth nor opportunity nor family loyalty, but a great love for the Oriental fusion that developed in the far north due to the influx of Chinese, East Timorese, Balinese, and Indians. Tony was fascinated by the way Asian people formed their mouths into sounds that were as different from the broad Australian twang as a human being could sound, by the way they cooked their food and played games with tiles and bits, by they way they drank wine instead of whiskey, and most of all, by the way they consumed tea.

Before his twenty-fifth birthday, he had a lock on the tea business in Darwin, an enterprise that grew with the population of the tropical city on the Timor Sea. At first, restaurants were reluctant to buy from him, figuring him for a know-nothing round-eye. In time, however, Tony won them over with his prices, service, and knowledge of the many-splendored bush. There was no estate he would not scour, no corner of the world he would not penetrate in search of newer and better tealeaves. His dream was to make Darwin the Tea Mecca of Australia, to lure not just the Asians to his coffers, but Australians with British roots as well, proper people who still took tea in the afternoon as a ritual instead of as a digestive.

It was in search of great leaf that Tony Tunstall went to

Indonesia, and it was with a good store of samples and stock that he returned just two days after the little son he never met perished in a hospital bed. Ordinarily, Tony would have gotten off the Garuda flight in Bali in order to see a girl he favored there–the fourth since abandoning Leili after she refused to have an abortion–but this time, when the plane landed, he felt achy around the knees and itchy on the belly, and so he stayed in the transit lounge, staring at the palms outside, making out a call list for his first few days home. By the time the flight left for Darwin, Tony felt lousy enough to suspect a relatively common Southeast Asian flu. He locked himself in the stinking airplane lavatory, railed under his breath about filthy foreigners and the simple, decent ritual of soap and deodorant, and raised his shirt for a look at what was itching so badly.

The round blotches gave him a shock. He was a ruddy fellow, just thirty, and never one for the sun. He dropped his shirttails in a rush, and leaned forward so his face was nearly at the mirror. He examined the tiny pores on the side of his nose, and exhaled against the glass to find his breath foul. Tony had visited tea plantations on the outlying islands, and although there was talk about some fever in Jakarta, everyone thought it was a government ploy of some kind. The infrastructure in Indonesia was so tenuous, half the city could die and no one on the edges of the archipelago would really know.

"You've got ringworm again, Tony Boy," he chortled.

By the time he cleared customs in Darwin, he was no longer laughing. He began to worry that maybe there was something to the plague rumors after all. Figuring that he might feel worse before feeling better, he hurried to get the new samples out to his restaurants. These included a couple of tourist traps, a handful of authentic local Chinese emporia, the six best hotels in town, and a high-end sushi bar where Japanese tourists could savor fine tea in the only Australian town they had ever bombed.

Tony struggled through his drops, stealing occasional glances at his reflection in windows and shiny spoons, praying that the pox would not migrate to his face before he made it home and curled up in bed. Tea's beneficial antioxidants bolstered his immune system and held the disease at bay long enough for him to brag about the products he returned with: the sweet *Gunung Rosa*, the golden tipped *Taloon*, the rich, dark, broken *Bah Butong.* "Indonesian tea is the next great secret," he confided to his customers, speaking in a hushed tone that conveyed conspiracy.

It is said the body knows it is going to die before the mind does, and perhaps it was that subconscious awareness that caused Tony to turn his Toyota Land Cruiser out towards his own father's base camp rather than go straight to his tiny beachfront *pied a terre* behind which, during the previous rainy season, in the car park at a high tide, a giant saltwater crocodile had taken his espresso-guzzling old nag of a neighbor just as she was getting into her Nissan Patrol.

His dad greeted him warmly, and made him glad to be home. Soon Tony was eating a hearty meal with the tourists, while outside a couple of rangers and more than a few aboriginals were feeling spotty. He had not brought the plague to Australia, he had met it there, and somewhere, as Tony Tunstall chipped away at his last two thousand breaths, the spirit of little Lombo Musi clucked on about a little notion called karma

30

Rachel Kleinman spread cream cheese over a toasted sesame bagel, took a bite, and shook her head in dismay. Hong Kong groceries carried American food, so cream cheese was no problem, but Chinese bakeries simply could not master the bagel. Rachel was not sure if water, baking temperature, or the air in the hole was to blame. She yearned for the deep ovens of St. Viateur Street in her native Montreal, Canada, yearned to watch thirty rolls being pulled out of a hot stove on a long wooden plank, pluck one off while it was still hot, and bite into it joyfully as the baker put a dozen more into a brown paper bag to go.

"You asked to see me?" Monica Farmore asked.

"You're spending a lot of time with Dalton Day."

"You mentioned that at the end of last week."

"And I'm mentioning it again."

"You assigned me to look after him. What would you suggest?"

Rachel looked up and sighed. She had anticipated this kind of trouble with Monica. Girls with her looks rarely stayed in middle management; they either zoomed undeservingly to the top or married up and off and away. She'd known this would happen, but the order to hire Monica had come from Billabong's new owners, with no explanation given, and no discussion had been solicited. Still, there were real marketing projects to run, and Monica had been hired to run them.

"The cosmetics book needs some work. We have to build relationships with some of the Korean retailers. These are the folks who used to charge five times the market for American and European products and are suddenly crying because customers can now go online to compare prices. Revenue is down and the idea of selling beauty books suddenly looks attractive. We have a good margin and we'll work with them, but you need to start answering their phone calls."

Monica plopped down in the Mission-style chair that was part of Rachel's desk set.

"I take it somebody complained."

"Indeed. The message is on your desk."

"I haven't been there today."

"My point exactly. There are other projects, too. The sailing guide…"

"I called on the Royal Hong Kong Yacht Club. They said they could sell thirty or forty copies."

"It's a backlist title," Rachel said. "We have to start somewhere, and word of mouth from that group means a lot. Not all our authors sell like Dalton Day."

"All the more reason I should take good care of him, don't you think?"

"Him and our other clients. It's your job."

Monica stood and saluted. "I'll tell him I'm tied up. He can do the next signing by himself. I'll let him wander around Hong Kong, take a taxi, pot luck if he shows up."

Rachel Kleinman's deceptions and schemes were executed on paper, and in boardrooms. She was a corpulent angler and a haughty smooth talker, but she didn't want to test her higher-ups by firing Monica, at least not just yet.

"How about we meet in the middle. Handle the Korean callback, and I'll have my secretary messenger some books over to the yacht club. We'll handle the billing later."

"All right," said Monica, sensing she had secured a victory, but not sure exactly why.

She rendezvoused with Dalton in the pouring rain, at the base of the Peak Tram, just out of Central.

"Any luck finding your electric man?" Monica asked Dalton.

"I had a lead, but it didn't pan out."

"Jimmy has another place he wants to take you. He's been asking around. He likes you."

"I like him too," said Dalton. "Look, are you sure you want to go to the top of the mountain in this weather?"

"It'll clear up. It's always different up there. Besides, I've got an umbrella."

He bought them tickets at the little booth, and together they climbed aboard a red car finished in gold leaf and wood.

"Rachel and I argued about how much time I'm spending with you, and she backed down," Monica announced as the old funicular began its steep, clanking ascent toward the mountaintop that Gao Zetian was attempting to clear of broadcasting antennae.

"Backed down?"

"It's almost as if she didn't want to push me too far on the subject."

"Maybe *The Boxer Within* is selling better than we think."

"That must be it, although we can't really be sure of the numbers yet. The system isn't that quick."

"I'm sure she appreciates your work and doesn't want to lose you."

"Maybe, but it feels like there's something else going on."

"Maybe she's getting ready to leave. It's been my experience that when an executive knows she's going to quit, she's reluctant to make waves."

"I didn't think of that."

The train stopped at the Peak Tower, a T-shaped building of buttresses and wings. There was a Ripley's *Believe it or Not* on one floor, cafes and tourist shops on another. Dalton and Monica climbed to the top floor for the view, and as they did, the rain stopped, the clouds parted, and the sun came down so strongly and quickly steam began to rise from the concrete.

"Everything looks so beautiful," said Monica. "It's hard to believe what's going on with the Indonesian plague. Have you heard it's cropping up all over?"

"I caught the report on CNN. Little pockets here and there all over the world, no apparent rhyme or reason to the spread. Third World healthcare's to blame for the big numbers, no doubt. Life's cheap in Asia. If people start dying *en masse* in London or New Jersey, there will be nothing else on the news, and they'll be using

NASA technology to save the day."

The pair found the footpath around the peak. At the start, they looked out over the city and down at the harbor, but as they continued walking, under the shelter of camphor trees and gums, they witnessed a view of Lantau–where the world's largest outdoor bronze Buddha sat–and past it the South China Sea and the Poi To Islands.

"Indonesia isn't that far away," Monica said. "People could be getting sick in Hong Kong tomorrow. All it takes is one businessman to jet over with the bug in his system."

The clouds closed in again, and as they rounded the last quarter of the dirt path that circled the lip of the peak, a great burst of rain soaked them. The wind gusted in, rendering Monica's umbrella useless; even the trees offered little protection. Dry rock faces turned into spouts for waterfalls the diameter of bedroom closets, and the dirt beneath their feet turned to mud. They quickened their pace to a jog, Monica's flat sandals slipped and slid, and Dalton's suede walking shoes were no better. They made their way to the shopping center across the road from the Peak Tower. Inside, they stopped in front of an electronics store window. Fifty television sets showed riots in Southern Thailand, where Muslims were blaming the plague on the religious transgressions of the Buddhists.

"Maybe you should rethink my offer about a job in New York," Dalton said.

"There's Reggie."

"Talk to him," said Dalton. "And sooner than later, while Hong Kong is still safe."

31

The morning Rachel warned Monica about Dalton, Zetian went shopping with Huangfu at Pacific Place. She preferred to go alone and melt into the crowd, emerging only to catch the eye of some attractive businessman, but Huangfu was taking her lessons to heart. Already he could read her pheromones well enough to anticipate her every whim, becoming such an agreeable companion that strolling arm-in-arm was actually pleasurable. She could tell the knot of her biceps and the iron of her waist astonished him.

"The buzz is the Jakarta plague is spreading to China," Huangfu told her. "I heard it on the BBC this morning. We should be developing emergency plans for the household, as I'm sure you are developing them for company employees."

Zetian was not known for making emergency plans. It had been a long time since she had crept out of the Imperial Palace in the snow.

"You worry too much," she said.

"I'm just doing my job. It's our responsibility, after all."

"Indonesia is far away. Everything will be fine.

"The plague has already reached Australia," Huangfu said firmly. "The news reports are really quite alarming. Nobody is immune, and the doctors can do nothing. I took the liberty of checking with the IT people about their emergency plan. One should be in place for typhoons and hurricanes anyway. I was surprised to find their plan quite weak, so I contacted a firm in Singapore and they are working to set up a more robust e-mail and telephone system for us on a priority basis. They promised me it would be done in four days, and then we'll be able to keep in touch with the entire corporate group should things break down in Hong Kong."

Zetian did not care whether all her people could chat with each other while some wicked wind swept the land; she cared what influence she could peddle, what favors she could curry if things turned sour, what assets she had put away. The notion of a responsibility to employees was more up her brother's alley, and the more she listened to Huangfu prattle on, the more she wondered whether all men had turned to mush in recent centuries, or did she simply have the misfortune to have surrounded herself with a bunch of dependent nursemaids, a bevy of males whose hearts were as soft as their bodies had become. Who cared about household employees, or workers at Crocodile & Crane? So what if it really was the murderous Banpo Smile?

She sighed, wondering where in the 21st century she might find a devoted warlord, a man who would slay a whole town just to please her. "I don't want my household or my business to appear cowardly."

"Of course not," Huangfu countered. "Just prudent."

"Do what you think is best," she agreed, just to shut him up.

The couple walked in silence until they reached the boutique of Salvatore Ferragamo. Zetian had a weakness for the Italian's designs. Decades earlier, she predicted his genius for blending fashion and comfort, and watched his career burgeon after he made Roman sandals for Cecil de Mille epics. Once, while on holiday to attend a croquet tournament at the Santa Barbara Biltmore in California–she loved the game, the precision of it, the pretensions, the excuse to see Western costumes–she commissioned Ferragamo to make a handbag. Inspired by the wicker birdcages Chinese intellectuals and aristocrats carried to teahouses during the Qing Dynasty, the bag was constructed of woven leather, with brass reinforcements for the oval handle and enough space to carry the creams and makeup so essential for maintaining Zetian's deceptions. She had many, many bags, but the birdcage remained her favorite.

Zetian remained loyal to Ferragamo's designs long after Salvatore died. She purchased his ties for her lovers, seeing them as a secret badge uniting her men in modern Hong Kong. With Huangfu in tow, she went right to the tie rack, where she selected a blue and red pattern of tiny laborers rendered with the Italian's typical whimsy. Their features were invisible; their backs were bent with the weight of the buckets hung over their shoulders, and their heads bowed in subservience to the overwhelming poundage of Chinese emperorship and taxation. As she knotted the tie around Huangfu's neck, the clerk, a young girl from Dublin, mentioned that the tiny figures might represent midgets or fairies or leprechauns or dwarfs. Although he didn't say anything, Huangfu was sure they were coolies, and unaware of the club into which he was about to be inducted, felt vaguely insulted.

What appealed to Zetian about her chauffeur was his neck. Huangfu reminded her of a certain infantry general she had known during the siege of Kaifeng in 1126. Sequestered with the forces of the Song emperor Huizong as they fended off the Jurchens, Zetian had seen her prey riding proudly along, just inside the city wall, on the day the starving peasants began to eat dirt. The general had the torso of a water buffalo. Huangfu was not as big, and these days, Zetian reflected ruefully, it was just as well. The relationship between size and brains had changed. In the old days, big men were true alpha males, but in the modern world success seemed to have as much to do with brains as brawn.

"Will there be anything else?" the sales girl inquired.

Shaking her head, Zetian pulled out a wad of cash. Credit cards were hell on immortals. They threatened the veil she had so carefully constructed around herself. Although Zetian had always embraced new toys, modern technology did make anonymity harder and harder to maintain.

"Now it's time for me to buy *you* something," Huangfu announced, as they stepped back out onto the promenade.

"Don't be silly."

"Come on. It'll be fun."

"All right," she said through clenched teeth. Huangfu was emerging from his servile chrysalis and turning presumptuous.

What he found was a lavender pants suit. The mandarin collar was high, imperious, the way she liked her look, but the pants were tight and svelte, and the blouse emphasized the bustline. The clerk cooed over Zetian's figure.

"It's perfectly *divine* for you," he cried, touching her sleeve with manicured fingers. "You're so *elegant*."

"Everything I know, I learned from eunuchs," she replied.

"Ouch," the clerk giggled, withdrawing his finger as if it burned. "Nasty!"

Zetian took the outfit into the changing room, and beckoned Huangfu to follow. He waited obediently outside her cubicle, sneaking glances at her feet. She had high arches, and beautiful toes.

"Huangfu?" she said, seductively raising her blouse over her head, giving him a peek at the white skin of her underarms and the blue-veined tops of her breasts.

"Yes," he croaked.

"I am very worried about my brother."

"You are?"

"He seems to have taken the Jakarta losses hard."

"Everyone feels that way," Huangfu managed.

"Hmm," she said, dropping her black silk panties where she knew he could see them. "He's not acting normally. I'm concerned he may be in a situation."

Huangfu swallowed at the sight and tried to think about Sanfeng. He could not imagine the man as anything but unflappable and in perfect control. "I'm sure he's all right."

"Even so, he may need my help, and not be willing to ask for it. I want you to follow him."

"Follow him?"

"Yes. I want to know his every move."

With that, she pulled the curtain aside with a flourish, and motioned him in. "Tie this drawstring for me, would you? Just a simple bow."

Huangfu fumbled his way through it, leaving one end far longer than the other.

"How am I in this color?" she asked, pirouetting.

"Perfect."

"Good. And you will stay close to my brother?"

"Of course."

"Thank you," Zetian said, touching his cheek gently. "You've been very good lately, Huangfu, and I've been thinking about us."

"Us," he repeated.

"You and me."

At those three words, Huangfu blinked his eyes rapidly, open and shut, open and shut, like a diving cormorant trying to squeeze out the salt of the sea.

32

After 24 hours, the protective suit's filters were clogged, and Dr. Henri Eonnet breathed through his mouth to avoid the reek of his own sweat. He could no more escape the suit than the outbreak. It was the big one; the one he had dreaded all his life, the one he knew was coming when he begged the World Health Organization to build Third World plague labs; now, there was nothing for it.

While the labs at the Pasteur Institute and the CDC undertook the standard evaluations of the problem, Eonnet honored his hunches. That was what made him such a fine scientist. A believer in Occam's razor, he kept whittling away at cause and effect in search of a simple explanation for the plague, despite complex and numerous variables.

Leili watched Eonnet search for clues in the data. She saw him run his own bacterial cultures just to be sure of the results, and do his own micro-fine cuttings of affected tissue as well. Even the watching exhausted her, and she realized she was running on energy borne of Zetian's *qigong*. Leili feared it might cost her later, maybe even take time off her life, but she could not tear herself away from the doctor. She could not fathom his French ramblings, but she sensed he was some sort of a magician and when he finally stopped shuffling papers and scrolling through lab results, she figured that he was on to something.

"Is there some news?" she asked.

He sat very still for a long time, then took a drink from the plastic straw by his face. Leili heard a slurping sound, and realized his sterilized canteen was almost dry.

"I have a hunch," he said.

"Tell me."

"Suicide," Eonnet said simply.

Leili grew angry at the word, so angry that she wanted to throw herself on the Frenchman, to rip through his suit with her fingernails, to scratch him and bite him and pull out the tongue that would so blaspheme the passing of everyone she loved, the memory of her serious young genius, her little Lombo.

Instead she just stared at him. “Explain that,” she managed at last.

Eonnet chewed on his lip. It was crusty. The suit did that. The little fan dried him out. He had not noticed that in the preparedness drills run by the institute in cooperation with the World Health Organization, but of course those drills had lasted less than an hour. The suit wasn't made for prolonged wearing.

“Let me check e-mail first,” he said wearily. “I am waiting for some news.”

The first letter that came up was from his ex-wife, forwarded through the institute. She asked him to increase his child support payments, as their daughter required extra tutoring in math. Eonnet could almost feel the venom the woman put in the letter, the satisfaction that the daughter of the famous scientist would require help in something so banal as high-school math.

There was another letter from his current wife, this one bearing the news that a colleague of his–a man with white teeth, a broad smile, thick forearms, and a trim waist, a doctor who took a rowing shell out on the Seine even in the winter ice–had just been written up in *Paris Match* as one of Europe's most eligible bachelors. Eonnet's blood boiled. He was sure his wife was sleeping with the guy. He tried not to imagine what they did in bed.

“Suicide,” Leili repeated. “I'm not going to sit here forever in the dark with you in that suit. Please. Tell me something.”

Eonnet raised his hand in a bid for her patience. An urgent e-mail missive from the CDC had just appeared in his in-box. His instincts had been correct. Lombo Musi's blood showed characteristic ladder-shaped DNA fragments. At first, the lab men figured the serum was breaking down and the fragments of genetic material caught in their filters were artifacts of normal cellular degradation, but after using electrophoresis gels on newer samples and labeling the DNA 3_ ends with biotinylated thymine analog, the answer was clear. For some reason, the cells were indeed killing themselves.

"*Nom d' un chien!*" he breathed.

"What is it?"

"The worm!"

"A worm is causing this?" Leili shook her head incredulously.

During the last few years, she had gotten the pharmaceutical company to pay for continuing education courses in bacteriology, virology, and parasitology. She knew most parasites were symbiotic organisms whose presence was either non-lethal–if the host died, the parasite did too–or harmed the human host very gradually over the course of a near-normal life span. She did not know of any worms that killed people in a few days.

"No, no," Eonnet waved his hand. "*Caenorhabditis elegans.* It's a nematode, but not a killer. It merely taught us about apoptosis."

"Apoptosis?" Leili repeated.

"Programmed cell death. It's a natural process that occurs during embryonic development, and later in life, after a sunburn, for instance."

"You mean when skin peels?"

"That's right. Skin cells damaged by ultraviolet rays are killed by apoptosis, and then shed. In the worm, the genes remove 131 of 1090 types of cells to form an adult worm from a larva."

"What does this have to do with what killed my Lombo?"

"His blood shows evidence of the process, evidence that his body may have killed itself."

"Why would a six-year-old body kill itself?" Leili asked numbly.

"That's the big question. But it is a hypothesis that fits the data, including the unpredictable way the disease is spreading."

"Unpredictable."

"Yes. There are people left alive in Jakarta, but not many. The authorities are using helicopters with infrared sensors to locate them, as well as military satellites. When the individuals are found, they are terrified, and usually expire quickly from the disease."

Leili paced the nursing station. There was a world beyond her tiny enclave, but she preferred to pretend it wasn't there. The wards smelled awful, the lighting was fading, and insects had begun to win the war they waged with the staff of every hospital between the Tropic of Capricorn and the Tropic of Cancer. Twice now, giant winged cockroaches had rushed at the crumbs left from her snacks, sometimes brazenly, right at midday. Too, there were the moths. Some were bizarre *Eipplimma* species with rolled legs that made them look like tiny, winged, hammerhead sharks, another looked like a preying mantis. But it was the seven-inch Atlas moths that intimidated Leili and kept her walks in the corridors brief. When the giant bugs stopped flying, their hooked, orange-and-black wings resembled the head of a snake. Leili had no idea where they came from or why they found the deserted hospital so enticing, but they buzzed fearlessly around the fluorescent lights at night, and had a habit of hitting her in the face whenever she nodded off. Some got tangled in her hair, and when she swiped at them they left a fine powder on her fingers. She established a defense perimeter against them with a flyswatter, paper, and a spray bottle, but when she left Eonnet for a moment–just to clear her head–they zoomed back in.

"In other words you're finding people who are just the last to go," she said.

Eonnet nodded.

"And you're getting all of this from your e-mail?"

"Yes, but you're missing the important part of what I'm trying to explain. Contagious diseases spread according to mathematical models. My daughter may not be good at math, but I am, and I can tell you there are epidemiologic models and this plague doesn't fit them."

"Your daughter?"

He frowned. "Never mind that. I'm trying to say I don't believe the disease is contagious."

"If it's not contagious, how can it spread?"

"That's what I'm saying. It's not spreading. It's just popping up."

It was Leili's turn to frown. "I don't understand."

"Did you keep a fish tank as a child?"

"I grew up in the country. But my little boy had fish."

The cumbersome yellow hood moved up and down as Eonnet nodded, and his breath fogged the plate. "Did you ever try adding more fish to the tank once it was up and running?"

"We tried it all the time. Lombo was a fiend for pets."

"And what happened?"

"They died."

"Which ones, the new one or one of the old ones?"

"I don't remember."

Eonnet smiled through his helmet. It was good to see, even behind the faceplate, and it made Leili smile too, if only at the incongruousness of it.

"That's because there's nothing to remember," the scientist said. "Your son's tank had what scientist's call a 'carrying capacity.' Every environment, big or small, has a number of animals it will safely hold. After that, the ecosystem breaks down and animals move out or die. In the case of your home fish tank, moving out was not possible, so they died. But there's more, so pay careful attention, *s'il vous plait*. You might think it would be the most recently added fish that died. You might also think it would be the weakest fish, or the smallest fish, or even the *biggest* fish. None of those guesses turns out to be true. Figuring out which fish will die is very, very difficult. It is, at best, a prediction without mathematical certainty."

"You're saying the plague can jump around the world and there's no more effective way to predict where it will go than there is to say which fish will die."

"Because the killing doesn't come from the outside, but from the inside, from our DNA. If there is communication, it is on a quantum or energetic level. It is not contagiousness in the sense we ordinarily think of it, but rather multiple manifestations of the same problem."

"In just the way the fish dying is because of a problem with the tank, not the fish."

"Very good," Eonnet smiled.

"And the fish probably wouldn't die if the tank were bigger or if it were living somewhere else."

"Correct."

"You are saying our whole planet is the fish tank," Leili said, growing pale.

"The earth has a carrying capacity too," Eonnet said. "Perhaps we have reached it. Until we are able to move off to Mars or shuttle away to the moon, there's no way to cut down on our numbers."

"I can't think about this any more," Leili said.

"Can't, or won't?"

"What does it matter?"

33

Hong Kong was cosmopolitan, but Hong Kong was also definitely Chinese. Accordingly, different socio-economic groups rarely mingled in the city. Old-guard Chinese made their liaisons at private clubs and karaoke establishments, where consorts attended them, and liquor flowed freely. Entrepreneurial wheeler-dealers, forced to do business with foreigners, met at dim sum lunch emporia, particularly in Central, and at the best of the Kowloon hotels. The truly rich–the empire-builders, shippers, real-estate magnates, and high-tech moguls–conducted their most important business in plush offices, or at estates in Sai Kung, a beach colony thirty minutes from town.

The young up-and-comers, however, were different. They watched Western movies and television, read American magazines, and noticed that the American business icon was fit and hard-bodied. They sought to emulate the steely-eyed commando look by becoming hunks and babes, and so they exercised with gusto, never in martial arts or *qigong*–choices seen as blue-collar, old hat, and even low-class–but in state-of-the art gymnasia that were also important meeting places. Dressed in Spandex and Lycra and wearing cross-trainers, headbands and mp3 players, they played racquetball and squash, ran on treadmills, huffed and puffed on stair-climbers, and groaned and grunted through aerobics classes that showed no Asian influence at all, classes with names like "high-impact" or "ab-burner," "thigh-buster," and "boot camp."

Monica Farmore was a member at Fittest HK, the best of these downtown gyms, an establishment with a waiting list for membership and a juice bar offering tropical fruit smoothies. It was not a gym for the faint of heart; one had to be young and brave to work out there, because the required uniform was revealing and every available surface was covered in mirrors.

Monica peeked into the aerobics room, where the class was almost ready to start. Most people spent a few minutes stretching on the mat before the action, knowing they would need every available calorie, every molecule of oxygen in their lungs, and ATP in their muscle, to get through this particular workout. Ordinarily, Monica would be in there with them warming up with the rest, but tonight she was indecisive, preoccupied with how she was going to keep her boss happy, and more than a little worried about the plague.

The instructor clapped his hands to signal the start of the class. It was now or never. Nobody came in after the music started. That was the rule. A tow-headed beach boy from San Diego, his eccentricities were indulged because he had a physique any man would envy, endurance enough for a Channel swim, and strength that let him squint knowingly at the prospect of hauling a Sequoia log barefoot up the Pacific coast.

Monica sighed, knowing she'd hate herself if she skipped the class. She pushed through the door, and the instructor smiled at her. Monica had soundly and repeatedly rebuffed him, but he continued to think she was just playing hard to get. When she told him that he was too dumb for her, that brains turned her on more than a resting heart rate of forty beats per minute, he figured she was only trying to draw out their thrice-weekly courtship until neither of them could take it any more. In moments alone, he imagined that with all the drama, when they finally made love, the world would rock and roll like an eight-point shaker. "Punch," he said viciously, putting out one big fist after the other to the pounding beat of P. Diddy. Hip-hop was big at Fittest HK, probably because there was something so blatantly un-Chinese about it.

He waited for Monica's eyes to move to his swollen biceps, and notice the snap he put in his punch. He waited for her to notice how light he was on his feet. To his considerable disappointment, she paid no attention to him at all. Nor did she pay attention to the slim, elegantly dressed man in the black bowler hat staring at her through the observation window.

She had not noticed Sanfeng all day, nor picked up the fact that he had tailed her from her apartment to the mall, to the corner coffee shop, and finally the gym, where he gained admittance with a bribe at the door.

A new track came over the loudspeakers, a faster, more

demanding tune. The class groaned as if with one voice. Every woman in the class could lock her knees, bend over, and put her palms flat on the floor, and there was a young male banker in the back row lithe and rubbery enough to leave a black heel smudge on the glass behind his head. All the students were running out of steam, though, and none of them were sustaining any power; Monica, on the other hand, had everything the teacher had: flexibility, speed, and strength.

"Come on baby, kick," he said, catching her eye and holding it.

She did, and the heel of her cross-trainer nearly caught the end of his nose. Left foot, right foot, left foot, right foot. She lifted her pins like a Rockette, one after the other. Thomas moved back to give her room. She fascinated him, in part because she was a half-breed, and in part because she played so hard to get. The rest of the class–which by the count of any reasonable man held more than a little beauty and talent–receded from his view until it was just Monica and he, pumping it out.

The selection changed to something even faster–Donna Summer singing *Bad Girls*. Classic Disco was making a comeback in Hong Kong, and the class hooted and clapped enthusiastically when the tune came on.

"KICK!" the instructor roared.

He and Monica were closing in on one hundred on each side by halfway through the song. These were not easy low kicks; the instructor wanted tight buns on his students; they made his classes popular. He wanted them on himself because he was vain. Midway through the song, most of the class had given up.

But not Monica. Turning negative energy into positive and fantasizing about finally seducing Dalton, she felt she could go on all night. The instructor took her small smile for encouragement–the two of them were the only ones moving now–and he smiled back, smugly, even though his legs felt like lead, and his chest felt like it might burst.

Sanfeng pressed his nose to the glass, unable to help himself. He had kept away from all the others, and indeed would have kept away from this one had recent events not put her repeatedly into view. Of course it was not coincidence driving his engine, but change. The status quo of centuries, of millennia, was now in peril. The Banpo smile was upon them again, and while Zetian might not understand the consequences, Sanfeng did.

His exquisitely honed sense of irony, propriety, connection, and threat made watching Monica an elating experience. He had not seen spirit like that since he was a Han imperial insider privy to the chambers of courtesans and queens. Compared to her, the pretty-boy teacher moved like a like a hippo with a thorn in his hoof. Personal feelings aside, the immortal simply could not accept that such a woman would die smiling the terrible smile. Sanfeng clenched his fist as Donna Summer reached for a crescendo, and he began hammering it into his open palm in beat to the music. The drums grew louder, faster, stronger, and for Sanfeng, Monica suddenly embodied everything that was right for him, innocence, resolve, beauty and promise. Such things mattered, even if Zetian did not see that they did–mattered as much or more than anything left in the waking world.

Monica forced her legs higher, remembering her tough dance training back in Enid, at the hands of a burned-out, cigarette-smoking vamp with a flat chest and wide hips, and a history of two or three dance companies in Chicago just after the vaudeville era. Keeping her back straight, she forced her legs high enough for the fronts of her thighs to touch the dark circles her nipples made in the damp fabric.

As he faded into exhaustion, the instructor from California tried to convince himself that because he was bigger and his legs were heavier, he was really doing better than his amazing student. Power-to-weight dynamics were in her favor, he told himself. His forte was not raising his magnificent foundation off the ground, but he could beat her if they were sprinting or pumping iron. Then too, he had been teaching all morning and she had been fresh when she came through the door.

Monica's determination sustained her long after the lactic acid in her calves and hamstrings had assembled into crystal palaces that would take days to melt away. The rest of the class lay gasping, but she kept going and going. The instructor's legs turned to stone. His feet barely reached as high as his waist. The last medley came up and he drove himself to keep going, knowing there was only fifteen or twenty seconds left.

He could not do it.

He fell.

The class, as if possessed of a single voice, broke out in a cheer.

Oblivious, Monica kept right on prancing until the music ended, and with it the class.

"Lunch?" The instructor offered, putting his arm around her shoulders as they stepped out of the classroom. Being gracious seemed the best way to save face. Besides, he would have paid a million bucks to have sex with her right then and there.

A moment of weakness overtook Sanfeng. As it happened, he marveled that it did. He was centuries past moments of weakness, had learned the painful consequences of violating his own rules, regulations set up to save him from suffering, guarantee that his next life would be transcendent on account of the power of the karma he had accrued through so many years of good deeds. Losing all that in this present moment, he recognized a shift, knew it was a natural and correct consequence of his decisions.

"I'm afraid Monica's company at lunch is already spoken for," he said, taking her arm.

The instructor frowned.

Monica looked puzzled. "Do I know you?"

"I have a boat waiting to motor you to my waterfront home," Sanfeng said. He was on a roll now, and flushed with tremendous excitement. This could be his time! The loneliness could end now. He could now roll out his plan like a giant red carpet, and everything would be all right.

Monica was fascinated with the way Sanfeng talked. His lips barely moved, yet every word was perfectly clear. More, he had very little physical presence at all. Even standing a few inches from her body, there was no scent of hair or cologne, no heat, and no fidgets or twitches whatsoever. He was a little bit spooky, but probably very, very rich. The last time she had seen a hat like that was in a Charlie Chaplin movie, and his suit was perfect, hand-tailored, and of 160 point wool. Too, there was that fancy wristwatch with no hands, just a block of gold with little numbers showing up in tiny windows.

"Take a hike," said the instructor.

Some of the women from the class were watching, in particular a brunette who wore her long hair up in a bun. Thomas loved the chaste librarian look. If this thing with Monica did not work out, the brunette was next on his list, and he wanted to impress her.

"I shall wait for you here," said Sanfeng.

"Dude. Are you deaf?" the instructor asked. "I said take a hike."

"It's not a long ride," Sanfeng said. "The boat is fast. You'll be comfortable at my place. I will show you a world of wonders."

Monica noticed Sanfeng's hair. It wasn't long, but it stood out in a strange way. It made her think of something, but she couldn't place what it was.

"I'll show *you* stars," the instructor said, putting a hand on Sanfeng's chest.

Sanfeng looked down, closed his eyes for a moment, and sent the young man reeling back.

"Sonofabitch used a stun-gun on me!" the instructor cried, bending to put his hands between his legs.

Monica stared at Sanfeng. There had been no gun, and she knew it. "What did you do to him?"

"Will you accept my kind invitation?"

"I need to know what you did."

"Nothing. He fell."

"He shocked me," the instructor moaned, writhing on the floor. "He's got some kind of electric weapon."

A crowd gathered. Sanfeng began to back away. He did so without cowardice, not excited, still calm, just taking little steps backward, his gaze fixed on Monica.

"Please," he said, extending his hand.

"Tell me."

"I did nothing. He lost his balance. Please come with me."

There was something in his eyes. Monica found them hypnotic.

Warm, yes, but more than that. Bottomless. Infinitely deep. Compelling. There was command in the glance. She had a hard time moving her gaze from him, but when she did, she knew she had to run.

She made it to the locker room, and once there collapsed onto a bench. She found it hard to breathe. Every time she closed her eyes, she saw the man. His vision filled her head, expanded, ballooning, creating a feeling of pressure she had never had before, at once frightening and completely new, alien and yet strangely familiar. Composing herself, she dialed Dalton's hotel room on her cell phone. The number rang and rang. She hit the locker in frustration. A woman changing looked at her fearfully.

"Dalton," she cried, when the answering machine picked up. "I think I've found your electric man. Call me right back." When she went back out, Sanfeng was no longer in sight. The brunette librarian was ministering to the aerobics instructor, stroking his forehead and asking if he wanted an ambulance.

"Where is he?" Monica demanded.

"Who, the guy with the waterfront home? You don't believe that creep really has one, do you? It's a line. Waterfront is out-of-sight expensive in Hong Kong. I'd be careful if I were you."

She searched the club in vain, then showered and changed. She checked her phone, saw no message, and went down to the garage for her car.

Sanfeng's Aston Martin was parked by the elevator. He sat in the driver's seat with the window down, playing a wooden flute. He put it down as she stepped close.

"Have you decided to join me?"

"I know someone who wants to meet you," she said.

"And what about you?"

"I don't get into cars with strange men."

He regarded her thoughtfully. "Do I seem strange to you?"

"I don't get into cars with men I don't know."

"We could become acquainted, then that would not be a problem."

"My friend saw you on an airplane. He saw fire come from your hands, and just now you electrocuted that idiot aerobics teacher.

That was you, wasn't it? On the flight from New York?"

"We could discuss it," he said.

"If there's something to discuss, the answer must be yes."

He smiled. "Come to dinner. We can get to know each other."

"I've got other plans," she said. "I'm waiting for a call. How can I find you?"

"You can't," Sanfeng answered. "But I'll find you."

34

The Capital City of Chang'an, Tang Dynasty, 730 CE

Pounded-earth walls thirty-five feet tall, and fifteen feet thick, fortify the city. From the west, access is through Jinguang Gate, the celebrated start and end of the Silk Road. Just inside the gate, southwest of the administrative city–which is, in turn, southwest of the Imperial Palace–there is a market, and in that market, within a strong stone courtyard of its own, is Gao Zetian's shop, final destination of many Silk Road traders. The place is a veritable compound, with an inn and residences. Emperor Li Longji's economy is booming, and many exotic valuables find their way into Zetian's hands. Traders appreciate Zetian because she pays fairly for quality merchandise, and also because her brother, a fearsome *gongfu* master, lives with her and guarantees a safe haven from ruffians and thieves.

Zetian always provides a woman for the dirty, weary traveler–someone to wash his feet, and offer him scented oils: a good massage, and for the right price, additional services. Even if no agreement is reached and a trader does not bed down for the night with a courtesan of the capital city, there is Zetian herself to consider. The woman possesses preternatural beauty, moves like water, and is a favorite with palace ministers and aristocrats. Rumors of her high-level affairs abound, but no trader would ever dare ask her about them. It is enough simply to bask in her presence, and to survey the goods she has assembled for her customers, so as to know what to seek on the next trip afield.

Sanfeng's life is simple here. He loves to drink tea, play music, and contemplate the turning of the blossoms in the courtyard trees. Among his friends are such Academy of Poetry greats as Li Shangyin and Du Fu. By day, they come to him for what he calls "cultural training," that is to say intellectual discourse–often he finds himself defending his beloved Daoism against the rising popularity of the Buddha and Confucius–and by night they train with him in martial arts. He chooses his students carefully, but never carefully enough for his sister, Zetian, who does not understand Sanfeng's urge to share knowledge.

"Why bother?" she often asks him. "They're just going to die, and then your whole investment will be wasted. Now if you have to reveal some meaningless detail in order to get something you want, that I can understand, but to have *disciples*, that's asking for trouble."

"You don't understand," Sanfeng replies. "I'm bursting with the desire to share! It's natural. Ideas and skills are like water. If they don't flow, they grow stagnant."

She sighs heavily. "Share this, desire that. If you love these ideas so much, why don't you just take them to bed?"

Although he has plenty of space in his indoor training hall, Sanfeng likes to instruct in the abundant elbow room of the open air, where the scale of long weapons is more realistic. Inside, blades and staffs seem impossibly long, creating bridges between combatants supported by pylons of fear and imagination and unnatural lighting and angles of view. Under the sky, proportion is restored, and crisp air keeps delusion to a minimum.

Zetian forbids action in the courtyard before dusk. She is afraid that if Sanfeng's reputation grows too large, questions will follow. Where are you from? Who was your teacher? How long have you studied the sword? How long have you studied the staff? Such inquiries lead to gossip, and gossip leads to problems. The siblings have long sown, watered, cultivated and massaged their reputations. Flight from Chang'an would not be as easy as it was from the steppe, the forests, or even the primitive villages of the Shang Dynasty.

The night they are forced from the capital, Sanfeng is busy deepening the relationship between the deft strokes of his calligraphy brush and swipes of his double-edged *jian*. His blade and his feet are dancing like mated fireflies under the full moon, and he is discoursing to his students on the role of the wrist and the importance of just the right balance between a firm grip and a light one. Suddenly there is a loud commotion from the direction of Zetian's shop. Four of the five students in attendance immediately dash off to her aid, eager to put her in their debt. Sanfeng is more casual in his response. Unless she faces an army, he is unable to imagine his sister needs help.

It is not an army, as it turns out, but a giant of a man dressed in the custom of the far Western provinces, Transoxiana, beneath the Pamirs, or maybe Khotan in the Taklamikan. He wears a yak pelt, and his beard is curly and luxuriant, suggesting he has been raised on animal fat. He has the scent about him of a true Mongol, which is to say of bitter milk, but also some musk. His complexion, even in the night, is clear but weathered, lending the impression that he has spent years in the Hindu Kush, his eyes relaxed to far off peaks. The giant wears twin broadswords, one on each side of his belt, and his stockings do not disguise the fact that his bandy legs are as thick as trees forced into a protracted war with a tireless wind. His nostrils flare when he breathes, and there is a bit of crust on his lips, revealing that he has been traveling in the cool weather, and has not recently had a drink.

"Gao Sanfeng!" the giant roars as the immortal sidles up. "Is this all there is of you? A little sprite of a man with a needle for a sword?"

"There can be no business now! I told you to come back in the morning!" Zetian cries shrilly.

She lacks her usual composure, and her hair and makeup are a tad off. There is a man in her room, a merchant from Champa who has come up with shark's teeth from the South China Sea, some special woodcarvings from the Philippines, and the special treasure of six shrunken heads from Borneo. He is a favorite, a lively lover with laughing eyes, and Zetian licks him up and down and sideways whenever he makes it to Chang'an. He is, however, no fighter. The roar of the big Mongol at the door only sends him deeper under her heavy quilt.

"I'm not here to trade, woman!" roars the giant, "I'm here to fight!"

Sanfeng sighs. This is the very reason he wishes to stick to poetry, the very reason he wants a place out of town, in the mountains, where he does not have to put up with the baggage of a reputation. Travelers often come straight to his school, thinking he is the best Chang'an has to offer, and if they beat him they will be able to set up a school of their own, and live off the spoils of their victory.

"We are thinkers here, not fighters," Sanfeng says, pushing his way past the students, who have formed a protective ring around him. "You're in the wrong place."

Moving far faster than anyone could have predicted, the giant swats Sanfeng's sword arm hard enough to cause the blade to clatter to the ground, then wraps a hand around his neck and lifts him until there is air under the immortal's feet.

"I know what you are," the giant spits. "I watched you beat my father, although I am certain you don't remember the inn where you did it, and the way a squirrel lit on your shoulder when the fighting was finished, and you stroked it with your hand. You look the same, even though you should be gray now, and bent with age. I heard you described, hiding here with your sister, and I have come to unmask you as a freak of nature who shows no years."

This kind of unlikely recognition, the Gaos fear most. It evokes their entire hidden history, their myriad flights across the face of the Middle Kingdom.

"You mistake me for another," says Sanfeng.

"You call me a liar?"

Sanfeng glances at his sister. "I call you confused," he says. "Now put me down."

The giant closes his hands around Sanfeng's neck. All five of his students run to his aid. The giant shakes them off like fleas, sending two across the courtyard with the back of his fist, crumpling a third with an elbow to the ribs, and running the last two down while still holding Sanfeng aloft. Through all this, Sanfeng can do no more than keep his airway clear by digging his chin into the fleshy part of the giant's arm.

Zetian joins the fray, and receives a knuckle sandwich. The

sight of her choking in the dirt as he himself dangles ignominiously as a dinner duck has a unique, alchemical effect. Something grows in Sanfeng's hands, something that centuries later he will be able to conjure at will, on the battlefield, in the forest, in numerous back alleys, and in the cockpit of an airplane. When at last it comes out of him, it coalesces as a red bolt straight to the giant's heart.

The huge man's eyes open, as if he has finally seen the firmament of Heaven, or the fruit of the Bodhi tree, and he falls. Two ribs penetrate the lungs, but that does not matter, because Sanfeng's bolt has already destroyed him, and he is dead within seconds of hitting the ground.

The students, witnesses, pay no attention to the corpse. They have seen the red light, all five of them, and they are amazed. Sanfeng runs to Zetian. He raises her up, lays his hand on her jaw, adjusting it carefully until the mandibles align, ignoring the teeth spilling into his hand as he does so, knowing they will grow back.

"Sister," he whispers, holding her to his chest.

"Master!" the students cry, dropping to their knees before him, as if he is the Buddha himself.

Sanfeng tries to raise them, but they insist on staying down. He frowns. He does not care for groveling. It reminds him of his father's death, of the villagers and the evil priest, of the insane power of crowds and illusion.

Zetian stirs, and tries to speak. Sanfeng kneels and puts his ear to her lips. They whisper to one another, so no one else may hear.

"Did the others see what you did?" she asks.

"Of course."

"And they heard what the giant said?"

"Obviously."

"Then you must kill them."

"No!" Sanfeng shakes his head violently.

"They are like children to you."

"Of course they are. Look how they love me. Look how they follow me."

"Why do you protect them so?" she asks. "The possibility of children was taken from us when we were still children ourselves."

"The *qigong* stops my body from having them, but not my heart from wanting them. The students are dear to me."

"I don't see the attraction," Zetian sniffs quietly.

"Can that really be true?"

"We've been through this so many times. The subject bores me. Your desire for offspring bores me. Men want them for immortality's sake, and you have immortality already."

"And women?"

"I have immortality too, though most women bear children against their will."

"They draw power from the nurturing," Sanfeng says. "With their men, and for themselves, in their bodies and their souls."

"I find it quaint that you still believe in souls, although someday I am sure I will find it tiresome. As for power, it's true that bearing his child does give a woman power over a man, but I have no such coarse and simple need."

"Because you have power enough over every man."

"Except you, Brother."

Already her jaw is healing. If the students dared look up from the ground, they would see her flesh resolving before their very eyes. "Kill them now," she says.

"I can't."

"Then I will."

"Please," Sanfeng implores. "There has to be another way."

Zetian's eyes flash, catching the moon. She makes her way to the students–at first unsteadily, and then with increasing certainty and power–and enthusiastically breaks their necks.

Sanfeng feels his breath coming in gasps. He feels his chest burning, then turns away and vomits.

"We will say they died at the hands of the barbarian," she reassures him calmly. "We will describe a terrific fight."

"No," Sanfeng replies. "You had your price. Mine is that we leave Chang'an."

"Leave all this?" Zetian gestures toward her shop, and gives a crazy smile. "Never."

"Oh yes," Sanfeng says "Tonight." He points at the doorway where Zetian's lover stands with a sheet wrapped around him, eyes frozen in disbelief. "And make sure you kill your little friend too."

Later, digging graves in the courtyard, Zetian starts singing, and Sanfeng, with a heavy heart, asks her why.

"The moon, of course," she answers. "It's so beautiful this evening. Is there some reason your eyes don't see it?"

35

"I don't understand why you're still in China," Annabelle said.

"It's complicated," said Dalton, wiping the sleep from his eyes and sitting up on the bed.

"By a cute blonde with short hair is what I hear."

"We're a little past this, aren't we?"

"The funny part is you think I'm jealous. I've got bigger fish to fry, mister. In case you hadn't noticed, the world is falling apart. Everyone's in a panic, all those students of yours, all those seminar attendees, all those readers and fans you worked so hard to get…."

"*You* worked so hard to get."

"*Excuse* me? You make it sound like I did something wrong."

Dalton went to the window and pulled back the curtain. Far below, tourists lay bronzing around a turquoise pool. It was sunny, lovely day. Hong Kong seemed not to have a care in the world.

"I'm sorry," he said. "I appreciate you very much, and I'm grateful for all you do. I know perfectly well I'd still be teaching in my little school without your creativity and drive. It's just that I'm onto something stunningly important here."

"Must be pretty earthshaking if it beats out your community here. Don't you care about your business, your reputation, your community? I'm trying to say people need you. I *need* you."

He let the curtain fall back because he couldn't see a way to secure it. The room seemed suddenly small and dark. He reached over and turned on the desk lamp. It didn't help much.

"Annabelle."

"I don't know what it's like over there, Dalton. I can't tell what news you're watching or what they're telling you. I read somewhere the Chinese control radio, TV and the Internet. Maybe you don't realize the plague has arrived. It's in Cincinnati. It's in Ojai, California–that's some little rich town outside LA with hot springs and horses–and it's in New Jersey. It's even in New Orleans, as if that poor city hasn't had enough."

"New Jersey? I didn't hear anything about New Jersey."

"I'm sure you didn't. But it's right across the Hudson River. People are panicking and they can't get answers and they can't find anyone to calm them down and they can't find any good news and so guess what? They'd like to hear from their guru about now, the man who calms them down. You're like a shrink to thousands, like a TV doctor but calmer. You can't believe the calls here, Dalton. I had to hire someone else for the phones."

"You hired someone?"

"You got a problem with that? Ten bucks an hour."

"I just meant it doesn't seem like a time…."

"Why, because it's the end of the world? Do you know something I don't? 'Cause if you do, you should get your famous ass back here and start helping people like you say you want to and cash in on misfortune a little bit but do it in a way that makes a contribution, in a way that's helpful."

"I suppose I should be glad you're off the clothing line for now."

"Forget the clothing line. Right now, you can help folks who are worried about something they can't control, something that could kill them, something that's killing everyone it touches. Killing with a smile like some sick assassin."

Dalton clicked the television on, then hit the mute button so he could watch it and still hear Annabelle.

"I'm not sure it's a germ," Dalton said.

"What does that mean?"

"I'm not a scientist, but I've got a feeling there's something different about this plague."

"What do you mean by different?"

Dalton straightened the bedclothes. He had stayed in quite a few hotels since the publication of *The Boxer Within* but he still couldn't get used to other people making his bed for him.

"I'm not sure, exactly. Perhaps it's the fact that it doesn't resemble any known disease, that they can't find an agent, that they can't predict where it's going to show up next, that people die so quickly."

"You're learning something over there; I know you are. I know you, Dalton Day. I can tell something's going on, and maybe I've been wrong to think it's the charming Ms. Farmore."

"Local news is blacked out, but I see the same international TV you do. It strikes me as a kind of biological neutron bomb."

Annabelle's voice had been steady, even indignant at times, but now it grew more tight and tense. "You're scaring me," she said.

"What I mean is, the neutron bomb kills with radiation in addition to its blast. Its wartime rationale is to leave infrastructure like factories and cities intact. During the Cold War, NATO threatened the Russians with it and the Russians threatened back. The posturing was all about casualties and assets."

"Assets," Annabelle repeated.

"It's military talk. I read military history."

"I never knew that."

"Every martial artist does."

"So what are you saying? That this is a biological weapon?"

"Maybe one that ran amok."

"If the infrastructure stays, I'll be able to talk to you no matter what," Annabelle said.

"That's right. And e-mail.

"E-mail," she gave a small laugh. "That's going to be about the dirtiest word in your vocabulary when you get home. You're not going to *believe* your inbox."

"More than a hundred?"

"Send me some of what you're smoking."

"The food's fabulous here."

"I've been worried about your stomach."

"If you're worried, you're not listening to my teachings."

"You say."

"Can't you answer the messages for me? Put in a form response or something?"

"I can forward them to you at the hotel."

"Please don't do that."

"Say pretty please."

"Pretty please."

"All right, but I've got one piece of news you want to hear."

"Give it to me."

"Book sales are through the roof."

He smiled. "Lucky timing."

"If you call Armageddon lucky."

The phone line beeped to let him know he had a call waiting. "I have to go," Dalton said.

"Just keep in touch, will you?"

He promised he would, and clicked the phone over.

"Did you get my message?" Monica asked, breathless. "I met your electric man."

"I've been sleeping. I had the do-not-disturb on the phone. What do you mean you met him? What are you talking about?"

Monica explained what had happened.

"So you actually saw fire from his hands?"

"Not fire. But the instructor kept screaming he'd been shocked by an electric weapon. I know this is the guy. And he does have pointy hair."

"Physique?"

"Not a health club body, if that's what you mean. He's thin and elegant and very light on his feet and also very rich, I think."

"You didn't even ask his name?"

"I feel like an idiot, but if you had been there, you'd understand. I did ask him questions, but I didn't get anywhere."

"So then we wait."

"I can't believe you said that. I figured you'd be jumping up and down."

"A man like him has a reason for everything. If he said he'd contact you, he will."

"He drives an Aston Martin," Monica said.

Dalton sat down at the hotel room desk. "Blue convertible?"

"That's right. How did you know that?"

"I asked you whether Rachel drove one, do you remember? That car or a blue Aston just like it has been at two of our presentations."

"Oh my God, you think he's following us?"

"I think it's an interesting coincidence."

"Great. A stalker who shocks people."

"I have an idea how we can find him," said Dalton. "Or at least narrow the field."

"I though you said we should wait."

"This is something to do while we're waiting."

"I don't like the idea of him following me around, Dalton. He's powerful, scary and sad at the same time. I can't explain it. Look, the plague is on the news again this morning, and it's getting closer. They're going to close the airports any minute. You don't understand China; it's not like home. They can do anything they want here. It's like the Wild West except it's the East; there are no constraining laws. I think we should go home."

"Home?" Dalton said.

"You feel at home in China because you love the culture so much. But the culture you love is old and dead. This is communism, or whatever communism is morphing into, totalitarianism with capitalist stripes. Anyway, politics don't matter now. What matters is we don't get sick."

"I think we have a better chance of not getting sick if we find our man again. Imagine what he must know about health, Monica. Imagine what he must know about power."

"And if we don't find him?"

"If the end is coming, arcane knowledge seems more important to me than ever. Personally, I don't want to die without taking one last hard crack at the world's marvelous secrets."

"So what's your idea?"

"The passenger manifest," said Dalton. "I don't know why we didn't think about this before, but there has to be a list of the people on the plane with me, and the list of those in first class has to be small. Take away women and children and folks with American names, and I bet we can zero in on him."

Monica was silent for a moment. "The airlines won't give that out," she said at last.

"Not to us, but they can't deny the police. You said it yourself. It's a totalitarian country. The authorities get what they want. How about asking Reggie? I bet if anyone can get that list, Reggie Pritt is the man."

36

The Sandwich Islands, 1985 CE

Sanfeng stares out of his private jet, and tries to ignore the painful heat in his groin. Outside, the water is a stunning shade of blue, and the beach off Oahu's Diamond Head is pristine. "So many tall buildings," he says to himself.

The pilot overhears him. "Hawaii is much more developed than most people realize. Most of the islands are not as bad as this one, though. Theres no place more alone in the sea."

"Perth, Australia is actually the most remote city," Sanfeng replies.

"Have you been there?"

"I have," Sanfeng says. "It took weeks by sailing vessel on rough seas."

It is, indeed, the very remoteness of the Hawaiian archipelago that has led Sanfeng to choose it. He wanted to be far from his sister as he withdraws from three thousand years of practice, but he does not want to travel too far from China. He fears being as truly alone as he would be on New Caledonia, say, or Ulan Bator, and he knows Hawaii is friendly and busy.

The general aviation facility is near the terminal. Waiting for a taxi, Sanfeng sees nothing but children. It's a new experience for him, being conscious of youth this way, and indeed it colors his world.

He asks a taxi to take him around the island. The trip takes some hours, particularly on account of the traffic around Honolulu. In the taxi, his sense of agitation grows. He can't seem to stand the fit of his own skin. His groin is on fire, and at the same time the region between his *dan tian* the area below his navel, and *ming men*, the spot at the small of his back, feels so empty a river wouldn't fill it. It has been only one week since he stopped his *qigong* practice, only seven short days since making the biggest decision of his long life.

It's a reversible decision, he knows it is, but changing course so soon would be an act of cowardice and Sanfeng does not fancy himself a coward. He has had a growing conviction about nature and life and death, a conviction that has strengthened within him over the centuries. He wants to have children, his father's *qigong* won't let that happen, and so the *qigong* must stop.

He has the cab drive him over the washboard, rutted causeway past Makaha, up toward military land and a stark, dramatic beach, dream palace of surfers the world over. While the driver checks the taxi's undercarriage, the immortal stands against the wind. A chill enters him through *feng shi,* a point on the gallbladder energy meridian that is vulnerable to the invasion of wind. He notices the disruption in the flow of *qi,* but isn't quite sure what to make of it, because for the whole period of his astonishing life, he has rarely experienced weakness or a sense of vulnerability.

Sand whips around him. The giant Pacific swells roll in. He takes a measure of the volcanic energy of the island and he makes a decision.

"Take me back to the airport," he tells the driver. "This is not the island for me."

His airplane is still there, but his pilot is not available. The man has gone off duty and is resting at a local hotel. Sanfeng goes to the ticket counter and buys himself a ticket to Maui, the island his guidebook says offers the "best balance" among the popular tourist locales.

Sanfeng confirms this balance from the air. The island is shaped like the modern yin/yang, with two volcanic peaks and a valley in between. More subtle information comes to him in veiled fashion, partly as a direct consequence of the reduction of his powers, and partly because, as the commuter plane descends, he feels a pain in his ears and a thickness in his nasal passages.

He is getting his first cold.

He holes up in a modest resort across the street from the beach in Kihei, on Maui's south shore. When he travels with Zetian, five star accommodations are the rule–she would have chosen one of the giant hotels just down the road in the wealthy Wailea development–but that is because Zetian craves insulation from the world around her, while Sanfeng enjoys engagement. The details of people's lives–which island fruits they enjoy most, what dry cleaner they use, what percentage of the local population is descended from royalty, how many of them now work as busboys or bus drivers, which board shorts they favor, and which boards, what strain of marijuana they deem best, and which beach offers the best sunset–compel Sanfeng and repel Zetian with equal force.

The room is moldy, and although he doesn't know what mold is and doesn't understand why it would bother him, his symptoms are worsened by it. There is a rule in Chinese medicine that says variations in health are desirable and normal, that over time the ups and the downs equilibrate so that the downs never become too sharp. The goal of qigong practice is to increase vitality so downward plunges are shallower and life is extended. Without his practice, Sanfeng's plunge is long indeed, and although it does not take his life, it proves an unpleasant experience.

In the yellow light of the yellow bathroom with its yellow shower curtain and its yellow tile, Sanfeng has never looked so yellow himself, nor so old. Aging doesn't catch up with him at once–he doesn't turn to dust like any other 3000-year-old human body would–but he sees faint lines on his face and suffers his first fever. His joints hurt and his teeth chatter and he sweats against the relentless blow of the air conditioner, which he cannot seem to diminish no matter what dials he turns nor what buttons he pushes.

"It's centrally controlled," the night clerk tells him on the house phone. "Open a window."

He opens the window, but the air outside is not much warmer. It is winter and there is a stiff breeze by the beach and the palm trees rustle and there is salt on the air. Unable to sleep, he gets dressed and walks to an all-night drugstore. He knows traditional Chinese medicine intimately, but has never had to treat himself and has not brought along herbs. When it comes to Western medicine, he has no familiarity whatsoever with the pharmacopoeia, and thus finds himself standing underneath a big sign that says colds and flu desperately trying to decipher what might be best.

A woman stands ten feet away. She wears a short skirt and her legs are lovely. She is blonde and she has a red plastic basket in hand. Sanfeng notices the smart, quick way in which she picks products from the shelf, this one and that one, high up and low down.

"Excuse me," he says. "I wonder if I might ask your help."

"You've got a flu, haven't you?"

"You can tell by my eyes?"

"You *are* in the flu section," she smiles.

"I have a high temperature," says Sanfeng.

If anybody's eyes are revealing, they are the woman's, which are lined and bleary from partying. She is there to stave off a hangover, having sat all night at the bar thinking she might meet an interesting man and leaving disappointed.

"I'm not familiar with these pills," Sanfeng says.

"Where are you from?"

"China. Probably, you should not come near me. I don't want to make you ill."

"I'm Cherylanne. I'm not usually out this late."

"You drank too much and you're looking for a pill."

"Oh. Is it that obvious? I hate to be obvious."

"It is late and you are here alone and headache medicines are here."

"You're funny. I don't usually drink so much."

"I'm Sanfeng. I'm not usually sick."

"Buy these. They bubble, and that makes them work faster."

"You are a doctor?"

"A nurse. Or I would have been. I went to nursing school, but I didn't finish."

"No?"

She looks at the floor. "I ran out of money. My mother got sick and I stayed home to take care of her. I didn't need the degree for that."

"In China, we honor the elderly," he says. "Our filial duty is the highest priority."

"Filial duty," she says. "I expect you went to college."

"Once or twice," he says. She laughs, not knowing he has gone through many, many years of school, in different provinces and in different fields.

"There are herbs too," she says. "They're getting more popular again. I take vitamin C. You might try that for your cold too."

He pays for his selections and they leave the store together. She asks where he is staying and he tells her.

"May I come by and check on you tomorrow?" she asks.

"You would do that?"

"I'd like to."

He coughs. It's a deep cough, and it leaves him bent over and red in the face and embarrassed by his own weakness. She sees his expression in the streetlight.

"Poor man," she says.

He goes back to his room and takes the medicine she has given him and goes to sleep. He is surprised by its power, and by the way it clears his nose. It makes him dizzy, and he's a bit frightened by that, by the sense his body is running away from him. Normal human beings are accustomed to less than optimal function, to the aches and pains of growing old, to the changes from childhood to puberty and beyond. Sanfeng has suffered none of these, or if he has, they have been subliminal and below his radar. At night, he feels more alone than he has in thousands of nights, perhaps tens of thousands, and disconnected from the world.

The next morning, he is worse. The fever is up and his joints ache as never before. His sheets are soaked with sweat. He lies in misery despite the brightness of the day, and when the maid comes to make up the room, he sends her away.

There is no room service, and he grows hungry, but feels too faint to go out. He drinks from the tap like a horse come in from pasture. At lunchtime, Cherylanne knocks on the door. She wears a bikini under a gossamer wrap, and even in his stupor, Sanfeng notices that her curves are restrained but ample, her gray eyes set widely are clear and caring, her features classical, her mouth small the way upper class Chinese men like a woman's mouth to be. The night before, he took her for a pretty girl; in the light of day he sees she is a beautiful woman.

"You look awful," she says.

He wipes his hand self-consciously over his chin. There is stubble there. His mouth tastes sour.

"The bubbling medicine worked well, but my fever is high. You should stay away from me still."

She walks past him into the room, takes a look around, and picks up the phone and calls for the maid. He watches her. She fluffs the bed, opens the window, and points at the bathroom.

"Into the shower with you, mister," she says.

Sanfeng has not seen such forward, American, self-possession before, as he has traveled rarely in the United States. He finds it charming, and in any case is too weak to argue with her. Under the water, he half expects she might open the door and join him, but she doesn't. He is too sick to be disappointed, but wishes he wasn't.

When he comes out, he is freshened, although he doesn't feel much better, at least he is clean. The maid gives him a dirty look for making her come back.

"You are two in here or one?" she asks.

"One," Cherylanne answers.

Sanfeng rests on the clean bed.

"You didn't take the vitamin C, did you?" she asks.

"I've never taken a vitamin."

She goes to the bathroom and finds the bottle and brings him two capsules and sees he takes them. Then she sits with straight posture at the desk and crosses her legs properly and withdraws a paperback novel from her straw beach bag.

"*Shibumi*," she says. "It's the story of a man with a Chinese girlfriend. She's blind and he's a hired killer and he loves to explore caves. Close your eyes, and I'll read to you."

He does as she says and he finds the sound of her voice soothing. He opens his eyes, but makes slits of them so she doesn't notice. He gazes at her breasts and her belly and her legs. The herbs begin to take effect and he is stimulated first and then relaxed. He sleeps.

When he awakens, she is still there, and she has brought fruit. "Papaya will help your stomach feel better."

It does, and he eats. She reads some more. This time, the protagonist of her book plays a round of *Go*, a Chinese game of great complexity. From the description, Sanfeng recognizes the author is a mere amateur, but he does not offer this comment. He falls asleep again. When he wakes it is nighttime, and she is gone.

The next morning, he finds her on the beach outside his hotel. He is much improved, and they have a swim together. In the gentle surf, with sand between their toes, they kiss.

Sanfeng has long pondered the mechanism of action of his father's *qigong*, and the manifestations of its power. The way the practice works runs counter to a general understanding of Chinese medicine, which has *qigong* creating *jing*, or sexual essence. This essence is the root of *qi*, life force, which in turn leads to *shen*, or spirit, which most disciplines claim is the path to immortality. Crocodile and Crane *qigong*, however, remains a mystery and a paradox, as over the years, while Sanfeng has remained virile, he has produced almost no jing at all.

Cherylanne insists on taking care of him again that night. He wants to invite her into his bed, indeed he is literally bursting with desire, but he honors her with his patience. She will be the first woman into whom he will deliver what there is of him, and while on a physical level he is very much in a rush, on a deeper level he is aware of the possibilities, and he wants all energies in line.

He falls asleep. Again he wakes, but this time she is asleep on his chair.

Now he takes her to the shower and pleasures her there, and in time, and with tropical juices and fresh food to propel them, they become intimate. Sanfeng is as skilled a lover as has ever lived, having had more partners and more passions than anyone, and he leaves no part of Cherylanne unexplored or untended. They move together standing, kneeling, lying. They vary rhythms and investigate patterns. At times, Cherylanne falls into unconsciousness from sheer exhaustion, but when she wakes he persuades her again, surprised to find that while he has so recently been ill there are long pent up forces at work to invigorate and sustain him beyond her comprehension.

"Who are you?" she gasps as he supports her from underneath as if he is the ocean and she a slender ship.

"You bring out my best," he says, kissing.

At times, when he moves within her, she feels she is in a dream. The idea she might tell her friends about him comes and goes in a moment, as she realizes there is nothing to tell that can believably be told.

"A beauty pageant sent me here," she tells him, against the crook of his arm.

"I don't understand."

"The trip. All expenses paid. Ten days in Hawaii. I won the beauty pageant at the tractor factory in Enid."

"Enid?"

"My home town in Oklahoma. It's a state a bit down from the center. Corn, cotton, and wheat."

"How old are you?" he asks.

"Twenty. How about you?"

"A little more than that."

"I can tell. You look young, but you know so much about so many things."

He hires a car and they drive around the island. They go north past Lahaina and Kaanapali and into the lush forests of Honokahua, then to the wind-swept cliffs at Kahakuloa, where they find a labyrinth delineated by white stones laid out by some New Age tourists and made sacred by gifts at the very center: a golf ball, another golf ball, a silver necklace, a tattered twenty-dollar bill, a garnet in a little plastic box, cushioned by cotton.

"Why would someone leave jewels and money here?" Sanfeng asks. "It seems wasteful."

"But you notice no one has stolen the goods. That's because they are offerings to the island gods. This is a power place. When we walked the labyrinth we alerted the spirit of the place to our love."

"Our love," Sanfeng repeats.

"Don't be afraid. I didn't mean anything by it."

They drive down through Waihee and into Wailuku, where they have breakfast in a bakery. A little girl is there with an older woman. Eating authentic European pastries made by an expatriate Frenchwoman, the couple watches the little girl in silence. The older woman notices.

"Her mother works," she says. "She's my job most days."

They are together three more days after that. They eat, they sightsee, and they make love. At ten thousand feet, and in a frigid morning with a tiny dusting of snow, they huddle together under a blanket and watch the onset of morning atop the dormant volcano known to the islanders as Haleakala, the House of the Sun.

"I'm not using protection," Cherylanne says, very quietly, as the day comes to light. "But if I get pregnant, I won't bother you about it."

"If you get pregnant, you *must* bother me about it," Sanfeng replies.

37

"I understand why the plague is happening," Leili said. "But I still don't understand how it kills us."

"The worm part, you mean?" Dr. Eonnet asked through his isolation suit.

"The worm part," she nodded.

"In apoptosis, cells in the afflicted organ systems kill themselves, and then one by one, the affected systems shut down. Connective tissue is involved, and that's causing the joint pain and facial rictus. The actual cause of death is most likely either the collapse of the diaphragm or failure of the valves of the heart."

"Can't you get them to stop shutting down?"

"I'm trying, but not having much luck so far. Chemicals called proteases are released when a healthy cell is damaged. It is those proteases that actually destroy the cell. I've asked my colleagues to focus their efforts on deactivating them, but they don't seem to be doing so."

Privately, Eonnet was not sure anyone was listening to his theory. A new team was on the way to Jakarta, vowing to manage the epicenter better than he was, accusing him of spending too much time on a crackpot theory, and in particular on one lone test subject. The argument was specious, and everyone knew it. For one thing, Eonnet was an epidemiologist, not a general or a politician. For another, the concept of epicenter was increasingly irrelevant as the disease popped up in far-flung and disconnected locations world-wide.

"Do you mean other scientists have different ideas?" Leili inquired.

Eonnet spread his gloved hands. "I'm sure they do."

She tossed her hair back "I'm going home. I can't even remember when I last had a shower."

"You can shower here," the scientist said, so quickly it came out as a plea.

She studied him, understanding he was afraid to be left alone. Through the glass faceplate his eyes were glassy and his beard was growing in, salt and pepper, high up on his cheeks. "You need a break too," she said carefully.

"I'll take one right now. We can watch TV."

Before she could respond, he turned on the little set in the nursing station. CNN was reporting that the plague had reached Japan, and people were dying in Osaka and Toyko. Organized criminals, *yakuza*, had taken over the country's supply of disinfectants, soap, and waylaid professional shipments and surgical masks. Warehouses were being held up, and markets pilloried.

"Have you ever been to Japan?" Eonnet inquired, trying desperately to make conversation, so Leili would stay.

"Never," she answered. "I traveled a little with Lombo's father, before he left me, but we didn't get to Japan. After that, I was busy raising Lombo and trying to hold down a job."

Eonnet tried to imagine the father of Lombo Musi, the boy who brought Western medicine its final test. He tried to imagine what kind of man would leave a woman like Leili, not to mention a young son. As he conjured Tony Tunstall's unnamed soul, he had no way of knowing that across the South China Sea, Tony's physical body–tea dust under the fingernails, eyes still full of baobab leaves, ears still full of the twilight cry of heavy-winged fruit bats–was being tossed onto a bonfire of infected corpses.

"I am aware the world has a difficult opinion of the French, but I myself have always found Japan a more challenging country. They say the Japanese like humor, but I so rarely see my Japanese colleagues laugh."

"There are Japanese in Indonesia," said Leili. "Or at least there were. I always liked them. They're very polite and smart and helpful."

Eonnet frowned. "They're always worrying about preservatives, radiation, chemicals in the air, any kind of pollution. It's a result of Hiroshima and Nagasaki, I guess, so you can't blame them, but there's a real national obsession with cleanliness."

The CNN reporter turned her attention to Fiji, where the

plague had appeared among the island nation's Indian minority. There was a long history of the lackadaisical natives resenting industrious Indian immigrants, and racial violence was spreading. The Indian government had launched a formal protest in the Fijian capital of Suva.

Australia was also in the news, having declared a state of emergency. There were plague outbreaks in Darwin, on the mostly-Aboriginal Cape York Peninsula, and in Cairns, Broome, and Brisbane; all in the continent's northern half. In an attempt to protect the major cities of Melbourne and Sydney and the rest of the highly populated "Boomerang Coast," the Australian government had restricted domestic travel with roadblocks and flight cancellations.

As if all that were not enough, the two million Moslems in Myanmar were burning the nation's flag and blaming the plague on scientific experiments conducted by the infidels of the West. The government in Thailand was expecting similar action among its own Moslem minority.

"Let me go home and clean up," said Leili. "There's nothing else I can do here."

"As a matter of fact, there is."

"And what might that be?"

"I need fluid from your joint capsules."

Leili frowned. "You already scraped my skin and nose."

"Yes, but the joint capsule is different. I need to look at your serum, your lymph, all the different cells I can find."

Leili had been expecting something like this. "There's nobody left alive out there, is there?"

Eonnet shrugged his shoulders in a very French gesture. "Not in Jakarta. At least, we don't think so."

"But I'm still here."

"And perfectly healthy."

"But filthy," she said.

"You're alive."

"So the fish tank doesn't need me to die."

"Apparently not, although I can't explain why."

"You've been waiting for me to go."

"Preparing for the worst, but hoping for the best."

The report droned on. New Zealand was now on the list of afflicted countries. Because of its remote location, low population density, and the prevailing winds expected to keep nuclear fallout at bay, the island nation had long been an apple in the eye of survivalists. Despite heated health directives from Wellington, containment proceedings were simply too little, too late. New Zealand was no bigger than Colorado, but its vast, crooked coastline was nearly impossible to patrol, and most of the 111 airports were rural unpaved strips, making radar monitoring of low-altitude flights from elsewhere in Polynesia difficult. Refugees were making landfall on tiny islands in the chain, and at remote agricultural stations and South Island fjords. The infection was spreading to schools, businesses and city gathering spots.

Eonnet took Leili's hands in his black, black gloves. "Listen to me for a minute. Sometimes cells kill themselves to protect the organism of which they are a part. Some viruses and some cancers have ways of tricking the cell into not killing itself as a way of ensuring the survival of the invader. But except in the case of metastatic disease–which takes far longer than a couple of days to kill someone–these conditions are tissue specific. They don't affect the skin, the joints, the connective tissue, and so on."

Leili withdrew her hands. "What's your point?"

"Everyone is looking for a bug, something transmitted between people, or from some common source. There's even talk of an extraterrestrial toxin entering the atmosphere. But the apoptosis model makes me think this is an autoimmune problem. You seem to have some genetic predisposition *not* to get this sickness, and that's a fact I can't ignore. I want to compare your synovial DNA to diseased samples, and see if I can find where they differ."

"You're hoping to find no bacteria or virus because it would prove your theory."

"That's correct."

"And you're entirely certain you're right, that I am not contagious."

"I am."

"So why are you wearing that yellow suit?"

He stared at her. She kept going. "If you're wrong, if there *is* a virus or a bacteria, the suit is what's saving you. If you're right and there's *no* infectious agent, the suit is useless."

"*Mon Dieu,*" he said, slumping down.

"If DNA talk to each other, or response to some global signal, surely the suit can't stop it. So the question is, how sure are you of your theory?"

"Very sure," Eonnet whispered.

"Well then. If you're going to succumb to some force from within, then the suit makes no difference. It isn't protecting you, not from me or from anything else in this hospital. Wouldn't you like a shave, and something to drink besides water through a plastic tube?"

"Yes."

"You're asking me to stay, and let you put a big needle in me. You're asking me to trust your theory. Show me you believe what you're saying. Take off the suit."

He put his head in his hands for a minute. It seemed to Leili that he had disappeared in the big yellow outfit. Finally he straightened, nodding.

"Your logic is inescapable," he said. "Science is logical, and I believe in science."

He began with his gloves.

38

The rooms in Gao Zetian's Victoria Peak estate reflected the range of her moods, and were arranged in a sequence of declining good humor, becoming bleaker the further a visitor ventured from the front door. While there were many great masterpieces and *objets d'art*, nothing had been selected for its own sake; everything was present as a contribution to overall effect. The foyer was painted yellow, and featured an exquisite beige and blue Persian rug spread over a floor of light hardwood slats. The pictures on the wall were Impressionist, and showed mostly bright flowers and kindly pastoral scenes–young girls holding umbrellas standing on arched wooden bridges overlooking clear ponds holding gay fish with flowing fins and generous tails. The room to the right, a gallery of figurines, was just a tad dimmer. It housed sculptures of wood, bronze, plaster, and stone, some painted in garish colors, some flat gray, some man-sized, some the size of toadstools.

Next came the library, which was paneled in cherry wood. Two rolling ladders made accessing any of the thousands of books a simple matter of climbing a few steps. Low-wattage picture-frame lamps lighted the fourth room. Zetian's Goyas lived here: masterpieces from the great artist's macabre late period, a time when he suffered keenly from meningitis and drew souls fully as tortured as his own. The colors on the original canvases were dark, and revealed images lost to history during the Spanish Civil War and unknown even to experts at Spain's much-vaunted Prado Museum.

There was a rosewood writing desk in the corner of that room, and Huangfu found his mistress sitting there. She had her back to him, but he could see she was wearing a navy-blue business suit and stiletto heels. He had to say her name twice before she turned around, and when she did, he saw that she was heavily made-up with magenta lipstick, white powder, dark eyeliner, and almost no blush. Any makeup at all was unusual because her skin was perfect, and she had no need to hide it. The effect that day was positively cadaverous, and Huangfu wondered what mood had prompted it.

"You haven't come about the plague, have you, Huangfu? I'm tired of hearing about it."

"No," he said. "I've come about your brother."

"Aha. And what news of the great Gao Sanfeng?"

"Master Gao has been spending much of his time in a suite at the China Bank Tower."

"The China Bank Tower? Why? We have no business there."

"This is not about business."

"He has a woman there?"

Huangfu looked around uncomfortably. He wanted to make this easier on himself. Bad enough he had been reduced to spying, but the reporting was even worse. He wished she would say something about his tie. It was the Ferragamo she bought for him.

"Not exactly, no."

"A man?"

"No, no, certainly not."

"Sit down, Huangfu."

He lowered himself into the only other chair in the room, a high-backed metal affair that looked medieval, and perfectly complimented the Goyas.

"Please explain what he is doing, then," she said.

"He spends time with his telescopes," Huangfu began.

"The hygiene of distance," she muttered. "Give me your opinion, Huangfu. Do you think there is a grand plan to the world?"

"Are you asking me if I believe in the gods?"

"Maybe I am."

"I don't believe that things and events are just strung together randomly," Huangfu replied slowly.

He hoped Zetian did not dwell on the subject. He knew she was an agnostic, knew she had very little religious tolerance, and knew she would never keep him on if she discovered he was secretly a devout Buddhist.

"Of course they are," she snapped. "How else would you explain duck carcasses, and diamond jewelry, fish shit, croutons, the roots of trees, lightning balls, snake fangs, capitalism, curry, and the billowing jibs of sailboats in the wind?"

Huangfu smiled. "Madame is a poet."

She rose. "Life is chaos," she said. "It's best to keep on an even keel and thread your way through. The key is to not get attached to anything."

"You sound like a Buddhist," he said.

"I hate Buddhists," she said. "Tell me, do you think I was attached to Jou Yuen?"

"I wouldn't presume to know."

"He was crooked," she said.

"I beg your pardon?"

"He hung crooked. But he was gloriously endowed."

Embarrassed, Huangfu looked at the floor.

"So tell me, what is my brother watching?"

Huangfu dug into his vest pocket, and produced one of the surveillance photos. "There's no way to be sure," he said. "I was able to look in on him from another building after I tailed him to the tower, but not, of course, to actually see through his telescope. I can tell you his target is in the Mid Levels, though."

Zetian looked at Sanfeng in the photo. "He looks old," she said.

"These days, it is hard to sleep."

Zetian wondered if Sanfeng might not be right about the Banpo Smile, if the damn thing had not come back to haunt them. Well, so what if it has, she thought. We escaped it once, and we will do so again.

"When he leaves the tower, where does he go?"

Huangfu spread his hands. "I don't know. I shall follow him more closely."

She put a finger under his chin. "Don't fail me. I've been looking after my brother for longer than you can imagine. He needs me."

"Of course, Madame."

"Not Madame."

Huangfu blushed.

"Of course, Zetian."

39

Waiting for Jimmy Ngo, Dalton and Monica watched TV in the hotel lobby, which buzzed with a far different energy than a week earlier, when Dalton had checked in. Management had set up a bank of sets along the north wall, and a line of chairs as well. According to reports, the plague had reached Africa, with Uganda, Kenya, Namibia and the Ivory Coast all reporting significant outbreaks. The Pope had come out with a speech experts were calling a veiled announcement of the Tribulation and Rapture and the End Times outlined in the Book of Revelation. South America was blanketed in the smoke of burning corpses, plumes of which eclipsed even the greatest of the long-decried timber fires in Brazil. The news commentator said the smoke made for sunsets so beautiful it almost made the dying worth it.

"He'll sing a different song when he starts smiling," Dalton told Monica.

Around them, guests in high gear lugged suitcases through the lobby, and the flutter of passport pages and the waving of cash gave rise to little puffs of wind. The talk was all about hiding in remote areas like Death Valley, the Canadian Rockies, the White Mountains of New Hampshire, and a plantation near Moultrie, Georgia. A man in a business suit mentioned a hideout in the former Soviet republic of Azerbaijan, but another said the hideout had been taken by militant Islamic extremists and held for the faithful. Russia, it seemed, was degrading into its component parts, as was Iraq, which had begun the process after the American pullout. No continent or country, it seemed, offered a truly safe haven.

Jimmy arrived. "I've got a strong hunch we're going to find your man tonight," he said.

"Where are we going?" Monica asked.

"A video arcade."

"You can't be serious," said Monica. "How can you think of video games at a time like this?"

"The world is ending and there's not a damn thing we can do. Why *would* I be serious."

"I like that attitude," Dalton grinned. "It has a Daoist flavor to it."

"I'm telling you, this place is special," Jimmy insisted. "Plague or not, all the *gongfu* jocks go there. Somebody's bound to know your electric man."

"At a video arcade?" Monica repeated doubtfully.

"Kids here are video crazy, Monica. It's a cultural thing, like karaoke, and this is the biggest gaming center in Hong Kong, the place the Japanese test out their hottest new products. If you haven't seen one of these games lately, you won't believe how realistic they are. They require reflexes, skill, judgment, and technique, and are used to learn to drive, fly, play music, even fight. It's practice without the bruises."

"It's okay with me," said Dalton. "I'm still hoping Reggie Pritt can get access to that passenger manifest, but in the meantime I love the idea of going to a video arcade. It's perfectly crazy, like fiddling while Rome burns."

"Should be fun, too," said Jimmy.

"You and Jimmy go," said Monica. "I'm going home to wait for Reggie. He'll come through, I know he will."

The Diamond Gaming Center was on Carnarvon Road, in Kowloon. A giant wooden statue of General Guan, patron god of the martial arts, guarded the door, seeming out of place in front of the flashing lights and the smoke. Air conditioning kept the place freezing cold, and Dalton noticed groups of teenage girls huddled together on stools, smoking cigarettes and watching their boyfriends compete along a wall devoted entirely to golf games, some named for Nicklaus, others for Woods.

"The Japanese love their golf," Jimmy said. "It's all about the romance of open spaces. Nobody has room to breathe in Asia. Dreams are made of elbow room."

"The plague is going to make all kinds of elbow room if someone doesn't stop it soon," Dalton muttered.

In another section of the center, a pair of teens dueled with computerized guitars around their necks, while more young girls watched. There were no strings on the faux instruments, only sensors to register the heat of hands and the pressure of fingertips. Looking at the place, one would have no idea the end of the world was just outside the door.

"You play anything?" Jimmy asked Dalton.

"I'm better at listening to music than making it."

They watched a pimply kid in a denim jacket play a football game, and Dalton learned that Jimmy was a veritable encyclopedia of gridiron trivia, this down and that, field goals, career yardage, the personal history of coaches, one of whom he suspected might one day be President of the United States.

"*Punisher*," Dalton said, inspecting the single-player control console of a nearby martial arts game. "Check this out. It looks new. You put your hands inside these gloves and your feet on the pedals to kick. Your life-size silhouette is projected into the game. How do they do that?"

"And look at that gorgeous, giant, flat screen monitor. If any of us survive past next month, I'm going to make sure everyone at Billabong Books gets a desktop model," Jimmy said.

A kid wearing a Harley Davidson motorcycle jacket, pointed at Dalton. "I know you. I was at your book signing at Pacific Place. I remember your face."

"Did you buy a book?" Dalton asked.

"Yeah. And I like it. It's pretty cool the way you understand all the old stuff."

"You think he talks well, you should see him move," said Jimmy, slipping coins into the machine and preparing to play.

"The old stuff is never newer than right now," Dalton said. "Masters in those old days didn't have video games and parties and movies to distract them, so they had loads of time to think and practice and explore the power of nature."

"I think that's a myth," the boy answered. "I think the old guys were too busy bringing in the crops to have much energy left over. I think *my* generation is going to find the truth of the universe, and we're going to use technology to do it. We're going to gather the evidence with electron microscopes and gene sequencers and atom smashers and radio telescopes."

"High-tech tools are great," Dalton said. "But interpreting the data is still up to us, using our brains. That interpretation is limited by our world view, and by what we think we know."

The big speakers rumbled, and the screen lit up. A tall biker girl with a matching motorcycle jacket appeared, and linked arms with the boy.

She winked at Jimmy. "Wow, are you going to get your ass kicked."

A life-size Viking filled the screen, his pupils richly rendered. He wore a horned hat, and his ankle-length leather coat was open to the words *It's Dead, Whatever It Was* tattooed across his hairy blonde chest. His pants were baggy over Doc Martens, and he held a broken bottle in one hand and a length of motorcycle chain in the other. "Ready to die, little man?" he boomed.

By way of reply, Jimmy moved the gloves landed a virtual punch on the Viking's mouth.

The Viking laughed. "Is that all you've got?"

A right cross from Jimmy brought a welt to the virtual Viking's forehead, and the kick that followed left a dust mark on his shoulder.

The Viking stepped forward, swinging his chain. Jimmy grinned, but then suddenly jumped backwards, a look of pain and astonishment on his face. His digital facsimile, no more than the back of a head and arms and legs, kissed the floor.

"Hey!" Jimmy cried. "I got an electric shock!"

"Why do you think they call it *Punisher*?" the biker girl taunted.

The Viking's chain hit Jimmy's digital forehead, and the real Jimmy cried out again.

"Harder hit, stronger shock," the biker explained to Dalton.

"Take this, you Nordic prick," Jimmy panted, working the pedals to loose a flurry of kicks.

The Viking rocked back on his heels, but was up and swinging again. He somehow managed to get the chain around Jimmy's computerized neck, and there was a loud crunching sound.

"Ow," Jimmy cried, letting go of the controls.

"You're dead," the Viking intoned.

The screen went blank. Jimmy pointed at Dalton, enjoining him to take up the battle. Dalton looked around the center. "No sign of him," he said.

"We haven't been here very long."

"Maybe I should listen to Monica and give up looking for this guy."

"Why the sudden impatience?" Jimmy asked. "The plague will end up there too. At most you'll buy the two of you a few weeks of life, but at the expense of fulfilling a lifelong dream before you die. I say, keep looking. If he doesn't exist and you don't find him, so what? Better than dying without trying your best."

Dalton regarded him for a long moment. "Thanks for saying that."

Jimmy smiled. "Just telling you what I would do."

Dalton turned to the kids. "Listen, everyone. I didn't come here to play video games, I came looking for a *gongfu* master with hair that sticks straight out: a guy who can make electricity come out of his hands for real. Have any of you seen someone like that?"

The motorcycle couple exchanged a look. "If you live through a couple of rounds of *Punisher*, maybe we'll tell you," the girl said.

"So this is a test?"

"You got it," said the girl.

The last video game Dalton had played was *Pac Man*, when he was a child. *Punisher* was decidedly more complex. "All right," he agreed, a bit reluctantly.

He put his money in the machine. "Ready to die, little man?" the Viking asked again.

"I hate a cocky Viking," said Dalton, knocking the Viking's horned hat off with a punch.

The biker girl hooted. A few other kids heard the commotion, and drifted over. Dalton feinted to the Viking's ear, hit his knee hard, and the virtual character went down for the count.

The video screen created a new opponent for Dalton, a Chinese girl in a purple *gongfu* uniform decorated in little moons. She moved so quickly, Dalton did not know whether to duck or parry, so instead he just started punching back. Some of his punches met their mark, but she was terribly fast, and before long the game jolted him, making the teenagers laugh.

"Go for her tits!" the biker girl jeered.

Dalton obliged, and a red blotch appeared on the character's chest. He chicken-kicked her collarbone by jumping fast on the pedals, and she went down faster than the Viking had, only to be replaced with a sword-toting thug.

"Pretty good," the biker boy admitted grudgingly. "But watch out for this guy's sword."

The blade came in strong and fast. Dalton tried to sweep the thug's leg by moving the pedal sideways, but it didn't work the way he planned and Viking cut off his virtual arm cut off. The resulting shock was strong enough to make him cry out.

"Say goodbye to your head," the thug smiled cruelly.

Dalton struggled at the controls. The electricity had numbed him. There was this terrible rushing sound, his screen head rolled off with a geyser of blood, but mercifully there was no shock.

"You're lucky," the biker girl said. "A bad beating gives you terrible shocks, but when you lose your head you don't feel anything."

"Did I do well enough to earn some information?" Dalton asked.

"I guess so. My boyfriend didn't get that far in a week. The guy you want comes in here sometimes. He walks like he's floating and never says a word. He used to play all the fighting games, but since *Punisher* came out, he's stuck on it. One of my friends said he saw sparks in his hands."

"In his hands, or coming out of his hands."

The girl shrugged. "I didn't see it. I think he said in his hands. Probably it was just static. It happens sometimes if you don't wear rubber shoes."

"Our boots have rubber soles," the biker boy said.

"But he's got the crazy hair," the girl said. "We always laugh about the way it sticks out. We say the game did it to him. We say he has it because he's been *punished*."

Everyone laughed, but Dalton stayed quiet. So close to an answer, with the world closing in, nothing seemed funny right then.

40

"She's not the only one," Sanfeng said quietly.

On the other end of the line, thousands of miles away, his old lover came up out of midnight's sleep "Oh," she said. "I've always wondered about that."

"I haven't taken any better care of any of the others."

"I never said you had. I never even asked."

Sanfeng pulled his chair closer to his desk in his apartment and began inputting websites into each of the three computers. It was his practice to check the news in this fashion every day, but since the recurrence of the Banpo Smile he had taken to checking the spread of the disease several times a day, using sites around the world. It was just after noon in China, and early morning updates were streaming in from the west.

"They don't all work in China," Sanfeng said quietly.

"I'm afraid it might not matter where they are," Cherylanne sighed. "The way things look right now, they say we'll all die, no matter where we are. I don't mind so much. I've had the life I was after and the life I deserved, but thinking about Monica...."

She started to cry.

"Please," said Sanfeng. "She'll be all right."

"How can you know?"

"You trusted me the night you met me, and you've trusted me ever since. Am I right? Is that true?"

"I've trusted you."

"I sent you a message on the Internet. You didn't answer."

"We had a lightning storm," Cherylanne said. "My computer is dead. I'll get another one soon. I've been worried you've been trying to reach me, but I thought you might call if it was important."

"Things may happen in the weeks to come. Life may become difficult."

"Some people say there may not even be weeks left. I trust in

God to take care of me. I trust in Him to do what he would do."

"I have heard it said that your God helps those who help themselves," Sanfeng replied. "This is a good and practical philosophy. Get some food in your house. Stock up now. I'll put some money in your account for a new computer. I want to be able to reach you. And buy an uninterruptible power supply for your computer. Do you know what that is?"

Cherylanne fought the need to go to the bathroom. Her bladder was a bit harder to control now, and being awakened out of a sound sleep brought the need on keenly. "Sure," she said. "A battery back-up."

Sanfeng laughed. "You're charming," he said.

"Of course I'm charming. I'm not so young any more, but if anything, I'm even *more* charming."

"I would like to see you again," Sanfeng said.

"You've said so before."

"Even more, this time."

"I'd like to see you too."

"If the power goes off, use your back-up and keep checking your messages. There will be a message about the plague from an American."

"There are already plenty of messages about the plague," Cherylanne said. "They show up every five minutes. They call on us to repent, they call on us to buy some kind of iodine, to make cash purchases of property in remote locations like Alaska and flee."

"Don't go anywhere," said Sanfeng. "It won't help. The message to look for is one that promises to heal the plague."

"I don't know what's going on over there," Cherylanne said, "but every telemarketer in the world is on late-night channels promising the curing diet, the healing pill."

"I'll have Monica send it. That way you'll know."

"You've spoken to her? Oh God, that's what you called to tell me. You've spoken to her. All these years I've kept you a secret, as you asked, and now she knows about you."

"She does not, but the message will come from her."

"If you know how to save me from the plague, maybe you'd

better do it now."

"Soon," said Sanfeng. "Just watch the computer."

Cherylanne bent over and squeezed her legs together. She could barely hold her water, but she had not heard Sanfeng's voice in twenty five years–had received messages from him in writing only–and she found herself clinging to ever word.

"I've always waited for this day," she said. "I've always hoped for it. I know she will love you. I know you will be proud of her."

"I'm already proud of her," Sanfeng said. "I am proud of all my children."

"Sometimes I think you are an alien from another planet and I wonder whether there are more of you."

"I am not, but there is one."

"One what?"

"One more like me."

"Years ago, I hired a detective to find out about you."

"I know."

"He cost me a month's pay. He couldn't tell me anything about you at all. Did you just say you know?"

"Yes, I know about the detective."

She laughed. "Of course you do. Do you know I went back to school?"

"I know that too. You graduated at the top of your class."

"That wasn't easy. The others were younger and more eager, and most didn't have kids to cook for during study time."

Sanfeng toggled between the website of the BBC and *Business News America,* watched a live news telecast from Japan, and scanned hard copies of *The Christian Science Monitor, The Sydney Morning Herald,* and Capetown, South Africa's Cape Argus.

"You've done well with your life," he said. "People love and respect you. Monica loves and respects you."

"How can you know that?"

Sanfeng got up from the desk and went to the window and looked through his telescope and saw Monica doing dishes near the kitchen window.

"I just can."

Cherylanne stood and dragged the phone toward the

bathroom. She ran out of cord. She put the body of the phone down and stretched the receiver cord as far as she could. She could not reach the toilet. She could not even get close.

"Sanfeng?"

"Yes?"

"I hope you're all right."

"I'm fine."

"Is this the last time I will talk to you?"

"Don't be silly."

"It is, isn't it?"

"I will try to call again."

"Only try?"

Before he could answer, her sobbing took her over. It was all he could do to understand her.

"I beg your pardon?" he said.

"I will pray for all your children."

41

Hong Kong under the British had been perfect for Reggie Pritt. There had been order, Chinese efficiency, and no limit to experience and opportunity. He commanded good men, he fought the good fight against the Triads and street scum, and he never had to worry about being busted while driving home drunk.

Reggie was charming when sober, funny and generous too, and his circle of friends–who regarded him with a mixture of alarm and affection–extended far beyond law enforcement and far above his station. He had wowed Monica with a mixture of *savoir-faire*, machismo, persistence, and, of course, the romantic appeal of a broad Australian accent clipped by years among Hong Kong's Brits.

She had been a diversion for him at first, and he nibbled at her as if she were candy merely there to sweeten the bitter loss of prestige and power that attended coming under Beijing's purview. In time he found she was more than that–tough and smart and struggling to make a meaningful mix of the cultures within and around her–and he fell in love.

When his communist masters in Beijing transferred him from Central to the boondocks of the New Territories Reggie needed Monica more than ever, but his mood swings and drinking pushed her away. After the degradation of the spurned proposal, he would have liked to just tell her to sod off, but loved her too much to do it.

So they met at an outdoor restaurant between Exchange Square–home of the Hong Kong Stock Exchange, the General Post Office, and the once-noble Jardine House–Hong Kong's original clearing point for tea, silk, fruits and opium. She saw him coming in fast across the plaza, his eyes drinking in the curves under her green dress as if the mere sight of her would re-hydrate him, restore the vital elixir that booze and the adhesive muck of unappreciated police work had drained from him.

"I'm sorry, Monica, but I don't have much time."

Monica noticed the bulge of the gun in his shoulder holster. Generally he carried only a small revolver at his ankle.

"You're working? Isn't this your day off?"

"All that's changed," he waved. "We've got so very much to do. The brass is going crazy trying to keep the infrastructure intact. They're setting up duty logs for people you never think about: street sweepers, traffic coordinators, bridge tenders and the like, and they have us working 24/7. The British Prime Minister was on the telly this morning. The plague's in London now. He wasn't hopeful. Vaccines take years, he said. Said half a thousand Englishmen are dying every time Big Ben sounds. I grew up hating the poms and now I find myself shedding a tear."

"We could have just talked on the phone," she said.

"You broke my heart but I still jump at the chance to see you."

"Are you all right?"

"I'm not half so good without you as with you."

She took him in her arms. "This is so difficult," she sighed. "Why can't you just be more positive about things? Do you really like what you've become? You go around blaming everyone but yourself for your unhappiness. You're better than this. I know that you are. The more I learn, the more convinced I become that attitude is everything, that we decide how we live our lives, that not sinking into despair at the impermanence of things takes a disciplined mind."

"You read this in the Yank's book? That I'm not disciplined enough for you?"

"No, he didn't write about you. But he did write that we can train ourselves to look at the world with a sense of wonder–to be childlike. He's older than I am, but seems younger."

"So you're in love with him?"

"He's admirable, that's all. He walks his talk. What he does is hard to do."

"You didn't answer my charge."

"No, I'm not in love with him. I thought I might be, but then I realized I was in love with *you.*"

Reggie's face lit up. It was something for Monica to see, that softening in his rough edges, the lightening of his usual, almost brutish expression, the creasing of a smile on his tough and loyal face, a face marked up and hacked down by the transition from freedom to totalitarianism, even with its capitalist stripe.

"You are?"

"I am," Monica said solemnly.

He pushed back from her so he could see her better.

"This is *jolly* good news," he said.

"It doesn't mean I'll marry you, though. At least not right away."

Reggie rubbed his hands together. "Not right away is good. Not right away is fine. Gives me something to focus on, yes? Something to work toward."

"Be true to yourself," Monica said. "Out with the down Reggie, in with the happy Reggie. Not bullshit happy, not talk-yourself-into-it happy. The Reggie I know wouldn't let a measly thing like a new world power get the better of him.

"Count my blessings happy," Reggie interrupted. "It could have been worse, right? I could have lost you forever. I could have been kicked off the job. I could be in the dole line back in Melbourne right at the time everyone is dying."

"Now I need a favor," said Monica.

"Anything, luv."

"It has to do with the airport, with Cathay Pacific Airlines."

He narrowed his eyes. "You're traveling."

"Don't worry. I'm not going anywhere, at least without you."

"You should at least have a plan. The plague is raging. Have you seen today's news?"

"I was late getting up."

"You remember the North Korean submarine that ran aground in 1994."

She shook her head. "I was in school back then, too busy studying to follow the news."

"Pyongyang sent a sub full of commandos south to Kangnung that year. They were supposed to reconnoiter a power plant, an airport, maybe take out some politicians. Sub got stuck on a reef, crew abandoned ship, half of 'em killed each other before the

South Koreans even found 'em. You think Arab terrorists are bad? You think Afghanis are tough? They've got nothing on the Koreans."

"What does this have to do with the plague, Reggie?"

"They're at it again, that's all. North Korea's got nothing to lose. They're blaming Seoul for the disease, and they've sent out another fleet of subs to guard their shores. Seoul isn't taking kindly to anything having to do with submarines. Pretty soon, the madness will start here. Just watch. Taiwan versus Beijing is only a few days off."

Monica noticed his hands trembling. This was not a man who trembled, not even when drunk. She wondered if he was nervous seeing her, or whether he was simply terrified of the plague.

"You're really worried about this, aren't you?"

"You asking me if the end of my world concerns me? I guess the answer would be yes, even if it's a world without Monica."

"You've stopped drinking," she said, suddenly comprehending his twitches.

He shifted his shoulders in his brown seersucker jacket. "Even before you said what you said today. I did it for me. I don't want the feeling anymore, that feeling at night when I'm alone and the whole world goes black but I have too much crazy energy to turn away from it, can't even go to sleep and dream. I don't want that anymore. I want peace, and I want it with you."

She gave him a good kiss then, a real kiss, disappearing into the smell of him, his arms and his lips. She realized it would be good to spend whatever time was left with this strong man who loved her.

"I'm proud of you," she said.

"You make me want to beat that damned plague," he said when they parted. "Beat it so we can have the dream, you know, after all this. We're still young, luv. We could really have it. Now what is it you need with Cathay?"

"The passenger manifest," she said.

He frowned. "Now that's an odd one. Could be a problem, too. It's a document for the national authorities, as a rule. What do you want with it?"

"We're looking for somebody."

"We?"

"Dalton Day is looking for somebody, and I'm trying to help him. It could be important, Reggie, and if it isn't, well it's still my job to keep him happy while he's in Asia."

"Who is it he's looking for?"

"He saw someone on the plane he thought might have something to do with the plague?"

"Something to do with it how? Terrorism? You better have him talk to me, then, or go to the authorities."

"It's not like that," Monica hesitated. "It's complicated."

"Give me a try."

"Dalton saw a man who had certain martial powers. Sometimes those powers can be used to heal."

"He's trying to save himself, is he?"

"He's hoping to do more than that. Look, Reggie, I know it's a strange request and I know this is a bad time, but there's a lot more behind this than you know. Will you trust me on it, just this once? Just do it because I asked you to and because you love me?"

"The love card," he said.

"I'm playing it," she smiled.

"I'll see what I can do."

42

When researchers at the Pasteur Institute received Henri Eonnet's first e-mail message, they began a systematic assessment of his hypothesis. They knew apoptosis could be initiated either through the withdrawal of positive chemicals needed for continued cellular survival, or through the presence of negative substances that gave the cell the message that it was damaged beyond repair. They searched for the negative substances first, tumor necrosis factor, lymphotoxin, and Fas ligand, which bound to the cell surface. When they did not find them, they stopped taking Eonnet's theory seriously. Withdrawing positive signals was not something a pathologic invader could do. Such signals were generated by the body itself, and were not the waste products of an invader's metabolism.

Eonnet continued to insist there *was* no invader, and demanded the labs look for markers of *internally generated* cell death, markers such as Bcl-2 and Apaf-1. The longer he stuck to the notion of a genetic source for the apoptosis–something that told the body to take away the positive cell messages and begin killing its own organ systems–the more he alienated his co-workers abroad. By e-mail, Eonnet finally came out and said he thought human beings were killing themselves as a result of some genetic programming, some doomsday switch.

The proposition had an immediate and galvanizing effect. A section director at the Institute wrote back, telling Eonnet he should be ashamed of himself for advancing wild theories at such a sensitive time. Staunch, long-time supporters abandoned him, clucking about how poor Henri must have snapped in the dead zone that was Jakarta.

The ridicule hurt Eonnet deeply. "It's as if this damned plague attacks the rational brain!" He ranted. "It usurps clear thinking!"

All the same, he had a hard time proving his point. His mobile virology lab was good for running hot PCRs and other standard virologic tests, but useless for sophisticated genetic testing. As a result, he was nowhere close to finishing analyzing Leili's tissue samples.

Leili did more than donate the fluid from her joint capsules. She fed Eonnet, consoled him, listened to his ranting, and ultimately came to believe in him. While he took a steamy hot shower, she went out to the empty half-dark hospital hallway, and performed the exercises she had learned from Zetian.

Eonnet whooped triumphantly when his testing found Leili's interleukin levels unnaturally high and plague victim's levels disastrously low. This was it! Positive signals *were* being withdrawn! It *had* to be genetic. Genes were the only controllers of such systems. The only question now was what was activating the gene that controlled the system.

He sent his results over the Internet in a massive mailing, exhorting scientists to look into that activator, and a genetic reason for the body to start killing its own cells. He knew no invading organism had been identified, no bacteria or virus at all, and that his results were therefore all the more compelling.

In his triumph, he was able to sit back and relax a bit, and when he did, he found his knees had become painful. He knew at once what the pain meant.

"It has me," he told Leili.

"You're sure?"

"I'm sorry," she whispered, biting her lip until it bled so she did not decompensate in front of him, wishing she had more and better to say than that, but finding herself drained beyond comprehension.

Eonnet was as compassionate and empathetic as he was diligent and curious, but the one mystery he had never been able to unravel was the mystery of death–more specifically, what it felt like to die from one of the diseases he studied. All that had now changed. His primary goal was to finish his research before he died, and he went at it with a vengeance. Even as his joints came apart he tested for levels of the chemicals that told cells to keep on living, growth factors in nerves, and interleukin-2 in white blood cells.

"Does this mean you were wrong to take off the suit?"

"Taking off the suit was fine," he said. "Don't worry, don't feel guilty. There is no bug, but there is a switch, and I have been switched off. The question remains why *you* have not."

Now that it had him, the plague surged forward with breathtaking rapidity. He felt as if he were going to explode. His breathing was labored, his hips ached as if a machete was slicing them, and his skin lesions burned as if in an acid wash. All the same, there was a certain satisfaction in the experience for him, as if it made his life's purpose complete.

"Is there anything I can do for you?" Leili asked. "Some way I can help?"

"Take me to the hospital president's office. He has paintings there, and a sound system. I saw them when I first arrived. I want to listen to good music one last time. I'd also like to gaze at beautiful art, so I'll remember it when I'm dead."

He was too weak to walk the long dark halls, so she helped him into a wheelchair. There were no corpses in the stinking wards they went through, but there were rancid bedpans and disconnected machines, tubes of congealing blood lying broken on the floor, and vases of dried flowers sitting by empty beds in empty rooms. Night was falling, and moonlight was beginning to make windowsills glow. Due to the lack of power, she couldn't take him down in an elevator, so when they reached the stairwell she put him over her shoulder and carried him down.

Eonnet was amazed by how strong she was, but even more startled by what had happened to Jakarta in the few, short days since he arrived. Because he had been so keen on his research, he had not so much as glanced outside, and thus had not realized the city was no longer conducive to human life. The streets–generally malodorous because the sewers often ran over–had become totally fetid in the absence of public works, and he saw shattered window glass everywhere. Firefights between the military and a public convinced their officials were withholding a cure had left victims strewn across the streets.

"This is too much," he said, covering his eyes. "It is the horror that faith in only science brings."

Leili carried him to the president's office. The door was unlocked, but the place was untouched, a veritable Eden of wood paneling, and carpet. A lamp burned on the desk.

"How typical," said Leili. "A generator for the man in charge while the rest of the hospital is dark."

Eonnet fell face down on the dark Berber carpet. The fuzziness of it was heaven to him. He had not felt anything soft in so long, and his fingers reached out to rub the fabric. "Music," he pleaded. "Turn on some music."

The stereo on the credenza behind the desk was an old British audiophile system set up for the president's extensive collection of LPs. Leili was unfamiliar with the needs of a tonearm and the delicacy of a fine needle, and there was a crunch and a howl as the final choice of the outgoing executive came over the speakers.

Eonnet adored Anton Dvorak's *New World Symphony*. He loved the images it summoned of America as a vast and undiscovered country, a place of tall pines and hooting Indians, raging rivers, deep chasms, and exotic wildlife. His imagination imbued the carpet fibers against his cheek with the vibrant colors of high desert clay, a bit of shale, browns and reds interwoven as they might have been in New Mexico, or Utah. As he imagined how the Czech composer must have been awed by his first visit to New York–a place the Frenchman himself had never visited and now never would–the melody transformed the steel legs of the file cabinet before him into great skyscrapers.

When he wept, Leili wept with him, holding him tenderly and trapping his legs with her own in an effort to quell the awful spasms overtaking his body. The symphony was loud enough to shake the crystal reproduction of the Rolls Royce Flying Lady on the desk, causing it to tremble as if it might take wing.

"I know I'm a stranger," Eonnet whispered, "but do you think you could love me before I go?"

Carefully, Leili undressed. Eonnet struggled to rise and kiss her, but failed because his abdominal muscles were melting. She wrapped her arms around the back of his head, and brought his mouth up to her breasts.

Knowing she was a miracle, he suckled in hope of a cure.

None came.

43

The telephone rang just as Dalton was finishing his morning round of *qigong*.

"It's Annabelle."

"You're up early," said Dalton, taking the hotel towel from around his waist and pulling on a shirt.

"The National Guard is all over New York, Dalton."

"I saw that on television."

"Why didn't you call?"

"I tried your home. You didn't answer."

"I slept in the office last night because of the soldiers."

"Are you practicing your *qigong*?"

"At a time like this? Are you crazy?"

"It's more important now than ever. You're under stress, there's a plague out there. You need to do everything possible to bolster your immune system."

"I tried meditating, but my mind's a tornado."

"Not good to force it, but remember, meditation does for the mind what *qigong* does for the body. We always need our practice most when we least want to do it. Do the Eight Pieces of Brocade set I taught you, just that simple warm-up routine. It will keep your circulation going."

"You're not afraid?"

"I'm scared shitless. It just doesn't make me feel any better to panic."

"This isn't the way I imagined the world would end. I had all kinds of ambitions and dreams."

"We get attached to our dreams," Dalton said. "It's hard to let them go."

"You could be reassuring, boss. You could tell me everything's going to be all right."

"I've never lied to you," Dalton said, leafing idly through the room service menu.

"So you don't think it's going to be all right."

"I'm staying busy with things here. It helps me avoid despair."

"What could be keeping you busy? The girl, right? Tell me it's not the girl."

"This demeans you, Annabelle."

"So I'm demeaned. At least I'm not dead yet, and you might notice I haven't bugged you about coming home."

"You're taking pharmaceuticals, aren't you?"

"Just a little Valium, so I go out in comfort."

Dalton's finger froze on a listing for buckwheat pancakes. "Stop taking the pills. The one thing you don't want is to die in a fog. You have to be clear, you hear me? When you come to the bardo, you have to know whether to turn right or left."

"The bardo?"

"The place between worlds, the life between lives."

"You never told me about any bardo."

"Please stop."

"Now? Did you catch the President's State of the World address? He's sending the Pacific Fleet to cordon off Indonesia."

"It's not going to help," Dalton sighed. "And it doesn't have anything to do with your habit."

"I'm sure there's pressure on him to act, to look as if he's still in charge, like America is doing something. They should be developing a vaccine, that's what they should be doing. Forget the fleet. Come to think of it, I don't think a vaccine will work. We've been a cancer on the planet for a hundred years now, poisoning the place. Nature tried to kill us off with strokes and heart attacks, cancer and AIDS, but we keep coming up with cures, making more babies, dumping radioactive waste, polluting the rivers, killing the seas, choking the air, killing off four species an hour. She's finally had enough. She's tripped the doomsday switch."

Dalton decided on breakfast, then noticed he was running out of clean clothes. He donned a yellow oxford and a pair of designer blue jeans. "Where did you hear that?" he asked.

"What, the doomsday switch? Environmentalists have been quoting it for a week now, and I think it makes perfect sense. Are you coming home?"

Dalton switched on the television set. The news showed fundamentalist Christian groups preaching Armageddon in Texas, orthodox Jews praying *en masse* in Jerusalem, and the outlawed Falun Gong marching in Beijing.

"All flights are canceled," he told Annabelle. "I'm stuck here until this thing blows over."

"I knew that would happen. I begged you to come back."

"I'll be just as safe here," Dalton said.

"It's not about you, mister, it's about me."

"I'll be there as soon as I can. In the meantime, please stop the Valium, and don't work alone. Don't stay home alone either. Be with a friend."

"I've been working too much to have a friend, isn't that strange? And you know what else? I thought the friend might be you. I actually thought that might happen, stupid me."

"I'm sorry, I didn't…."

"You didn't know, huh? Because I've been too pushy? So all about business? You couldn't see through that? There goes another dream I'm attached to that I'm going to have to give up, because right now CNN is talking about an outbreak in China."

"I don't see it."

"State controlled television, remember?"

"We can talk about things when I get back. Tell me about New York."

"Even with the soldiers on the street, it's like a blackout or a blizzard here, but a hundred times worse. The mayor closed all the restaurants, and grocery stores are out of everything. I thought only cops and criminals had guns in New York, but suddenly everyone is armed. The lady who cleans your office came in here with some kind of huge revolver. Where do these people find weapons?"

"Go home, Anabelle," he said.

"Don't make me leave, Dalton. At least here I can work on the books."

Dalton pulled the curtains open. Low clouds hung over the city, and he saw a fire on top of a mountain in the distance.

"Listen. If things don't work out, I mean if bad things happen,

I just want you to know how much I appreciate…."

"You're welcome for all my hard work. You're welcome for pushing you toward good things. And what I said before? Forget that. It's a bad idea to shit where you eat, and I said it in a moment of weakness. You're not my type, boss. You live too much in your head. Hey look, I've got to go."

"Stay in touch," he said.

"Sure."

44

On his way to the video arcade, Sanfeng huddled under a brick overhang to wait out a summer shower. He remembered another overhang, a bridge under which he had practiced Crocodile and Crane *qigong* back in the tumultuous Yuan Dynasty. That bridge had been a poorer choice of refuge than this one, as a powerful Mongol general had been resting not far off and witnessed his practice. Building on the previous three hundred years of incursions, defeats and invasions, the Mongols inside the nearby great wall were constructing the political and military machines they needed to conquer all of China. They were a fierce and tightly knit group, and when Sanfeng killed their leader for what he had seen, they hunted him relentlessly.

He and Zetian took refuge in Dadu–later to become Beijing–but things quickly grew hot there, and he fled to the Temple at Shaolin, where many of the monks were disciples of great masters who had taught on Wu Dang Mountains in generations past. He was comfortable masquerading as a simple cook for a time, but the political situation degraded there too, and finally the Red Brigade, a group who would later evolve into one of the Triad gangs, laid siege to the temple, and Sanfeng was trapped inside.

He stayed in the background, preparing meals and lifting spirits with his music. Nobody noticed him until one morning, when the attacking army broke through and caught him in the courtyard with nothing but his bamboo flute in his hand. The flute was a sturdy instrument, and Sanfeng used it to devastating effect in the fray. He slung it one way and then the other, coming down in fast arcs on the unprotected heads and sword hands of the marauders, driving the hard end of it into bellies, smashing knees, and deflecting arrows. He destroyed a tight, well-organized phalanx of seventy men with sheer animal ferocity and apparent disregard for his own safety. No one had any idea how little he had to fear being wounded, and his apparent courage served as a rallying point for the monks. The tide of battle turned about him, and in the aftermath–the celebrating, the beheadings, the planting of banners, and giving of speeches–Sanfeng slipped silently away and made off downriver.

Much later, he learned that the monks had honored him by persuading the emperor to confer upon him the mythical name Jin Na Luo Wang, the name, ironically, of an immortal. He also discovered they incorporated the savage movements Sanfeng made with his flute into their famous sequence for the short staff, a sequence practiced to this day by old men with canes in the parks of Taipei, Beijing, and Hong Kong.

Such clear and detailed memories were becoming more and more inaccessible to the immortal. Increasingly, he could not remember facts that just a few years ago had seemed as vivid as day: the first opponent he killed in combat–was it with a broadsword or spear?–the last time he caught a lobster with his bare hands, tasted fresh snow on his tongue, or put his nose to a fragrant flower while on a mountain walk in spring. Sanfeng had read somewhere that the average person uses no more than a small portion of his brainpower. He wondered if over the course of 3,400 years he might actually have begun to use up his mind. How else could he explain the fact that his memory was shedding details the way his long black raincoat shed water?

Dalton watched the entrance to the gaming center from the greasy spoon across the street. He had been there for hours, swallowing wet and nameless pork products, and spiking flat, tasteless rice noodles with red pepper sesame oil. The restaurant's windows fogged up in the rain, and he cleared circles on the glass with his palm so he could see out. Once, he let out a shout when an old man with the plague pressed his gruesome, smiling face against the glass and pleaded for help. Later, he saw a teenage boy convulse and fall into the gutter, but knowing there was nothing he could do, he did not go to him.

And still, perhaps because it had become the last escape, a parade of characters went in and out of the gaming center: guitar hackers, faux golfers, starship pilots, kickers, archers, oarsmen and snipers, cigarette-smoking boys, teenage girls pierced with pins and baubles, jaded, dim-eyed couples in their thirties who had nothing better to do with the night.

At two in the morning, after the noodle shop closed and he had endured countless rounds of a mindless target-shooting game called *Police Academy*, Dalton headed for the arcade exit disappointed to the point of desperation. He was about to step out into the hot rain, when without any fanfare or herald, Gao Sanfeng came through the front door.

Dalton saw his hair, and knew him at once. He felt weak in the knees, unsure of what to do despite imagining the moment at least a hundred times. Should he go right up and ask how the electric man had saved an airplane full of people from falling out of the sky? Should he say, "Look, I've written this book, and I've taught all these people, but compared to you I don't know a damned thing?" Should he say, "I figure you've got to have all the answers, like why we are here, and what we're supposed to do, and by the way, maybe you could teach me how to light up the Christmas tree at Rockefeller Center, the big one by the skating rink in New York City, just by touching it with my fingers, because from what I hear, the people of New York could use a little miracle right now."

Instead, Dalton kept quiet as the kids fell in behind Sanfeng as if he were some kind of pied piper. Sanfeng loved the children, indeed he could have afforded his own video arcade, built one right in his home or at the office, but he loved the company of youth, and he led the kids straight to *Punisher.* There was a boy at the controls, far too young to be out so late–but with Armageddon afoot, what parent would deny their child a last game? The kid struggled with the electronic Viking, tapping the soles of his oversized yellow-laced Caterpillar work boots against the pedals, in anticipation of the shocks to come. As the Viking swung his chain, the boy yielded the gloves to Sanfeng like an autumn leaf falling from a tree. Sanfeng's virtual hand grabbed the chain, and pulled the Viking forward.

"IS THAT ALL YOU'VE GOT?" the kids chorused.

As if in answer, Sanfeng's virtual palm drove the Viking's nose out the back of his head, leaving a black gory hole with teeth and splintered bones. The kids cheered. The flyweight girl in the purple uniform appeared on the screen next, and Sanfeng parried her blows easily, stepping in with a concatenation of techniques the computer was not programmed to handle.

Dalton watched in amazement. The immortal's movements were not limited to his hands, but encompassed his entire body. His ribcage heaved, his shoulders turned, his hips sank, his abdomen twisted. His kicks came from his hips, not his feet, and his punches came from his core. Finally, he threw the girl across the screen. She cartwheeled into a stone pillar–something Corinthian, occidental, and entirely out-of-place–then fell in a heap, arms and legs twitching like a beetle's.

The bearded video swordsman appeared. In a flash, Sanfeng stole his weapon and cleaved him in two with it. A fire-breathing video dragon came next. Dalton saw a little smile on Sanfeng's face. He could not have known that fighting imaginary creatures with power to shock him was all that was left for a man who had battled his way across the great expanse of China's land mass and history. Nor could Dalton have known that ever since losing his dragon-etched sword to the King of Yue, Sanfeng wanted nothing so much as to fight a real dragon, especially one that looked squat and solid the way this electronic one did.

The truth was, the dragon was Sanfeng's real reason for coming to play the game. He met it with incredibly fast hand movements. The kids stepped back. The electronic creature erupted in a fountain of green blood. Its wings stopped mid-beat, and it dropped like a stone, its eyes rolling backwards, mouth falling open, drooping yellow tongue licking air. Dalton could see that Sanfeng was sorry he had slain it so fast. He surmised Sanfeng usually stopped there, because when he stayed at the controls, the kids put out their cigarettes in attentive anticipation of the next electronic enemy.

She was a demon of some kind; that much was clear, possessing a woman's eyes and a woman's breasts, but with blue skin, a werewolf's snout, a colt's mane, equine, muscle-bound legs, hooves on her feet, and talons on her hands. Sanfeng couldn't help thinking that on some mythic level, she resembled his sister, Zetian.

"I'm so happy to see you," the virtual Zetian said, looking straight at her brother.

"And I you."

Sanfeng attacked immediately, going straight for the knees, but his attacks lacked the vigor of his previous movements, and Dalton wondered if the crazy-haired man was tiring. He could not know that the resemblance to his sister took the wind out of Sanfeng. In short order, the demon shocked Sanfeng with amperage so high a pacemaker warning appeared on the bottom of the screen. The children gasped in approval.

Punisher could stop your heart!

The fighting resumed. Again, Sanfeng was knocked back.

Give her the fire, Dalton wanted to scream.

One more kick, one long electrical buzzing sound, and Sanfeng fell away from the console, his palms smoking and his eyes glazed. He would have hit his head on the sharp edge of the tennis game behind him if he had not landed, light as a scarecrow, in Dalton Day's surprised arms.

"I'll always be stronger than you," laughed virtual Zetian. "It'll take you a thousand years to beat me."

Sanfeng worked to control his breathing. He had been injured in myriad ways over the centuries, but he had never been so roundly electrocuted. It was, despite the porcupine appearance of his hair, quite a new experience for him. He drifted out of consciousness.

Suddenly, his father's face floated before him, and Sanfeng smiled. It had been so long since his father had visited him! Years!

"The time has come. You can avoid it no longer," the blacksmith said.

"I cannot bear the idea, Father. She is my sister."

"But she is flawed, my son. And she has turned into that which I have always feared she would–and hoped she would not."

"There has to be another way," Sanfeng said.

"Then find it. But if there is not…."

"I will find it, Father."

"One more thing, my son. Don't do what you are planning to do."

"The world has changed, Father," Sanfeng answered. "There are new circumstances…."

"Circumstances change, but principles do not. Surely you have lived long enough to learn that."

"I've learned that principles evolve, Father," Sanfeng answered. "They grow as consciousness grows, as knowledge grows."

"No," the blacksmith shook his head. "Principles are what they are."

"Principles may indeed stay as they are, but their application may become irrelevant. There are cycles we can see, and larger, longer cycles we cannot. We are in the grip of something bigger than your experience, and bigger than mine, too."

The blacksmith frowned, and looked as if he had more to say, but it was Sanfeng's time to return to the material world, and he did return, feeling sad, empty, and more than a little chagrined at having been felled by a machine. His ears were ringing, and his eyesight blurred. He blinked a few times, wetting his eyeballs, licking his lips, showing small, even teeth.

"Are you all right, Master?" Dalton inquired.

"I'm fine," Sanfeng replied, struggling to his feet. "Thank you for asking."

45

Alone in her apartment, Monica Farmore remembered a quote from Albert Einstein: "The definition of insanity is doing the same thing over and over and expecting different results." Even so, she dialed her mother in Oklahoma repeatedly, only to get a recording saying her call could not be completed. After half an hour, she tried Dalton Day's room at the Hyatt. He didn't answer, so she left a message, and then did it again, and again; and again until his electronic mailbox was full. Melancholy seized her as she thought about her days back in Oklahoma, the excitement and promise of Harvard, the high hopes she had for her job with Billabong. She saw what little was left of her life spiraling toward plague, pain, and death, and she wondered fleetingly if she would be better off lighting some candles and putting some chocolate bath oil into a nice hot tub, climbing in, putting on some soothing music, and slitting her wrists. She remembered reading somewhere that the key to a successful suicide was to make longitudinal cuts, and she figured she could dull the pain by taking a handful of aspirin.

Instead, she lay numbly on the bed and watched the news, as she had been doing for days. The Chinese government news station reported Nigeria had closed its borders, and Uganda was putting people in camps. Kenya was in total chaos as blacks, blaming pharmaceutical manufacturers and chemical plant testing for the disease, tried to eliminate every white face in South Africa. India–that most densely populated of nations–was having the worst time of all. Crying out for deliverance by a bevy of Hindu gods, crowds swelled the streets of Agra, Hyderabad, Bangalore, Delhi, and Pune. International observers said the number of those trampled underfoot might possibly exceed the number of plague victims. There was a glaring absence of any mention of outbreaks in China, which Monica assumed meant they had started.

She had never been more aware of the addictive quality of the television set, of how transfixed she became by the same doom-and-gloom scenario playing out all over the world, hour-by-hour, day-by-day. She was jolted out of ennui by the sight of Denise Howard, the senator who had attended Dalton's first book signing. Howard had been appointed chairwoman of the United States Senate Plague Task Force, and her C-Span interview with a noted scientist was being broadcast live on CNN International.

The scientist's name was Dr. Gary Broten; he worked at the Centers for Disease Control in Atlanta. Monica wondered if the southern venue accounted for his jaunty, python-skin boots. The boots caught Senator Howard's attention too, and she pointed them out.

"I wanted to look stylish for the End Time," said Broten. "We're making an indelible record here. Thousands of years from now, aliens from another planet will probably watch a DVD of this chat to find out what happened to the human race."

"You really think our world is coming to an end?" the senator asked.

"Not the world. Just the people."

Monica saw he had missed a patch shaving, and it struck her as funny he'd gone to all the trouble to dress up, yet failed to notice a rough patch on his chin.

"I'm sure you know that every emergency preparedness plan this country has in place has failed."

"I've heard that, yes."

He didn't seem worried. Monica wondered if he was a religious nut, happy to be preparing for heavenly deliverance.

"And you know that the best and brightest scientists from our think tanks and facilities have given up hope of combating this plague in a timely manner?"

"I've heard that, too."

"Until yesterday, when the news came in from our colleagues in Europe, some of us were still thinking that an aggressive quarantine of the worst pockets of infection might help. Now it seems we're too late for that."

"The plague is on every continent save Antarctica," said Broten. "Quarantines won't help."

"Not even to slow it down?"

"I wouldn't say so, no."

"You received the Nobel Prize in Epidemiology last year. My committee is looking for some ideas, anything at all, no matter how wild it might sound. Do you have some to share?"

"We could freeze people in giant cryogenic tanks until scientists working in sealed underground shelters can find a cure," he said, trying his best to keep his expression sober.

"We don't have cryogenic tanks, do we?" Senator Howard asked.

"Not as far as I know. Of course, we could destroy the ozone layer with a mass release of tropospheric Freon."

"And that would accomplish what, precisely?"

"The cosmic ultraviolet radiation might precipitate a random, lifesaving mutation."

"You mean a handful of special people might survive."

"That's the way it's going to be anyway," said Broten.

The senator looked around the interview set as if seeking advice from someone off-camera.

"Of course, we could also put healthy babies underwater in one of the Navy's super-secret deep submergence labs," Broten continued.

"I find your sarcastic attitude offensive, Doctor," said Senator Howard.

"We could shoot genetic samples of our best and brightest into space on a rocket and hope they land somewhere and flower," said Broten.

Monica surprised herself with a laugh. She liked the guy's brand of black humor.

"Do you have any notion at all as to how to destroy the pathogen?" the senator asked.

"There is no pathogen."

"I've heard that nonsense, and I refuse to believe it."

"Forgive me for saying so, Senator, but you're not a scientist. What do you know about the Gaia Hypothesis?"

"The Earth is the organism, and humanity is a cancer run amok? The reports I've read say that's nonsense."

"Hardly," Broten countered. "It's based on the concept of carrying capacity, something every biologist understands. Put too many goldfish in a pond, they die off. Put too many rats in a cage, they develop tumors, kill each other, or become homosexual."

"That's not very politically correct."

The scientist rolled his eyes. "You're worried about political correctness now? I'm trying to tell you that every ecosystem, from the one on the head of a pin to the one that includes Heaven and Earth, has a built-in, shockproof, failsafe device. It's in our genetic material. It's in the genetic material of worms and birds and bromeliads and elk. To save the whole thing, genes can be switched on or off to preserve a species or eradicate it. It's what you might call a doomsday switch."

Senator Howard frowned. "I object to that phrase. I cannot imagine God would allow such a thing."

"God, or no God, it's one hell of a system."

"You sound as if you admire it."

"If it saves the whole rest of the planet, then maybe I do."

"If it's a switch, tell me what triggers it."

Broten leaned forward. Monica thought he looked interested in the conversation for the first time. "It could be an environmental stimulus. We don't know. We *do* know it works through apoptosis."

"Programmed cell death: the Frenchman's discovery."

"Programmed cell death," Monica repeated. She sat up on her bed.

Broten shook his head. "Henri Eonnet didn't discover apoptosis, but he was the first to assess its occurrence. He's a very senior man, very qualified. All of us at CDC were searching for a pathogen. That was reasonable, because there are tumors, and even viruses, that control apoptosis. But they do it by turning cell death off so the body can't kill them, not by turning it on. No bug would turn on a mechanism that resulted in its own death. Eonnet saw that before any of us."

"He's dead," said Senator Howard.

"I hadn't heard, but he was in Jakarta, so I'm hardly surprised. Anyway, we've isolated the doomsday gene now, the switch, if you'll permit me the expression...."

Monica watched the senator sit up in her chair. "I don't permit it."

Dr. Broten smiled a forbearing smile. "Are you familiar with the phrase ontogeny recapitulates phylogeny?"

"No."

"Perhaps you'll permit me to explain *that.* Ontogeny refers to an individual animal's development from a simpler to a more complex level. Phylogeny, by contrast, refers to the evolutionary path of a given species, or group of species. Now, where we see the relationship between these two notions most clearly is in embryology. As an embryo develops–and forgive me if you already know this, Senator, but our viewers may not–it goes through the same evolutionary phases as did the species to which it belongs."

Senator Howard leaned forward impatiently. "You're saying that soon after conception we look like a fish, then later like a monkey."

Broten nodded enthusiastically. "Exactly. And an amphibian and a reptile and all the other stages in between."

"What does this have to do with a doomsday switch?" the senator asked.

"How do you suppose we get from a flipper, for example, to a hand with fingers on it? That question intrigued embryologists for decades, until finally, some time ago, researchers discovered that we don't exactly grow fingers. Instead, the fingers are present inside the flipper, and the skin between between the fingers–the webbing if you will–disappears. The mechanism of that disappearance entails the killing of the skin cells in the web. In essence, the body kills cells in order to shape itself. That killing, that programmed cell death, is embedded in our DNA. Not only that, but the development of an embryo, a human fetus, for instance, follows the proscribed path with absolute certainty."

"Nothing is absolutely certain," said the senator.

"This is, because there is a backup gene to start this cell death, this cell suicide, and if you turn *that* one off, there's another. There may well be another one behind that, and another, and another."

"You're saying cell death is a natural phenomenon."

"Thank you, yes. And we don't fully understand how it all works, because ninety-five percent of our genetic material is still a mystery."

"But we've mapped the genetic code."

"Mapping and understanding are two different things. What we're looking for may not be on the map."

"Not on the map," she repeated.

"No, and we don't have time to draw another one. Apoptosis is incredibly quick."

"You're saying what is happening to our species is a natural phenomenon?"

"Yes, Senator. That is what I'm saying. And it fits the data, the randomness with which it pops up globally, the rapidity of action, and frankly the way it spares the planet. It's not like a tsunami or some other natural disaster; indeed, it's not like anything we've faced before. There is no enemy to shake our fist at, no tornado fast approaching, no giant storm or wave. The enemy is inside us–in a very real sense the enemy *is* us–and when we are gone, the earth will be fine without us. New species will evolve, new niches will be filled, and if anything of humanity survives, it will become something entirely new and, we hope, something entirely better."

Monica began to cry. Senator Howard stood up from her chair as if she had someplace to go, and then abruptly sat back down. The camera on her shifted a moment, then stabilized. Monica wondered if one of the cameramen had walked out.

"Why the smile?" the senator asked. "Can you at least tell me that, Doctor? Why is everyone dying with this horrific grin on their face?"

"I'd say it's just a nasty coincidence. The collagen in ligaments and tendons are the first to go, and that decline is most visible on the face. The actual cause of death is the disintegration of the heart valves and the suspensory ligament of the diaphragm. The circulation fails, or breathing does."

Monica ran her hands over her cheeks. She wondered what collagen felt like when it turned to Jell-O. She wondered what it felt like to be terrified, but unable to stop smiling. Once, she and

Reggie Pritt had laughed about his erection when it would not subside. An hour later, with him wincing and making jokes about the God Priapus, son of Dionysus and Aphrodite, they went to the emergency room. She felt a sudden, desperate desire to see the Australian.

"Everyone agrees you're the best molecular biologist at CDC," the senator said. "This is your last chance, Doctor. Tell me what we can do to save our country."

Broten did not want to tell her that in addition to being a molecular biologist he was also a veterinarian. He definitely did not want to tell her that for him, the sorriest aspects of seeing the human race come to a close was that he would never be able to bring to profitable fruition his dream of creating the ultimate food for his beloved Persian cats, Sadie and Rachel.

"People watching us right now need to know this is not anyone's fault. Unlike violent behavior, which we could curtail, there isn't anything anyone can do about this doomsday switch. I said the enemy is us, but I didn't mean any one of us personally. At our final hour, the best we can do is abandon our separate egos and take as broad and loving and philosophical view as possible, a view that embraces the marvel of *life*, not the marvel of man."

"You don't have children, do you?" Senator Howard regarded him tiredly.

"Children? No. I have cats," he said.

Monica switched channels. A Chinese news station showed the United States Public Health Service Metropolitan Medical Strike Team assisting in the orderly evacuation of downtown Chicago. Commentators talked about technical assistance from the Department of Energy, and of mobilization procedures, medical treatment areas, decontamination, and assigned localities. There was talk of incident commanders, of quarantines, and of the Federal Emergency Management Agency.

A knock at the door interrupted her reverie.

"Monica, it's Reggie."

She ran to the door in excitement and relief. He made a beeline for the couch and plopped down, disheveled and exhausted.

"You've been watching the news. You know what's going on. We're covering it up as best we can, but the plague has arrived. They put up a cordon around a whole town in the New Territories, and soldiers surround every hospital in the city. They're taking people away, Monica. You're not hearing about it, but they are."

"Taking people away? What does that mean?"

"What do you think? Interest of national security and all that. They're lining them up by trenches, luv. It's the old days all over again. Look, here's that list you asked for. A little late, I expect, but I went through hell to get it."

She tore it open and started reading. "There are only sixteen people in first class. Seven of the passengers are women. That leaves nine."

"Hasn't Mr. Day gone back to America yet? Oh. Right. He can't leave. The airports are closed. What's it about then, Dalton's fascination with this fellow?"

"He saw him perform a miracle."

"Miracles are a bit of a stretch for me right now luv. What kind of miracle was it?"

"Something about *gongfu*."

Reggie rolled his eyes. "All this for a *gongfu* lesson?"

Monica went back to the list. "Three Chinese names."

"Check the addresses. There might be a clue there."

"Not that I see."

She got up and went to the computer. She entered the first name into the search engine and came up with a picture of the national sales manager for a shoe company based in Minneapolis. A headshot of a corpulent man came up. Monica shook her head. No. That's not him.

The second name brought up a list of Internet hits, all connected to business. Monica was about to continue the search when the name Crocodile & Crane caught her eye.

"That's the company that bought Billabong," she said.

"Pardon?"

"Crocodile and Crane. That's the company that bought Billabong Books."

She went deeper, clicking and scanning on myriad articles.

"The man's an executive," she said. "A principle."

Reggie leaned in, pointed a finger. "He's a principle all right. He's the company's president."

There, next to a brief bio, was a small black-and-white photo of Gao Sanfeng. Monica gasped.

"That's him!"

46

After Eonnet died, Leili found food in the hospital cafeteria and returned to her nursing station. She was unwilling to face the carnage she and Eonnet saw out the front door. Alone, she could nurse the pain of losing Lombo without worrying about donning a game face, remaining in the cocoon she had created, stinking and dim as it had become. She continued her e-mail correspondence with the Pasteur Institute, although she made clear how little she believed in scientists and their theories. When she sent news of Eonnet's passing, the director himself wrote to her.

"You're incredibly important to us. I am beyond sorry to have to tell you that the population of Jakarta is no more. You are the only survivor in the city, and we cannot help but think, as Dr. Eonnet did–may he sleep on the bosom of God–that you are critically important to our investigation."

"There simply must be others."

"Rumors, nothing more," his Internet message came back. "We are coming for you, and will bring you back to the Institute. Please believe me when I say we desperately need your cooperation."

"I've given all the tissue samples I care to give. I will not be your prisoner."

"Prisoner? Of course not. You will be our honored guest."

Leili could almost hear the desperation in the director's voice. "Call me," she said, giving her phone number.

He called at once.

"Dr. Eonnet was right," she said. "You should have listened to him."

"His notion of a doomsday switch doesn't help us."

"But what if it's correct?"

"We have not yet discovered the mechanism of transmission, but we do know that once the disease strikes a community it spares no one. You are the sole survivor."

"Nonsense. There are plenty of people left alive."

"On the planet, yes; inside an affected community, no. Even Dr. Eonnet's theory, the notion of a switch, would have you dead along with everyone else. Tell me, is there something special about your diet, your family tree, anything we could start working on while we wait for you to get here?"

Leili had been keeping the *qigong* to herself, had not mentioned it to Eonnet, had not allowed herself to actually believe it was the critical factor. Now, faced with news of the extinction of her city, she admitted to herself there could be no other explanation.

"I exercise," she said.

"Exercise is important," the director replied.

"Don't patronize me. This is a special Chinese program."

"Tell me about it, please."

Leili knew he was trying to keep her on the phone, afraid she might bolt at the last minute. She had watched enough television to know a team was already on the way, and indeed when she went to the end of the hall and looked through the window, she saw a van pull up front and two men in yellow suits emerge.

"You work fast," she said. "Your men are here."

"The stakes are high. Tell me about the exercises."

"Where will you take me?"

"To the World Health Organization operations center in Hong Kong."

"Not France?"

"We have everything there that we have here, and time is of the essence."

It took her some time to remove the barricades from the hospital's front door, even though the director's men were working at the same task from the outside. When the task was done, she stepped outside. The sun was shining brilliantly, but the stench of corpses nearly knocked her over. The men grabbed her at once.

"Let me go," she said.

Through their visors, she could see signs that they were struggling to hold her. She found that curious, and gave an experimental tug. One of the men fell down. The other one drew a gun from the flap pocket of his suit.

"It's no use resisting," he panted. "We're taking you to the airfield."

She relaxed and let them put her in a Humvee marked with a red cross. One man drove, the other kept his pistol trained on her.

"Red Cross workers with guns," she said.

"We're not Red Cross," said the driver.

"The Red Cross workers are all dead," the guard said. "Maybe they wouldn't be if they'd had guns."

The field was private, far from the commercial airport. For once, Leili appreciated the odor of jet fuel, because it blanketed the smell of decaying bodies. The plane, a gleaming corporate jet, bore no insignia. A lone soldier standing by a chain link fence waved them through. The men followed Leili carefully up the steps into the cabin. She sank into a plush leather chair and ran her hand over the polished burl trim decorating the plane. She was impressed. She had taken two business trips with Jou Yuen to Hong Kong, but they had flown commercial, he in first class, she back in coach.

"If you know who I am and why you were sent for me, you know I'm far too valuable to shoot," she said. "Why don't you put that gun away?"

The guards smiled politely, but kept the guns trained on her until the co-pilot retracted the stairway and the aircraft was in motion. Once in the air, they relaxed, went to the back of the plane, and brought her drinks and snacks. Leili had ginger ale, her first cold drink since the crisis began. Savoring the taste, she closed her eyes and did an inventory of her body, a process she adopted after Zetian's exercises began to take hold. Familiar with the concept of the CAT scan and the MRI, she started with her head, and moved down in cross-section, checking her inner ears, her sinuses, her hyoid bones, her throat, lungs, breasts–she always spent extra time looking for suspicious lumps there–then dipped below her diaphragm into her abdominal cavity, her viscera, kidneys, and liver. She checked her arms and hands, and then she scanned lower, checking the muscles and bones of her hips and legs, making sure all her joints were clean and clear and free of obstructions.

It was after sundown when the plane landed with a hard thump, and the guards, who had been playing cards, came to attention. Leili saw they were using a private field, and as a consequence of their official status, the customs and immigration process was perfunctory. The guards escorted Leili to a waiting car, and together they zoomed off in the direction of Hong Kong Central.

"Where's the lab?" Leili asked.

"The driver knows," a guard told her. "I haven't been told."

Leili was struck by how quiet the city seemed compared to the last time she had been there. The skyline was still beautiful, and neon light still flooded the streets, but while the streets were still busy by western standards, it was a different sort of busy; most folks moved slowly, almost aimlessly, as if acutely aware of the futility of their lives; another, smaller group seemed industrious to the extreme, as if they had much to do before the end, or sensed how very insignificant their lives had suddenly become.

Leili watched the street signs zip by, looking desperately for one she recognized. During her previous trips, she had been in a hired car with Jou Yuen and had relied on the driver for bearings. To her dismay, nothing seemed familiar.

"Why the frown?" the guard nearest her asked. "From what I hear, you're in Hong Kong to save the world."

"If Dr. Eonnet couldn't do it, nobody can," she answered.

"Never heard of him," said the guard.

They passed a tall black building with the logo of a crocodile and a crane emblazoned on the cornerstone. Leili gasped in recognition.

"Now don't panic. Nobody's going to hurt you," the guard said, his automatic pistol at the ready in his lap.

Leili reached over and grabbed the gun, moving so quickly, she surprised herself. She leaned forward and put the barrel against the driver's head. "Stop the car," she said.

As the driver slowed, the second guard came forward with a sap, taking aim at her cheek. It seemed to her as if he was moving in slow motion. She turned away from the blow, rolling her shoulder and following his momentum so his arm went over the back of the driver's seat. When she yanked down on his hand, she felt his shoulder come out of its socket. The guard screamed, and the driver brought the car screeching to the curb.

Dropping the gun onto the floor of the car, Leili grabbed her purse, leapt out, and ran. The uninjured guard jumped out after her. Leili used to enjoy jogging, but the uneven hours of her job with Jou Yuen were hell on her exercise routine, and since the day Lombo fell ill she hadn't done more than walk up and down a flight of stairs at the hospital. Her life had been too busy to indulge in aerobic exercise of late–lethargic sex with Jou Yuen didn't count, nor did Zetian's *qigong*, which was mostly about breathing and twisting–and she was delighted to find that her heart rate barely budged. Dodging crowds, she quickly left her pursuer behind.

She ducked into a doorway to get her bearings, too rushed to notice the small figure huddling there. It was a man, bent in half like a monkey, holding onto a walking stick and beating it into the stoop in a staccato rhythm. The overpowering odor of fish was with him, but also fainter traces of urine and feces familiar to her from the hospital. When he looked up at her, she saw the beginning of the Banpo Smile on his face.

"Please," he said. "Help me."

His fever was so strong she felt it in her palm before she actually touched his forehead.

"It won't last long," she said. "There's nothing I can do."

"I have the tall power," he muttered.

"I don't know what that means."

"And I can sing like a bird. Everyone used to ask me for that."

"Your singing?" Leili asked gently.

"The tall power. All my children came out tall. Women want that these days. Did you know there is a Chinese basketball player? Do you know the money they make in America playing that jumping game; the shoes they wear?"

The man's speech was slurred by the deformation of his lips and the collapse of his collagen.

"I don't know the game," said Leili.

"How women want me," he said.

Leili smelled his smell and saw his rotting yellow teeth and the way his hands were clasping and unclasping. She steeled herself and drew him close. "I know," she said.

She felt the tremors come to him. His words became more and more incomprehensible. "They took us all away," he said.

"Who took you?"

"The police. They come in the night and take us off the street. If we smile they take us, and if we don't smile they take us. They put us all away in a van, but I jumped out."

Pressed against her he bared his leg, showing her a long, angry red scrape where he had hit the ground.

"It doesn't matter," she said.

The shaking grew stronger and the smile broadened. Leili instinctively understood the old man had been holding off the plague because he didn't want to die alone, holding it off as it built inside him, pressured him, heated him, twisted and tortured him. He held it to his breaking point, and his breaking point had come. He tried to sing as he died, fighting it to the end, his words mere gasps and whistles.

They stayed clasped like that in the doorway, while outside the hustle and bustle of Hong Kong continued. They were like a mop and a broom thrust together, Leili the mop because of her rich hair and because she had moisture in her while the man, now dead, was dry. After a time, feeling numb, she disentangled herself and let him down slowly onto the stoop. He weighed nothing, but she did not marvel at his lightness; she had seen so much of it lately.

She went another block, then ducked into another stoop, trying to stay out of sight in case her pursuers regrouped. It was the entrance to a dress shop, the kind of outlet savvy ladies with money frequented, not a brand-name boutique on the boulevard, but a vendor of fine cloths with a good seamstress on tap. While Leili smelled remarkably fresh for someone who had, within the previous twenty-four hours, made love on a dirty carpet, flown across the ocean at gunpoint and then been stuffed into a car, she was hardly ready for an emporium devoted to image creation. A cluster of high-class customers and two salesgirls froze at the sight of her. Leili touched her hair self-consciously. She could not remember the last time she had washed and conditioned it, and blown it dry.

"Can I help you?" the salesgirl nearest the door asked timidly.

"You're shopping," Leili said, looking past the salesgirl at the customers. "Everyone in Hong Kong is about to die, and here you are worrying about dresses."

The self-righteous looks she received told her she was preaching to deaf ears. She looked up and down the alley, then left again, suddenly conscious that she was penniless and filthy in a city that glorified money and style. She turned and left and made her way back to the Crocodile & Crane building. The security guard stopped her at the elevators.

"I'm here to see Madame Gao," she said.

The guard gave her a dubious look.

"From the Jakarta office," Leili went on. "Jou Yuen sent me."

The security guard picked up the phone and spoke into it. "She's not in the office," he said, putting the receiver down.

"Then I'll wait," said Leili, suddenly very tired.

"The man you mentioned?"

"Jou Yuen?"

"The girl upstairs says he's dead. She says everyone in Indonesia is dead. She thinks you're lying."

"I'm not lying, but I am tired."

"They'll skin me alive if I send you upstairs."

"I don't usually look like this," Leili said. "It's the times. The dying."

"Why do you want to see Madame Gao?"

"I have an important message for her. Won't you please help me?"

When Leili rubbed her eyes and stretched, the guard suddenly saw how beautiful she was.

"Rest in the security office," he said. "There's a cot in there. I'll let you know when Madame arrives."

47

Dalton watched the outlines of Hoklo fishing boats pass in a foggy blur as Sanfeng's speedboat blazed through the waves. "Looks like weather's coming in," he said.

Sanfeng took the harmonica from his mouth and gazed at it admiringly. "A great invention, this little instrument. So many keys in such a compact package."

"Where are we going?"

"You'll find out soon enough."

At one point, Sanfeng thought he heard the sound of a helicopter, and doused the lights on the boat. They rocked quietly in the dark, but did not hear it again. Dalton did not dare ask who they might be hiding from or why. Instead, he closed his eyes, imagining he was asleep in his bed at the Hyatt, and dreaming. He opened them when the sea spray hit him in the face. He had been up all night, and the mock battle at the Diamond Gaming Center was a blur. He was keyed-up and hungry, but felt a warm and passive contentment that might have been Sanfeng's energy and might have been his own martial ambitions teetering on the edge of fulfillment.

"So. Where did you learn your *gongfu*?" he asked the immortal.

"Here and there." Sanfeng smiled faintly.

"Tell me about the airplane. How did you save us from crashing? Since when do *qi* emissions affect avionics? That is what you were doing, right? Emitting *qi*?"

"I blocked your memory. How did you unblock it?"

"With meditation."

"Where did you learn such meditation?"

"From a teacher named D.D. Mo in New York Chinatown."

"I see. And was this Mo your only teacher?"

"Henry Huang taught me in the Bronx for years. He was one of Mao Zedong's bodyguards."

"My sister knew Mao very well. He was a coarse man, and a

thug; a connection to him is not a high recommendation. What was teacher Huang's style?"

"*Xingyiquan.*"

"Aha. So that's where you get your alignment. I noticed your posture when you were speaking at Harbor Plastics."

"You were there?"

"And at End Zone Illumination. They are my companies. I own Billabong Books, too."

"Was it you who ordered the foreign rights for my book?"

Sanfeng nodded.

"Do you drive an Aston Martin?"

"An extravagance," Sanfeng allowed. "There are things about Hong Kong that are contagious. I draw less attention driving such a car than I would if I listened to my urges in the direction of simplicity. Of course, I continue to believe the world would be better off without cars altogether. I remember when the air was free of exhaust and the sound of engines and horns. People these days don't know what it is to hear the sounds of the land, to hear wind in trees or their own heartbeat in the quiet of morning."

"You remember a time before cars?"

"China came late to the automotive age."

They drew near land, and as they did the water roughened, and the first sun of morning illuminated Sanfeng's hair in an imitation of the pines on the steep cliffs ahead. The sight reminded Dalton of the lightshow in the cockpit over the Arctic.

"Tell me about the finger fire," Dalton urged.

"Finger fire?"

"What you did on the airplane."

"Ah. The airplane lost its balance. I returned it."

"That it?"

"Yes."

"That's all you have to say?"

Sanfeng turned to him and smiled. "For right now, yes."

"Do any of your students know how to project power that way?"

"I haven't had any students for a long time."

"So we're not going to your school?"

"My school? I have no school."

"I was hoping you did. Why don't you teach?"

"Family issues," Sanfeng replied. "A clash of philosophy."

The immortal maneuvered the speedboat through the sharp rocks off the beach. Kelp scratched the hull. A fish jumped out of the water and landed again with a faint crack. The tide pulled back, and when it did, the entrance to the cave showed its rocky teeth.

"What is this place?" Dalton asked.

"Kat O Chau. Now duck your head."

The immortal happened upon the island in 1539, while smuggling weapons from the mainland on a small trading ship. Fleeing a six-masted Imperial warship captained by a eunuch and propelled by five hundred men at oar, Sanfeng ducked into one of the island's sheltered coves. He saw what appeared from a distance to be a set of teeth, but which, up close, turned out to be stalactites guarding the entrance to a cave. He rowed in for a look. While exploring its depths, his ship was discovered by the Imperial lookout. In a fierce and bloody battle, the Imperial sailors confiscated his booty, butchered his men, and threw their bodies overboard.

When the warship departed, Sanfeng retrieved the remains of his crew from the fierce surf and brought them into the cave. Set to bury them there, he noticed a small shaft of sunlight, and followed it to a hole in the rock ceiling, and thence to a passageway to the headland above him. It was there he staked the gravesites, buried the dead, and marked their resting place with headstones. Years later, he built a mausoleum over the tunnel so access was disguised. A cemetery grew up around it, but the cave remained his secret hideaway, in part because it was remote and defensible, and in part because he knew his sister hated dank places and would never trouble him there.

"You knew the plague was coming, didn't you?" Dalton asked

as he stepped off the boat and onto dry ground.

"I have seen it before."

"I thought it was something new."

Sanfeng shook his head. "It is as old as man, and perhaps as old as nature."

"Do you think the world's scientists know that?"

"I think they will figure it out."

Dalton followed Sanfeng through a watertight hatchway and into the bowels of what he realized must be an extensive cave system. The greeting room was brightly lit and filled to the brim with computers and other electronic equipment. Suddenly, Dalton wondered if Sanfeng might not be an electrician rather than an engine of *qi*. Maybe he does not fly on wings of will, or operate on frequencies of magic, Dalton thought. Maybe he is more James Bond than Superman, carrying a tiny high-tech generator in his pocket for use on errant airplanes and challenging video games.

"I hadn't figured you for a technologist," he told the immortal.

"Why? Because you don't think martial arts and technology go together?"

"I don't know much," Dalton answered. "But I know that learning to do the kind of things you can do requires years of study and an inward orientation."

"No matter how deep inside you look, there is still the world out there," Sanfeng said. "And even if the world out there is just the projection of the world inside, as you say in your excellent book, the world outside remains. A fascination with the *nature of nature* ultimately leads to technology, because technology is the fruit of exploration."

"So no clash between science and religion?"

"Who said anything about religion?" Sanfeng seemed genuinely surprised by the question. "Certain skills are certain skills. They take hard work to acquire, they take practice to acquire, they take proper instruction to acquire, but they don't take belief in the supernatural nearly so much as a proper philosophy, a proper understanding of the way things work."

"You have an Internet connection here?"

"Internet, television, radio, everything. This is a communications center, a retreat. I've been coming here for a long time. The salt air corrodes the printed circuits and switches and such, so I control the environment. It's not air conditioning–the cave keeps naturally cool–so much as purification and dehumidification. The hum you hear is the fans."

"Must take a lot of power."

"This island doesn't have much in the way of a power grid," Sanfeng smiled. "There's enough power, I suppose, but it's not stable, and using so much would draw attention I don't want."

"You don't draw much attention," said Dalton. "You have no idea how hard it was to find you."

Sanfeng smiled. "I bet I do. In any case, I have my own generators. They run on wave action."

Dalton stared at him. "Wave action?"

"There's a tremendous amount of energy in the sea. The tides have the power to raise and lower floating objects, and harnessing that power to generate electricity is not so challenging as your expression would suggest. A cam-shaped buoy rolls with the passing of waves. The rolling action drives hydraulics, which run a hydroelectric generator."

"You're self-sufficient. Nobody knows you're here."

"Perhaps there is someone who knows, but if so, he is the only one, and that is almost entirely the point."

Mystic or technologist, Dalton learned Sanfeng was a Renaissance man whose eclectic interests spanned centuries and continents. The evidence was in an underground gallery full of Mondrians, Kandinskys, Pollacks, Miros, dripping-clock Dalis with their casual disregard for time, Ming Dynasty bronzes, Grecian urns, a sculpture gallery replete with statuettes of Daoist gods, primitive renderings of animals, tiny jeweled Buddhas, and last but not least, a cavern full of flutes, jaw harps, ehru, gaohu, and enough other rare stringed instruments to warrant a wing at the Glinka Music Museum in Moscow.

Leading Dalton to another chamber, Sanfeng paused.

"What is it?" Dalton asked.

"I'm not sure. We are deep underground, and there is the constant hum of the generators and air handlers, but I thought I heard an aircraft."

Hearing nothing, Dalton looked around. The chamber brimmed with weapons. There were battle axes and steel fans–their blades sharp enough to shave the light from a starry sky–and spears decorated with the remains of the animals they had killed. There was a clump of boar hair, a chip of bear pelvis, and two tiger claws. Fashioned from woods that grew as far away as Tibet, there were wooden staffs for blocking, thrusting, smashing, and parrying. Dalton's gaze lingered over one particular pole without knowing it was fashioned from the oar with which the treacherous fisherman, Ahn, had batted Sanfeng into the cold ocean 2,200 years before.

"Why do you collect all these things?" Dalton asked.

Sanfeng sighed. "I used to say it was because I like to surround myself with beauty, and to remind me to maintain a constant state of wonder at the world. I don't think that's the reason anymore. I'm aware of a unique energy in each and every object, imbued by the craftsman who made it. The vibrations are powerful, if one is sensitive enough to feel them."

Dalton pointed to the blade Sanfeng had used to dispatch the turtle on the bank of the Yellow River the day he saved the monk.

"That broadsword has a vibe. It's beautiful."

Sanfeng smiled. "Thank you. It happens to be my own work. It took me a month to fold the steel."

"It looks worn."

Sanfeng smiled. "It's seen some use. You can't get swords like that in China anymore. For a couple of hundred years now, you've had to go to Japan. It's the island nation syndrome. The Japanese are accustomed to defending themselves from invasion, accustomed to finding great joy in small things because they are crammed together and don't have much. The natural resources of China, by contrast, are endless. A good Japanese sword-maker of the last century would meditate for forty days, ritually cleanse himself in preparation for making a blade, then devote his mind, body, and soul to nothing else for days, weeks even, until it was executed to perfection. No one bothers with that kind of craftsmanship in China anymore. There's too much else to do–wine, women, mah-jongg, politics–big houses, expensive cars."

Dalton's eyes came to rest on a certain, primitive, giant halberd. It stood alone, in the center of the room, within a tall, velvet-lined umbrella bucket, illuminated from above by a single spotlight. The wooden shaft, the same one the murderous Banpo priest had held in his hand, was cracked, splintered, and in some spots burnt nearly to charcoal. The blade was chipped and scored, but mainly well-preserved, given its mission of cleaving horse legs. The insignia of Gao, the blacksmith, was still clearly visible on the blade's base.

"This mark looks very old," Dalton pointed out.

"Yes. I lost that weapon for some time, but finally recovered it."

"It must be valuable. You give it a place of honor."

Sanfeng took a deep breath. "My father forged it," he said slowly.

"Your father? It looks ancient."

"He forged it, and I brought a bucket of water to cool the blade. It made a tremendous hiss. That was back in the Shang Dynasty. It is one of my first memories."

Dalton frowned. "The Shang Dynasty?"

"That's right," said Sanfeng. "Just about thirty-five hundred years ago."

48

The Imperial Palace, Beijing, Qing Dynasty, 1899 CE

The dowager-empress Cixi floats on pillows in her private chamber. Over her right shoulder is the portrait of a crane, and chrysanthemums and peonies surround her. She waves her fan, moving a stray strand of hair that has escaped her elaborate hairdo.

"I am the cleverest woman in the world, am I not?" she asks, gazing fondly at Sanfeng, who sits at her feet with his legs crossed in the lotus position.

"You certainly are, Empress."

"Am I cleverer than Queen Elizabeth of England?"

"Her life cannot possibly be as interesting as yours, Empress."

"You don't answer my question, eunuch."

"You are cleverer than she by the length of a river," Sanfeng says, looking up at her gently.

"What river?"

"China's Sorrow, Empress."

"I hear our Yellow River is not the world's longest. I hear the world's longest is the Amazon, eunuch. Am I the cleverest by that much?"

"Begging the Empress' pardon, but the Amazon is the world's *greatest* river. The world's longest is the Nile, in Africa. Compared to those giants, our Yellow River is not so very much."

Cixi is silent for a long time. Sanfeng winces. He knows all about her silences. In private conversations, he has likened her to a volcano, able to lie dormant for centuries and then suddenly explode with great fury. Of course the dowager-empress does not function in geologic time, so her outbursts come far more frequently than any volcano's, although they are mercifully shorter in duration.

"Are you correcting me, eunuch?"

"Of course not, Empress. I am agreeing with you, although even to do that is above my humble station."

"Good," Cixi says, her voice barely a whisper. "Now tell me, am I the cleverest woman in the world by a margin as long as the length of the Nile?"

"You are the cleverest woman in the world by a river the length of the Nile and the Amazon strung together," says Sanfeng.

"Ha," Cixi chuckles, but without real mirth. "You are clever yourself, which is why you are my favorite. But tell me something. Am I as clever as the Pearl Concubine?"

"Lady Tatala is no match for you in any way, Empress."

"Even though she is younger?"

"She was born a commoner," says Sanfeng. "How can she compete with the marvels of heaven?"

"Come pleasure me, eunuch."

Sanfeng approaches, scuttling like a crab, keeping his head far lower than Cixi's. When he is within range, he removes her silk slippers and begins to gently knead her feet. They are tiny and bound, the arches sharpened by the torture of training, the toes turned downward.

Cixi sighs. She slips lower on her throne. "Your hands are like no others, eunuch."

"They could never equal your feet, Empress."

"Lady Tatala never bound her feet. I have seen them. They are hideous."

"As I said, Empress, she is of common birth."

"But she has the emperor's favor. I wonder, eunuch, how she and her sister could be of the same stock. Her sister's feet are lovely, and the two of them do not look alike in the slightest."

"The emperor has married both, Empress, but if I may be bold enough to say what many others think, your nephew's tastes are not so fine as your own."

"You say that, yet I know you and Tatala are close."

"I exist to serve you, Empress. Were I not close to the emperor's favorite consort, I could not serve you as well as I do."

"You do serve me well, eunuch. Better, I am certain, than any of my nephews' wives serve him. Now come closer, and pleasure me another way."

The dowager-empress' appetites are legend. Sanfeng knows them all too well, although he is far from the only one with whom she is intimate. He lets her feet gently down onto a pillow, and lifts the hem of her robe, sliding beneath to use his tongue.

"Ah," Cixi leans back. "Like that, but harder. Good. Harder still."

When she climaxes, the dowager-empress stiffens and gives a cry. Afterward, she moves away. "Tell me, eunuch, do you think I am right to support the rebellion of these so-called boxers?"

"The Empress is hoping to shore up the country against all foreigners, I know."

"I am not confident of China, eunuch, though it pains me to say so. Our government is outdated, and the countries of the west outstrip us."

"The relationships between nations move in cycles, Empress. We Chinese were pursuing architecture, mathematics, and medicine when the forbears of the western kings were crawling around in the dirt chasing pigs. There will come a time when China rises to the top again."

"But perhaps not while I am alive. France, Germany, Austria, Belgium, Holland, the United States of America, they all have their feet in our bedchamber."

"The *Dao* moves in strange ways, Empress."

Cixi takes Sanfeng's face and lifts him from the floor. "Make love to me, Sanfeng," she says.

"How I wish I could obey, Empress."

"But you can, eunuch. I sense these things, and I know you can."

"I am but a humble eunuch."

"You are humble, that is true, and it is why you have become the most powerful man in my court. But I doubt you are a eunuch."

Sanfeng feels a rush of fear. He has made not one mistake, ever. There is no one in the Imperial City who has ever seen him undress. "You are too kind, Empress. If there are two things I regret about my condition, one is that I might not make love to you in the manner you wish."

Cixi reaches down and touches between Sanfeng's legs. Sanfeng does what he has learned to do, which is to retract the contents of his sac. "And what is your other regret, Sanfeng?"

"That I cannot have children."

Cixi nods. "It would be better if you could pass your wisdom down, Sanfeng, although there are those in the court who find you enough of a threat all by yourself."

"It is not for power I wish children, but for company," he says. "There is no bond like that between parent and child."

"Were you close with your mother, Sanfeng? You do not speak of her."

"She died giving birth to me, Empress."

"And your father?"

"Was knowledgeable in medicine, and also a magician with steel. I remember the feeling of being held in his arms, and perhaps I may say I miss him more keenly with every passing day."

"He is gone, then?"

"Yes, Empress. Some time ago, when he was still a young man."

"Longevity not in the family tree then, is it?"

Sanfeng shifts slightly, but dares not pull away from her. "I yearn to know the love of my own offspring."

"You will have to be satisfied with the love of an empress."

Any man would harden at her skill, but self-control is Sanfeng's forte, and he remains limp in her hand. Just as she reaches for the sack she is certain is there, a commotion erupts at the door as Zetian pushes the guards aside and enters.

Sanfeng hastily straightens himself. Zetian instantly understands what is happening, and struggles to hide a smile. Cixi is furious.

"You dare enter my private chamber?" she screams.

Sanfeng shoots his sister a worried glance. He has repeatedly warned her about baiting the dowager-empress. He knows they are birds of a feather, these two: equally manipulative and power-hungry, equally scheming and deceptive. There is only the small matter of three thousand years of experience between them.

"I have heard you have a plan to send my cousin to Xi'an in commoner's disguise," Zetian says without preamble.

"The dowager-empress' only concern is your husband's safety and the integrity of our government," Sanfeng interrupts. "The plan is only for an unthinkable foreign invasion."

"Kneel in my presence, you insolent girl," Cixi thunders.

Zetian kowtows, but haughtily, deliberately stopping her forehead half an inch from the floor.

"I'm sick of your attitude!" Cixi shouts again. "I should have your head right now."

That particular phrase gets Zetian's attention, and she makes a loud business of sniffing. "Your incense burns strong, Cixi. Perhaps it is to cover up some other smell?"

Cixi comes off the throne ponderously. Long a student of her every move, Sanfeng can see she is still weak from her orgasm. She walks to where Zetian still kneels, and bends slightly so as to be closer to her. She puts her extremely long fingernails on Zetian's face.

"Empress," says Sanfeng. "If you scratch her as you recently did the maid, the emperor will know it was you."

Cixi grits her teeth and lets her fingers fall. "Not a day goes by I do not plot your demise," she hisses. "When I send the emperor out of the city to protect him from dangerous forces, you will not go with him. You will be left here, with me, and then we will see how strong you are."

"Indeed," Zetian smiles. "When we are left alone together, we will see."

"Get out of my chamber," Cixi commands.

When Zetian is gone, Sanfeng returns to massaging the dowager-empress' feet. "Beheading is too good for her," he says. "I say throw her down the well."

Cixi laughs harshly. "What a fine idea," she says. "Let her drown in her own tears, while the water rats feed on her flesh."

"A perfect idea, Empress," he says. "Truly, you are the cleverest woman in the world."

49

When Huangfu came to the door with the news of Sanfeng's secret retreat, Zetian was sitting in a silk dressing gown at her kitchen table, enjoying a morning repast of fresh-baked croissants, kumquat preserves, and a pot of Golden Monkey Darjeeling tea.

"Good morning, Huangfu," she said. "Isn't it a beautiful day?"

He fingered his tie, wondering how she could possibly seem so happy? Hadn't she heard the news about the bodies? Couldn't she see the pillars of smoke around the city and smell the bodies burning?

"I'm worried about the plague, Zetian," he said. "I think we should leave the city, all of us, go to one of the islands for the duration."

Zetian gazed out the picture window at the view of Tung Pok Liu Hoi Hap, the East Lamma Channel, and beyond it, the islands of Lamma, Cheung Chau, Shek Kwu Chau, and Lantau.

"That hardly seems necessary, Huangfu. Look what a fine morning it is. My China is still beautiful, and beautiful it will remain."

Huangfu chewed his lip in frustration. "I saw a little girl on the way to you this morning," he said. "At first I thought she was dancing by the side of the street, but then she went sideways onto the road, clutching her head and screaming. I nearly ran her over. She had this terrible smile, Zetian. I've seen it on the foreign broadcasts, but in person…."

She poured him some tea. "I know; it was grotesque. Don't fret, Huangfu. It doesn't become you. Tell me, is my brother still in Hong Kong?"

"He's in the area, yes."

"The area?"

"That's what I came to tell you. He has an island home, a cave not far from the mainland."

"How do you know this?"

"I used the company helicopter to follow him early this morning. He was with an American."

"You could tell that from the helicopter?"

"He is very tall, this American. He's the writer who has been in the paper so much lately. Billabong Books brought him over. He interprets philosophy for ordinary people. He does *qigong*."

She put down her cup.

"The American does *qigong*?"

"He's a writer. You may recall Hop Ting mentioned him at a board meeting. They say he's very good, that he has an uncanny understanding. He's been written up in *TIME* magazine, and he has a book which one of our companies publishes. He has quite an audience, I'm told, or at least he did before the plague."

She fixed him with a stare. "How large an audience?"

"He teaches rich and famous people. He's been on TV. His book is a bestseller. Probably millions of people have seen him."

"And this American with a large audience is on an island with my brother?"

"As I said, they went there late last night. I've had the place under surveillance."

"Where exactly is this island?"

Huangfu took a folded map from his jacket pocket, along with the pictures he had taken from the helicopter. The latter had been taken at night, with infrared film, so light was dark and dark was light. Zetian inspected the images of the boat.

"The American *is* tall."

"Quite tall, yes."

Next, she looked at Huangfu's landscape shots. The silhouette of the coastline was clear. A tiny black arrow marked the cave, the cemetery, and the mausoleum. Wordlessly, Zetian compared the photos to the map, tracing the marine route with her smallest finger.

That finger mesmerized Huangfu by the dainty whiteness of it, the translucence of the skin, the perfect application of dark red nail polish. He felt his mouth go dry with desire.

"What are these white flares?"

"It's infrared film. The bright spots are heat."

"Gadgets," she snorted. "Computers and gadgets. You know how he loves them."

"From the look of it, it is a network of caves with many chambers. This is a cemetery on top. The film didn't show that, but I made a low pass."

"A very clever location," Zetian said thoughtfully. "Hidden in an obscure corner of the archipelago, not accessible by ferry, but close enough with a fast boat. This is very good work, Huangfu. And may I say, you look dashing in Ferragamo."

Beaming with pleasure, Huangfu gave a small bow.

"I always want to look good for you, Zetian," he said, his voice cracking.

Smiling, she stood and stretched, arching her back so her breasts pressed against the silk of her dressing gown. She relished drawing things out like this. She was preparing to steal his vital essence, and she knew there was no better way to increase the density and volume of that most precious liquid than by teasing. She reached out, and stroked her driver's cheeks. Making raindrops with her fingertips, she gently traced the sides of his face, touching and then not touching, then touching again. She stroked lower, massaging his jaw line.

Huangfu closed his eyes. He had no way of knowing Zetian had used the falling raindrop technique across thousands of years, and was more practiced in the movement than a pigeon is at flapping its wings.

"It's all right about Sanfeng's hideaway," she whispered. "We're all entitled to our secrets."

Leaving his tie in place, she unbuttoned his shirt and slid her cool fingers in. She pressed her palms to his chest, at the bottom of the rib cage, over the acupuncture point known as *zhong men*, a key juncture in the energy highway, a place where nerves and blood vessels ramify outwards.

"Zetian," he murmured, reaching for her.

She led him to the kitchen counter, to the gas burners, and the stainless steel flue rising above them like a steamer's smokestack. Careful not to hit his head on the hanging pots and pans, she laid him down and turned a burner on. She brought his hands close to the flame, and when the heat was too much, when he began to struggle in protest, she guided his hot hands inside her robe, and placed his *laogong*, the energy gate at the center of his palms, directly onto her nipples.

He was shocked by how cold she was, and by the electricity he felt in his hands. Breathless at realizing his fantasy, he ran his hands gently over her breasts, looking at them, wondering how her pearly skin could possibly be so fine, so devoid of any defects. How was it possible there were no birthmarks, no moles or marks of any kind at all?

She bent down to kiss him.

"I love you," he mumbled into her mouth. "I have loved you every minute of every hour since the day we met."

By way of answer, she raised him, and led him down the long hallway, through the chambers of her moods, to the bedroom. It was a starkly simple room, a windowless chamber lit by sconces holding candles. But the elaborate bed Huangfu had always imagined would be there–the four-poster with sheer curtains and silk sheets–was missing. In its place, in the face of untold wealth, in the inner sanctum of one of the most expensive homes in the world, was a simple straw mat. Above the straw mat was a mural, a riverside battlefield scene done by the same artist who had created the screen in the Imperial Museum of Fine Arts. There were Manchu troops rendered there, with glorious steeds and gray weather above.

Zetian lay down with him on the hard straw. She pulled the belt on her robe, freeing it, and sat astride him. Instead of heat from her, he felt cold. She freed him from his trousers, and lowered herself down.

What was this? She was wet, but frigid as a mountain stream inside.

"Cold," he gasped.

He was closer to it now, and in the candlelight the painting was revealed. He saw the tiny men on horseback, some with spears in hand, some with arrows protruding from their chests. Huangfu saw the thick clouds and a stand of oaks beside the battlefield and a tall brown deer running through a nearby stand of oaks. He saw a woman bursting forth from the shelter of the trees, her hands in fists. She was running toward the soldiers even though she had no weapon, her mouth open in a battle cry.

It was Zetian! She was in the painting! There could be no mistaking that aquiline nose, those high and wide cheekbones, those eyes. Huangfu was about to ask her about it–the work looked impossibly old–when suddenly she pulled off of him and moved down, taking him in her mouth.

"My love," he croaked.

Her fingers crept up his chest. They found his collar. They found his tie.

And twisted.

As she worked her mouth, he felt more alive than he had ever been.

Twist.

He was having trouble getting a breath. Ferragamo's damn bent-backed coolies were cutting off his air supply. He reached up, trying to release her grip, but she was too strong. Finally understanding, Huangfu grabbed desperately for a fistful of hair, tried to pull her away.

He could not budge her. She was like a bronze cast around him.

Huangfu's world started to flutter. He felt the pulse of her lips around him, cold and hard and insistent. He arched his back, crying out as he finished, but she kept on twisting, swallowing every last molecule, taking in his heart, his soul, his brain, his love.

When he was dead, feeling as if nothing could stop her now, she rose, and made preparations to meet her brother.

50

Leili was still fast asleep on the cot in the security office when Monica and Reggie Pritt showed Sanfeng's picture to the guard at the desk on the ground floor of the Crocodile & Crane building. The guard squinted for a better look, because while everyone else at the fancy dinner table stood out in sharp relief, Sanfeng was somehow indistinct, as if there had been a fingerprint on the lens when the photo was snapped, blurring only him. Monica had noticed this when she downloaded the picture from the Internet, but it was the only photo available, and she was unsurprised at the quality of his image; she keenly remembered how it felt to be near Sanfeng, how he evidenced no smell, noise, or heat.

"That's Mr. Gao," the security guard said, frowning. "He's the president of the company."

"We need to see him," Monica said.

"I'm afraid that won't be possible. We're in lock-down mode with the plague."

Reggie produced his police ID. "Official business," he said. "We're going up."

"Mr. Gao is very busy," reiterated the receptionist who met them when they got out of the elevator. "He sees outsiders only rarely, and always by appointment."

"We're friends," said Monica. "He invited me to have dinner on his yacht."

"I'm not privy to Mr. Gao's private life," she said. "If he invited you, perhaps you should go."

"This is a police matter," Reggie interrupted.

"I'm afraid Mr. Gao is not in the office."

"Very busy, or not in the office. Which is it?" Reggie demanded.

"Perhaps I can find someone to speak with you," the receptionist said, indicating they should wait in a pair of antique lacquer chairs.

"Look at this artwork," Monica breathed, pointing to the series of ancient scrolls on the wall, each flanked by potted plants, with a cold light shining gently on it from the ceiling. "Look at this mountain, and the waterfall. If you see it from a certain angle, it's like the human body. I think the river is supposed to be the circulation, and these boulders are organs and the trees the lungs."

Reggie regarded her with fascination. "I didn't know you were into art."

"For a guy who notices everything, how could you not know that? You notice people's faces, you always know if they're lying, you can *smell* lies, that's what you told me, and I know you can do it to, because without those skills a policeman would be dead. Anyway, treat the art like a clue, okay? Treat the whole office that way and tell me what you can about Mr. Gao."

"Maybe I'm not paying attention because I don't know what we're doing here," said Reggie. "Chasing another man's dream is the best I can make of it. There are so many things I'd rather be doing with you right now, so many places I'd rather be."

"All right," Monica said. "If you want to put it in cop terms, let's do it like this. I've been calling Dalton, and calling him some more. Nobody knows where he is. I'm sure he hasn't left, because he can't fly out and he doesn't know anyone else in Hong Kong, and besides, he wouldn't go off somewhere without telling me. Jimmy Ngo turned him onto a video arcade and he was going to go there and watch for Gao. I know it's a long shot, but Jimmy heard all the top *gongfu* guys go there because there are fantastic games. Dalton knew I asked you for the airplane manifest, so if he didn't find Gao he would have called me for an update."

"Maybe something else happened to him," Reggie said. "Hong Kong has gotten awfully rough with the plague going on. We've told tourists to stick to their hotels, but people are starting to panic."

"He didn't panic. He's not the panicking sort. And as far as something happening to him, he's a good fighter, and more than that he has this talent I've noticed, which is he always knows where his body is. Do you know what I mean by that? He's very sensitive to his surroundings, to where other people are and where other things are, too. He's not the kind of guy to lose his balance or not sense someone sneaking up on him. No, if something happened, I'm betting it has something to do with Gao."

"So this is a missing person investigation?"

Monica smiled and touched his face. "You're cute," she said. "Predictable, but cute."

"I bet you didn't predict I'd come to think more about love than anything, more about love than police work, and more about love than even the plague. If we die, it will be because we don't love others enough."

Monica looked at him suspiciously. "I know why you're doing this," she said.

"Why?"

"You're softening me up. You're trying to get me to change my mind and marry you."

"You've already changed your mind," Reggie grinned. "The rest is only a formality."

"Maybe to you, bucko," Monica hit him playfully on the arm.

It was then that the two of them noticed Brush. He stood in a doorway next to the chairs in which they had been sitting. Tall and thin and dry and spare, he might have been part of the doorjamb; indeed, he was nearly the color of fresh wood.

"You have police business with Mr. Gao?" he inquired.

"A friend of mine wanted to meet him," Monica explained. "Now that friend has disappeared while looking for him. On top of that, I know this sounds crazy, but I think I'm important to Mr. Gao, and I think he's important to me."

Brush stepped out of the doorway and looked at Monica more closely. He took a step to one side, then the other, taking in her profile, and her clear eyes and skin.

"You say you're important to him?"

"He watched me work out at the gym," said Monica. "He invited me for a sail."

Brush jumped. "A sail?"

"On his yacht."

"He doesn't have a yacht."

"His boat, then. He was on an airplane with a friend of ours," said Monica.

"Where is your friend now?"

"I told you, he's disappeared. Last time I saw him he was going out to look for Mr. Gao."

"Why is he looking for Mr. Gao?"

"The plane was struck by lightning, and it was going down," Monica said impatiently. "Mr. Gao went into the cockpit and did something to the controls. Fire came out of his hands, or at least some kind of electricity. Then he turned and took away my friend's memory, but my friend got it back. He remembered the whole thing."

"I see," said Brush.

"He thinks you're daft," said Reggie. "We're wasting our time."

Monica took Brush's arm. "Don't you think this is the time for long shots? The world is coming to an end. He said he'd take me to his waterfront home."

Brush straightened up. "His waterfront home?"

"He said he would show me a world of wonders."

"Christ," said Reggie. "How rich *is* this Gao?"

Brush sat down in one of the lacquer chairs. He put his head in his hands and stayed there a long time.

"Bugger's nodded off," Reggie whispered.

Brush suddenly sat up. He pointed his finger at Monica. "You should listen to your friend," he said. "He's right what he said about love."

Reggie's face changed with a sudden understanding. "How many people have you lost?" he asked softly.

"My whole family," Brush answered. "They were in Indonesia. I'm thinking differently about things now. The old rules, I fear, no longer pertain. Not even the rules I've held most dear."

"I don't understand," said Monica.

"I'm saying I'm going to help you," said Brush. "I'm not entirely sure why, but I believe Mr. Gao would want me to."

"You're going to tell us where he is?" she asked.

"I'm going to do better than that. I'm going to take you to his island."

51

The longer Dalton was around the immortal, the more questions came to mind. Lost in a hurricane of awe, he wanted to memorize every inch of Sanfeng's flesh, catalogue every burgeoning liver spot on his hands, and mentally record every line on his brow. Most of all, he wanted Sanfeng's knowledge and abilities.

"Is there anything you don't know?" Dalton asked.

"That is a ridiculous question."

"All right, then tell me something you do know. Just one thing."

"The rational brain is a dangerous toy."

"But you love technology and science."

Sanfeng nodded. "I didn't say I don't *like* the toy, I said it's dangerous."

"What other toys do you like?"

"My tastes are eclectic."

"I talk about the balance between the rational and intuitive brain in my book," Dalton said.

"I know you do. And you're on the right track. But it goes much further than that. People rely too much on the five senses, which are like a primitive telescope: they allow us to see only a narrow slit of the world out there. A tiny percentage of light falls into the visible spectrum–you can't imagine how a bat sees these caves–and in any case vision is just one sense, and after you add taste and touch and hearing and smell, you're still leaving out a huge chunk of the available mind. To imagine life, and please hear the word imagine, Dalton, to *imagine* life properly, you must forget the limitations of the senses and strive to break through the confines of what you think you know. You must experience the world through movement, because in truth, the way the material world appears to you is delineated by your size and the length of your step and your reach. To grasp the infinite, or even to grasp what is just beyond the hard corner of your mind, you must transcend your frames of reference."

"I follow some of what you say," Dalton said slowly.

"There's a discipline required, and the discipline is hard to find these days, particularly in America, which craves busy-ness above everything else. It is hard to find in China as well, which is trying so hard to be America."

"Won't the plague change all this?"

"We can hope it does. Hard to imagine a silver lining to such a tragic occurrence, but if there is one, it is the possibility humankind may redefine itself and explore anew what it means to be alive."

"By learning more?"

"By learning less," Sanfeng said. "In the beginning, I cataloged everything, made a game of remembering everything, drew tangential lines from one event to another, one time to another, just to help me keep track of it all. Eventually, all that learning became an enormous castle in my mind, and unlike my sister, I wanted to know less and less, to have less and less, to make things ever simpler, to pare down the experience of living until I transcended the borderlines I just talked about, and got behind it all."

"You have a sister?"

"Oh, yes."

"Tell me about her. Is she like you?"

Sanfeng smiled a smile full of a hundred lifetimes. "No," he said. "I wouldn't say that she is."

"Older or younger?

"She was born six years before I was."

"Tell me about her."

"Zetian prefers the company of rich people, when she tolerates company at all. Personally, I favor the poor. Rich people tend to preoccupy themselves with things that are of utterly no importance whatsoever. Poor people are more likely to live in the moment, whether it's a miserable moment or a joyful one. They are closer to the animal survivalist in us."

"So that's the most important thing? Our animal grit?"

"The most important thing is innocence," said Sanfeng. "When innocence is lost, wonder is lost, and when wonder is lost life becomes less worth living."

"And you? Have you preserved your innocence?"

"It has been my greatest mission, my greatest battle too. I have striven hardest of all to keep my childhood alive into my old, old age–to keep my sense of love and fun and wonder. Do you understand what I mean by a sense of wonder? I don't merely refer to gawking at a sunset like a drunken tourist, or marveling at a snowcapped peak. I'm talking about marveling at the very fact of life itself."

"The fact of life," Dalton repeated.

"The phenomenon itself," Sanfeng said. "It is vanishingly unlikely."

"With all those solar systems out there, all those planets and suns?"

Sanfeng smiled. "It's not a question of odds so much as of natural laws. You see, everything in the universe tends toward maximum entropy."

"Goes from a high-energy state to a low-energy state."

"Correct. After the release of energy scientists call the Big Bang, matter was flung away from the point of the explosion at unimaginable speed. Writhing, spiraling galaxies were spawned and combusting stars formed planets. Everything cooled down. The bonds that held things together broke, which means the complex became simple, and everything in the universe became less well organized."

"Lost energy," said Dalton.

"Right. But not life! While absolutely everything else in the universe fell apart, life fell together. You could think of the universe as a big river flowing away from the point of the Big Bang, and life as the tiny fish swimming upstream. Life organizes itself while everything else disintegrates. So, energetically, life is precisely the opposite of every other natural process. On top of that, the component parts are huge in number, and the system incredibly delicate and complex. It's fantastically improbable, which just makes it all the more wonderful. You must tell your readers to marvel at that, Dalton."

Dalton considered Sanfeng's words for a moment, then stretched out his arms as if to wrap them around the books and art and musical instruments in the gave. "I'm caught up in the unlikely," he said at last.

"This is a collection of my favorite things."

"I find possessions a burden," said Dalton.

"And you're wondering why I don't."

Dalton nodded.

"I passed the need, and I came back to it. And do you know why? I *do* need them. I need them to remember. There's been so much, you see, and so many...." His voice trailed off.

"Dostoyevsky?" Dalton read from the spine of a volume.

"The Russian, yes. A keen comprehension of the dark side. I read him over and over to better understand my sister."

"She's dark?"

"After millennia of evolution, instead of rejoicing in life as I have described it, human beings have become so good at killing that we can wipe each other out in unthinkable numbers."

"I asked about your sister."

"Of course, there's no need to worry about killing each other," Sanfeng said. "The plague is going to do the job for us."

Dalton picked up Jack London's *The Call of the Wild.*

"I like wolves," Sanfeng explained. "I don't know why, I just do."

"Maybe because their society is so well lubricated," Dalton offered. "Their pack systems work so well, their combat is so perfectly ritualized, their pecking order so efficient, they rarely hurt each other."

"Would you like to live at the bottom of a pecking order?" Sanfeng asked. "Would you like to be the last one to get a scrap of food? Would you like to be pushed aside, pissed on, marginalized? We're not so different from them. Millions of children don't have enough to eat. Millions will never know love. No, I like wolves because when you look into a wolf's eyes, you really see something. Wolf eyes are deep. There can be anger and distrust in them, but love and loyalty, too."

"Do you remember your first love?"

"Ha," said Sanfeng.

"Ha yes, or ha no?"

"She was twelve," Sanfeng replied. "I probably looked about the same age. She tasted like almonds. We lived in a little hut of twigs and straw. We made rice cakes together, and hunted mushrooms and grubs. I remember I loved her so much I would have jumped down a tiger's throat for her. I would have wrestled a crocodile."

"What was her name?"

"There is that," said Sanfeng.

"You've forgotten?"

Sanfeng walked the perimeter as if he were picking berries in the woods, touching books and artifacts with his finger. Dalton was struck again by what he noticed first on the airplane and then again at the video arcade–Sanfeng glided more than walked, seeming barely to touch the floor, his movements so light and his joints so mobile he might have been a ghost, and an athletic ghost at that.

"The Japanese are making robots that so resemble people we won't be able to tell the difference," the immortal said. "Robots will have perfect memories, or at least be able to back up their hard drives."

"I don't think anybody's working on robots anymore. They've got more important things to worry about."

"The Japanese are like us Chinese. And like the Russians, too. They take a long, strategic view of everything. Maybe they've already developed robots to which they can transfer consciousness, so at least their politicians will survive the plague. They've been fascinated with robots for centuries. It goes back to puppets that moved with the subtlety of humans. In the West, you fear robots will steal your soul. In the East, we think less fragile bodies might be a good idea."

"To live forever."

"Nothing is forever," said Sanfeng. "Not even me."

"You were telling me about your sister."

"I wasn't telling, you were asking."

"Does she marvel at life? Is she an innocent?"

"No," said Sanfeng. "I'm sorry to say she is not."

Dalton waited for more, but there was none.

"Have you always been a musician?" Dalton finally asked, gesturing at the cave's array of instruments.

"Always. I played for the court, and I played for mountain people. Now I play only for myself. Music is the key to life."

"Will you play something for me?"

Sanfeng picked up the bamboo flute that had turned the tide in the Yuan Dynasty battle of Shaolin. The ragged mouthpiece was bitter with age, but to Sanfeng it tasted sweet. Swaying like a snake charmer, he closed his eyes and began to play.

Dalton was mesmerized by the melody. It was like a poem evoking the aroma of chestnuts and cherries and other delights that grew on trees, the feel of moss between the toes, the feel of rough stone on his bare haunches, the sight of birch trees swaying on the taiga.

"What do you call that piece?" he asked, when Sanfeng finished.

"I just made it up. I haven't given it a name."

"And what do people call you?"

"My family name is Gao. My given name is Sanfeng."

"May I call you Master?"

Sanfeng smiled. "You are in love with traditions long dead."

"Is that a bad thing?"

"No," Sanfeng said. "I deny it, but I am as you are."

"Would you tell me why you brought me here, Master?"

"I've made some inquiries," Sanfeng said. "Your books sell well. You have a following."

"I'm not exactly a household word."

"Perhaps not yet, but you have made Chinese philosophy and movement accessible to Westerners in a way no one else has, and you give a hip, Western stamp to things young people no longer respect. I believe you have a special understanding."

Dalton opened his mouth to demur.

Sanfeng shook his head impatiently. "Do you remember the lecture you gave at Harbor Plastics?" he asked.

"You heard that?"

"I enjoyed it immensely–especially the part about our intuitive and rational sides needing to be in equilibrium. You are more right about that than you know, and it is more important than you realize. Let me give it a Darwinian perspective for you. Like every species on this planet, the human race is evolving. But, unlike all other species, we are consciously involved in our own evolution."

"Part of the wonder," Dalton interrupted.

"Just so. And by choosing to concentrate on the external world rather than the internal one, on materialism and technology rather than instincts and feelings, we are unknowingly diminishing the importance of our most critical faculty, the subconscious intuition, the thing you refer to as the inner boxer. You are quite right to say if we stay on the material path, we will lose our strongest weapon in the fight for survival."

"Another way of saying our rational mind is a dangerous toy."

"Yes."

"You've got a plan and the plan involves me."

"More and more," said Sanfeng.

"Since you say that, I have to tell you I'm not sure I share your love of technology. The way I see it, we've been relying on technology to get us out of the messes we get ourselves into. All that's done is make bigger messes. We haven't grown the spirit; we've just become more dangerous animals. The thing you call our dangerous toy makes us more dangerous to ourselves, and more dangerous to the rest of life on earth."

"You are confused about the evils of technology," Sanfeng replied. "The fact is our entire frame of reference, everything we know and understand about the world is, as I mentioned, determined by our biological limitations, the limits of our senses, and our reach and our scale. By scale I mean, for example, that a concrete wall ten feet high is a barrier for us, but not for the giraffe, who can see over it. The surface tension on a lake is a barrier to a waterbug, essential to support the bug's skating, too, but it is not a barrier to us. Are you with me so far?"

"I don't understand what this has to do with technology."

"*Gongfu*, *qigong*, energy exercises, athletics, these are our attempts to push back our limits so we can deal better with the world. We want to live longer, to avoid illness, to be able to climb and see the view from atop the hill. Intellectual activity, including scientific inquiry, is our way of pushing back our limits, too, of understanding things better. Technology, being a manifestation of science, goes hand in hand with the work you do. X-ray machines and telescopes give us a window into worlds we don't see with the naked eye; cyclotrons and supercomputers do, too."

"Where does spiritual work fit in?"

"What is spiritual work if not another way of pushing back our limits? Meditation, prayer, philosophical inquiry, these are ways of pushing back our limits, too. Eventually, uniting physical, scientific, and spiritual work, we may push our limits back so far we can actually understand what's going on."

"If the plague doesn't wipe us out first."

"Indeed."

"So we have to do something."

"Yes."

"And that's why I'm here. That's why you're giving me a crash course in the metaphysics of three thousand years."

Sanfeng laughed at that, and took Dalton by the hands as if he might at any moment break into a waltz with him.

"Yes!"

"But you didn't know about the plague when you found out about my book. You didn't even know about me, did you?"

"No, I did not. But I have indeed seen the plague before, and I knew someday I would see it again."

"But it caught you by surprise," Dalton said.

Sanfeng's expression grew breathtakingly sober. "It did," he said. "Nature, it seems, has forced my hand."

In that moment, Dalton understood what he meant.

"You're going to share what you know," he whispered. "You're going to tangle with the plague."

"I'm part of nature," Sanfeng said. "If the plague is a doomsday switch, I am the reset button."

52

The security guard shook Leili gently. "Wake up," he said. "Madame Gao just got here."

Leili's eyes came open, and she sat up, tousling her hair. "How long have I been asleep? I don't remember…."

"You lay down and you were out. Madame Gao's Bentley just pulled up. She's driving herself, too. I've never seen that before."

"How long does she usually stay in the office?"

"Every day is different."

"What's the *shortest* time she's been here?"

"Sometimes she comes and then leaves again. It's not my job to follow her."

"Could you find out how long she plans to stay? Call her assistant, maybe? I have to clean up. I can't see her like this."

The guard glanced at Leili's legs, and licked his lips nervously. "All right," he said.

Leili watched while he dialed the number, spoke briefly, and hung up.

"She wanted to know why I was asking. Everybody's jumpy these days."

"Could be because everybody is dying. What did she say?"

"Madame has two appointments. She will be here for a couple of hours."

"I need a shower," Leili said. "And a change of clothes."

The guard shrugged and pointed her to a restroom.

"Do you have shampoo and a razor?"

"No. There's only soap."

"That will do. Will you do me one more favor and get me something to wear to at the street market?"

"I can't leave my post."

"The other guy is outside. The market is close, I saw it on my way here."

"Dresses cost money," the guard said.

"I don't have Hong Kong dollars. I don't even have a toothbrush."

The guard sat down on the bed beside her. He was a chubby young man with a pimply face. He reached out and touched her leg very gently. "I might be persuaded," he said. "But I need to know there's something in it for me."

Leili felt a wave of desperation. "The whole world is dying," she said.

"That's not my business."

She took his hand off her leg.

"At least let me watch you shower," the guard said.

Leili looked at the clock on the wall. She was keenly aware of the passage of time. She felt trapped in the tawdry negotiation and burdened by the ongoing struggle her great beauty brought. "I've had a child," she sighed.

"I don't care. You're still pretty," said the guard.

"Don't you have a girlfriend? A wife?"

The guard frowned. "Do you want the clothes or not?"

Leili nodded.

The guard got up. "Then don't start until I get back."

While he was gone, Leili lay on the dirty cot and looked at the ceiling. She thought of the sex she had seen between Jou Yuen and Gao Zetian. She thought of Tony Tunstall, and of a boyfriend she had while in nursing school. She tried not to think of Lombo, but she couldn't help it. Images of him flowed to her as if through an unrestricted tap: holding his stuffed elephant, splashing, laughing in the surf, curled up asleep with an astronomy book on his lap, fighting to get a piece of broccoli onto his fork. As if the images were not enough, if she closed her eyes Leili was sure she could smell his hair, the skin on his neck, the little-boy aroma of his dirty clothes. Shaking her head violently, she wiped back her tears and stood up. Movement on the monitor console caught her eye, and she went to it and sat down in the chair in front of the panel.

Zetian was on camera, but only for a moment. Emerging from her office, the camera showed her walking to a conference room. There was no audio, but another camera showed the room. A man sat waiting at a table. He had a portfolio case in front of him, and when Zetian entered, he stood and gave a deep bow.

The monitors were black and white, and the quality could have been better, but even so, Zetian in motion once again fascinated Leili. The immortal seemed to walk to the table without actually touching the floor, and when she lifted an arm in a brief greeting–she didn't actually shake hands–her flesh seemed to float in the air. All Leili could think about was the way Zetian moved in her *qigong,* and seeing her for the first time in over a year, she was struck by the fact the *qigong* suffused everything she did.

The man showed Zetian pictures from the case. They were an advertising campaign for a waterfront development in Macau. Leili wondered how Zetian could be conducting business as usual when the whole world was falling apart. Who would buy condos in this development, Leili wondered, and why would anyone be thinking about long-term investments at this time?

Leili continued watching her unwitting mentor until the security guard returned.

"Here," he said, putting a nice print dress down on the counter. "Blue to match your eyes. They're your most unusual feature, you know. And I've brought you a toothbrush and shampoo and a razor and some cream."

Leili took the supplies into the bathroom. She hung the dress at the end of the shower rail to steam the wrinkles out of it, and got undressed while the security guard stood in the doorway. She tried not to look at his face, but she could hear him breathing, and saw him touch himself when she turned the water on and raised her arms to the spray.

At one point, while her eyes were closed against the shampoo, she felt his hand on her breast. She pushed him violently away. "No," she said.

He brought up his other and started to force the issue, but she grabbed his wrists and brought him to his knees in a joint lock she had never learned but somehow instinctively understood. Soapy water sprayed his uniform as he whimpered to be let go. After that he sat on the toilet while she got dressed. He hadn't brought her underwear, nor a hairdryer, and she had no makeup with her, so the process was brief. She ran her fingers through her tresses to help them hang straight after she toweled them dry.

Afterward, he brought her some breakfast from the lobby coffee shop, and she watched television while she ate. "The plague will be here within twenty-four hours," she said.

"The government won't allow it in," the guard said confidently.

Leili hated the cynical sound of her responding laugh. When she had eaten her fill, she locked herself in the bathroom and did twenty minutes of the *qigong*, constraining some of the movements due to the lack of space. The lack of confidence she felt at the prospect of confronting Zetian eased as she went through the set.

"It's time to take me to Madame Gao," she told the guard when she came out.

They took the elevator up in silence. The guard spent most of the time looking at the ground, although Leili sensed he was staring at her legs. When they got out, he took her to the receptionist. "This lady is here to see Madame," he said.

"I'll see if she's available."

Leili didn't wait. She strode to the conference room, where the advertising presentation was just winding up. The room was paneled in dark wood, and mostly taken up by a gigantic table of Brazilian rosewood, the rich hues of which had not been rendered on the monitor. Zetian, wearing a red silk suit of lustrous tones, started to snap at the interruption, but then stopped and stared at Leili.

"I know you," she said.

Leili had forgotten the sheer power of Zetian's presence. "We have met before," she said. "I worked for Jou Yuen."

"I heard he was dead."

"So is most of the rest of Jakarta. I, however, am alive, and I have come here to talk to you."

"I'm in a meeting."

"Please finish it now. I have things to say you don't want this gentleman to hear."

"Wait outside."

"Exercises I saw you do while you were in my bedroom with Jou."

Zetian's face tightened. It occurred to Leili that the

chairwoman looked even more beautiful when she was angry than she did when she was making love.

"We're done," Zetian told the ad man. "My assistant will call you."

When they were alone in the conference room, Zetian came close to Leili, and appraised her. She reached out and touched Leili's face with a cold finger. She brought her nose close to Leili's skin.

"You copied my *qigong*," she said. "You've been practicing it."

"I watched through the keyhole. You were in my bed with my boss, after all."

"You slept with him, too." It was a statement, not a question.

Leili shrugged. "Part of the job. I never loved him."

This brought a small smile from Zetian. "That makes two of us."

"Where did you learn the exercises?" Leili asked.

"They are a family set."

"I have questions about the movements, things I couldn't make out, and sounds I heard you make. Will you teach them to me?"

"This is a first," she said. "In more years than you can imagine, nobody has ever seen those exercises."

"How do you know?"

"I know," said Zetian.

"You didn't know about me. Maybe there are others."

"No," said Zetian. "There aren't." Closing in, she put her hands on Leili's hips. "You're very fit."

"And I survived the plague. I'm the only one. Scientists studied me. They took pieces of me for analysis."

"Of course they did," Zetian said, reaching for Leili's breasts.

Leili pushed her away. Zetian tried again. Leili resisted.

"You're strong," Zetian smiled.

The pushing grew more intense. It turned into a wrestling match. Leili was amazed at her own strength, and at Zetian. At last, the immortal prevailed, pushing Leili down onto the table. Grabbing the fabric at the shoulders, she ripped the dress from her, then ran her fingers, like raindrops once more, over Leili's flesh. "So lovely," she said.

"Stop."

"If you want to learn the rest of the system, you won't resist me."

"You yourself said I'm the only one who knows what you know. You're curious about me; I'm special to you. If you treat me this way, you'll never see me again."

Zetian took a deep breath and relented.

Leili pulled her dress back up. "I'm getting younger," she said.

"No, you're not."

"I'm not getting older, then."

"Yes, you are, but very, very slowly."

"Just how old are *you*?"

By way of answer, Zetian picked up the telephone on the table. "Cancel my next appointment," she told the secretary who answered. Then she turned back to Leili.

"Come with me," she said. "You can help me tend my garden. After that, I am going to take you on a little trip."

53

Brush looked like a scarecrow in an oilskin slicker, while Monica, leaning over the prow of the old junk, might have been a compact, green-eyed bowsprit.

"Where are you from?" Brush asked.

A salty slap of the South China Sea hit Monica. "I grew up in Oklahoma," she said, wiping her face. "Fields of gold and all that. A world away from here, not that any of that matters now."

"Fields of gold?"

"Wheat, corn, soy. In the autumn, the crops turn colors, and in the distance, the high plateau was red. It was beautiful. I'm sure I'll never see it again."

"Tell me about your family," said Brush.

"My mother, Cherylanne, is a nurse."

"And your father?"

"Mom met him on a trip and never saw him again. I never knew him."

Reggie called Brush back to a consult at the wheelhouse. Keeping one hand on the wheel, he pointed at the nautical chart with a dripping finger.

"The GPS says we're here. I can't push this crate any faster, so I don't think we'll arrive where we're going until dark. Do you know if there is safe harbor? The map shows nothing on the island."

"Perhaps we can anchor," said Brush.

"We've got a depth finder and we've got charts, but I'm no sailor. Anchoring without being able to see where I am doesn't make me too happy. Are there pirates? Smugglers?"

Monica climbed aft to join them. "Why worry about pirates now. Isn't the real danger people out on the water trying to get to China from the sea? Who knows who might be out here?"

Brush looked at her, and tears rolled down his cheeks.

"What?" she blinked at him.

Reggie saw what Brush saw, which was how fresh and lovely Monica looked, with the sea spray on her face, and how her youth and promise were excruciatingly poignant in the face of the looming end of the human race.

"I had a granddaughter your age," Brush said. "She was going to be an architect. Madame was going to give her a job designing a new project. She died in Jakarta."

"I can't believe it," Monica said, shaking her head. "I can't believe this is how it ends."

"It might end sooner than you think," said Reggie, pointing at a puddle under their feet. "It looks like this old shit pile is leaking. If there is water this high up, I'm afraid to go below."

So Monica did. The cabin of Brush's brother's old craft was flooded. The velvet, overstuffed furniture, which looked as if the owner had bought it from a thrift store in Morocco, floated back and forth with the pitch and yaw of the boat. Monica ran back up to the wheelhouse.

"We're sinking," she said. "The cabin is under water."

"Jesus Christ," Reggie exploded at Brush. "Your brother is trying to kill us."

"My brother is dead," Brush said.

"When was the last time you were on this boat?" Monica asked.

"Many months. I know the timbers leak, but we've always just run the bilge."

"We're going to need more than a bilge pump now," said Monica. We're going to need a miracle."

Brush practiced calligraphy, and held the wheel on course, while the younger two went below and started bailing. As dusk fell, they were still at the job. They became aware of the sounds of the sea: the flapping of the sails, the throb of the motor, a change in the splashing made by the bow. Despite their best efforts, the junk sank deeper and deeper into the waves.

A couple of hours after midnight, a fog set in. Not long after that, the trio heard the sound of powerful engines, and the radar showed another craft closing in.

"Get below and keep bailing," Reggie told Monica.

As she went through the hatch, a ship appeared. A single red strobe on the bridge created phantasms in the murk. It bore red stripes on the side and a helicopter on deck. Brush cut the engines.

"Maritime Security Agency," said Reggie.

"What does that mean?" Brush asked.

"A combination of customs, navy, and police."

"Will your badge help?"

Reggie put his bucket down as the frigate-sized vessel pulled alongside. "We're about to find out."

Sailors swept the deck with a searchlight. An armed officer appeared, peering over to the junk. "State your business," he said.

Reggie moved slowly toward the gunwale, identification in hand. "We're taking the boat over to one of the out islands."

The officer shone a flashlight over onto Reggie's shield. "Throw it over," he said.

Reggie closed the cover and tossed it. The officer made a grand show of close scrutiny. "Plague victims aboard, Captain?"

"None," said Reggie, inclining his head in Brush's direction. "I'm taking my grandfather home."

The officer snapped the case shut and tossed the identification back over. "Dangerous night," he said.

"We've got radar," Reggie said.

"You're listing badly."

"It's an old boat. The bilge can keep up with it."

"You're off the shipping lanes. Nobody around if you go down. Sure you don't want a tow?"

"Thanks, but we don't have too far to go now."

The frigate moved off. The junk rocked in its wake. Reggie returned to bailing. Brush kept the boat on course. A few hours before dawn, the engine quit.

"The water's drowned it," Reggie cursed. "We're dead in the water."

"We've still got the sails. We're nearly to the island."

"There's a raft," said Monica. "Let's get it loose just in case."

They put the raft out behind the stern on a tether line. Reggie consulted the GPS for their position, and then slung a hand compass he found in the emergency locker around his neck on a lanyard. “In case the power goes,” he explained.

Before first light, but when a very optimistic eye might have found a cerulean hint on the dark horizon, the junk dipped its starboard flank into the ocean like a drunken lady, and did not straighten. “Free the raft,” Monica cried as the lights went out, circuits shorted by the seawater.

The end came up far more quickly than any of them expected. Reggie went for the line at the stern cleat, but the junk lay down just then and he was thrown into the sea. Monica clung to the high railing at the back.

“Jump,” Reggie cried from where he flailed in the swell. “When she goes down, she’ll pull you with her.”

“Where are we?” Monica yelled back.

“Close to the island.”

“Save the raft!”

He took a few strokes toward where he thought it might be, but found nothing. “Brush!” he yelled. “Can you swim?”

No answer came. The sails hit the water. Reggie saw them coming at the last minute, felt them would be more accurate, and dove under before he was smothered. He swam along the edge, feeling with his hands, until he came up at the trailing edge of the thick canvas, where he found Monica. She wrapped her legs around him.

“Let go of me and kick,” Reggie gasped. “You’ll drown us both.”

The mast cracked from the opposing forces. Monica let Reggie go. “Brush,” she cried.

There was a loud noise as one last air pocket escaped the junk, but Brush was gone.

54

Dalton Day and Gao Sanfeng stood together before the immortal's enormous television monitor, watching the local news. In a vain and horrific attempt to stop the spread of apoptosis, the Chinese government dynamited an all-girls school in Beijing with the children inside. Total anarchy seized Paris and Rome. Someone poured thousands of gallons of blood onto the street in front of Buckingham Palace. Radical Islamists lit a bonfire under the arch in St. Louis and immolated themselves in search of the virgins of Heaven. The President of the United States disappeared from public view, and there was speculation he might be smiling.

"This plan of yours," Dalton said. "Don't you think we'd better get it in motion?"

"It already is in moving. Now, let's continue."

"We've explored the metaphysics of our race, but there is evolution to consider."

"Back to Darwin?"

"Yes."

"And the doomsday switch?"

"Right. The DNA molecule works like a Lego toy. It has simple building blocks, fits together a certain way, and can become large and complex with relative ease. So, starting back when the Earth was an organic soup with DNA floating in it, there were plenty of resources. DNA began by building cells, then single-celled organisms, then multi-cellular organisms like slime molds and lichens, algae, and so on. Life dimensionally increased after that, and plants bloomed and covered the Earth and did their own terra-forming."

Dalton wiped his brow. He was exhausted, overwhelmed, vibrating with excitement. Seeing the look on his face, Sanfeng put down the flute. "I've been a terrible host. Would you like something to eat? You must be hungry. I don't have the appetite I did when I was your age."

"Yes," Dalton admitted. "But I'd rather you finish your thoughts first."

"Let's jump right to cycads, then, and the proliferation of insects. This was followed by primitive creatures such as trilobites and, later, complex invertebrates such as *Limulus*, the horseshoe crab. The system worked because it was young and fresh, and resources abounded. After that came the fishes, the amphibians, the stem reptiles, and the dinosaurs. That world grew full and ripe and warm and wonderful, at least so long as you were top of the food chain. Then something upset the apple cart."

"The apple cart?" Dalton smiled.

"An American expression, yes? From eighteenth century New Hampshire?"

"I have no idea."

"The dinosaurs, then. That party ended when meteors hit the planet, threw dust up into the sky, blotted out the sun, and dropped the temperature below dinosaur operating range. There is an impact crater under the Arabian Sea, off the coast of India, near Mumbai, and another in the Yucatan Peninsula. The meteors provided a cosmic pruning, a cataclysm that put an end to the dominance of any one group of animals and cleared the path for another–specifically, the mammals. Life on Earth has always featured this cycle. Trouble is, we humans have destroyed the subtleties of the global ecosystem so quickly, there hasn't been time for a natural cataclysm to reign us in."

Dalton got up and stretched. He was too self-conscious to move in front of Sanfeng, even though he knew the immortal had seen his demonstrations. Instead, he just rubbed his back. "So you believe the plague is a natural cataclysm?"

"I think the doomsday switch notion is accurate. In just the way earthquakes and tidal waves are features of our dynamic geology, population control is intrinsic to biology."

"Like Europe's Black Plague, or AIDS."

Sanfeng clapped his hands. "Exactly. And cancer, cardiovascular disease, diabetes, malaria, cholera, even exotic viruses like Hanta. But each time we control them with medical science, we gain the upper hand and unbalance the cycle."

"What about war?" asked Dalton.

"Excellent question. Violence is a terrific population control. We kill each other far more effectively than any bug can kill us."

"I've got a problem with the model," said Dalton. "It seems so nuts-and-bolts. Earlier, I had the impression you had a much broader view of the human experience, that you believed we had a destiny, which was to grow and evolve and do what you called push back our boundaries."

"Evolution and destiny seem at first to be at odds, but actually, they are not. Evolution is just the mechanism whereby we achieve that destiny."

"So here we leave pure science and move into metaphysics again."

"Scientists believe in only what they can see and test," Sanfeng replied. "It is what I cannot see and test, but can nonetheless sense, that leads me to my conclusion."

"So you consider yourself a scientist?"

"Of sorts, yes."

"And you see things most don't because of your longevity."

"Yes."

"And that longevity comes from…?"

"My family *qigong*."

"And this *qigong* will work against the plague?"

"It will."

"Now I'm hungry," said Dalton.

They followed a low tunnel to the kitchen chamber, which was set far from the sea. "After a time, you come to see food differently," Sanfeng explained.

"Don't tell me you don't enjoy eating."

Sanfeng opened a refrigerator to reveal a panoply of fresh fruits, vegetables, nuts, and grains. "On the contrary. I daresay I enjoy it more than most people. Food is energy, and different foods provide different *kinds* of energy."

They ate in silence, relishing a pomegranate at first–Sanfeng ate each seed with care, spilling not so much as a single drop of the staining juice–then zucchini with a strong nutty flavor, and a mix of nuts and berries, many of which Dalton could not identify. They drank a few sips of wine made from lychee fruit, and enjoyed the most exquisite *pu'erh* tea Dalton had ever tasted. Through all this, Dalton felt a sense of urgency, a need to address the problems of the world, but he noticed Sanfeng appeared unhurried, and he took the cue.

"The tea gets its smoky flavor from additional roasting," Sanfeng explained.

Dalton reached up and touched the rough ceiling of the cave. There were sharp places in the rocks, lending a primitive feel to the chamber. Sanfeng saw his expression. "Best to do only what you need and no more in building a dwelling," he said. "If you do otherwise, you become too comfortable. Comfortable, you become attached. Attached, you become unhappy."

"But you've becoming attached to living," said Dalton.

"Not so much as I used to be, but you're right, it has long been my weakness."

55

The junk disappeared from view so quickly it took Monica's breath away. There was no sign of Brush in the water, and the raft was gone, dragged down by the stern line before she or Reggie could reach it. There was a small cushion in the water nearby, and Reggie let Monica hug it to her chest. He held the compass, following it toward the Kat O Chau's coordinates.

"Take off your pants," said Monica. "I'll show you how to make a float out of them. I learned it in my basic survival class."

She tied the legs together and scooped air into the seat. When she put it back in the water, it provided something for Reggie to rest on. They watched the compass by starlight.

"There's a current," Reggie said. "You can see the way it moves us against the fog."

"How do you know the fog's not moving?"

"I don't, but we can't fight the current; we're going the only way we can go."

"We should have taken the frigate's tow," Monica said.

"You don't know those guys like I do. They could have taken us anywhere, done anything they liked with us–with you. They're the one and only law out here, and now, with the plague, it's every man for himself."

"We'll make the island."

"Brush won't, that's for sure," Reggie said.

"I have a feeling he wanted to go," she said. "The last time I saw him he looked amazingly peaceful."

"We're not joining him," Reggie reassured her. "Things will look better when the sun comes up."

"I'm afraid of sharks," Monica said. "I can't think of anything but what's under my dangling legs."

"I could sing Australian bush ditties," Reggie said. "Although there's a real risk my singing voice might lead you to try and drown yourself."

"I don't know how you can joke at a time like this."

"That's rich. First I was too morose for you, and now I'm too jovial. There's a lesson in this, luv. Perspective, I suppose. You've exhorted me to try and rise above it all, and here I am, floating adrift in a dark sea, minus a boat, probably minus a job for just disappearing while I'm on duty, facing the ruin of a country and maybe the ruin of humanity as a whole. I'm chasing after a man I don't know or particularly like, a man I figure is more my rival than you'll admit, and yet, with all that, I'm a happy bloke because I have my sheila with me and she's beautiful in the glowing fog. I'll take this moment, yes, I will, and the sharks won't come near me because they know I've got Aussie blood, and there's no shark in the world, not even a white pointer, that isn't scared stiff of an Australian man in the water."

"You're a bit crazy; you know that, don't you?"

"That's all you have to say? I'm crazy?"

"And you're right. And if Brush hadn't drowned, I suppose this would be some kind of romantic. But I'm still worried about sharks."

"Tell me about your men, then."

"You know I'd never do that."

"This might be a good time to violate the rules, luv. Start with the first one to express undying love."

Monica kicked vigorously as if resisting the idea. "A boy in high school named Phillip."

"Where is Phil now?"

"He died. He bought a rocket engine from a junkyard and strapped it into the trunk of his Plymouth Roadrunner and lit it. He smashed into a rock outside of town. The local sheriff said he was going like two hundred miles an hour, but he couldn't steer because the front wheels were off the ground."

"You sure can pick 'em."

"I didn't pick him, he picked me, but there's no need to be nasty."

"And Dalton Day?"

"It always comes back to him."

"We are swimming in the open sea in the fog at night with

sharks all around because of him, luv. Doesn't seem unreasonable for an officer to ask for more information."

"You don't understand him."

"If he wasn't trying for your knickers, I don't understand him at all. I do believe I've made that clear."

Monica splashed at him. "He didn't come to Hong Kong to get laid, Reggie."

"Every American comes to Hong Kong to get laid, as you say."

"Not this American. Remember, he arrived before the plague. It's like this whole trip, the book he wrote, everything he's been studying, everything he knows and loves, his *gongfu*, his love of Chinese culture and history and philosophy, it all came down to meeting that guy on the plane. There's no way he could do anything but hunt him down, and I'm completely sure we're going to find he's with Gao now."

A large swell picked them up. Floating, they rose higher in the fog. The smell was different up there, and density of the air diminished. Monica took a deep breath. "Morning's coming," she said.

Suddenly, the surface roiled and fins appeared. Monica cried out.

"Hush," said Reggie. "They're just dolphins."

"How do you know?"

"They swim like they're on a teeter-totter. Sharks stay steady because they don't come up to breathe."

The mammals circled, gamboling and spouting. Sea birds squawked overhead. As if on cue, the sun broke the fog, first in spots and then in great swaths. A whole new world came to light, bathed in warm yellow and cleaned by a salty breeze. It was a deliberately innocent world, a world clean and pure, with an internal intelligence, with its own perspective on the wisdom and the rightness of the ebb and flow of species, the importance of balance, and the rise and fall of man.

"Land," Reggie cried. "Good Lord, if it isn't land."

"You think He delivered us?" Monica said, joining him in a redoubled kicking effort.

"I'm allowing every possibility," said Reggie. "Most of all, I'm grateful. Don't know how else to explain it, luv, and I don't know what else to call it. I'm grateful for all that I see and smell and hear and taste. I'm grateful for everything I feel. I'm grateful for you, more than anything else, no matter what you decide to do with me."

An hour later, they felt rough stones under their feet. Monica began to cry. "I've been shipwrecked and I've lived," she said. "I'm a damn Navy SEAL."

"That you are," Reggie grinned. "Any fighting force would be proud to have you."

The policeman found he'd lost a shoe. His feet were so numb with the cold, he hadn't noticed before. They disrobed on the deserted beach, wrung out their clothes, and lay them out on the sand to dry. Reggie stared at Monica's body.

"Don't get any ideas," she said.

"Too late."

They went down on the sand. Reggie licked the salt from her, starting at her feet. He made love to her fingers and her toes, to her neck and her eyelids and her ears. Squirming with desire, she pulled him back to the bordering beach grass, and coupled with him there, violently, explosively, with all the frustration and fear of not only their trial at sea but the days and weeks before, the backdrop of the world falling apart.

The Chinese government was expert at keeping things from its population, and for at least a week it had been hiding the full truth about the Banpo Smile, which was that it had arrived, and people were dying. On the beach, in Monica's arms, Reggie dove into her beauty as if it would cleanse him of the things he had seen on the street, horrors he had kept from her because a policeman's instinct is to protect and he protects most fiercely the ones he loves.

Most of all, Reggie tried not to think of the children–there had been lots and lots of dead children–nor of the elderly, who when the plague took them seemed to dry up as if all their fluids had been sucked out and to lie in heaps like matchsticks. While Monica thought he was doing administrative work–and well a captain would have, under ordinary circumstances–he had in fact been coordinating blockades, curfews, and containment. He had seen and smelled the bodies up close, and he had seen the final frightful dance of the plague victims before they expired, nervous systems running amok, all the while wearing the terrible distorted grin.

When their lovemaking was over, the wind picked up, but it was warm and gentle. Monica came up on her elbows, and shook the sand out of her hair, and watched Reggie stand to face the sea and spread his arms, eyes closed.

"Grateful!" he cried, because he was.

They made their way to a road they saw running some distance off, and walked along, waiting for some traffic. At length, a girl came by on a bicycle.

"Is this Kat O Chau?" Reggie inquired.

The girl nodded.

"A miracle," Monica said.

"Not really, luv. We had GPS and we had a compass and we had a current. Most of all, we had faith."

The bicycle girl began to move off. "Wait," Reggie called after her. "We're looking for a man in a cave."

The girl frowned.

"I'm a policeman," Reggie said.

"Where is your gun?"

"Our boat sank. The gun went with it."

Monica dug into her pants and pulled out the picture of Sanfeng she'd found on the Internet. It came out in bits, a sodden jigsaw, and she had to put it carefully together without tearing it further.

"This man," she told the girl.

The girl looked carefully at the picture, but kept an eye on Reggie as if she was afraid the big round-eyed foreigner, the big *gweilo*, might suddenly do something untoward.

"This is such a long shot," Monica sighed.

"It's a tiny island, luv, and he's a rich man who lives in a cave.

The long shot is we found his island. Finding him on it shouldn't be too hard."

The girl nodded. "I recognize him. But he's crazy. He lives in the cemetery."

"Perfect," said Reggie. "Redemption from a ghoul."

"You're sure it's him?" Monica asked.

"I'm sure," the girl said. "He has hair like a porcupine."

56

"This plan of yours," Dalton said. "It's about the *qigong*, isn't it?"

"You have no children," Sanfeng asked.

"A statement, not a question. You've investigated me, then."

"Of course."

"I've never been married."

Sanfeng smiled. "Such an American response."

"You mean in China children and marriage don't go together."

"Sometimes they do, sometimes they don't. And not just in China–other places in Asia, and in Europe and Africa, too. Come with me, I want to show you something."

Dalton followed the immortal deeper into the underground cavern, passing through another door. He fingered the low, rough-hewn ceiling of a passageway literally dripping with calcium-rich droplets.

"This is a very extensive cave system," Sanfeng explained. "It's shaped like an octopus, and some of the arms go under the sea. I keep the electronics' chambers dry with the filtration device, but the natural humidity is such that I can't keep all the chambers dry."

"I thought the hatches were for flooding."

"Air and water both."

The destination chamber was full of plants. "This is my fern garden," Sanfeng announced. "I suppose most connoisseurs are interested in orchids, for their great beauty and diversity, and the fact is I do love orchids, and succulents too. I have great and fond memories of the northern plateau, where evergreen succulents make a soft bed in the cold woods, and of the southwest expanse, too–where in many great adventures I suffered from succulent thorns–but the fern to me is the most glorious of plants because it primitive and delicate at the same time. These particular ferns relish the cool temperature of the cave. They like humidity and they sweeten the air. That's a Man fern you're standing next to, one of the larger species. Comes from the island of Tasmania. That's another Australian species, the Bat-wing fern, and another, the Kimberly Queen fern. That Christmas fern is American. Some species are simple, others complex."

They stood in the jungle of delicate fronds, a cluster of fiddleheads framing Sanfeng like a halo. Dalton looked overwhelmed. "So the contrast between the electronics and these plants...."

"Yin and yang," Sanfeng finished. "The balance. Balance is so important. Ferns reproduce by alternation of generations. They are asexual in one generation, sexual the next."

"Those asexual generations must be lonely," said Dalton.

"Yes. They are. Do you want children someday?"

"When the time is right, yes. It's an American trend to have kids later. It has to do with an emphasis on career, I guess, on getting things done, on accumulating wealth, on security."

"Security is an illusion, wealth is something for others to steal, and careers are merely trading time for money, which is to say trading a non-renewable resource for a renewable one."

"I would think someone with all the time in the world would trade it for anything."

"I'm going to teach you my family *qigong*," said Sanfeng, tasting the sound of the words on his lips.

Dalton felt a tremble. "You say it like I'm the first."

"My father made my sister and me promise never to share it."

"You've kept that promise?"

"Through hundreds of lifetimes."

Dalton leaned against a heavy flowerpot. He was closing in on what he'd been hoping and dreaming about since he could remember, and yet somehow the thrill was not what he'd expected. "It stops you having children, doesn't it?" he said.

Sanfeng's eyes opened wide in surprise. "How do you know that?"

"Family is everything for the Chinese. Your father gave this gift to his children, but you haven't passed it on. If you could have children, it would go to your eldest son."

"The *qigong* is a tripartite system. If you practice all three parts, you get the complete benefit, but you cannot have children. Pieces of the practice came from my mother's side. Apparently, she knew how to countermand the effects. I tried for centuries without result. My sister never cared for children."

"You don't think well of her."

"Of Zetian? She is my sister. We have been together for three thousand years."

Dalton had never felt such a yawning gulf between him and another human being. The sense that Sanfeng was alien, perhaps more alien than someone from another planet, the dizzying panoply of reference points they did not share, the sharp edge of the realities separating them were suddenly excruciating. "You brought me here for this," he said. "You've had the plan all along, but the plague pushed the timetable."

Sanfeng nodded. "Every population has a critical minimum. Dip below it, and there is not enough genetic resilience for the species to survive."

"You want me to go out and share it, teach it to others."

Sanfeng put his hands on Dalton's shoulders. Dalton was amazed by the great weight of the touch.

"I am a very old Chinese. I have thousands of years perfecting invisibility, and I have nearly done so. Nobody will accept my authority. Nobody will believe how long I have lived. Without Western credibility, media credibility, the kind of credibility you offer, I might try to share what I know, but I would be ignored."

"And your sister has never taught anyone."

"If you knew my sister, you wouldn't ask. We've been terribly careful. Also, there are additional elements to the practice, dimensions you must be taught, aspects you cannot see."

Sanfeng opened the door out of the fern garden, and Dalton followed him to another chamber, a quiet place with a reading table and a reclining chair, a library of sorts, though filled with as many CDs and videos as scrolls and books. While Dalton gingerly examined one of the scrolls, wishing he could read Chinese characters and marveling at the beauty of the calligraphy, Sanfeng picked up a copy of *The Boxer Within.*

"Remember," Sanfeng read aloud, "the external world is

entirely the creation of the internal world. The concept of objective reality is exactly that–a concept. Everything we think we understand is our own creation. Make peace inside, and you will make peace outside. Learn to stand quietly without judging anyone, and harmony will reassert itself. Meditate for an hour instead of giving in to the urge to pick up the gun and kill, and wars will never get started."

Dalton put the scroll down. "That is what the Chinese classics teach, but you say it as if you disagree."

"I agree entirely. I'm trying to show you I have good reason for having chosen you. I have been planning this day, as you said, for centuries. You appeared. Increasingly, I am certain there are no coincidences. You have an audience, and the audience knows you for your mastery of Eastern activities and ideas."

"Activities," Dalton said. "That about says it. I want to learn what you know, but you don't need me to share it with the world. Share it yourself! Show the world and, believe me, they'll listen to you. They're scared, they're dying, they're desperate, they're grasping. Just demonstrate your power and you will make believers overnight."

"My power is in my mind," Sanfeng said softly. "It is in the lessons I've learned, the people I've loved, the wonders I've seen."

"What you did to the airplane...."

"Parlor tricks."

"Some will think that," Dalton nodded. "Others will follow you and survive. When they do, more and more will follow."

"They will follow *you*," Sanfeng said.

With that, the immortal began to demonstrate his moves. The techniques were familiar at the start, reminiscent of many different *qigong* systems Dalton had studied, but there were subtle differences.

"Think of wringing water from a towel," Sanfeng explained, without pausing. "It's the most efficient way to move fluid, and the most efficient way to distribute life energy, too."

The immortal ducked low on the ground, slithered in precisely the part of the set Leili had seen Zetian perform through her bedroom keyhole, then went up on one leg to imitate a bird. He flapped his arms vigorously, making a deep hollow of his chest each time.

He paused then, and bade Dalton to repeat the set. Dalton froze. All he could think about was that he was learning an immortality set from a man who had been alive for thousands of years. He was stultified into inaction by the implausibility of it, the self-consciousness that came from knowing he was being watched and judged, and that the stake was far, far higher than simply his own performance; it was, indeed, the future of the human race.

"Your mind is in the way," Sanfeng said. "Don't think now, just do."

Dalton had heard the same advice from all his teachers, and remembered plenty of times he had striven to engage his subconscious mind and stop thinking about what he was doing.

"The movements come from watching animals," Sanfeng said. "Try again."

The process was slow for Dalton, although at times in the past he had learned sequences quickly. After a while, he began to relax, and the power of the movements took him.

"The sequence must be full of *qi*," Sanfeng explained, showing Dalton a particular turn of hand. "The mind is the general, the intention, the *yi*. The *qi* is the army, the troops; it follows the intention, energizing the action."

"You're saying that the flow of energy actually makes my arms and legs move."

"And your waist, your hips, your shoulders, neck, and torso."

"And how much daily practice does this require?" Dalton asked, eyeing the precise position of Sanfeng's hand, then moving to the angle of his toes.

"Once you memorize it, the whole sequence takes less than an hour a day. I will teach you the rest tomorrow, but now it's time to exact a promise."

"Aren't promises what got you into trouble in the first place?"

"My promise caused me great pain, but it didn't get me into trouble. Anyway, this is something I require."

"Whatever it is, I agree," said Dalton, slightly breathless.

Sanfeng brought his face close to Dalton's, and his expression held great intensity. "The first person you teach this to must be Monica Farmore."

Dalton could not hide his surprise, but before he could say anything, Sanfeng continued. "This is not a negotiable point. She must learn this as soon as I take you back to the city."

"She told me you met at the sports club."

"Do I have your word?"

Dalton gave his best approximation of a traditional kowtow. "You have my word."

"Then show me what you've learned."

Rising, Dalton repeated the set. He did a credible job of it, slow, but with attention to the details he sensed were important.

"Good," Sanfeng nodded. "Now tell me what you feel."

"I feel opposing energies working inside me," said Dalton.

"You feel both heavy and light?"

"And both quiet and restless."

Sanfeng took Dalton's hand and led him back to the kitchen, where he put the kettle on to make fresh tea. "Your body is taking to it smoothly because of all your training. Some people have a more difficult time. My father took yin/yang theory one step further than anyone else had ever done," he said.

"What does that mean?"

"He applied it to reality," Sanfeng explained. "Understanding that since everything we see is a creation of our mind, he deduced there must be something here when we are not."

"Sounds like quantum physics," said Dalton.

"A few millennia early, but yes. Scientists are just now exploring the existence of dark matter and dark energy, the yin to the yang of heat and light, of what can be measured and weighed. My father understood all that thousands of years ago."

"You mean the universe and not-universe express alternately, in a cycle; we're here and then we're not?"

"Very good!" Sanfeng smiled. "Our existence blinks on and off like a piece of movie film with black lines between the frames. The film is moving so quickly that sitting in the theater you don't see the line, but the film is nonetheless being redrawn, frame-by-frame, as you watch."

"Who makes the film?"

"That is a Western question, asked by someone raised to believe in a Creator. There is no knowing those things except by direct mystical experience, and if you have such an experience you know you cannot speak of it. Lao Zi wrote of this in the opening of his *Dao De Jing*."

"The *Dao* that can be spoken is not the eternal *Dao*," Dalton said. "If you can talk about God, you don't understand Him."

"Exactly," Sanfeng nodded. "If you insist on knowing the why of things, the how will continue to escape you."

"Sorry," Dalton spread his hands.

"Perhaps someday you will discover what you seek. I don't know the answer myself. What I *can* tell you is that the blinking on and off leads to change. A car turns a corner. A butterfly flaps its wings. The sun goes down. A child smiles."

"What an elegant concept."

"The better you understand it, the more elegant you realize it is. Now pay special attention here, because the next bit of information is the key."

Dalton put down his teacup and leaned forward. "I'm listening," he said.

"Quantum physics tells us that better than seventy percent of the universe is comprised of a combination of what we call dark energy and dark matter. The black line, the blink-off phase, works by different rules. Natural laws don't apply there: no space, no gravity, no magnetism, and no time. If you gain access to the black line, you can affect a redrawing of the frame. You can literally remake yourself."

"And in the remaking, eliminate the effects of aging and sickness."

"Yes. This meditation is the second part of the *qigong*. But remember that the black line is the edge between objective, external reality and the simulacrum your brain has created."

"The world is in the mind," said Dalton.

"Yes. And finding it requires focus and peace, and attention and practice."

"I understand."

"Not everyone can focus deeply enough to redefine themselves, Dalton, but everyone can do the movements they need to do to beat the plague. The movements are the first part of the three I mentioned. I will teach you the other two."

Just then came a sudden roar that sounded to Dalton every bit like the end of the world had found them, *qigong* or no.

57

Zetian loved to fly, but she was not the pilot she wanted to be. Partly, it was a matter of practice–she had not had much lately–and partly it was a question of getting accustomed to the new French helicopter Crocodile & Crane purchased a month earlier. She impressed Leili with the way she took off and crossed the water to Kat O Chau, but landing at the cemetery in a crosswind was a different story.

"I've thought about growing wings," Zetian said. "But I would be at a competitive disadvantage to technology."

"You could do that?"

Zetian shrugged, finessing the stick as the helicopter hovered over the landing site. "I've never tried. I'm not one for exploring all the different possibilities. My brother does that sort of thing, takes off for years at a time and stays in a cave trying to figure out how to become this, that, and the other thing. I've always been too involved in business to spend time alone meditating."

Leili looked out the window and marveled at how far she had come and all she had been through, at the way her aching heart continued to beat, at the liaisons she had made and lost, at the suffering and death she had seen, at the fact she had outlived her boss and come to consort with the likes of Zetian. She felt tired past exhaustion, but she also felt bold.

"I don't think business is what drives you."

Zetian looked at her, amused. "No?"

"I don't think sex or money do either."

Zetian reached out to touch Leili's thigh. "Not sex?"

Leili put her hand lightly on top of Zetian's in a fashion neither encouragement nor rebuff. "No," she said. "It's power you like. If the power comes from money, so be it. If it comes from your body, that's fine too."

"You're clever," said Zetian. "But you're wrong about sex."

"Does your brother know the *qigong*?"

"Oh yes," Zetian smiled.

"And can he do the things you can do?"

"I know when people are arriving," Zetian said. "And sometimes when they are thinking of me."

"When the telephone rings, do you know who it is before you answer?"

"Yes," said Zetian. "Like that."

"And your brother?"

"His attentions are elsewhere, and his concerns are different. As you will see, his mind is weak."

Leili had a thousand more questions, but saw Zetian busy herself with preparations to land. They went down and down and down, more like an elevator than an airplane, and the change in pressure took its toll on Leili's ears.

They were only ten feet off the ground when a gust of wind tipped the helicopter to the side, driving the rotor into the mausoleum Sanfeng had built for the sailors lost under his command all those years ago. The top of the structure gave way and chips of marble flew into the air, some striking the helicopter's windshield. Leili was pitched forward against the glass. She struck her head, and Zetian watched her beautiful features go slack as she lost consciousness.

The immortal turned off the fuel and listened to the whine of the avionics spinning down. She knew the mausoleum led to Sanfeng's cave because she had seen the infrared pictures. She got out, peered down into the blackness revealed by the decapitation of the building, and saw the hint of a trapdoor in the ground. She kicked the stone bits aside and pulled up hard on the door. It would not give. She closed her eyes and concentrated, drawing on her memories as a reservoir of strength, thinking of all that she had seen and done with her brother, all the way back to the day she stood beside him on the riverbank and saw in the confrontation between the reptile and the bird a harbinger of the very life she and Sanfeng would come to lead. She wondered if it had been fated to turn out this way, or whether they had created their own path with the myriad choices they had made, most small, some big, but adding up, over the seconds and minutes and hours, days, months, years, centuries and millennia, to something so complex as to be beyond her full comprehension.

At last she defeated the thick tongue of the steel lock and the trapdoor came up in her hands. She took a long look into the blackness, began to descend the steps, then paused and turned around and returned to the crashed copter.

Zetian never flew with a harness herself, but she extracted Leili from hers and took her out of the cockpit and laid her out on the rough ground. The sea sparkled, and the mountains of the mainland were dark green and visible in the distance, but Zetian was too intent on her prize to notice. She had dressed Leili in a pants suit of the finest green silk, and added a Ferragamo jacket for the flight. She began to undress her with the speed and skill of a woman who knew every possible manner of costume.

"My Amelia Earhart," she said, undoing the snaps on the front of the jacket, which was of quilted, distressed leather, the indentations the size and shape of coins.

Leili's breasts heaved under Zetian's hands, a consequence of being in a twilight state between consciousness and oblivion, but knowing, on some level, that a violation was near. Zetian set to work on the frog buttons of the top. Leili wriggled. Zetian moved up to kiss her, starting at her chin and then working the length of her neck.

"So beautiful," Zetian murmured, noticing that Leili's skin showed translucence similar to her own.

She bent and pressed her ear to Leili's breasts, feeling her heat and listening to her heart. Despite her foggy state, Leili felt the coldness, as Zetian's ear was as frigid as a stethoscope, or a gynecological instrument. Zetian listened to the steady sound of Leili's heart, and synchronized her own heart to its rhythm. She wanted them to be together that way; it was something she savored in a lover.

She turned her lips to Leili's flesh and moved downward, nuzzling the taught skin of her belly. She was working the zipper on Leili's pants when an eccentric piece of motion caught her eye. Beyond the instrument pod, she saw a bedraggled couple, a man and woman, entering the cemetery grounds. Holding hands, they covered the uneven ground awkwardly, moving straight toward the helicopter.

Zetian rose to her height, toying with the idea of killing the interlopers, but understanding it would not help if she did. This moment with Leili was a moment only, and the moment had passed. She gave a sigh for what might have been, darted back to the helicopter for something she needed, and slipped off toward the crushed mausoleum.

She had work to do.

58

As she floated down the ruined steps, Zetian kicked aside the human remains the rough landing had dislodged. Watching, Sanfeng rushed to the bones.

"I knew when you finally came here, you would do something like this," he said, picking up a femur. "This was my first mate."

"I don't care," said Zetian.

"These dainty fingers belonged to my cook," Sanfeng said. "And these long toes, they are all that's left of a boy who could climb a mast faster than a pelican could pluck a fish from the sea."

"You brought the American here," Zetian said. "I want to know why."

"This rib was around the heart of my tiller man," Sanfeng continued. "He had such a sense of the wind, he could simply turn to the horizon and determine a tack, foretell a squall, predict the hour of landfall."

"The American," said Zetian.

"How did you find me?"

"You know I keep tabs on you."

"Huangfu?"

"No longer among the living, I'm afraid. He gave me this lovely lavender suit. I didn't care for it much at the time, but it has grown on me."

Sanfeng sighed. "It's a wonder he lasted as long as he did."

"He was a good driver," Zetian said, reaching behind her head and pulling a short sword from a sling around her neck.

"A good spy, too. Tell me, where did you get that blade?" Sanfeng asked, squinting through the bone dust at the beautifully folded steel blade lit up by the shaft of sunlight coming in through the shattered mausoleum.

"A gift from the King of Yue," she smiled innocently. "In appreciation for services rendered."

Sanfeng looked at the squat, round dragons emblazoned on

the steel. It was the very sword he had coveted for millennia, the sword he had hoped the vendor Chou had found. "So many men have given you so much," he sighed.

"Not as much as I've given them."

A lone brick tumbled down from the cemetery above, riding the dust motes and the lines of sunshine. Zetian cleaved it in half with the blade as easily as if it were made of pressed flowers. "You live in the damp and the dark like a mole," she said.

"The crash seems to have affected the lights in here. Come, I'll take you to a more comfortable place."

They went back through the door, passing Dalton, who remained alert beside a giant fern. Sanfeng glanced back and made a barely perceptible motion with his finger, indicating Dalton should go up and out of the cave.

Sanfeng led his sister through the maze to a room Dalton had not seen, the repository for his vast collection of ancient porcelains.

"It is light and dry in here, no? Do you feel like a mole now?"

"I didn't know you liked porcelains."

"There's much you don't know. Their delicacy intrigues me."

"You criticize me for my passion for business, yet you are the ultimate consumer," Zetian said, shaking her head.

"You misunderstand me. Your love of commerce has to do with taking advantage of people."

"Serving their needs."

"We both know you don't serve anyone, Zetian. That's a line you use on customers, a line you use in interviews and speeches–please don't insult me with it. As for porcelains, I love them as a reminder of impermanence. So much effort goes into creating so much beauty, and yet it can all vanish at any moment."

To illustrate his point, he lovingly lifted a tall flask from its place on the shelf. "Yongle era," he said. "Do you remember it?"

"About fourteen hundred," she said.

"That's right. That's a cobalt blue underglaze. These black spots mean the cobalt spread into the overlying glaze during firing."

"I know all that," said Zetian. "I had many like it in my day.

Probably it was sent to Persia. The Persians liked those big handles. Not a Chinese design."

Sanfeng nodded. "I bought it from a dealer in Tehran. It was crafted in Jiangxi Province. The dragon design, as you know, is imperial. It was probably a gift to a dignitary."

"Expensive these days," she said. "Expensive even back then."

"Very."

With that single word, Sanfeng let go of the handles. Zetian was too shocked to move quickly enough to save it, and the flask shattered on the hard floor of the cave, sending bits and shards flying.

"Change is life," he said. "The beauty of the thing is no less because it was and is no more. The preciousness is no less because it's gone."

"This is why I have been the businesswoman and you have been the idiot."

"As you say," Sanfeng smiled. "Come, there is more to see."

He took her next to the weapons gallery. The museum cavern was redolent with smells even Sanfeng's sophisticated air handlers could not totally eliminate: the citrus tang of hundreds of pounds of bronze, iron, and steel, the sweet smell of the camellia oil Sanfeng employed for the protection of his blades, and the horse-sweat stench of tanned leather tassels and handles and scabbards and braids.

"You and your collections," she said.

"Collections and souvenirs are not the same," Sanfeng replied. "As with the porcelains, I keep things for a purpose."

"Every collector says that."

"I'm not a collector. I take souvenirs. Souvenirs help you remember, collections help you forget. Take that *guan dao* over there. It's the very one that took our father's head.

Zetian's eyes darted to the huge sword.

"You're crazy," she said.

"Not at all. I went back to the Banpo village for it."

She went to the giant old sword and regarded it closely. Bending to it, she sniffed it loudly, then stretched out her free hand as if to feel its energy.

"Go ahead and touch it," said Sanfeng.

Watching her expression, he could almost see the memories pour into her head, the flickering of the night torches, the stench of the valley, the grunts of the Banpo, their father's face, impossibly calm, his body, bruised and beaten, stretched out on the slab, the deerskin leather wound again and again around his ankles and his wrists to secure him.

"I don't want to," she said.

"If you don't touch it, you won't know it's real."

"Yes I will."

"No, you won't."

"There is no difference between touching a thing and almost touching it," she said.

"That is not a thing. That is the instrument of our father's murder. And more than that, there is a difference. If you had gone to school with your *qigong*, if you had spent time looking inward to develop yourself instead of turning outward right away, you would know this."

"Inward and outward," Zetian spat. "Your old monk mumbo-jumbo. Look at what I've built in the world. Look at our empire! You have a seat on the board because I gave it to you. You are president because I appointed you. I gave you everything you have, and that's the way it has always been."

"Not everything," said Sanfeng.

"You should honor your older sister."

Sanfeng bowed to her. "I honor you, Sister. But all I have is not yours. You have no idea of the worlds inside me."

"I suppose you're going to tell me about your special abilities, the way you can sense things and know the future before it happens, the way you see patterns in things, tiny whorls and eddies. I've heard it all before. You say your life is nuanced. I say your life is idle. You say you see the future. I say you're obsessed with the past."

"Do you remember clawing our way out of that little valley? It looked much smaller when I went back, Zetian. The forest was still there, as was the big stone table. I found fireplaces and graves. I found the priest's bones. The *guan dao* was with him."

"I hope you shit all over them."

"I just took the old sword."

"A great opportunity missed. The story of your life."

"Opportunities that you seized? Shitting on the dead? Whoring? Peddling skins? Outmaneuvering lovers? A chance to turn a profit?"

"If this *is* the Banpo Smile, we owe them thanks."

"So you care nothing for the world?"

"I care greatly for the world," Zetian said, hefting the King of Yue's sword. "I look forward to calling it mine."

He closed the distance between them. Gently, he reached out and took her free hand. "The world you will have will be hell. You think you want to be alone, but you have no power without others to worship you. You are stuck, Zetian. You replay the same story over and over, only the lovers change, and the kings, though your kings of corporate fiefdoms are not nearly so good with arms. You don't really want that world, and neither do I. What we thought would be glorious, what *was* glorious at first has become tragic. I'm done with the tragedy of it, Sister. I'm ready to move on, to find out all I don't know."

Zetian pulled her hand away, but not roughly. "There isn't anything I don't know," she said.

"You don't know what it is to make a child," he said.

"A child?" she blinked. "The *qigong* makes that impossible."

"True, which is why I've stopped the practice."

"Stopped!"

"Part of it, yes. It's time for a different kind of immortality, Zetian. I wanted a child, and for years I tried to have one. I succeeded. In fact, I have a daughter and she's here in Hong Kong."

Zetian lowered her sword and stared at her brother in total incredulity.

"You didn't know," Sanfeng smiled. "You think you sense things, but you didn't sense this, the biggest change of all, the largest, most significant monolith in your universe, and mine."

"It's impossible. You can't have stopped."

"You see that I'm getting older. You've said it yourself. It's not a switch, Zetian, although fertility returned to me almost at once–a fact I take to mean my body *craved* reproduction, wanted what was natural and right and true. In all other ways, I have been in a slow decline, and I have felt it, but I have not resumed."

"You must start again at once! Don't be a fool!"

"You don't hear me, Sister. It is time for my daughter, and for other children I have, too."

"Others!"

"There are a few more. They are scattered around the globe. I was careful. I chose their mothers well, and I have supported them, made moves to assure their futures."

"Why didn't you tell me?"

"It was because of you I haven't been a father to them, Zetian. I feared what you might do if you learned of them. You remember what you did to the students in Xian."

"Xian?"

"You had a lover in the shop. There was a giant."

"Ah," Zetian murmured. "The students who saw your power."

"All dead."

"They would be dead anyway."

"But after living."

Zetian's expression grew dark, and she was silent a long time. "I suppose that means you want to give the children a share of the business," she said at last.

"Poor Zetian," Sanfeng chuckled. "Still living in a zero sum world. There's enough for everyone; you've never understood that."

Zetian ignored her. "Who are the mothers of these children?"

"Never mind."

"I will find them."

Sanfeng blanched. "Stay away from them, Sister."

"You can't give me orders. You're old and weak. How does it feel?"

"I hurt sometimes. And I'm stiff when I get out of bed in the morning. I tire easily, too, and I get up often during the night. Still, you must stay away from my family."

"I'm your family."

"Not if you wish to kill my children."

"I know about the American writer," said Zetian. "I know why you chose him, Brother. You think you are going to share our *qigong.* You want to use his big audience. You're going to die and so you no longer care about your promise."

"Mortality does that," said Sanfeng. "It changes the way you look at things, forces you to change and grow, to discard old ideas and replace them with new and better ones. Our father had no idea what would happen to the world. Today's problems and complexities would be beyond his wildest imagination. We have to share. Sharing is the reason we know what we know. Sharing is the reason he developed the *qigong* in the first place, even though he didn't know it all those years ago, on the empty steppe."

"I can't allow this," Zetian shook her head. "It simply cannot be."

"Please, Sister. Let me teach the *qigong* and save the people I can save. They are the next generation. We can't go on forever."

"Speak for yourself."

"You should see how perfect your niece is, Zetian. How beautiful and good. She is the future, and we are the past. Humankind is evolving into something wonderful. We have to help!"

Zetian struck a martial pose, suddenly tired of the rhetoric. "I am Queen Mother of the World," she screamed, lifting her sword. "I don't have to help anyone!"

59

A crowd gathered at the perimeter of the cemetery, local people of the island, fisherfolk with straw hats and cell phones. Some held oars as weapons, and some held machetes. Most were simply staring quietly at the cemetery, which was marked by flowers and photos in the usual way, and now by the fine dust of the helicopter crash. They were too late to see Zetian disappear underground, but not too late to see Monica and Reggie arrive and go to the barely conscious Leili.

Reggie tried not to stare as Monica closed Leili's blouse. Leili woke slowly, her head pounding and filled with vague images of Zetian's predation. She touched her forehead lightly.

"Your helicopter crashed," Reggie said.

"In a cemetery," added Monica.

"There was a woman with me," Leili managed.

Reggie pointed at the wrecked mausoleum. "She's under there."

The three of them tottered toward the yawning stairs. Behind them, the crowd drew closer, but slowly, carefully. A young boy pointed a video camera in their direction, walking with it as he shot footage.

"We're looking for a man named Gao Sanfeng," said Monica.

"The woman you saw was his sister," Leili replied.

As they neared the stairs, a piece of rubble fell in, breaking way from the crust of the damaged earth. The helicopter leaned a bit further with the drop, and one of the rotors nearly touched the ground. The crowd jumped back a bit, and then, like a tide, came closer. When they did, Leili saw that some of them were smiling the Banpo Smile. The disease was subtle still, a level of disruption the victims themselves had yet to notice: a tiny spike in temperature, a twitch, an initial softening of connective tissue, the oxidation of hyaluronic acid that would lead, inexorably, to joints coming apart.

Leili turned to face them, full of compassion, wishing there were something she could do. Because she had her back to the hole, she was the last person to see Dalton Day emerge from the ground.

He came out slowly, blinking at the daylight, an expression of wonderment on his face. He had wanted to follow his master, sensing the brewing storm, but obeyed Sanfeng's orders and come up to the sun.

The people saw him and gave a collective gasp. The boy with the camera took a step backward but used his zoom to bring the record forward, figuring to have a tape of a man emerging from the dead. But Dalton was no zombie or ghost, had no chains, no tattered flesh, walked with no limp, bore no unkempt beard. Nor did he carry a sword, like Zhong Qui, the ghost-hunter of Chinese legend and patron of moon cakes and the autumn festival and the abundant harvest.

Monica ran to him and embraced him and Reggie Pritt reluctantly followed. "Dalton," he said, offering his hand.

"Pritt," Dalton said, taking it.

"You found your master, didn't you?" said Monica.

"I did," Dalton nodded. Then he noticed Leili. "Are you all right?" he asked her.

"I'm fine," Leili answered.

"These people are just starting to smile," said Monica.

Dalton nodded and walked into their midst. He seemed so simultaneously foreign and caring, they made way for him and then closed around him again. He took a deep breath. "Follow me," he said in rough Chinese.

Without explanation or instruction, Dalton began the slow routine he had just learned, the movements he had striven to commit to memory with effort hotter and more intense than any effort he had ever put into anything.

At first the island people did not know what to do, but there were a few members of the crowd who recognized the movements as *qigong*. These were older people who had come from the mainland, a couple of them elderly natives of Taiwan who had been there before Chiang Kai–Shek. Certain Mao's forces would follow–or at least certain that their freedoms would be lost–they had fled to the outlying rocks of the South China Sea and given up farming in favor of fishing. Now, they began to copy Dalton's movements.

"Follow me," he told Monica. "I made a promise that I would show you this."

So she and Reggie joined in, and eventually Leili did too. Dalton felt her presence keenly, moving as he did, with grace, power, beauty, and certainty. He noticed her eyes were closed, and he felt energy radiate from her, the same energy he had felt from his master, and he wondered at how she could possibly know what she knew.

The group performed together on that remote piece of rock, far away from television cameras or any other promotional machine, unprotected from the salty ocean wind, with marble dust blowing in the air and a damaged aircraft for company. Their hats–conical, snug-fitting and straw–bobbed up and down in unison. Interlopers and islanders alike, they were the first people on Earth to do Crocodile and Crane qigong without knowing what it was or why it was important.

As they swooped and hopped and twisted and bent, Leili and Dalton exchanged glances. There was a world of detail they would later share, but as the morning sun grew warmer and stronger, they came to realize they were linked. In Leili, her blouse misbuttoned, her hair disheveled, her face enchantingly asymmetrical–the left side of her lips slightly down from the right, the right eye a tiny bit closer to center than its counterpart–Dalton saw riveting beauty, and fathomless compassion. In Dalton, gracile, confident, and quiet, Leili saw the other half of herself. She knew him before she ever met him.

If there existed an instrument of science, something to measure the quantum effect of a certain type of biological emanation, the needle of that device would have been pegged by the radiation of the moving group. If there existed a viewfinder that could take biological energy and make it visible to the naked eye, the villagers would have seen that which Leili and Dalton felt–the beginning of a twist in the *Dao.*

Full of serenity, purpose, and hope, Dalton finished the set, then turned and went back down beneath the surface to find his teacher.

60

Sanfeng suddenly had his father's *guan dao* in his hand and was wielding it against Zetian's ancient blade.

"I can't let you share the practice," Zetian hissed.

"It's too late."

"Then I have to kill your students just the way I've done before."

"And will you kill my children, too?"

"I will do what I need to do to keep my promise to our father, even if you have broken yours."

Their weapons did not seem to meet directly, but twisted one about the other instead, like snakes. Sanfeng's face was impassive, but Zetian's jaws were working, her eyes wet and blinking, her tongue wiping spittle from her lips. She pulled her sword back toward her body in preparation for what Sanfeng recognized as the strike of a sword mistress, a strike founded in the collapsing power of the ribs and the sinking of the tailbone and the forward settling of weight into the leading leg, femurs rotating inward together to create the consummate arch.

"You've always been weak," she said.

"And you have always been cruel."

"You've always left everything to me!"

"You have always done what didn't need doing."

"I hate you!" she shrieked.

"I love you," he said. "And if you make me a promise, I will let you live."

"*You* will let me live! *You* want a promise from *me*?"

"I want a promise because I know you will keep it. Promise to keep away from my children. Promise to let them live their natural lives without threat of violence. Allow them the world to come."

Zetian thrust, but not quickly, and Sanfeng moved his father's halberd aside and let her come. The tip of the sword of the King of Yue touched his throat, and he felt a trickle of warm blood begin. “However did you dream you could dictate terms?” she whispered.

Sanfeng shook his head, and when he did, the razor steel made a line on his neck. “When we were children in the forest we came to a lake. Do you remember the lake?”

“I remember many lakes. What of them?”

“It was the first lake we came to after we left the cold country and headed south. I was used to seeing the lakes frozen over in the north, and in summer, with the plants blooming, the water appeared as only a shiny green field. But that lake was different. Beneath the surface I saw minnows, frogs, snakes and turtles gamboling in an underwater forest of lilies and weeds. I saw fish navigating a three-dimensional universe, Zetian, a world completely invisible unless, as I did, one took the time to dive in with eyes open.”

“You’re blathering,” she said. “It’s age taking your brain down, piece by piece.”

She tried to hold her sword against his neck but he gently moved it aside with the blade of the *guan dao*. “That lake helped me realize the world is not what we see,” he said. “We operate on the surface, each and every day, but there is far more underneath, an endless and repeating depth whose entirety eludes us even if we sing for it.”

She brought her face close to his. He could sense the violence emanating from her, the cloud of energies collected each time she killed, each time she violated, wounded, or harmed. It was as clear to him as her features, which had become blurred over time, at least to his eye, as if they were symphonic notes blending backward into background noise.

“You and your music,” she said. “You and your singing. Tell me something that eludes me but not you.”

“I see that you are the same as everyone else. The people you think of as insects are connected to the pine trees and to you. Indeed, they are the same as you, suffering the same helpless limitation, identical to you in every way save that you are dead to the link and many of them are not, and that your play is longer.”

“You talk like a poet who eats the wrong mushrooms. My

curtain call hasn't come. I have much more acting to do."

"Acting," he nodded, drawing the back of his hand across his bloody throat. "That's just what it is. Moving according to a script long-written, something stale and out-of-date and devoid of your own free will."

"That cut should have healed already," she said, pointing at the line her sword had made below his throat.

"It will," he smiled. "A little more slowly than it did, but it will."

"How long has it been, Brother?"

"Not so long as you have been hiding your selfishness behind supposed allegiance to a man you hardly remember."

Zetian moved the sword slightly to the side and regarded it carefully. "I've kept this sword all along," she said. "Perhaps on some level I knew I would kill you with it."

"Thinking of killing," Sanfeng shook his head. "What a waste of a life. How sad for you, poor girl, missing everything but targets, a horse with blinders."

"I *do* see targets," Zetian smiled, "even though you've always been the *gongfu* teacher."

"It doesn't have to be that way," Sanfeng said, searching her face for a hint of regret. "You have another choice. Every moment we are remade, you understand that all too well. Every moment, you could fashion yourself differently."

Zetian looked around the room. She noted the low ceiling, not conducive to *guan dao* play, and she noted the way the floor rose to meet the walls at the edge. She noticed, too, the particular play of light in the chamber, the way the small, halogen spotlights illuminated what Sanfeng claimed were his memories, but which she believed were really his fancy. It was a warrior's appraisal or, more precisely, an assassin's appraisal, and when it was done, she lifted her right foot and sprang toward him, sword held at her chest.

Drawn by the sounds of battle, Dalton stepped into the chamber. He recognized Zetian's maneuver–*Wild Horse Leaps the Ravine*–from his *Taijiquan* training. Zetian's version included a sliding step and a drop in altitude that brought her in under her brother's protective downward *guan dao* sweep, but while Sanfeng failed to catch her blade, he did manage to turn sideways in time for the thrust to harmlessly pass his torso.

Zetian's swordplay, however, was far more sophisticated than the average fighter, who saw the straight sword as limited to thrusting movements. She dropped her elbow, flipped her wrist, and pivoted her hips, turning the plunge into a slice. It would have gone right through the ribs and into his heart, had he not brought his father's giant halberd up in time. Sparks flew from where the iron met the steel.

"I feel our father's intention," said Sanfeng. "He protects me from your folly. Please stop!"

Zetian's next move was to attack his wrist with a tiny, vertical movement of the tip of the king's sword. Had it struck home, it would have severed the tendons of Sanfeng's wrist, rendering him unable to hold a weapon, but again he evaded it by twisting the huge halberd into position.

"I will not strike you!" Sanfeng cried. "You are my flesh and blood. Stop this now, please."

"You are only an obstacle now," Zetian whispered, turning around and bringing her sword to bear once more.

Her blade turned blue-hot as she worked to pierce his defense, and the flesh of her sword hand began to burn. Sanfeng redoubled his efforts. Zetian moved the blade so fast it began to wail, then to howl, the heat creating *schlieren* in the air. The dragons on her sword relinquished their grip on the steel. No longer etchings in folded steel but creatures of ethereal substance, their wings beating slowly, their mouths breathing fire, they hovered in front of Sanfeng.

On another day, the sight of them might have distracted him. He might have wondered who and what they were, prudently taken them for enemies while hoping, as he had when he first saw them on the sword, they could become friends. This day, he kept his equilibrium, the very calm center he had vaunted to Dalton Day.

"Please stop," he said.

"There is no stopping. You are my brother no longer. Your choice has made you one of *them.*"

Despite aging and dying, despite having embraced his own

mortality as deliberately as any parent, soldier, sailor, or duke, Sanfeng was still strong. Hearing her words, seeing he had no choice, he swung the halberd outward with one hand, using a reach and a horizontal circle that struck his sister in the abdomen.

"*Tiger Flies At You Suddenly,*" he whispered, rotating the shaft in his hand at the last minute so that the dull spine of the ancient iron blade, rather than the sharp edge, hit home.

Zetian was drawn inward by the decreasing radius of the circular strike, and she ended up very close to her brother. She might have been halved by the maneuver had he used the edge, but he sought only to disarm her, which he did, although it cost him the thumb on his left hand, as she managed to bring her weapon into play at just the last minute.

They were close enough to inhale each other's histories as the thumb hit the floor. The halberd clattered down and he thrust the bloody hand that had held it into his pocket, taking up her sword with the other.

Under other circumstances, he would have rejoiced to finally hold the weapon he had coveted for so long, but there was no time for that now, or for much else, as Zetian was upon him with a flurry of deadly punches and kicks, taking advantage of the fact she had him two hands to his one, staying out of range of the blade; dashing in, then hopping away.

She used death-touch point strikes, *dim mak,* aimed at key places along acupuncture meridians, and they interfered with the flow of *qi.* In Sanfeng's case, they had less effect than on an ordinary mortal, but one of her well-aimed, single-knuckle attacks landed on the brachial nerve plexus under his raised arm, and in doing so cost him command of the sword. It dropped, but he covered it with his foot before she could catch it.

They stared at each other, too fit and too relaxed to be breathless, but every cell in a highly aware state. Zetian searched her brother's eyes for weakness, but found only compassion; Sanfeng searched his sister's eyes for love, but saw only emotionless purpose. He defended against the chokehold she put up by issuing a wall of fire. Watching, Dalton Day had the incongruous thought that it looked like a New Year's Eve sparkler.

"Impossible," said Zetian. "You can't…"

"The negative effects are slow," he answered. "Only child-making returns in a hurry."

"Child-making," she spat. "Like a common rabbit. You dye your hair now, don't you? All those years we colored the black gray, and now you do the reverse like one of *them*."

"I won't color it any longer," he said. "I did it only to hide my choice from you."

Her energy flared up then, and it was no less than his own. The museum chamber filled with the crackling of their fire and the smell of ozone and something else: a pine-forest smell like something burning. Despite that, there was no heat, as the forces the immortals conjured were more like a particle beam or maser, not causing damage until they reached a target, barely heating the air.

Indeed their struggling auras were nothing more than their struggling wills manifested, and thus there were two distinct energies at work. The air above the siblings began to darken. It was as if a tiny, tropical storm had come to rest on her crown. Strands of hair stood up on Zetian's head as if drawn skyward by the electrical charge of invisible miniature clouds. As part of the process, her attack on her brother grew more concentrated. Her brow furrowed with concentration, and even though she rarely perspired, beads of moisture appeared on her brow.

"You can't beat me," Sanfeng said. "Your skills lie elsewhere, in collusion and persuasion and manipulation and charm."

"Die, old man," she answered.

In response, he just smiled, and began to hum.

"No," Zetian gasped. "You said you quit."

He kept humming. He had a certain melody in mind, and he produced it with joy. A dark line appeared around him. The untrained observer would not have seen it until it grew more distinct, but Zetian recognized the earliest hint of it and intensified her attack. Her fire turned blue, then white. It grew narrower and sharper, focusing in like a dagger.

But Sanfeng was stepping out of phase, and her attack passed through him. She yelled in frustration and began to hum herself, seeking to chase him to whatever dimension he used as a refuge, intending to track him through time.

He remade himself quickly, and was back and strong. He could not replace his thumb, that level of ability had gone when he abandoned his practice, but he could stop the bleeding and the pain. He took advantage of the first moment of coalescence–the *qigong* of the Gao family was not intended for use during the heat of battle–and he found Zetian where she had worked her magic, and he put the *guan dao* to her neck.

"Surrender," he said. "Do it now. You can't shift as fast as I can move."

Fury on her face, Zetian shimmered one last moment, then grew solid and still, relinquishing the idea of dimensional retreat. "Everything about you is wrong," she said.

"It's not too late for you, Sister. Consider what I've said. Consider letting me do what I can to save those who will follow. Promise to leave my children in peace."

Now that she had density again, her power cohered. She brought energy to the surface of her body, channeling her *qi* so as to make her flesh invulnerable to strikes or cuts. Sanfeng saw in her gaze the truth that had haunted him for more than 3,000 years, the truth that had clung to his back ever since the crocodile and the crane had wrestled for the fish, all those years ago along the ancient riverbank. There was no persuading Zetian. There was no changing her. She was what she was, and he had spent hundreds of lifetimes denying it. The sharp tragedy of the realization washed over him, galvanizing him to do the thing he had been born to do, the only thing he could do.

Using the *guan dao* forged by the man who had created the two of them, putting all his will into the iron, he raised the *guan dao*, brought it down with all his force, and cut his sister's heart in two.

61

The master met his students beneath the ruins of his monument to the past, amidst the bones, illuminated by sunlight filtering down, and coated by a salty drizzle from the sea. The four of them saw him, but only Dalton noticed that the *qi* Sanfeng had so long and carefully cultivated–the elixir nurtured and protected until it was an essence as unique, distinct, and complex as the finest liquor–was leaking from him too quickly to stop. He ran to Sanfeng and helped ease him down onto a chunk of marble. Monica came, too, and the once-immortal's eyes fixed on her and he extended his hands.

"Your father," Dalton said quietly.

There was no more explanation than that. Monica felt his flesh, which was nearly her flesh, and lowered herself to his feet with her legs crossed, sitting as a disciple might or, of course, a child.

"My mother…." Monica began.

"Has much to tell you, and she will once I am gone."

"But…."

"I don't have long," Sanfeng said. "Please let me speak."

It was then that Monica saw what Dalton had seen, and what was now increasingly obvious. Sanfeng was collapsing in on himself, not dehydrating like a victim of the Banpo Smile, but diminishing vertically, as if the weight of all his years was at war with the liberation of all his insights, and his skills, as marvelous as they were, and as numinous, could not support his frame. What only Dalton understood right then was that Sanfeng was doing what he had chosen to do, transcending the physical world for the incorporeal.

"I wish…" Monica whispered.

Sanfeng touched her hair and she experienced the tiniest shock, barely more than the static of a carpet, a tiny, barely perceptible charge, not because he wanted to give her less, but because this was all he had left. "I loved her," he said. "I loved her and she loved me–and all these years I have loved you too without seeing you or hearing you. I stayed away to protect you from my sister, to keep her from discovering what she would see as my betrayal. She couldn't recognize the way the world was changing–the way *we* were changing. Wherever she is, I hope she forgives me."

"Where *is* she?" asked Leili, coming forward.

Sanfeng sighed and pointed over his shoulder. "She lies down there. I have killed her."

To everyone's surprise, including her own, Leili burst into tears.

"You will think that this is about good and evil," Sanfeng said. "You will think I killed her because she wanted to stop me from saving what part of humanity I can. You will think I killed her because she wanted to kill my child, my children; yes there are others, and I have made provision that you shall come together. You will think she died because she was a monster, but the truth is she suffered from the same blindness that seizes us all. We are blinded by the material world. We think that the atom is the basic unit of the universe, and that we should claw and scramble and kick and scream our way to the top of the heap of atoms so we can have our brief time in the sun. The truth is different. The truth is that the basic unit of the universe is information."

"Knowledge," said Dalton.

"A fancy word," Sanfeng gave a wan smile. "In any case, I have chosen the four of you to use information to save those who wish to be saved."

"You don't know us," said Leili.

"I know you came here with my sister. I know you learned from her."

"How could you know that?" Leili demanded.

Sanfeng smiled again, but more weakly this time. Dalton propped him up, and stayed with him so he wouldn't fall over. "You cried when you heard she was gone," he answered. "You were the only one. And you have the glow."

"I stole the movements without her consent," Leili whispered.

"You didn't steal them, you copied them. You can't steal something that belongs to everybody. You can't steal the air."

"My name is Reggie Pritt," the policeman said, coming forward and doing his best version of a kowtow.

"I know who you are, and I know you love my daughter. Now if the four of you will forgive me, I haven't much time. There are three parts to the practice. One is the movement, one is the black line meditation, and the last is the melody. Dalton will teach you the first two parts, I will teach you the other. When I am gone, please follow Dalton's counsel, as he will stand in my place."

"This *qigong* you're talking about, this will cure the plague?" asked Reggie.

"It will do that and more, according to your desire, according to what you practice. Dalton will explain."

"I'm worried...." Dalton began.

"You're worried about where I will go when I leave you," Sanfeng said gently. "I don't know where I'm going, but I will know when I get there."

"Is there an afterlife?" Dalton asked, suddenly desperate to know. "Can you tell us? Have you seen...?"

"Your hand," said Monica, touching her father's finger. "Your thumb is gone."

"Shh," said Gao Sanfeng. "Just hum with me, child. The four of you need to learn the tune."

What he gave Monica in those last moments was a gift almost as great as the gift of life he had given her a quarter-century before, greater perhaps than the gift of continuing life and immunity from the plague. The gift he gave her was the gift of identity, of an interior circle completed, of a sense of who she was and where she had come from and why she was unique. It was the feeling of being loved.

In his passing, the immortal was effulgent. At the moment of transition, when the *qi* finally quit him, he stopped humming. His eyes fixed open, his thumbless hand dropped away from his daughter, and as his body sagged, he smiled.

62

When they returned to the surface, the disciples saw that the island's population had closed in on the mausoleum. Some people smiled, some twitched, some cried, and some died. Scattered among them–as the few blooming flowers on a bent and dying stalk–was the small group Dalton earlier led in *qigong*. The shocking reminder of what was left to do in the world hit Dalton harder than the others, because his was the heaviest task, but it struck Leili only slightly more softly, and still hard enough to rock her back on her heels.

Reggie found a piece of the wall of the mausoleum, all that was left standing after Zetian's hard helicopter landing. His Chinese was good enough to read that the structure had been built in honor of Sanfeng's shipmates, and that he had committed them to the earth out of love and respect. He shared his discovery with the others, trying to digest the date, which showed Sanfeng had been alive for centuries.

"It's not just hundreds of years," Dalton said quietly. "It's thousands."

Reggie found his breath coming in shallow gasps. "The sister, too?"

"The sister was born first."

"We should bury my father and aunt rather than cremate them, Monica said sadly. "He buried his shipmates. It was the ritual he respected."

Using the bloody *guan dao* as a shovel, Monica and Dalton dug the earth for Sanfeng, and Leili and Reggie dug for Zetian. The bodies of the immortals were as light as *papier maché*, the result, no doubt, of their etheric alchemy. Villagers helped move the broken marble into a pile over the bodies, which were positioned side by side in interlocking semi-circular pits.

"I turned down his dinner invitation," Monica said, tears streaming down her face.

"You didn't know," Reggie said.

"My mother should have told me."

"It is pretty clear your father didn't want that."

"Nobody will ever believe what happened here today."

"Nobody should ever hear about it," Reggie put in.

"I had a son," said Leili. "He died of the Smile. I couldn't help him. There was nothing I could do. If I let myself think about him, I hurt so much I can hardly stand up."

Her words were their signal to begin again to train the now growing crowd, and they began the movements. The crowd moved along with them. There were some people who found the movements difficult because they were old and there was bending, and others, including the very young, who were confused by the spiral movements and by the direction of certain circles. But with repetition and patience everyone muddled through the set, and sank to the ground when it was over, warmed by the effects of their gathering energy.

It was only the physical part of the system, but the result was still strong. Some of the islanders were stunned by the onrush of *qi* they felt, the sudden, vibrating power awakened within them. A few folks fell to the ground and were still, unable to absorb everything at once, waiting for the feeling in their body to settle down. One woman writhed on the ground. Others set to leaping and dancing, and one man howled at the sun like wolves calling for the pack.

Dalton took the others to the underground chamber after that, and when he was certain no one had followed, he talked the group through the black line meditation. Leili was the first to achieve it, but the others soon followed. When they all got it–Reggie and Monica did so simultaneously, and the black line around them was one line not two–it was time to hum Sanfeng's melody.

They did so with their eyes closed, repeating the tune until it brought visions of forests to their heads, and of brooks babbling and oceans roaring, of scenes from ancient China that could only have been the residue of the Gao siblings: a deer running through a forest so tall and clean and pure, the clatter of assault hooks thrown up and over a defending wall, a long trail winding through the mountains of the Himalayas, disappearing in the distance as a blizzard closed in, a close-up of a moth hiding in camouflage against birch bark, the cluttered, stinking market of some northern Chinese town when the streets were a toilet and a thoroughfare both. They saw stalls rife with exotic goods on the backs of camels and horses and mules, the soft interior chambers of some palace, and they saw jade figures on a shelf and the moonlight prying its way in.

They kept singing as visions of past loves came to their heads. Leili saw Lombo and felt her tears come; Dalton saw the lovely face of Grace; Monica remembered the kiss of rocket-engine Phillip, and the caress of another boy named Michael who carried an empty syringe in his pocket. Reggie remembered a redhead he met on Sydney's Bondi Beach during a spring break from university, in particular the soft whiteness of her breasts as they necked against the stonewall below the boardwalk.

Dalton saw the view of his mother's ankles from under his bed, where he hid, cowering after sneaking a cigarette in his room; Leili smelled the tropical aroma of her grandfather, the *dukun*; Monica saw a peregrine falcon that once settled on her Oklahoma windowsill; Reggie saw his teenage older brother beat another school kid so hard his ears bled.

They kept singing and singing, each doing the work they needed to do to make themselves whole. One put a kidney into harmony. Another cleared the clouds from her spleen. One smoothed a blood vessel plagued by turbulent flow. Another repaired a malformation of the cochlear ducts of the inner ear. Monica filled a tiny, leaking crack in a fallopian tube.

When Dalton finally brought them up and out of the trance, they had no desire to leave or move, but sat huddled together while the fans worked the room, cleaning and clearing what the sea brought in, struggling now against the world settling in through the hole made by Zetian's crash landing.

63

Wild-eyed and unwashed, Annabelle Miller huddled under the bedclothes in her Greenwich Village apartment. With the world outside a great bubbling stew of anarchy, terror, and death, she was in a state of siege. There was a police bar across her front door, and her fifth floor windows were locked and sealed, tacks glued to the sills. She had kitchen knives and pepper spray strategically placed throughout every room, and a bathtub full of rusty dark water in anticipation of the inevitable, dark day when even the most basic services would end. When the telephone rang, she snatched up the receiver.

"What?"

"Annabelle, it's Dalton."

"You're alive! Where are you?"

"In a cave in China."

"A cave?"

"Annabelle, I need you to listen to me very carefully. Does your Internet connection work?"

"Of course."

"Good. I was worried the network might be down. Do you have broadband?"

"Cable modem."

"Fine. Turn it on now. I'm sending you a video file."

She told Dalton when the download was complete.

"The file shows exercises," he said. "Turn up your speakers, play the file, and follow along with the movements. Do it now."

"Dalton, what's this all about?" she asked as she hit the speaker button on the phone.

"These exercises bolster your immune system. If you do them, you won't die."

"Are you serious?"

"More serious than I've ever been about anything."

"Then you have to tell the world."

"That's why I need you to please send the file to everyone on our mailing list. Folks who know me are more likely to do the routine. Send it to our media contacts, too. You never know, they might just play it on TV. Of course, you must send it to your friends and anyone else important to you."

Annabelle started mimicking the motions, which at first looked reptilian to her, and then birdlike. She felt ridiculous, especially in her nightgown, but she did not stop.

"When are you coming back?" she asked, slightly breathless.

"No plans right now. There's so much to do."

"Is this your new e-mail address?"

"For the time being. I really can't say I'll be reachable, and I really don't know what's going to happen."

"Do I still have a job?"

"Not only do you still have a job, but it's more important than ever. You are the world's gateway to me."

"But the water only flows in one direction, is that it?"

"I'm sorry, but until I figure out what to do from here and exactly where to go, that's the way it has to be."

"I feel something," Annabelle said. "Like there's an alien in my stomach. I'm not kidding. A roiling, but not like I'm going to be sick."

"You'll have all kinds of sensations," Dalton said. "Just trust that they are signs you're getting stronger."

"This can't save everyone, can it?"

"No," Dalton sighed. "It's already too late for that. There are places technology can't reach, and millions are already dead."

Annabelle moved to the window. Below her, the streets were full of trash, and small groups of youths ran huddled together as if in some new game, seeking a goal. She saw a police car turned on its roof at the end of her street. An old man stood next to it, turning one of the wheels by poking the tip of his umbrella into the hubcap. A young woman crouched next to the flowers planted around a tree across the street from Annabelle's building. She had a long plastic lighter in her hand, and she was using it to set fire to a stand of tulips.

Annabelle heard the drone of an airplane overhead, and

crouched down to get the right angle to see up past her metal fire escape to the sky. There was a biplane in the air, the kind used in air shows, with old-style chrome exhaust pipes issuing from the cowling and wires between the wings. It made tight, purposeful circles, turning nearly sideways to manage them. A flurry of white papers dropped from the cockpit, and Annabelle watched as they spread and fell. One came to rest on her window ledge. She read the message.

The End Time Is Here–Repent And Be Saved

"People won't believe you, Dalton," she said toward the phone. "I spent days online when the plague began. Everything and anything is spinning around out there right now, this cure and that cure, conspiracy theories, confidence games. It's the end of the world."

"We can't be responsible for the actions and decisions of others. All we can do is our best."

"I love you," said Annabelle.

But Dalton had already hung up.

She went back to her computer and started the video again.

She moved.

EPILOGUE

Pah.
Hooosh.
Pah.
Hooosh.
Kursh. Pah. Pipipi. Krak.
Ar muves n.
Ar muvs ot.
Bld floes.
Fngrs tingl.
Tose crmp.
Doe noweriam. Doe nohuiam. Doe nowadsdisplace.
Kule nd blk it is.
I m so lone.

Can zee mor cleerly now. Tis a forist uv zum kind. Treez tall nd all da same kind. Oshins uv treez so purfect they don look reel. For al da quiet nd da stilnez I feel zum beaudy here, but I m al lone. No burdz. No bugz. Der z no time here. I jus am here. I jus be.

Storm comes. Ran nd lideneng bd no lideneng smel. Lowd dundr. Im kold, jes me. Still feel lone.

The trees r gone. The forest z gone. There is no kumfirt. There is no eart. Can't get kumfordable. Still don no where I am. Where am I? I speek questyuns bud no won anszers. Do u heer me? Why don u speek du me? Don u kair I feel dis way?

Now where am I? Who are these people, standing on tiers, looking down at me and pointing? I know some of them. How dare they judge me?

There on the first tier is my father's brother. I know that stern, reproachful look. My uncle always loved my mother, and yet he foretold her death with satisfaction. How can you love someone and be glad for her passing? I know about love, even though people have said I do not.

My uncle is at Sanfeng's birth. Right out of the womb, my brother favors my father. I see my uncle twist in rage at the resemblance. I see him cut the cord while my father weeps for joy. While my father's eyes are wet and my mother's eyes closed in relief, I see my uncle shove something inside my mother. His movement is smooth and quick and small, but terrible. No one but me sees the last tiny hint of a curved, venomous tail as the bug disappears. It is a scorpion. My uncle put a scorpion inside my mother.

On the second tier, I see the emperor child. I was his wet nurse. I had nothing for him in my dry breast but said I had milk. I bribed a stable boy to work a goat and bring me the warm nurture and I gave it to the little Prince of Heaven, that whiny, helpless, hungry brat. It was a dangerous game I played. The boy's father would have had my head if he'd known, and I can't survive without my head, can't put it back on in my quiet time. There were so many people to bribe, maids and consorts and soldiers and guards—even though it was a small secret compared to my big secret, my real secret. The boy grew up and I stayed with him, to serve him. I knew he would be emperor someday and he would love me, but I did not know he would be cruel and flawed. When he first discovered what I had done, he used his knowledge to force me to perform unspeakable acts for him. He was still a child but fast becoming a wicked man. Oh, those things he did to me. Oh, those cruel things. I remember my tears. I remember my screams. I remember how everyone pretended not to hear.

I see Xiao Chan on the third tier. She worked for me when I ran a protection agency and provided guards to noblemen and to governors and to merchants. She was my best friend and my best fighter. We would often ride together on the same horse, and I took in her smell and she felt my heat from behind. All the men wanted us but we wanted only each other. So many passionate nights. I loved her so much. I thought she loved me—I let down my guard, which I swore I would never do, not after what the Banpo did to my poor, dear father. She was my partner in every way. We practiced fencing together; we shared a fortune, we shared a life. I could not even hide my special practice from her. She asked about it and I wouldn't tell her and she pouted and closed her legs to me but I stayed with my promise and she became angry, and then angrier still. I had made up my mind to share it with her when she tried to murder me in my bed. I had to kill her. I took her body out in the desert. With only the stars to see me, I burned her to a crisp and poked her body with a stick. After I did it, I cried.

On the fourth tier, I see four old men I know. They ran an inn by the road by the beach and everyone had to come past that inn, even princes, even generals. The men allowed me and my brother to sleep in a little room near the stable. At night, the old men murdered travelers in their beds, then chopped them up and used the human meat for dumplings. They caught me spying. I was just a girl and they were going to chop me up, too, and they were going to chop up my brother but I promised to keep silent and to help them with their terrible work. I added herbs for taste.

The tiers are gone and I am in a dirigible floating over Vietnam. I see people in Ho Chi Minh City and Saigon dying of the smile. I see people in Cambodia and in Laos and there, in a small clearing beside a rice paddy, I see a laptop computer glowing on a clump of palms and I see people practicing qigong, my qigong, my family qigong, and they are living, not dying, although there are not many of them.

Now I am over Paris. There are piles of burning bodies and there are fires in houses and there are cars stopped sideways. The bridges are clogged and swaying from the static weight of cars and buses and trucks. In a park off the Champs Elysees, I see a group of people following a young boy doing my qigong. Everyone is thin and weak and hungry, but they live and will keep living.

Now I am over America. I see Illinois and Nebraska. The Oklahoma panhandle is red and tough. Wild livestock grazes on wheat and soybeans and corn. The highways are packed with people not fleeing but milling, people with nowhere to go. People on bicycles and people pulling wagons of goods and people with pitchforks and spades and people with guns. I see a hospital damaged by fire. Behind the building there is a parking lot and a nurse leading a small crowd through my father's qigong. Those who do it are more alive with each passing hour.

I fly some more and I see Brazil. I see the forests are taking back the cities there, but in those forests are some people and they are doing the qigong too. I fly over Africa and see snakes and roaches and rats take Nairobi. People on rooftops practice my qigong there and I am glad for them because they are tough and because they are practicing not killing and fighting. I see they have time to couple, and am glad to know their children will survive.

The lightness in my heart somehow affects my airship. I rise, and as I do I feel better and cleaner and clearer and stronger. The higher I fly, the more unburdened I become. I don't want to fight anymore and I don't want to kill. I don't want to torture and I don't want to maim. I am simply glad there is life down there, beneath the clouds.

I see my beautiful young mother float toward me. Her belly is flat and her skin shines and she is so glad to see me. My father comes next, handsome and strong, no line on his neck. He forgives me for keeping my promise.

At last I see my dear little brother. He smiles his wonderful smile, the only smile like it in the world. He holds out his arms and he beckons to me. I run to him. Right out of the airship and over the clouds, I run into his arms.

We are together again, the crocodile and the crane.

About the Author

Arthur Rosenfeld is a martial arts teacher, writer, speaker, and coach. His martial arts training spans more than twenty-seven years, and includes instruction in Tang Soo Do, Kenpo, Kung Fu, and Tai Chi Ch'uan. Rosenfeld is a critically-acclaimed, best-selling author of six novels (Avon Books, Bantam, Doubleday Dell, Forge Books), two non-fiction books (Simon and Schuster, Basic Books), several screenplays, and numerous magazine articles (*Vogue*, *Vanity Fair*, *Parade*, and others). He consults for the pharmaceutical industry as a recognized expert on aspects of chronic pain. Arthur Rosenfeld resides in South Florida.